DARK PURPOSE

CHARLI CROSS SERIES: BOOK ONE

MARY STONE
DONNA BERDEL

DESCRIPTION

Everyone has a purpose. Some are just darker than others.

Always calm, cool, and collected, Savannah PD Detective Charli Cross compensates for her petite five-foot frame with an impenetrable exterior and pragmatic competence. It's an approach that catapulted her to the rank of detective at twenty-three and contributes to her and her partner's unequaled murder clearance rate. But when a bird-watching couple discover the remains of a teenage girl stuffed in a storage container, Charli's composure starts to crack.

Not only is the murder horrifying, it dredges up memories of Charli's best friend. Madeline was only sixteen when her body was found a mere half-mile from the grisly discovery. Add the sadistic sexual component to this recent crime, as well as the location of the body, and Charli fears they are facing the hallmarks of the worst kind of serial killer—one who's organized and thorough. One intent on fulfilling his dark purpose.

Charlie wants to stay unemotional. But when more victims are discovered, she is determined to stop the killer before he strikes again.

This time, it's not just her job. It's personal.

Spine-tingling and chilling, Dark Purpose is the adrenaline-charged first book in the Charli Cross series from bestselling author Mary Stone—guaranteed to ensure you never walk home alone again.

This book is dedicated to all those who go missing each year, and to the people who love them. My heart breaks for each of you.

1

Maddie Hanley walked down Brockman Street, sticking to the shade as much as possible as she followed the same route home from school she took every day. During the cooler months, she didn't mind that her route took her through the outskirts of Savannah's Historic District, one of the few places where the live oaks didn't explode everywhere like some tree lover's wet dream. Today, it was *hot*, though. She'd kill for a little extra shade.

She fanned herself with the hem of her t-shirt to try to cool off, not that it did any good. Even with the scattered clouds, the air was thick with humidity. The kind of weather that made being outside feel like hanging out in her cramped bathroom at home with the door closed and a steaming shower running at full force. The kind that only grew worse as May rolled into the hotter summer months.

Just one more week of school, and then she could swim in water instead of her own sweat.

She used her bare arm to swipe the moisture from her forehead, making a face when she realized how pointless it was. Her arm was just as gross as the rest of her, so she'd basically just mixed her arm and forehead sweat together like some kind of weird chemistry experiment.

Great.

She already regretted not accepting that ride home from Donny, the senior who lived a few houses down from her. He was so annoying, though. Always bragging about his grades and how he was going to get to UGA on a band scholarship.

That was why Maddie was planning on getting out of this hellhole. Not because of the senior or even just the heat, although that totally played a role. Mostly, she was sick of her parents, always up in her business. She couldn't wait to get her driver's license when she turned sixteen in a couple months, though she'd be shocked if her overprotective dad would let her get a car.

School sucked too. If it weren't for seeing her friends during lunch, she'd lose her freaking mind. What was the point of classes like Geometry? She sucked at math and had zero interest in being a mathematician when she grew up. Not that she knew for sure what she wanted to be, but definitely something cooler than that. Like maybe a journalist or a party planner.

She was pretty sure neither of those careers required knowing the hypotenuse of some stupid triangle.

Maddie crossed the empty street and hopped up onto the sidewalk. The only good thing about the heat was it meant the school year was almost over. Soon, there'd be no more classes or homework, freeing her up to spend more time with Kevin.

Kevin.

Tingles raced through her body as she thought about her boyfriend. So far, the farthest she and Kevin had gone was making out because her parents were freaks. Like, so uptight. They wouldn't even allow Kevin in her bedroom with the door closed. How stupid was that? Depriving teens of privacy should be against the law.

Maddie cut through the same abandoned lot she always did, veering over to a patch of weeds and kicking an empty beer can someone had chucked. Tonight would be different, though. Tonight, she and Kevin planned to sneak off to his older brother's apartment to mess around. No open doors, and definitely no nosy parents.

I could become a real woman tonight.

Giddiness made her dance a few steps onto the adjacent street before she caught herself and slowed her pace. Cheeks hot, she glanced around to make sure no one had witnessed her dorkiness, but the neighborhood was empty as usual. If any kids from her school lived on this block, she'd be surprised because she'd never run into them before. The homes were more beat up than the ones on nearby streets. The yards were a mess, with weeds as high as Maddie's thighs in places, and the driveways were full of junker cars. One of the houses even looked deserted, with boarded-up windows that creeped her out a little.

The black SUV across the street was probably the nicest car around, all sparkling clean and new looking. Maddie had first noticed the SUV a week or so ago, parked across the street from the abandoned lot, and it hadn't moved since. Probably belonged to a contractor from one of those construction companies her dad was always bitching about. He'd been all bent out of shape one day over the weekend when someone from that neighborhood tattle app complained that they'd spotted two construction workers sleeping in their truck at five in the morning.

Maddie rolled her eyes. Seriously? Who cared if someone wanted to sleep in their car? Adults were so weird, always sticking their noses into other people's business.

Her dad was a dick too, so there was that.

She spared one last glance at the SUV before shrugging. Whoever owned it was smart because they'd sprung for tinted windows. Probably because they wanted privacy from freaks like her parents. She could totally relate.

Maddie's phone blasted her favorite rap song from her bag, and she paused to dig it out from beneath a tangle of papers. "Abby, whassup?"

Her best friend launched right into her mile-a-minute babble. "Oh my god, can you believe it's finally Friday? That week took like a thousand years. I'm so ready to be done with school for, like, forever. Are we still good to hang out tomorrow night? There's a movie I really want to see, plus I need new shorts because it's already so freaking hot and all my old shorts from last year are gross. Oooh, and I heard Jeff Swanson talking about going to that party at Tyler's. I swear, could that boy be any hotter?"

Abby finally paused for air, making Maddie smile. "Could which one be hotter, Tyler or Jeff?" She shouldered her bag and headed into the empty street. The sidewalk was so messed up and uneven that the last time she'd tried to talk and walk, she'd tripped and skinned the shit out of her knees and hands.

She definitely did *not* plan to show up for her date with Kevin tonight with oozing scabs.

"Does it matter? I'd jump either one of those delicious man-morsels in a hot second."

Maddie giggled as the asphalt heated the bottom of her shoes. "Okay, big talker. I expect to see that in action next time we're out."

Abby was so funny. Anyone listening to her would think she was some kind of uber-confident sex maniac who'd tapped more ass than a rock star, when in reality, Abby froze up when it came to talking to boys in person.

She prattled on in Maddie's ear about some stupid thing

her mom had done while Maddie paused to wipe the fresh sweat off her face. Only a few blocks, thank god. The first thing she was going to do when she got home was jump into a cold shower and wash away the slime.

Showing up for her date reeking of BO was even worse than concrete rash.

"What you got going on tonight?"

Kevin. Lots and lots of Kevin.

Maddie stifled a giggle. "It's my mom's birthday, and we're supposed to go out for some family dinner."

Maddie didn't add that she planned on skipping out by saying she had a school project that couldn't wait. Since she really did have a project due on Monday, it wasn't a total lie.

Though, if she was lying, it was her parents' fault. If they weren't so controlling and weird about her personal life, she wouldn't have to sneak around like some freaking juvenile delinquent just to be with her boyfriend. Like, why couldn't her parents be more like her friend Gina's, who was allowed to have sex in her own room? Gina's mom had even taken her to the doctor and got her on birth control.

So not fair.

Abby babbled on about the last birthday party her mom had, where one of the neighbors drank so many margaritas they puked in Abby's kitchen sink. "It was so gross. Like, why not try to get to the bath…" Abby groaned then dropped her voice to a whisper. "I gotta go. My mom's screaming at me about something again, and I don't want to lose my phone. Later!"

"Bye." Maddie hung up and stuck the phone back in her bag.

Only a few hours until I'm at Kevin's. Oh god, what am I going to wear?

Good thing she'd done her laundry last night. At least she was sure she had clean underwear. None of them were

Victoria's Secret exciting or anything. She supposed that one black-and-white polka-dotted pair was kind of cute, except, ugh, were polka dots too little kid-ish?

As Maddie performed a mental inventory of the contents of her dresser drawers, an SUV flew past her before slamming on the brakes and blocking her path.

"Chill out, dude." Maybe those stories she'd read about delivery drivers being under too much pressure and having to pee in bottles instead of stopping for bathroom breaks were true because this person was driving like a jackass.

She hadn't reached the bumper yet when the driver's side door popped open. Curious now, Maddie checked out the person who jumped out. He was a tall man, wearing jeans and a gray, long-sleeved hoodie pulled up over his head.

No uniform. Maddie wasn't sure if delivery people even wore uniforms anymore. Damn, though. He must be sweating his balls off in that outfit today.

She took another few steps before stopping short.

The SUV was black, with dark-tinted windows.

The same one from down the block?

Beneath the sweat, Maddie's skin turned cold. *Not a delivery driver or a construction worker.*

She hesitated, telling herself not to be an idiot. The guy probably had a perfectly good reason for moving his car.

To the middle of the street, right in front of you?

Okay, yeah, that was a little sketch, but it wasn't like he was coming for her or—

Before she could finish the thought, the man charged. Panic froze her in place as every horror story from the news flashed through her head.

Kidnapping. Rape. Murder.

This was exactly how teen girls disappeared.

That split second of hesitation cost her. By the time she whirled to run, he'd narrowed the gap between them. Fear pounded her body, pushing her legs to pump harder. Blood thundered in her ears. Were those her shoes smacking the asphalt, or was he gaining on her?

Faster, faster, he's going to catch you.

Panting, she poured on the speed, craning her head to peer over her shoulder, and—

An arm wrapped around her neck and yanked her off her feet.

Maddie gasped for air as the pressure squeezed her throat shut. Her backpack was jerked off before she reached up to claw and pull at the arm, anything to release that iron grip.

"Help!" Her scream was useless, more like a croak as the stranger bent her over his hip and dragged her backward.

Maddie dug her heels into the asphalt, her lungs burning from lack of oxygen. She thrashed and struggled, but nothing worked.

Suddenly, he stopped moving, and she threw all her remaining strength into escape. She had to. She'd heard the stories of girls who were snatched off the streets and tossed into cars. No one ever saw them again.

Maddie bucked against his grip, and the pressure around her throat loosened. Hope barely had time to surge in her chest before he'd grabbed both of her arms and twisted them behind her back.

Zip! A stinging pressure bit into her wrists, and when Maddie tried to pull them apart, the pain increased. Her legs started to shake as an intense wave of terror swept her body. He'd zip-tied her arms together.

No more time.

Maddie gasped for air, trying to suck enough oxygen into her lungs to scream. The next moment, her body was wrenched sideways, and she was flying headfirst into the open back of the vehicle.

Her shoulder struck the floor, followed by her cheek.

White-hot pain shot through her face, stealing her breath as she rolled onto her back. Her scream was cut off by a thick wad of cloth stuffed inside her mouth, choking her all over again.

As she bucked and squirmed and tried to spit the cloth out, the man slapped a strip of duct tape over the gag, securing it in place. When he turned away, she kicked out at him. Her left foot struck his stomach, hard enough to make him grunt.

Take that!

Maddie's triumph died with the fist that smashed into the side of her knee. Pain exploded in her joint, and she screamed…or at least tried. The gag muffled the noise to a squeak.

She was still writhing in pain when her feet were bound a moment later.

Through tear-blurred eyes, she watched the man jump out. He jogged over and grabbed her bag. He dug around and pulled out a turquoise object.

Her cell phone.

"No!" The gag swallowed her shriek.

Within seconds, he'd dropped it on the ground and brought his foot down on top of it with a loud crunch. Her hope shattered along with her beloved device.

No one could find her now. She was completely on her own.

When he returned and started to crawl inside, Maddie wiggled as far away as she could, sweat dripping down her back as he slammed the rear door shut. She cowered against the second row of seats, whimpering.

This is it. This is the part where he rips off your clothes and rapes you, and then sells you into sex trafficking.

Tears streaked down her cheeks. Why hadn't she said yes when Donny asked if she'd wanted a ride home today?

The man scooted closer, so close that Maddie could smell his spicy cologne and sweaty armpits. Or maybe that was her sweat. Either way, she gagged.

It was a reminder that she would never get to shower or meet Kevin tonight.

Maddie sobbed harder, choking on her own tears as he reached for her jeans.

An object appeared in his hand. *A knife?* She started to shake violently, blinking to clear her vision.

Not a knife. A syringe.

Before she could flinch away, his hand swung. The needle stung her ass right through her jeans. The injection was still burning into her system when the man scrambled into the driver's seat, and the engine turned over. Fresh terror exploded beneath Maddie's skin when the floorboard rattled, and the SUV rolled forward.

Wherever this guy was taking her, it was nowhere good.

Last chance.

Maddie wiggled her bound legs closer to the rear window. *Almost there, almost there.* If she could just get close enough, maybe she could kick out the glass. Her legs were strong from walking every day.

She was so close when exhaustion crashed over her, worse than the morning after that last all-nighter she'd pulled with Abby over spring break. Her arms and legs stopped working properly.

So, so tired. If she could just close her eyes for a little bit...

Idiot, that has to be the drug! Get out of here, sleep later!

Maddie fought the grogginess for a few seconds, but her body and mind had other ideas. She was floating away. The sweet calm dragging her under was so peaceful that Maddie almost *wanted* to give in to the drug's soothing pull. She reclined on her back, staring out the window as the world turned hazy.

"There you go. Nighty night." A man's chuckle followed. "I can already tell we're going to have a lot of fun together."

Maddie frowned at the unfamiliar voice that seemed like it was coming from the far end of a long, hollow tunnel. Who was talking? Where was she?

A pinprick of clarity pierced the fog, giving Maddie time for one final burst of terror.

Mom, please, help me...

That was Maddie's last thought before she was swept away.

2

Detective Charli Cross slouched in the driver's seat of her four-door hybrid, polishing off the last bite of a double cheeseburger with ketchup only and washing it down with a slurp of soda. She wadded the paper wrapper into a tight ball and shoved it into the sack before carefully swiping her shirt to remove any crumbs and collecting them on the napkin spread across her lap. After she folded up the paper to trap all the crumbs inside, the napkin joined the wrapper in the bag.

She picked up the drink again, sucking on the straw as she studied the fancy house across the street from where she'd parked at the curb. This particular Savannah neighborhood was wealthy without being ostentatious, boasting traditional Southern-style houses set back on sprawling lots. The home she was currently scouting out was a two-story brick affair with white columns lining the porch. Deep green ivy climbed the sides and added a splash of color between the windows, and two large trees provided shade to a manicured lawn.

Dread crawled down her spine, making her slouch lower

in the seat. There were plenty of things Charli didn't look forward to—sticking her feet into those cold stirrups in the gynecologist's office, dental surgery, short people jokes—but this visit topped the list.

Her boss knew how much she despised this type of job duty, but had that stopped Sergeant Ruth Morris from sending Charli? No, of course not. When Charli had asked why they couldn't just take care of this at the precinct, Ruth had lowered her head and fixed her with that flat Terminator-esque stare that made even the most senior officers squirm before grinding out the favorite reply of peeved parents everywhere.

"Because I said so, Charlotte."

Charli cringed but didn't say a word. Ruth eventually explained that Charli showing up at the Briggs's house would make the matter more personal and comfortable.

Charli's eyebrows had shot up her forehead. "For who?" She might as well have been talking to a wall for all the good it had done. Fitting, since Ruth seemed about as persuadable as an inanimate object most of the time.

Charli expelled a sigh before sucking on the straw again. No liquid came up this time, which meant she'd officially run out of procrastination excuses.

Let's get this over with.

She climbed out of the car, brushed the few remaining crumbs off her pants, and headed across the street. Damn. It was only the first week of September, and it was still hot as a furnace outside.

She all but dragged her way up the three steps that led to the front door, stopping on the porch to smooth her blazer and her hair. Her finger hovered an inch from the doorbell.

Charli stared at the white circle for far too long before jabbing it. If the order had come from anyone but her boss, she might have dug in her heels. One didn't argue with

Sergeant Ruth Morris, though. As a fifty-three-year-old Black woman, Sergeant Morris had experienced more than her fair share of hostility over the years. As a result, she had no patience for "attitude" in the department. Mess with her orders, and she'd punt you to desk work faster than you could say "oopsies."

The musical "ding dong" was still echoing through the house when the door swung open, and a beaming face greeted her. "Detective Cross, so good to see you again. Please, come in."

Peter Briggs was an attractive man with deep brown hair and a strong jawline. He motioned for her to enter, so Charli stepped into a high-ceilinged entryway with walnut-colored hardwood flooring that matched the banisters on the dual staircases that swept upstairs from each side.

Peter's wife, Shelly, popped into view and ushered Charli toward the back of the house. "This way, Detective Cross."

Charli allowed herself to be herded between the stair-cases and into an elegant living room overlooking a lush backyard. Shelly gestured at a sunny yellow couch with skinny, delicate legs that seemed to defy physics in holding the piece up. Pretending like she hadn't noticed, Charli scooted past and claimed a sturdy yellow-and-blue wingback chair instead.

As soon as Charli's butt hit the cushion, Shelly rushed up, bearing a gleaming silver tray. "Please, help yourself to a cookie. I baked them fresh today."

Charli brightened, plucking a napkin from a short stack. After careful deliberation, she selected the biggest cookie with the most chocolate chips. Finally, a perk to this excruciating assignment. The double cheeseburger she'd eaten in the car had barely made a dent. "Thank you."

Shelly hovered a foot away, nibbling her lower lip and

watching her like a hawk. "Is the cookie okay? If you don't like it, I can get you something else."

Charli wasn't sure how she could possibly know if the cookie was okay since she had yet to take a bite. The intense scrutiny made her twitchy, though, almost killing her appetite.

Almost.

This cookie had better be good, Ruth.

Feeling a little like an animal exhibit at the zoo, Charli nibbled off a tiny piece. *Mmmm.* Okay, Ruth was vindicated. "It's delicious, thank you."

Shelly beamed at her. "I'm so glad." Turning, she set the tray back on the table and held up a finger. "Hang on just a second."

"Okay." Not like Charli could go anywhere anyway.

Shelly scurried over to the stairs and cupped her hands to her mouth. "Michael, come on down. Detective Cross is here, and I know you've been dying to thank her."

Charli chewed off a massive bite of cookie to hide her groan. *Sure, I bet that's exactly what the poor kid has been begging to do.*

A few seconds later, footsteps clanked down the stairs, and seven-year-old Michael appeared. The last time she'd seen the little boy, she'd been rescuing him from his biological father and Shelly's ex-husband, who'd decided to kidnap Michael when the courts refused to up his visitation rights. That night, he'd been trembling and pale.

Charli studied him as he entered the room, pleased to note the healthy pink cheeks and lack of fear. He did, however, tug at the collar of his short-sleeved polo shirt, his uncomfortable expression reflecting Charli's mood perfectly.

You and me both, kid.

She toyed with the idea of faking an emergency call and bolting, but Ruth's stern voice echoed in her head.

"Don't you dare mess this up, Cross! You sit your ass down and smile and suck up whatever that family has to say, and be glad it's not a damned complaint. The way things are playing out in the court of public opinion lately, we can't afford to pass up any good PR opportunities that come our way. Understand?"

Charli did understand. Unfortunately.

She forced her lips upward and prayed the expression didn't resemble one from her school yearbook photos. The photographers were forever nagging her to smile, a tactic that might have worked on her classmates but with Charli was an epic fail.

Even at a young age, she'd bristled whenever someone told her what to do.

Pretty much every school photo had ended up with her either appearing pissed off or constipated, to the point it had become an inside joke between her and her mom.

Pain twisted her heart, making the already fake smile even harder to hold. Luckily, Shelly and Peter Briggs seemed too tickled with her presence to notice. They both settled on the sunny yellow couch, with little Michael squirming between them.

Charli's gaze flickered to the spindly legs. How was that thing even standing? One day soon, those legs would cede the battle to mass and gravity. Designers who sacrificed form and function for the sake of appearance would never cease to baffle her.

Peter cleared his throat. "We just wanted you to come by so we could thank you personally for rescuing our little boy."

Shelly nodded. "Yes, we all owe you our eternal gratitude for helping us through that terrible time. There aren't very many true heroes in the world anymore, but you're definitely one of them."

Charli clenched her knees together to keep herself from

squirming. Ruth was definitely back on her shit list. "I'm glad I was able to help."

How much longer?

Shelly turned to her son. "You remember Detective Charlotte Cross, don't you, sweetie? Isn't there something you wanted to say to her, Michael?"

The little boy fidgeted with his belt loop. When he finally spoke, he mumbled the words without glancing up. "Thank you for saving me, Detective Cross." Michael scooted closer to his mother and buried his face in her side.

Charli wished she could hide her face too. So. Much. Awkward. "That's so kind of you to say, Michael, but really, I was just doing my job. And please call me Charli."

"Well, then, you perform your job exceedingly well." Peter Briggs ruffled Michael's hair while Shelly Briggs sniffled, her head still bobbing up and down.

"Yes, how can we ever begin to thank you enough? That whole ordeal was so awful. I knew that George," Mrs. Briggs gave a delicate shudder and checked on Michael as she uttered her ex-husband's name, but the boy didn't stir, "wasn't happy with the custody arrangement, but I never would have guessed he'd stoop to kidnapping."

A snort came from the opposite side of the loveseat. "Well, maybe you should have guessed. It's not like George has ever been a real stand-up guy, is it?"

Her husband's mild tone was belied by the accusation underlining his words. Charli knew it, and Shelly Brigg's flattened smile said she did too.

A tense silence followed. One Charli filled by mentally cursing Ruth for sending her on this painful excursion in the first place.

And by grabbing another cookie.

After a huffed breath, Shelly sat up straighter and jerked her chin toward Michael. "Like I've mentioned before, I'd rather save discussions of George for more private conversations."

Peter Briggs shook his head and gave a humorless chuckle. "Right. Because Mikey can't figure out for himself that his bio dad is a loser after being kidnapped by him for five days."

Charli stuffed another chunk of cookie into her mouth to prevent sharing a statistic on the percentage of children kidnapped by their biological parents each year. Not everyone appreciated a good statistic as much as she did.

Shelly Briggs cleared her throat. "I'm sure Detective Cross didn't come here to listen to us squabble."

No. Charli Cross didn't. The awkward gratitude session had been bad enough without adding a shot of marital strife. As a consolation prize, she snatched a third cookie. "These cookies really are delicious, Mrs. Briggs, and it does no one any good placing blame on each other." Poor woman. She'd just been through the wringer with her son and ex-husband, and now her current one was raking her over the coals.

Shelly shot her a grateful smile. "Thank you. I enjoy baking. It's stress relief for me." Her mouth tightened. "I used to do a lot more before Peter decided to go on a keto diet."

Charli stopped mid-chew, her gaze darting to the front door like a cornered animal.

Don't do it. Ruth will bench you for a month if you pull a dine and dash.

Still, the tension crackling through the room made her scoot her hips toward the edge of the chair. Just in case.

"Yes, I'm trying to stay healthy for Michael. Is that so wrong? I'm sorry if I'm raining on your inner Betty Crocker parade."

Charli choked on the last bite. Eyes watering, she pounded her chest and cleared her throat before grabbing a glass of sweet tea off the table and guzzling it down.

She slanted an accusatory glare at the silent phone in her pocket. Were all the criminals on vacation or what?

Somehow, she managed to survive another excruciating ten minutes of the Briggs's appreciation for her efforts, mixed with their needled barbs.

Her heart softened when she focused on the kid. Poor Michael. No wonder he hadn't wanted to come downstairs.

When Peter Brigg's phone rang and he rose from the couch to answer, Charli was prepared. She sprang to her feet and powered toward the entryway. "Thank you for having me over, but I really do need to get back to work now."

Shelly popped up behind her. "I understand. I'm sure you must be busy. Here, let me walk you out." She rushed past Charli to open the door.

Charli was almost free and clear when, without warning, Shelly flung her arms around her neck. "Thank you again for rescuing my baby."

The second Shelly's hands clutched her, Charli froze. *Oh no. Nooo. Shelly Briggs was a hugger.*

She probably should have guessed and kept her distance or faked a cough, but it was too late now. The hugging was already underway.

Thankfully, Charli had both enough experience with the loathsome squishing of bodies together and enough discipline to ignore the instincts screaming at her to bolt like a scalded cat, the way she used to as a girl whenever her hug-loving grandpa from Virginia came to visit.

Charli's hands hovered in the air, inches away from Shelly's back. She should probably pat the woman on the shoulder or something but couldn't quite bring herself to make that additional contact.

Shelly seemed too busy sniffling when she finally stepped back to notice. They exchanged awkward goodbyes before

Charli hurried down the walkway at about three times the speed of her arrival.

When she climbed into her car and slammed the door, she released a giant sigh of relief. That had been every bit as awful as she'd anticipated, but the ordeal was over now.

She patted her pocket. At least she'd managed to grab two cookies for the road before making her escape.

The cookies almost made the trip worth it.

Almost.

Charli snapped on her seat belt and released the parking brake before steering the car onto the road toward the precinct. She flipped through the radio stations, cranking up the volume when an old Beastie Boys song came on and tapping the steering wheel in time to the beat.

Just before the final chorus, her phone shrilled. The radio silenced as Bluetooth kicked in and commandeered the speakers. "Detective Charli Cross speaking."

"So, how'd it go, Smalls? Did the theme song from *Full House* play in the background while Mr. and Mrs. Briggs gushed over you?"

"It went fine, *Bigs*." Charli emphasized her partner's despised nickname as payback.

Smalls. She wrinkled her nose. Charli's short stature meant people already treated her like a cute teen or talked down to her. She definitely didn't need a cutesy nickname making things worse.

"Really? So, you didn't chew off your own leg and make a run for it? Damn, there goes my twenty-dollar bet."

Matthew's reply surprised a snicker out of Charli as she pulled to a complete stop at a red light, scanning for cars in both directions before making a right turn. "No, but I definitely thought about it. Especially when Mrs. Briggs gave me a surprise hug at the end."

Her partner's sympathetic groan filled the car. "Noooo, really?"

"Yup."

"What did you do?"

Charli rolled her eyes. "What do you think I did? I shoved her away and told her she'd better brush up on the basics of consent. Obviously." She was careful to keep her delivery matter-of-fact.

A second or two of silence followed her remark before Matthew cursed under his breath. "Dammit, Charli, you almost had me that time."

Charli smiled as she flicked on her turn signal. "I promise, I only *thought* about shoving her away, all while praying she wasn't crushing the two cookies I'd shoved into my pocket. The important takeaway is, both me and the cookies emerged unscathed."

"Whew, what a relief. Cookie crumbs can be a bitch to remove from pockets. Save one for me?"

"Not on your life. I earned those things." Charli's conscience pinged a little, and she sighed. "Mr. and Mrs. Briggs were very appreciative and seem like decent people. I feel bad for the kid, though. I'm not sure their marriage will survive the kidnapping."

They razzed each other a little more before Charli ended the call. "See you back at the precinct in a few."

Before the radio could retake control of the speakers, Bluetooth announced an incoming text from her dad in a robotic female voice: *We still on for dinner tonight?*

She dictated the return message: *Yup, looking forward to it.*

Not even a lie, as long as the meal at her dad's house turned out to be for dinner as advertised and not another opportunity for him to launch into a spiel criticizing her life choices. By now, she was pretty sure she could recite them by heart.

She curled her fingers around the steering wheel before easing her grip. Her dad loved her and meant well. Still, his disapproval of her job as a detective stung. Even when she was younger, Jason Cross hadn't quite understood Charli, always wondering why she wasn't bubbly like his friends' daughters, or more into dancing and dresses, or at least more into interests that fit the typical Southern daughter mold.

Her dad never seemed to see the real Charli. Or maybe he did and just refused to accept she was a little left of center.

She'd been lucky, though, and had a couple of friends in high school. Well, two exactly. Rebecca Larson and Madeline Ferguson. Charli and Rebecca had been fairly close, but Madeline was the only human who truly *got* her. Madeline had been her best friend…right up until some bastard murdered her at age sixteen.

The next person who'd come closest to grasping Charli's off-frequency wavelength was her mom. Pain sucked the air from Charli's lungs, wrenching her ribs and burning her chest.

Two years had passed since lung cancer had taken Carrie Cross from them. The diagnosis had come unexpectedly because her mom had never smoked a day in her life. The cancer hadn't cared, though, spreading like wildfire and stealing her mom so much faster than the experts had predicted.

Charli's eyes burned. Her mom had appreciated her for the daughter she was rather than the daughter she'd hoped her to be. Her dad managed to make Charli feel like a failure for staying true to herself instead of settling down with a family like he wanted.

She grimaced as she cruised down the street. Her dad didn't even get her well enough to understand her deep-seated drive to achieve. If he did, he'd know why she devoted most of her time to the job.

At work, she had a good shot at succeeding.

Ten minutes later, Charli parked in her usual spot and headed inside. Out of the four precincts in Savannah, this one was the oldest, with all the offices housed in an unimposing three-story brick building that sat on the edge of a graveyard.

Charli entered the lobby at a brisk pace and made her way upstairs toward the small office she shared with her partner. Several pairs of eyes tracked her progress, but she ignored them. Not her problem some of the uniformed officers were jealous of her quick transition to detective. She'd never win a popularity contest around here. She could live with that.

Especially since being popular typically translated into a willingness to bitch and gossip all day long. Charli would rather peel off her own skin and set it on fire than be subjected to twenty-four-seven whining about missing out on promotions or speculating over who was banging whom.

When she burst into their cramped little office, Matthew paused over his laptop keyboard to examine her. As usual, his button-down shirt and thinning dark hair were equally rumpled. One from his inability to keep his possessions tidy for longer than five minutes, and the other from his habit of dragging his hand across his scalp when he was deep in thought.

He chuckled. "What, no fruit basket or t-shirt that says, 'Best Detective Ever'? Gotta say I'm a little disappointed."

"Really?" She was tempted to flip him off but refrained. "When's the last time you ate a piece of fruit, huh?"

He scrunched up his broad face and pretended to think that over. "Does a protein smoothie count?" When Charli narrowed her eyes, he busted out into a grin. "Okay, okay, you win. I didn't really care about the fruit basket. The shirt is still a real bummer, though."

"Right. That'd go over about as well as that terrible elephant joke you told me yesterday did."

"Hey!" Matthew looked genuinely offended. "That was a great joke. I can't help it if you don't appreciate my sophisticated sense of humor."

Charli snorted as she arranged her bag neatly on the shelf below her desk. "It was a knock-knock joke. And it didn't even make sense."

He scratched his chin. "Yeah, come to think of it, that wasn't my best offering."

The smile left his face when she collapsed into her chair with a soft groan. "Seriously, though, you do okay on that visit?"

Charli softened at her partner's concern. He knew how much she hated the non-detective part of the job, like dealing with the public in a one-on-one capacity or accepting kudos for simply performing her job. Out of the few people she had left, Matthew probably understood her the best. Not as good as her mom had, or Madeline, but it was something.

"Yeah, I'm good. Thanks, though."

He grunted and returned his attention to his laptop.

"What're you working on there?"

Matthew shrugged. "Just wrapping up a report on that drug bust that went bad. Nothing new came down the pike except for some small-time stuff."

That meant no new homicides, a fact for which Charli was grateful on a personal level. Professionally, though, she enjoyed a challenge. "How small are we talking?"

"One of them is a vandalism case, if that answers your question."

Charli drooped. Ugh. Property crimes were the least interesting to her, especially lower-level ones like vandalism. She'd entered the police force to help solve murders and bring peace and closure to victims' loved ones. Ease their pain, if only a little.

Buildings didn't have feelings.

Three sharp raps rattled the door. Without waiting for an invitation, Sergeant Ruth Morris blew into their office, her cropped black curls gleaming beneath the artificial light. "I need both of you in Conference Room A, stat."

Her boss's full lips were flat, and a muscle near her right eye twitched. She glared at both of them before pivoting and marching out.

Matthew and Charli exchanged a glance.

Murder face? Matthew mouthed as they trailed their sergeant to the conference room.

Charli nodded. Definitely.

Looked like the vandalism case would be someone else's problem.

3

Sergeant Ruth Morris pounced as soon as Charli and Matthew entered the conference room, not even giving them a chance to pull out chairs from behind the beat-up table before launching into the news.

"At one o'clock this afternoon, we received a call from a fifty-eight-year-old woman named Sherrie Johnson. She and her husband were birdwatching over in the marshes by the mouth of the Vernon River when they stumbled across an oversized plastic container, like one of those bins people store dog food in, only bigger. They opened it, hoping to find something exciting to share with their buddies at the next birder shindig. Sounds like they were none too thrilled to find human remains instead."

Charli's stomach lurched, but she hid her reaction. She could picture the general area Sergeant Morris was describing. Back in high school, people used to joke about hiding dead bodies there, which was mildly amusing at the time. Before Madeline was abducted.

Charli shook away thoughts of her dead friend and

focused on the new case. "The recent rains might have uncovered the container, especially if the grave was shallow."

Ruth nodded. "That's what I'm thinking. Initial inspection suggests the body belongs to a young female. Possibly a teen, but we're still waiting on confirmation."

Charli's heart sank while Matthew frowned. All homicides were disturbing, but young victims were a particular kind of upsetting.

"They got a time of death estimate yet?" Matthew's voice deepened and turned gruff, a sign he'd switched into serious mode.

"No. Apparently, the body's in pretty bad shape, so we'll have to wait for testing for more details. Given the circumstances, I went ahead and called in the GBI to assist on this one. The DOFS will help, in case…"

Ruth's expression hardened back into her murder face, and Charli's pulse quickened. The Georgia Bureau of Investigation required an invitation to join a local investigation, except in very specific instances or by order of the governor. If Ruth had already requested the GBI's Division of Forensic Sciences to assist, then she had a good reason.

For instance, if she was concerned about a repeat killer.

"Was the body mutilated in a specific way, or a body part missing? Or did they find something else in the container?" Sometimes, the sociopaths who murdered for sport left a specific signature, which manifested in different ways.

The runaway muscle near Ruth's eye twitched. "Apparently, one of the first cops on the scene braved the smell and peeked around inside the container. He's not sure exactly what he saw, but he said the girl was naked, and the area between her legs didn't look like the rest of her. The skin appeared to be bunched together, possibly sewn together."

The hairs on Charli's arms lifted. *Don't jump to conclusions. There aren't nearly enough facts yet.* Still, if the cop was right, there was a good chance the murder had a sadistic sexual component to it.

"I'm assigning this case to you two. There are officers on the scene now, plus crime scene techs and DOFS. Janice Piper will be assisting with chasing down the paper trails, starting with missing persons reports."

Charli nodded. Janice Piper was a detective in their department who often went drinking with Matthew. Knowing her, she was probably already griping that she'd been assigned the grunt work while Charli and Matthew got to go out in the field.

Not Charli's problem.

Ruth crossed her arms over her chest and fixed each of them with the stink eye. "We need to stay on top of this one. I don't need to remind you that if the body does turn out to be a missing teen, the media will be circling like vultures sooner versus later. Do not speak to anyone who approaches you about the case, journalist or otherwise. On or off the record. Is that clear?"

Charli nodded. "Yes, Sergeant."

"Sure thing, Sergeant."

Ruth subjected them each to another glare before her posture relaxed a little. "I know I don't need to say this, but please remember this body belongs to someone's child. Even if the victim turns out to be twenty, that's too young and likely will rock the family and this community. Let's hope it's just the one body out there. Otherwise, you can bet your ass panic will follow."

"We hear you, Sergeant."

Matthew lifted his eyebrows at Charli, prompting her to agree, but her mind had already latched on to a new concern. "The location of the body worries me. The marshes are pretty isolated in that spot compared to most places around here, with soil that's soft and easy to dig, and the area isn't on the way to or from anywhere. Makes me think the killer is highly organized and did his research first."

Both the hallmarks of the worst kind of serial killer. Bad news, if they did discover other bodies out there.

Ruth's eye twitched. "The location worries me too. Why do you think I'm assigning the two of you? That was a rhetorical question, Cross." She added that last bit with a pointed finger when Charli opened her mouth to answer.

Right. Ruth already knew Charli and Matthew had the best murder clearance rate in the Savannah PD and surrounding counties. She'd never understand the logic behind people asking questions they didn't want answered. More than that, she found the incongruity irksome.

After several seconds when no one spoke, Ruth grunted and jerked her chin at the door. "Now, quit running your mouth and get to work."

4

A twangy country song played as Matthew drove them south in his truck on White Bluff Road, shooting Charli sideways glances every so often.

Most days, she would have teased him by now about the growing collection of fast-food bags on the back seat of his extended cab or the persistent eau de burger. And she was always the talkative one on the way to a crime scene. She liked to go over the existing facts of the case aloud so they were cemented in her head by the time they arrived at the location, leaving Matthew to jump in with whatever his gut instinct was telling him about the case. The fact that those gut instincts turned out wrong almost as often as they paid off was exactly why Charli favored facts and analysis over magical thinking.

Today, though, she was quiet, her mind drifting as she stared out the windshield at the marshland that sprawled to the east before meeting the banks of the Vernon River. The glittering water reminded her of the day Marcia Ferguson had sobbed on the phone as she gave Charli the dreaded news.

"They found her! They found Madeline's body, buried out by the Vernon. Some monster k-killed my b-baby and left her in the mud to rot."

"Everything okay, Charli?"

She flinched, her fingers jerking the pendant she'd been clutching. She opened her hand and stared down at the half of a golden heart nestled in her palm. Until Matthew interrupted her, she hadn't even realized she'd been touching the necklace again.

Charli flipped the charm over and stroked the engraved letters.

BFF.

"Charli? It's not like you to go silent. You're starting to worry me a little."

She slipped the pendant back under her blouse. "Sorry. This case is dredging up old memories, that's all."

"That friend of yours who was murdered back in high school?"

"Yes." Charli hated the sympathy in Matthew's voice. Hated that he knew about Madeline at all, along with the rest of the people at work. Her friend's death was personal to Charli. A hurt she wanted to mourn in private, not a scar for everyone to see and discuss.

She angled her body toward the passenger window. She didn't like feeling so exposed.

"Wanna talk about it?"

Charli shook her head. "Not really." Matthew was the closest friend she had these days, but even talking to him about Madeline seemed wrong and only upped her anxiety.

Although, ever since Ruth had filled them in on the case, not talking wasn't doing wonders for her anxiety, either. As the distinct odor of salt and sulfur trickled in despite the closed windows, the memories grew increasingly difficult to keep at bay.

She dug her nails into her thighs and blew out a quiet breath, sensing Matthew's gaze on her again.

"I hate cases like this one. That could be my daughter they found, you know?"

Charli winced. She'd been so wrapped up in her own trauma that she'd momentarily forgotten Matthew had a teenage daughter. "Sorry, that's such a terrible thing to have to think about. How's Chelsea doing, anyway?"

He lifted his broad shoulders. "Last I heard, she'd taken up the violin. Still totally into all the K-pop stuff, though. I just don't get it."

His bafflement made Charli smile. "You and half the dads in this country, but that's okay. Historically, the musical tastes of parents and their children have always diverged."

Matthew snorted. "Yeah, but at least the stuff *I* liked as a kid was good."

"Keep telling yourself that. Besides, have you seen some of those K-pop singers dance?" She bobbed her eyebrows at him. "Pretty impressive."

Her partner groaned. "Please, don't tell me you're gonna insist on playing K-pop now when it's your turn to pick the music."

Charli tapped her chin, pretending to think about it. "Depends on whether or not you keep calling me Smalls."

"Okay, okay, I'll quit!"

Charli's grin faded as they pulled up behind a long row of squad cars and vans on the side of the road.

Time to get down to business.

The murder site was already swarming with people by the time Matthew and Charli climbed out of the truck. Uniformed police officers dotted the area near the yellow crime scene tape stretched between strategically arranged pylons. Additional officers were off in the distance, mingling with Savannah PD's crime scene techs and the GBI's forensic specialists, some of whom were easy to spot in their white plastic Tyvek suits.

Charli scoured the area. "No news vans...yet. That's good, at least."

Matthew nodded. "Yeah. We'll see how long that lasts."

Charli was glad she'd worn combat-style boots as they picked their way through the swampy grass and mud toward the yellow crime scene tape.

Matthew waved at two officers who stood guarding the entrance to the scene. "Ronnie. Pat."

Savannah might be a city, but it had somehow clung to that small-town vibe, where pretty much everyone knew everyone, at least in the law enforcement circle.

"Hey, you two. Throw on some booties from the box and stick to the obvious footpath as much as possible, or else they're gonna yell at you down there. We already got an earful from the GBI about 'trampling the crime scene like a herd of elephants.' Can you believe that nonsense?" Ronnie, a lanky officer with a dark mustache, rolled his eyes, inviting Charli and Matthew to join in.

Much better at playing the game, Matthew cracked a smile while Charli frowned. "Did you trample the scene?"

Ronnie stared at Charli like she was some weird specimen beneath a microscope. She returned his gaze without blinking. If she cowered every time another cop gave her that look, she'd spend half her time on her belly.

She was close enough to the ground as she was.

"We walked up to the scene like anyone else would have. How the hell could we have known what we'd find?"

Matthew nudged Charli to move, but she ignored his cue. "Didn't the people who called tell you it was a dead body?"

Ronnie's cheeks turned blotchy. "People call in about dead bodies all the time, and more often than not, they turn out to be old chicken bones, or maybe a dead dog."

True. But until the remains were verified as human or not, the crime scene should be approached with caution.

Matthew cut in. "I hear you. Charli, we'd better get a move on if we don't want Ruth busting our balls." He lifted the yellow tape for her to duck under.

"I don't have balls to bust." She took his cue and scooted under the tape because her partner's sentiment was correct, even if his wording wasn't.

He contorted his tall frame to fit beneath it, and they headed down the well-trodden path.

Despite all the people milling about, the crime scene was quieter than usual. More subdued. Like ER doctors, most officers became detached when dealing with death after a while. Shouting and raucous laughter was frowned upon, but the intermittent chatter and an occasional joke to break the tension were standard fare.

Not today, though. Today, everyone was wearing identical grim expressions.

Even the most hardened cops weren't comfortable cracking jokes if they were potentially looking at a killer who targeted teens. That was Charli's presumption for the atmosphere until a breeze kicked up off the river.

The stench hit her a few moments later. Rotting meat that was foul and so strong Charli's eyes started to water.

"Jesus." Matthew made a small gagging noise and averted his face.

Charli's nostrils flared, but she kept her head high and picked her way closer to the large, mud-splattered container that held the body. Or what remained of the body. One glance inside the circular opening made the cause of the odor obvious.

These remains were long past the early stages of decomposition. She was no medical examiner, but based on the smell, lack of distinguishable facial features, and exposed bone, she'd be shocked if some of the organs hadn't liquefied already.

Something buzzed near her ear, and Charli swatted it away. More flies swarmed around the body. She checked the faces but couldn't pick out the GBI's medical examiner. "Where's Soames?"

John Haskins glanced up from where he was bagging a hair sample, his blue shirt marking him as part of the GBI. "He was already out on another case, so he sent me."

"I see." Not ideal, but that was how things played out sometimes. Charli had interacted with Haskins several times over the years and found him pleasant enough. He wasn't a medical examiner, though. Death scene investigators worked out of the same office and were skilled at their jobs of collecting forensic evidence, but she needed the medical examiner. Soames was the one who'd be best able to coax out any secrets from the body. "Got anything for me yet?"

Haskins finished with the sample and rocked back on his heels. "Not really. The heat makes it hard to get a good read on anything."

Charli had figured as much, but she made a point of always asking anyway. Overconfidence led to narrow thinking, and narrow thinking led to unsolved cases. "What about the flies? Do you know if they originated from inside the container with the body, or are they recent additions?" A body's exposure to insects had a huge impact on the rate of deterioration. The more insects, the quicker the flesh broke down.

"They're new. The plastic container must have protected her. Good thing. Otherwise, she'd be nothing but bones and hair by now, with this heat."

Along with insects, heat also sped nature along. Especially humidity.

Sweat rolled between Charli's breasts. Early September,

at close to four-thirty in the afternoon in Georgia, was still hot as blazes. The weird off-and-on-again drizzle only made the air stickier.

And the smell stronger.

The mix of factors would make establishing a time of death challenging outside of a lab. "Whoever she was, she definitely wasn't killed within the past few days."

"Yeah, my nose told me that already." Matthew popped up from behind her, his sleeve protecting the lower half of his face. Together, they watched the forensics team work. "Are you going to transport her in that?" He gestured to the plastic container she'd been buried in, which was large and unwieldy, with a big, round screw-off lid on the top.

Haskins nodded. "Yeah, I'm worried that we'll lose parts of her if we try to transfer to a body bag."

Matthew grimaced. "Great, thanks a lot for that visual."

Charli swatted at another flying bug, this time on her arm. When she glanced up again, her heart slammed against her ribs.

The victim's rotting face had vanished, replaced by creamy skin, a pointed chin with soft, rounded cheeks, and long, silky brown hair. Charli released a tiny gasp.

Madeline.

Charli blinked, and the decaying face reappeared.

Get a grip, Detective.

"Come on." Charli gave herself a mental shake. "Let's get in there for a closer look before they cart her away."

Matthew's sarcastic "great" trailed Charli as she squared her shoulders and forged ahead.

She had a job to do, and nothing could get in the way of that.

Not even Madeline.

5

S tepping closer to the body intensified the smell enough that Charli had to be careful to inhale through her mouth to maintain her poise.

Matthew wasn't nearly as worried about appearances. He made another gagging noise in his throat and stumbled back. "I don't know how that doesn't bother you. My nose must be more sensitive than yours."

"Yeah, that's definitely it." Charli respected her partner, but sometimes, he could act like such a man. At five feet tall and twenty-six years old, she couldn't afford to have a sensitive nose or anything else. As it was, most of the other detectives and LEOs side-eyed the hell out of her. Hitting detective younger than thirty was a rare accomplishment that tended to bring out the haters. The fact that she didn't always play well with others didn't help. If she carried on like Matthew did about the smell, she'd only give them ammunition.

Matthew stood more than six feet and had a linebacker's build. He could hurl on Charli's shoes right now and still not get labeled as weak.

He was a good guy. A little oblivious at times, but definitely not responsible for the systematic sexism within law enforcement.

"I'm gonna see what I can get out of forensics."

Charli waved him off, and he beat a hasty retreat over to where someone from the GBI forensics team was checking out potential tracks. She turned back to the body. The mud was extra soft from the recent rains, with pools of water scattered everywhere.

Recent precipitation coupled with the passage of time made viable shoe prints a long shot—a situation not helped by the first responders running amuck all over the scene. Maybe the GBI would get lucky and find some evidence snagged by the muck or caught in a patch of reedy grass.

She returned her attention to the victim but straightened after only a few seconds. In the body's advanced state of decomposition, analysis was far beyond Charli's expertise. Too far gone for her to obtain any vital information from a visual inspection. That and the body was awkwardly crammed inside the container, and no bits of clothes could be seen. They'd have to wait for the GBI's medical examiner to perform his autopsy back at his office in Pooler.

Her attention turned to the girl's makeshift coffin. It was made from some type of plastic and had a barrel shape. Like one of those old feed bins people sometimes repurposed as a rain barrel. Nothing special jumped out at her about the exterior.

Through watering eyes from the stench, Charli peered inside again, looking for identifying marks on the interior of the barrel. She was greeted with puddles of dreadful-smelling, reddish-brown fluid. The result of bacteria and heat feasting unchecked on flesh. Tilting her head, she studied the vat.

Why that container, and why here?

As she straightened, the dirty brown marsh faded from view. Images of a different day flickered behind Charli's eyes like frames from a movie reel.

Madeline, giggling and bouncing around by the statue of a female jogger…walking down the dirt trail near a wrought iron fence…the man dragging Madeline away…

No! She couldn't think about that right here, right now.

She had to give all her focus to another dead teen girl, her body dumped in the same vicinity as her best friend's. The police had searched for Madeline without any leads until several months after she'd disappeared. Until her lifeless body was found in the marshes, maybe less than half a mile from where she currently stood.

Would this case end the same way? Unsolved, with the killer still walking around out there, free to commit more heinous acts?

Even though no one else was privy to her mental interrogation, Charli shook her head. Firmly. A big part of why she'd been drawn to police work was to ensure other loved ones never had to go through what she and Madeline's family had.

Whoever you are, I will do right by you. For your sake, and for Madeline's.

After one last glance at the girl's final resting place, Charli approached a group of forensic techs who were clustered around the site, busy bagging samples of anything that might be of use. She noted any tiny bits of trash or otherwise out-of-place items collected from the area nearby were also carefully preserved.

That reminded her.

She retraced her steps to John Haskins, who was in the process of sealing an evidence bag. "Find anything unusual?"

He shook his head. "Not yet."

"Any preliminary estimates on time of death?"

"Ballpark, figuring in all the elements?" He shrugged. "I'd say she's been hanging out in that container at least one to two months, maybe even longer, but don't quote me on that. Soames will skin my hide."

Charli frowned. Not good news if their victim had been dead two months or longer. The more time that passed, the less evidence. Plus, the lack of certainty on the time of death made narrowing down their pool of missing persons more challenging.

Matthew was talking to one of the other officers, so Charli headed over to a middle-aged couple huddled near the police tape. They stood close together in matching mustard yellow waterproof overalls and over-the-knee boots, and their hunched posture and downturned mouths indicated they were anxious to get out of there.

"You must be the birdwatchers." Charli murmured her deduction aloud as she trudged closer, the marsh mud sucking at her boots with each step before releasing them with a *plop*.

A glance down confirmed she'd lost both disposable protective booties to the tug-of-war somewhere along the way.

Mental note: hose down boots as soon as you get home. Otherwise, the mud would dry and increase the probability that the marshy odor would linger. Charli would rather not spend the next year smelling like she lived in a bog.

She stopped a good five feet away to introduce herself. "Hi, I'm Detective Charli Cross of the Savannah Police Department. Are you the couple who discovered the body?"

The woman answered first. "That's right, we did." Her head swiveled toward the crime scene before she jerked it away, shivering.

The gray-haired man wrapped his arm around the woman's shoulders and pulled her closer to his chest. "It's okay, Sherrie." He pressed a kiss on the top of her blonde head before glowering at Charli. "The officer told us we needed to give a statement to the detectives, and we want to do our duty, but we've been waiting a long time now. We're hot and sweating, and this has been a big ordeal for my wife."

Charli nodded and pulled out her notepad. "I understand, and I'll do my best to get you both out of this weather as quickly as possible."

The man's chin angled up. "See that you do."

"Gerald, stop that!" Sherrie swatted her husband's arm. "The detective is just trying to do her job. I might wilt a little in this heat, but I won't melt."

Not melt, maybe, but Charli could understand why Gerald was concerned. The woman's face was bright red and sweat dripped from her chin. "Hang on. I'll be right back."

Ignoring Gerald's protests, Charli tromped over to a large cooler someone had set by a pylon and popped the lid. She returned with two ice-cold bottles of water and extended one to Sherrie. "Here, drink this."

She gave the other bottle to Gerald and waited for them to finish.

"Thank you, I didn't realize how much I needed that." Sherrie flashed Charli a grateful smile.

"Yes, thank you," Gerald mumbled.

The woman looked a little less ready to collapse at any second, but Charli still wanted to get her home soon. "First off, can you say and spell your full names for me?"

Gerald groaned. "We already gave our names to—"

"*Gerald.*"

At his wife's pointed glare, Gerald threw up his hands. "All right. I'll be quiet now. I just don't know why we have to give them the same information all over again."

His reaction didn't faze Charli. "I like to take my own

notes. That way, I don't have to rely on anyone else, and if I get any details wrong, I only have myself to blame."

Sherrie nodded. "See? Detective Cross knows what's she's doing."

Her husband's chin sank. "I suppose that makes sense. I'm Gerald Johnson, and this is my wife, Sherrie."

Once he spelled their names, Charli moved on. "I understand you were out here birdwatching today?"

"We were. We wanted to see an anhinga and thought there might be some in this area." Gerald elaborated when he noted Charli's blank expression. "An anhinga is a long-beaked bird that dives for fish and sometimes looks like a snake when it swims."

"Oh, shush, Gerald. Who's holding us up now? I doubt Detective Cross gives two figs about anhingas. She's got more important things to do in her free time."

Definitely. Very weighty pursuits like reading books about serial killers and binging whatever new Netflix series was out.

"So, you came here this morning looking for an anhinga. Did you stick to this area right here, or did you walk a while?"

"We walked around a little that way, oh, maybe half a mile." Gerald pointed south. "Didn't have any luck, although we did spot a couple of painted buntings. We'd circled back along a different route and were on our way to the car when we spotted that container."

"When you approached the container, did you notice anything odd? Maybe footprints or strange markings of any kind?"

Sherrie shook her head. "No, but we weren't looking for them, either. At that point, we were just curious about what might be inside."

"Did you notice anyone else out here? Other birdwatchers, anyone at all?"

"No, just the two of us, as far as I noticed. You see anyone else, Ger?"

Gerald sucked his lip over his teeth as he thought. "Nope, unless you count the couple of boats that passed by on the river."

Charli made a note, although she doubted the boats were relevant. Nothing so far seemed especially useful, but she kept her mind open. Sometimes the smallest details turned out to be the ones that cracked a case. "Okay, walk me through your process. As you're headed back to your car, you stumble across a large container in the mud. Then what?"

Sherrie started wringing her hands together and ducked her head like she was embarrassed. "Gerald and I were wondering aloud what could be inside. We figured it might have fallen off a boat and figured it couldn't hurt to take a peek. Boy, were we wrong."

She swallowed hard and shuddered, prompting Gerald to pull her close again.

"So, you opened the container, and that's when you saw the body?" Charli prompted, just to make sure she had the facts clear.

"Saw it, smelled it, all of the above. I always figured they played up how bad dead bodies smelled on those TV shows, but they weren't kidding. I about tossed my cookies." Just talking about the smell was making Gerald swallow repeatedly and lose his color.

Charli scooted back a couple steps, just in case. The muck on her boots was more than enough without adding vomit. "What happened after you opened the container?"

"Once we figured out what we were looking at, I screamed like a little girl, Gerald said a bad word, and then we hurried far enough away to escape that ghastly smell before calling nine-one-one. We never went back over there after that. Once was more than enough."

"And you didn't notice anything else? Find anything in the mud that you might have picked up or any other cars parked along the street when you showed up?"

"No, nothing."

Sherrie was sweating profusely again, so Charli finished scribbling and plucked a business card from her pocket. "All right, I appreciate your help. Here's my business card. If you think of anything else that might be helpful, give me a call."

Gerald took the card from Charli's hand. "Will do. Come on, Sherrie. Let's get you home."

With his arm still wrapped around his wife's shoulders, Gerald escorted her away from the scene, toward a white Toyota Camry that had been parked along the side of the road when Charli drove up.

She tucked the notebook back into her pocket and headed for Matthew's truck. Halfway there, the clouds began drizzling, so Charli picked up her pace as she followed the path recently trampled by the police. By the time she reached the car, the drizzle had turned into a sprinkle, splatting against the windshield and plinking into a nearby puddle.

Charli wrenched open the passenger door but paused, glancing down at her feet. "My boots are a mess."

Matthew motioned for her to get in. "You think mine are magically clean or something? Hurry up, hop in before you're soaked through. Don't need you catching a cold."

Charli did as he suggested while rolling her eyes in exasperation. "Okay, Grandpa." Matthew had a heart of gold, which she appreciated, but she could do without the mother hen routine.

One overprotective dad was more than enough.

"Aw, come on. Can't a guy worry about his partner?"

Matthew waited a beat. "Besides, if you call out sick, that's more work for me."

She snorted as he shifted the truck into gear. "Great, so now you're saying you only care if I get sick because you're lazy?"

"Just don't tell, okay? I gotta keep up appearances."

Right. Matthew was about as far from lazy as a cop could get. If anything, her partner was even more of a workaholic than her and skewed toward putting too many hours into the job, not too few. He'd told her once during a late-night work session over pizza and hot wings that it was one of the main reasons his ex-wife had divorced him.

As he drove them back toward the precinct, they shared what they'd learned at the scene, which didn't amount to much.

"They're going to be doing a sweep of the general area to make sure there aren't any more bodies nearby," Matthew said.

Charli rubbed her arms to chase away a sudden chill. "Let's hope it's just the one body."

"You can say that again."

She stared out the rain-streaked passenger window, watching the marsh flash by.

Who are you, and how did you get into that container?

6

Back at the precinct, Charli stuffed another bite of broccoli with beef into her mouth from a paper plate, chewing while she scanned the NCIC database on her computer screen. The FBI's National Crime Information Center was an information-sharing tool used by law enforcement agents across the country. Among the wide array of files housed within the records was information on missing persons.

Matthew was sprawled behind his desk, wolfing pork fried rice straight from the container and flipping through hard copies of the local missing persons files Janice had dropped by earlier.

With the time of death so nebulous, the search parameters were wider than optimal. After a brief discussion, Matthew and Charli had agreed on flagging any cases involving girls aged twenty-five or younger and included anyone reported as missing two weeks ago or longer. Just to be safe.

Janice Piper popped back into the office, carrying another couple of files. She bypassed Charli without a single glance and plopped the folders onto Matthew's desk. "Here you go. Found a few more that someone shoved in the wrong spot. Probably Louie."

Charli rolled her eyes. Ever since Louie had left happy hour early one time because his wife was sick and stuck Janice with the bar tab, he'd become her scapegoat around the office. The only thing Charli knew he was for sure guilty of was being a decent spouse, but according to Janice, everything from not replacing the last toilet paper roll in the bathroom to misfiled documents to a coffee spill in the breakroom someone neglected to wipe up were all Louie's fault.

Charli wasn't sure what Matthew saw in Janice, apart from their shared love of kicking back with a beer. To her, Janice was overdramatic and more than a little ridiculous. Plus, her work tended to be sloppy. Beyond that last bit, Charli had nothing against the older detective.

Janice almost certainly had it in for her, though.

The older woman hitched her hip onto Matthew's desk as he gathered up the files. "We still on for drinks tomorrow?"

Her back was to Charli, making it clear she wasn't included in the invitation.

Matthew rapped his knuckles against the folders. "As long as I'm not knee-deep in this at the time."

"Any word from Soames?"

"Not yet. We should hear something soon, though. Hoping the autopsy is done in the morning."

"Hope he skips breakfast. Heard she was a horror show, like a rotting zombie corpse out of one of those *Night of the Living Dead* movies."

Charli clutched her pen and briefly imagined using it to stab the woman through the vocal cords. Like a remake of the shower scene from *Psycho*, only with less nudity and mommy issues.

Do not say anything. Do. Not.

Janice was lucky, though. If it weren't for Matthew, Charli would definitely let Detective Piper know what she thought of her crude comparison.

People called Charli blunt, but Janice had no tact at all. *That's somebody's daughter you're talking about.*

"Yeah, well…" Pages flapped, and Charli guessed Matthew had opened a file. "Okay, gotta get back to work myself. Keep me posted."

The other woman stared at the top of Matthew's downcast head for a beat too long. As she pivoted, her expression was softer than the usual smirk until she locked eyes with Charli and the sharpness returned. Janice gave a curt nod as she breezed out the door. "Cross."

Charli waited until Janice's footsteps receded before swiveling in her chair. "I swear, that woman hates me because I spend more time with you than she does."

Matthew spluttered, choking on a bite of rice. "What?" He grabbed a napkin and wiped his mouth. "That's ridiculous. We're just drinking buddies. Unlike you, some people enjoy kicking back with a beer or two every night after work."

Yeah, no. She wasn't buying it. Janice's animosity toward Charli had only manifested once she and Matthew had been paired together as partners. Matthew was oblivious, although Charli wondered if his ignorance was deliberate at this point.

She didn't really care one way or the other about who people were dating…as long as their interpersonal drama didn't spill over into the job. On a personal level, there was no big loss. If Janice was the kind of person to act snotty to other women over a dude, she and Charli were never destined to be friends in the first place.

An ache settled in her chest. Some days, Charli thought it might be nice to have a friend in the department who wasn't

Matthew, like that red-haired detective from Charleston she'd helped with a case a while back, Ellie Kline. Too bad *she* didn't live closer. Charli had appreciated Ellie's candor and quick sense of humor. Plus, in the brief time they'd worked together, she'd witnessed enough to admire the Charleston detective's dedication.

Guilt guided Charli's gaze back to Matthew. Her partner was great and all, but beyond the job, they didn't have much in common. He was almost a decade older than her, divorced with a kid. He listened to country music while she liked everything but. He was someone who, in his spare time, liked drinking and watching pro sports on TV. Charli averaged a glass of wine a week if that, and the only sport she enjoyed watching was MMA because at least those had some basis in reality.

Unlike football. What was the point of running back and forth down a field, tossing a ball, and dogpiling each other, all for the joy of breaking down your joints by age forty and radically increasing your statistical odds of being diagnosed with CTE?

Charli made a face. Football, ugh. Another way she'd failed her dad, by not faking enthusiasm for the Bulldogs' games. In these parts, her refusal to pick any team to cheer for made her an anomaly.

Give her some popcorn and a good MMA fight, though, and she'd scream her head off.

She forked another bite of beef into her mouth before leaning back with a sigh. *Maybe this is why you don't have very many friends. You're too damn picky.*

Not that she didn't want to be friends with Matthew, because she did. She just missed having a close female friend to talk to. The kind of friend she could share all her weird observations and idiosyncrasies with, without them getting that look in their eyes that said she was a freak.

Someone like Madeline.

Charli shoved the plate to the side and grabbed her mouse. Now wasn't the time to let her mind wander or feel sorry for herself. A young woman was dead, and the sooner they identified the body, the sooner they could get started on bringing her killer to justice.

Except, *justice* wasn't the right word. Not like there was any true justice to be found in tracking down and prosecuting murderers. Catching and jailing killers didn't change anything. The victims were still dead. True justice would be if that girl out in the marsh, if Madeline, were still alive.

She clicked on the screen. So, no, she couldn't bring the dead justice, but she could help with accountability. With closure. Not nearly enough to heal a family's wounds and a pale shadow of what they deserved, but better than nothing.

Or at least, that was the belief Charli clung to all these years. Hard to predict how healing closure might be when she'd never had the opportunity to experience it herself.

Twenty minutes later, Charli pushed away from the desk, raised her arms overhead, and stretched. "All right, let's go over who we have so far who fits our net. I'll go first." She read through the two names she'd found. The first was Shana Feist, a seventeen-year-old who disappeared in February.

Regina Pugh was the other girl. A fifteen-year-old who'd been reported missing since March. As soon as the medical examiner inspected the body and narrowed down the time of death, they could start eliminating names.

There were several more who fit the initial criteria, but they were all from out of the area. She'd taken meticulous notes in case they extended their search parameters.

"I've got two also." Matthew scooted his notepad closer and began reading. "Jennifer Cahill, age eighteen. Reported as missing by her parents a little over three months ago, over near Forsythe Park. The report said she has blonde hair, not brunette, but could be the victim's hair was dyed."

Charli noted it all on her pad. "Got it. What about the other girl?"

"The other one I found is brunette, age fifteen when she went missing around four months ago, would be sixteen now. Her name is Madeline Hanley, goes by Maddie."

The pen slipped from Charli's hand. When she bent over to pick it up, her hands were trembling.

Quit acting irrational. Madeline is a common name. This means nothing.

Charli wasn't prone to attributing meaning where none existed or giving much credence to those gut feelings that so many cops, Matthew included, relied upon.

Somehow, though, this coincidence hit hard. It felt... significant. A sign from a typically impartial universe that Charli needed to solve this case if she ever hoped to gain that elusive closure for her old friend.

Okay, now you sound even sillier than Matthew when he's spouting off with one of his hunches. You don't even know if this is the right girl.

Her pocket dinged and vibrated, so Charli fished out her phone. She spotted the name on her screen and emitted a silent groan.

Oh, crap.

Her dad. She'd completely spaced on their dinner date.

She opened her texts to a photo of her dad's dining room table, all neatly arranged with place settings for two. He'd even used the good china plates with the little flowers twirling around the edges, an anniversary gift her mom had especially loved, and placed a bouquet of colorful flowers in a glass vase in the middle.

Before she could rattle off a quick apology, the three little dots appeared.

Uh oh. This isn't going to be good. Charli curled one hand over her desk and braced for impact.

The text popped up, and yup, it was a zinger all right: *I'd ask for a raincheck, but what's the point? You'll just take a raincheck on the raincheck.*

Oof.

"Something wrong?"

She lifted her glum gaze from the screen to find Matthew watching her with a crease between his brows. "Forgot to tell my dad I couldn't do dinner tonight, and he's a little peeved."

"So, basically, business as usual in the Cross family."

"That about sums it up."

Her thumbs hovered over the keys for another few seconds before she shoved the phone back into her pocket without typing a reply. There was nothing she could write that would appease her dad. Even an apology would bring on another lecture about her abysmal work-life balance, and she couldn't deal with that right now.

Not when there was a dead girl who needed her help. Her dad was going to be pissed no matter what. Knowing him, he'd be itching for his opportunity to list all the ways she didn't live up to his expectations.

He would just have to wait because the dead girl's family shouldn't have to.

"Toss me that file on Maddie Hanley, will you?"

Charli might have failed Madeline all those years ago, and she'd clearly failed as a daughter, but she would not fail this girl. Whoever she was.

7

M y truck rattled down the uneven road, the stereo blasting a catchy pop song as I cruised past the marshland flanking the Vernon River. Most of the cops and the work crews that had camped out along the area all afternoon had packed up their patrol cars and taken off already.

Up ahead, a lone black-and-white patrol car was parked on the side of the road. Probably there to keep an eye on things overnight, in case the person who'd killed that girl returned to his burial ground.

"Trust me, not gonna happen, folks. You'd have to be a real idiot to dump a body in the same place where the cops just found one, and the guy you want definitely isn't one of those."

I'd known something was up during my drive-by earlier in the day. Two squad cars had parked off the road, and a third one had come blazing down the street, sirens blaring.

I drummed my fingers on the steering wheel and shook my head. Sirens blaring. I'd never understood the logic there. Sirens were supposed to be for emergencies only: heart attacks, fires, active shooters. A dead body was beyond the help of emergency services. Especially one as dead as the girl they'd found.

Cops and I weren't that different, I supposed. I bet they liked to flash those red-and-blue lights and scream the siren because the act of forcing all the other cars around them to part at their command felt good.

Powerful.

I liked to feel powerful too. I just went about it in a different way. That was the beauty of our great country. We were all free to choose how we pursued our own liberty and dreams.

The police and I also both worked to help our communities become better places. It wasn't my fault no one had the vision necessary to legalize the type of assistance I provided.

I drove by the cop car at just under the speed limit, glancing at the area as I passed. The yellow crime scene tape was visible, but beyond that, the marsh descended into darkness.

Earlier that day, I'd driven to the back corner of a construction site I'd scoped out. A row of fancy townhomes was in the middle of being erected, probably some rich landowner's project who was hoping to capitalize on the real estate boom. They'd throw them up as quickly as possible, more than likely cutting corners to maximize their profits and sell them by boasting of river views.

The attention to money over people was one of the reasons I was forced to step in and act. If parents worked less and paid more attention to their kids, the current predicament wouldn't exist. Instead, they let their kids run wild. No supervision, glued to their screens consuming all sorts of filth.

No wonder they turned out the way they did.

Over the past month, I'd noted the construction crew's schedule the same way I'd memorized all my girls' routines.

The workers started at seven each morning and punched out at five o'clock sharp, so if I waited 'til around six to show up, I didn't need to worry about any Peeping Toms intruding on my...*peeping.*

The site turned out to be perfect. Far enough away from the cops to remain safe from scrutiny, yet close enough to see what the cops were up to with my high-powered binoculars.

I cruised north a few blocks before signaling to make a right turn. I still wasn't sure how the cops had found one of my girls already, but they had. I planned to perform my due diligence and study every news report on the topic to learn from this experience. That was the mistake so many people made, thinking life had nothing left to teach them.

No matter our age, we could always gain more knowledge.

I pictured the police opening the plastic container, and my breathing quickened. There was something exciting about someone finally catching on and discovering one of my offerings. After all these months, I was starting to wonder if my girls would end up in the ground forever, unnoticed and forgotten. What a shame that would have been. Maddie would have hated missing out on all the attention, and no one would ever have appreciated how nicely I'd gift wrapped her.

"See, Maddie? You're getting that attention you were so desperate for after all."

I turned into a drive-through, patted my flat gut, and ordered a diet soda anyway. Didn't want to squander my health on all that high fructose corn syrup. My girls needed me to help show them the errors of their ways.

The employee who waited on me at the window was young, maybe twenty or so. A little too old for my taste, but pretty. She smiled when she handed me the drink. "Here you go, sir. Have a nice night."

"Well, you just made it nicer, so thank you."

I winked before I drove away, making her giggle.

I loved girls. Their soft skin, sweet-smelling hair, boundless energy, and sly grins. I understood what made them tick too. No matter their background or economic status or family life, girls that age all shared the same drive for attention.

As I sipped my drink, I shook my head. It was so obvious. Of course, they craved attention...why else would high school girls dress in those short shorts and reveal so much skin with those barely there tops? Or spend hours applying makeup and fixing their hair every day? Before school, during lunch breaks. In the car on the way home. Before they took one of the hundreds of pouty, deliberately seductive selfies splashed all over their social media accounts.

The parents who flipped out about how social media had corrupted their precious daughters were oblivious to the truth. Social media hadn't corrupted teen girls. It was the other way around. Girls, with their need for never-ending validation, had corrupted social media. If society wouldn't step in to correct this worrisome trajectory, then I would.

I had a duty to uphold.

Teaching them where they'd gone wrong didn't mean disrespecting them. That was why I took such care after I killed them. I understood their desires and honored them, even in death. I stripped them naked and washed them clean, then I spent some time drinking in all that youthful beauty on display as a final tribute to their earthly but flawed desires. I even gave them each a special gift before I placed them in the ground. A little token of my affection, so they'd understand I was only doing this as a labor of love.

I turned up the radio, humming along to another chirpy pop song about kissing girls and liking it.

The moon had been three-quarters full the night I'd put

her into the ground. Its reflection had bounced off the nearby water so brightly that I'd barely needed the flashlight. Frogs and insects had been my only company as I'd shoveled into the mud, digging out a hole in the marsh. A little unsteady on my feet thanks to the cheap whiskey in my system, the same brand dear old dad used to guzzle by the gallon.

Like always, I'd made sure to pick a dry stretch before burying the container, so I could drive my truck out without fear of sinking into the muck. I'd dragged the container out of the back and slid it into the hole before pausing to catch my breath. The slosh of the river against the bank and the whistling wind had muffled the mud smacking the top of the container.

Once Maddie was hidden from view, I'd packed up and left, disposing of my gloves and the sneakers I'd picked up at a thrift store just for the occasion. No one would think to look in a dumpster twenty miles east.

"Nearly four months since I planted you in the ground. I was starting to fret you'd turn out like those girls from Virginia, but I can stop worrying. They found you."

At the next light, I turned left, heading down the street that would take me back to my house. This new development was all very exciting, but I couldn't let that go to my head. Now that Savannah's finest had found one body, the chances had jumped up that they'd stumble across the others.

All that extra scrutiny meant I needed to be extra sure to get a good eight hours of sleep.

That way, when I started the process all over again with a new girl soon, my mind would be well-rested and focused enough to avoid detection.

I couldn't afford to be caught.

My girls needed me.

8

When Charli lugged her weary body into the precinct the next morning, she didn't notice much of anyone or anything apart from the fragrant aroma of coffee, which she tracked like a bloodhound straight to the breakroom.

The first human she actually focused on was Matthew, who was hunching his big body over the coffee maker as he waited for the liquid to finish streaming into the pot and mumbling under his breath. Charli didn't need to decipher the words to guess what had triggered this morning's grumpiness.

"Still no Keurig?"

"No, and we're out of that hazelnut vanilla creamer I bought. All that's left is some cheap crap that probably tastes like dirty shoes." He grabbed the pot a little prematurely to fill his mug, and the coffee maker hissed when a drop splattered onto the hot plate. "And no, I don't need another lecture on how those individual cups lead to environmental waste and are less economical, okay? Let a man have his dreams."

Dreams. Ugh. Charli's dreams normally turned into nightmares.

When Matthew turned around, he took one look at her face, let out a low whistle, and set the filled travel mug on the counter in front of her. "Here, I think you need this more than I do."

"That bad, huh?" Charli grabbed the creamer he slid over to her next, pouring a generous amount into the mug and stirring until the liquid turned a rich caramel color. She followed that with a packet of sugar.

"You don't look bad for, say, an ER resident on her third all-night shift of the week." Matthew filled a second mug and added the tiniest splash of creamer. "You sleep at all last night?"

Charli shrugged. "Some." Not a lie. If she hadn't nodded off at all, then she wouldn't have suffered through her usual nightmares. He hadn't asked about the quality of her sleep.

Matthew subjected her to the same lowered brow, intense expression he used on suspects, one that often made people uneasy enough to open their mouths and start blabbing. Charli was immune, though. She blew on the steam that curled up from the cup and met his gaze evenly until he finally gave up.

"Fine. But you know if you ever need to talk, I'm here, right?"

She made a big show of rolling her eyes. "Trust me, you're kind of hard to miss. Anyway, I know you're here because you're always here. We both are, if you go by what my dad says."

When he snorted and accepted her deflection, she released a silent sigh of relief. This case had only just started, and she'd already thought of her late best friend far more than she'd like. Besides, there was nothing to talk about this morning. She'd spent a restless night fending off vague boogeymen in nightmares she couldn't remember as soon as she woke up, so what? If detectives went around whining each and every time they had a bad dream, they'd never get a chance to talk about anything else.

"What's the plan for this morning?"

Charli allowed herself a sip of coffee before answering. "I want to head over to that construction site across the way from where the body was found. Maybe one of the workers saw something." She took one more sip before popping a lid on the travel mug.

Matthew nodded. "I was thinking the same thing. Maybe we'll get lucky, and the perp will out himself the second we show up."

Charli wasn't banking on it. Still, someone had to be the optimist. "Has one of your cases ever played out that way?"

"A murder case? No. But there was this guy once who took one look at my uniform and immediately fessed up to petty larceny." Matthew slapped a lid on his own cup before trailing Charli out of the breakroom toward their office to drop off her laptop bag.

She paused just outside the door and turned, narrowing her eyes at her partner. "Petty larceny, huh? What exactly did that guy steal?"

Matthew mumbled something into his cup and took a hasty gulp. "Hot!" He yipped, waving his free hand rapidly while exhaling to release the heat.

Charli arranged the bag neatly on her desk's lower shelf in the same spot as usual and waited her partner out. Once he finished his theatrics, she was ready. "What did your guy steal?"

Matthew sighed. "A skateboard."

"And how old was he, this hardened skateboard thief who quaked in the face of your shiny badge?"

"Twelve."

Charli let her silence do the talking as she skirted around him and headed downstairs toward the entrance.

Matthew's heavy footsteps thudded behind her. "Okay, so maybe that's not the best example, but that doesn't mean it still couldn't happen one of these times...like today."

"Sure." A smile threatened to erupt, but she kept it at bay. "Just point out the twelve-year-old construction worker, and we might have a shot."

"What did I say, Charli, about letting a man have his dreams?"

Charli shook her head as she exited into the already balmy air, her lips twitching. "Who's driving?"

"I will."

Matthew loped ahead of her to the parking lot on his long legs, taking one stride for every two and a half of hers. As he beeped the remote to unlock his truck, he hesitated near the passenger's side.

Don't you do it.

Charli relaxed when he rounded the hood to reach the driver's door. For a second there, she'd been convinced Matthew was about to fall into his polite, Southern gentleman routine and open her door for her. She'd spent the first year of their partnership training him out of that undesirable behavior. She had no desire to backpedal now.

Her petite size and age acted against her in this line of work enough without her partner drawing even more attention to them through his misplaced gallantry.

Matthew keyed the ignition. The truck rumbled, and a man's twangy voice flowed from the speakers. "Ready for some Garth Brooks?"

"Is that who's singing now?" Charli couldn't tell one country singer from the next. Half the time, she was suspicious Matthew was messing with her when he told her a new song wasn't by the same artist as the previous one.

"I swear, Charli. Someday you'll appreciate country music. There's got to be at least one artist that you'll like out there somewhere. We just need to find them."

She shrugged, biting back a smile. Over the course of all their rides together, she'd already come across a couple artists she didn't mind so much.

She wasn't about to give Matthew the satisfaction of admitting that fact, though.

WHEN MATTHEW PULLED into the leveled dirt lot that led to the construction site, work was already underway. Power tools droned and whined, serenading them with a discordant symphony that made Charli wince as they climbed out of the truck and headed toward the chaos.

Ahead, a neat row of structures was just starting to take shape. Southern yellow pine beams crisscrossed to form the two-story skeletal frames of the townhomes to come. A jack-hammer kicked off nearby, sending a cloud of dust wafting toward Charli.

She coughed and turned her head to the side, grateful she'd popped on sunglasses to protect her eyes.

A lanky, red-cheeked man wearing a flannel shirt and a yellow hard hat approached, pushing a squeaky wheelbarrow full of supplies. He frowned when he noticed them and stopped, casting a nervous glance over his shoulder. "You guys shouldn't be here. Boss won't like it!" He shouted to be heard over the racket. "The units aren't ready for viewing yet. Come back in two months. We should have a model ready for walk-throughs by then."

Charli's eyebrows rose. Two months? Hard to believe that six or even nine months would be enough time to turn those bare beams into actual, livable homes, let alone sixty days.

Then again, building was something she'd always struggled with, much to her dismay.

Given her love of facts and logic, assembling raw materials according to a blueprint to form a structure should have come easily to her, except every gingerbread house she'd ever made as a kid would beg to differ. Her holiday legacy included a depressing collection of collapsing white-frosted walls, cracked roofs, and gumdrop-laden chimneys toppling to the floor. On the bright side, her gingerbread disasters meant she could eat the ruins guilt-free.

Then there was the residual horror she experienced whenever she remembered that awful bridge-building assignment from high school physics. Even her less academically minded classmates had managed to craft cool structures from all sorts of random materials. Their bridges had all managed to withstand a pound or more of weight.

Her sad, popsicle-stick creation had crumpled when the kid at the desk next to hers sneezed.

And that one time she'd purchased a new desk from Ikea had ended in unspeakable horror.

Charli shuddered at the memory while Matthew flashed an easy smile at the worker along with his gold shield. "Not house hunting at the moment, although I'm sure these will turn out nice. We need to speak to the foreman. Can you point him out?"

There was a lull in the commotion halfway through Matthew's question, so his last few words rang out unnaturally loud in the relative quiet.

The man wiped his sleeve across his flushed forehead before jerking his thumb over his shoulder. "He's on-site, at the next building over. Name's Tommy. Big guy, blue shirt. Prob'ly screaming at someone. Can't miss him. Make sure you grab a couple of hard hats from the table before you see him, though, else he'll chew your ass too."

Matthew flashed him a thumbs-up. "Thanks, man. Have a good one."

"I'd say you too, but he's in a mood, so…" The man lifted his shoulders before squeaking the wheelbarrow away.

Matthew watched his retreat for a moment before clapping his hands together. "Right. Sounds like this guy we're going to see is a real daisy, gonna be a fun way to kick off the day. Who's pumped? You? 'Cuz I sure am. Bring on the grumpy foreman. Let's do it." He shook out his hands as he jogged in place and then threw out a few punches, like a boxer warming up for a big fight.

Charli snorted and started walking down the dirt in the direction the worker had indicated. "Careful, Rocky. Remember, we're here to question this guy, not knock him out."

"Spoilsport." Matthew grumped from behind her, which she also ignored.

When he fell into step beside her, his forehead and neck glistened with perspiration, his face was flushed, and a dark patch already dampened the front of his rumpled, navy blue button-down. Charli smoothed her own crisp white shirt and straightened her gray blazer while worry pinched her lips together. A concerned comment sprang to her tongue, but she thought better of saying anything.

She'd started to notice the changes in her partner's fitness not long after his ex-wife began the divorce proceedings. Big life changes were hard at first, so she'd figured it was a transient thing. Symptoms of mild, post-break-up depression.

Except time hadn't improved the situation. If anything, Matthew seemed to be going downhill in terms of physical health. His waist had thickened, and his suits fit differently now. Tighter, with his belly straining the buttons of his shirts. Every time she rode in his truck, there was a new collection of fast-food wrappers and bags crumpled in the back seat. Based on comments he made about being out of shape and his commitment to hitting the bar for happy hour every day after work, she'd gotten the impression he wasn't exercising regularly, either.

Winded by less than thirty seconds of shadow boxing, though? Now she fretted that he wasn't exercising at all.

Charli didn't care about his appearance. Everyone's body was their own business. But all the factors together worried her, health-wise. Cops were already at a heightened risk of many ailments, and the stress of the job made heart attacks particularly common. The one time she'd suggested he skip a few nights at the bar and meet her for a jog or MMA class instead, he'd turned bright red and stiffly changed the subject, and for the rest of the day, their interactions had been stilted.

She bit back a sigh and kept walking. Her partner was a grown man, and his decisions were his own. Charli didn't appreciate anyone interjecting themselves into her life. The least she could do was extend Matthew the same courtesy she desired for herself.

She'd just have to add his health to the mental checklist of other silent worries to reassess at a future date. Not drop completely.

Not when her late-night research showed that, in a current study, one out of four officers suffered from symptoms of mental illness like depression. Even more disturbing...police were more likely to die by suicide than the general public.

Matthew pointed at a box of hard hats sitting on a portable picnic table. He grabbed two and handed her one. Once they were suited up, they approached the wooden frame for the second structure.

As Charli scanned the scattered workers for a blue shirt, shouting penetrated the *rat-a-tat-tat* of a jackhammer, drawing her attention to the left. The tool switched off a moment later, allowing the yelling to take center stage.

A burly, broad-shouldered man in a blue shirt poked his finger into a shorter man's chest. The lectured worker's unhappy expression suggested he'd rather be anywhere but there. He nodded, earning himself another finger-stab.

As the bigger man yelled, saliva droplets flew from his mouth and splattered onto the kid's hat and forehead. Charli wasn't sure how he managed to take it without snapping back. If she were in his shoes, she doubted her ability to remain so submissive. Yelling was one thing, but standing still while her boss rained bodily fluids down on her face? Nope.

When the foreman finished yelling and the worker had scurried away, Charli smoothed her jacket again and adjusted the plastic hat on her head. This was one of those days when she longed to be taller. Bullies always seemed to have the height advantage, especially over her.

Not that she'd ever let that stop her from putting one in their place before. Plus, she couldn't deny there was a specific type of satisfaction that came when men underestimated her based on her size, only for her to educate them on the dangers of prejudging someone on their stature alone.

Charli straightened her shoulders. "Come on. Let's get this over with."

As they headed over, Matthew couldn't resist a quick dig. "Bet you're rethinking nixing my Rocky Balboa thing now, huh?"

"In an effort to 'let a guy have his dreams,' I'm declining to comment." Matthew's chuckle made her smile. She flattened her expression before calling the foreman's name.

"Tommy?"

The beefy man stiffened—enough that Charli could tell he'd heard her—but didn't acknowledge them right away. He took his time, unscrewing his water bottle and chugging for several seconds. Only after he drank his fill, wiped his mouth on his sleeve, and set the water bottle back down on a chair did he turn to greet them.

A pair of deep-set blue eyes glared from beneath a prominent brow. His gaze skipped over Matthew but halted on Charli, traveling up and down her body at a slow pace designed to make her squirm.

Charli waited patiently for him to finish his obnoxious alpha male ritual. When his inspection finally brought him back to her face, she met his gaze with no reaction. As the seconds ticked by without any change to her expression, his leer turned into a scowl.

True to type. For most bullies, the thrill was in provoking their target.

"Wait, don't tell me, lemme guess. You selling Girl Scout cookies?" He smirked and patted his gut. "Too bad I'm on a diet, but hey, come back decked out in one of those cute little uniforms, and I might be willing to cheat."

Charli reached for her badge, but Matthew beat her to the punch, flashing his shield as he stalked forward. "I'm Detective Church with Savannah PD, and this is *Detective* Cross. We're here on an investigation and need to ask you a few questions. Name?"

No easy smile this time. Matthew was all business as he drew himself up to his full height and positioned his right hand in such a way on his hip to ensure his gun showed. A deliberate flex on his part. One that made Charli's face burn. She didn't want or need him to go into over-protective dad mode on her behalf. Especially not over this guy.

Charli made sure to plant her elbow in Matthew's waist as she edged around him. If he kept this nonsense up, he'd soon regret it. She could take care of herself.

The foreman's slack-jawed expression told her she likely

wouldn't need to this time. "Wait, *she's* a cop?" He swiveled his head on his squat neck to gape at Charli. "You're a cop?"

"Not a cop, a—"

Charli elbowed her partner again, with enough extra oomph to cut him off. He winced and took the hint by swallowing the rest of his sentence. "As my partner here started to say, I'm a detective. For someone who probably enjoys reprimanding his employees over their poor listening skills, you don't seem to listen all that well yourself."

The foreman's eyes widened before he forced a weak chuckle. "Oh, that. I didn't mean nothing. When you're in charge, you gotta lay into them sometimes, so they don't start slacking on the job." He coughed and had the decency to duck his head a little. "And, uh, sorry about that Girl Scout crack. I thought you two were a couple'a lookie-loos coming to snoop around the site. If ida known you was a cop...er, detective, I wouldn't have said nothin'."

Charli bristled and opened her mouth, ready to deliver an icy suggestion that he should consider keeping his Girl Scout comment to himself no matter what the profession of the woman he was dealing with, but Matthew nudged her shoe with his first.

A warning, to focus on the case.

Her partner was right, of course, so she smoothed her blazer and switched gears. "Your name?"

"Thomas Doleman, but everyone calls me Tommy."

In the space of a few seconds, the man's entire demeanor changed, from obnoxious and belligerent to almost too obsequious.

In her experience, that sort of rapid cycling meant one of two things. Either Tommy Doleman had a family member who was a cop...or he was nervous about something specific and hoped his cooperation would keep him out of trouble.

Charli was betting on the latter. She jotted his name on her notepad while Matthew took the lead again.

"Mr. Doleman, we're here on a murder investigation. A body was recovered within viewing distance of this site, and we were wondering if you've noticed any unusual activity lately, either at the location or around here."

As soon as Matthew mentioned murder, the foreman's shoulders relaxed. Whatever he'd been fretting about, chances were it wasn't a dead body.

Unless he was a skilled actor.

Charli could never discount that possibility when interviewing witnesses, but in his case? Doubtful. Tommy Doleman struck her as a brash, loud man who put just about every thought in his head out into the world.

Irksome, to be sure, but not really the hallmark traits of a skilled deceiver.

"A body? Damn." Tommy scratched his neck before his eyes widened, and he half-turned in the direction of the crime scene. "Oh, hey, is that what was going on across the marsh yesterday? I saw the cop cars, just sorta figured it was some kind of drug bust."

Charli mimicked his actions and peered across the marsh. From their current location, the spot where they'd discovered the body appeared much farther away than she remembered. If anyone was keeping tabs on the victim's remains from this distance, they'd need binoculars. "Did you notice anyone? Maybe someone skulking around who shouldn't be here or walking around carrying a pair of binoculars?"

Tommy was shaking his head before she finished. "Nah, I didn't see no one like that. If I had, I woulda sent them packing. I don't like people snooping around my construction sites before they're finished. Too much damn liability. 'Sides, most anyone who comes to sneak a peek early on is just looking for somethin' to bitch about, know what I mean?"

Not really, but he'd raised a good point. Based on his negative reaction to their visit, she believed Tommy when he said he tended to hustle any lollygaggers along. "And you haven't had to send anyone packing like that since this job started?"

"Nah. Before you two, only people I yelled at were a couple of kids cruising around on their bikes."

"How old?"

He scrunched up his face and scratched his neck again. "I dunno, maybe ten or so? They weren't on big kid bikes yet, so not too old."

Charli's perfectionist streak made her jot the note, even knowing it would amount to nothing. Transporting the body to the marsh would have required a car or similar vehicle. Kids that young wouldn't have the means or the strength. Even if their victim had been murdered at the site—and the forensics team had found no evidence yet to suggest that was the case—the container alone was too large to lug around on a bike.

"What about your men?" Matthew used his hand to shade his eyes while he studied the workers. "Anyone who seems a little off, or maybe a little too interested in what's happening over at the crime scene?"

"Not my guys." Tommy Doleman puffed out his chest. "I ride 'em hard, but they're a good crew. Got into a little trouble once when I was about ten years younger and twenty years stupider, hired this guy who talked a good game and had the right build for the job without double-checking his references. Son of a bitch split in the middle of the night with three grand worth of equipment, never saw him again. Gave me a fake name and everything. That came out of my paycheck, so you bet your ass I learned my lesson. Now, I background check everyone. I don't care how long they're planning on workin' for me."

Matthew glanced at Charli to get her take, and she dipped her chin. His story rang true.

Before he could jump back in, Charli's phone rang in her jacket pocket. She held up a finger and half-turned away from Doleman. "Detective Cross."

"Good morning, Detective. This is Randal Soames. I'm ready to update you on that delightful package you sent over yesterday afternoon if you want to stop by."

Charli smiled. Randal Soames was the GBI's medical examiner in their neck of the woods. She'd had numerous dealings with the man and his offbeat humor over the years.

By contrast, he was a consummate professional while performing his assessments and autopsies in the lab, always treating the bodies with respect.

"If by 'delightful package' you mean decomposed human remains, great. We'll finish up here and head on over."

Matthew was watching her when she hung up. "Was that Soames?"

"Yeah, he's ready for us to stop by. Let's wrap this up."

Her partner nodded and turned back to the foreman. "If you have nothing to hide, then I'm assuming you're okay with putting together a list with all your employees' names so we can look it over before the next time we drop by, right?" The mild taunt in his phrasing let both Charli and Tommy know that Matthew hadn't forgiven the foreman for his initial impropriety.

"Sure, I can do that."

"And how about letting us question a few of them should the need arise? Can you do that too?"

Tommy spread his calloused palms wide. "Hey, go for it. I'll even let 'em take extra break time to talk to you. No way any of these guys murdered someone. No freaking way."

Matthew grunted, his meaning clear. *We'll see about that.*

Charli inspected the makeshift parking lot. "And you haven't noticed any suspicious vehicles?"

"Nope, not a one."

"Do you recognize all the cars here now?"

The foreman turned to scrutinize the lot. "Yeah, those all belong to my crew, except for your black pickup. I can even tell you which guy drives each car if you want."

His eyes lit up like he was eager to show off his memory skills. Charli held up her hand to cut him off. She believed him, and she and Matthew needed to head over to the M.E.'s office. "Thanks, but that won't be necessary. You have anything else before we go, Matthew?"

Her partner shook his head and handed Tommy his card. "My email's on there. Send me that list of names as soon as you're done, and remember, we'll probably swing back by one day soon to take you up on your offer."

"Yeah, sure. Whatever you say."

Charli rolled her eyes behind her sunglasses. She still wondered what had caused the foreman's sudden about-face in attitude, but her curiosity would have to wait.

They said their goodbyes, and she and Matthew turned and started across the dirt toward his truck.

They'd only made it a few steps when Tommy Doleman hollered after them. "Hey, if you do come back, can I pick your brain about unpaid parking tickets? My freakin' ex got 'em when she was still driving my vehicle, and I'm worried my truck's gonna get impounded one of these days, or worse, they're gonna come throw me in the slammer."

The mystery around Tommy Doleman's attitude adjustment was solved. Lips twitching, Charli kept walking, leaving Matthew to respond.

As she retraced the path to the truck, some impulse pulled her attention back across the marsh toward the river, as if her gaze was being tugged by a high-powered magnet.

Uneasiness writhed in her stomach, and the back of her neck prickled.

She rubbed the spot, frowning as the morning sun glinted off the Vernon in the distance.

Good thing she didn't believe in inexplicable phenomena or superstitions like Matthew. If she did, she might actually be a little freaked out right now over the sensation they were being watched.

9

Matthew seethed all the way down Highway 204 East to the Northbound 95 and was still a little pissed by the time he signaled to hop on the 80 to Pooler. He'd had half a mind to haul that Doleman asshole in on those parking tickets and toss him in the clinker for a few hours to teach him some respect.

He might have too, if they weren't on a big case and if Charli wasn't riding shotgun.

As he checked over his shoulder before changing lanes, he caught a glimpse of Charli's profile. She stared straight out the windshield, quiet again.

He was tempted to pester her but held his tongue as he navigated them through Pooler. His rib still smarted from back at the construction site. Charli threw a mean elbow.

She was probably still pissed about how he'd gotten all up in that clown's face after he'd made that Girl Scout crack. No sense riling her again. Once they were in the M.E.'s office, she'd be too focused on the case to give him hell, Charli-style.

A few minutes later, he'd parked in front of the Coastal Regional Crime Laboratory. Built in a patch of Georgia wetlands, the forensic center had opened in 2019, after the GBI and state decided the southeastern counties needed more support.

Besides the M.E.'s office, Coastal performed services like toxicology and trace analysis, firearms examinations, and processing of DNA. Like a one-stop shop for key forensics.

Awesome that they had such a top-notch facility a few miles up the road. Matthew only wished the place wasn't such an eyesore.

He grimaced at the gleaming, geometric building looming over them as they approached the front door. "Why'd they have to make it so weird looking?"

Charli gave an inelegant snort. "You say the same thing every time we come. Just because it's not antebellum archi-tecture doesn't mean it's weird. I actually like the design, how they melded the old-fashioned brick with all those gray panels and glass."

"Not me. It looks like Space Mountain and one of the historic brick homes got it on and had a mutant kid."

His partner shook her head as she opened the front door. "I think you got confused somewhere along the way back in science class. *Invertebrates* are the ones that reproduce, not inanimates."

Matthew grinned at his partner's back as she approached the circular wood and glass reception desk. Charli razzing him again meant she was over any irritation from before.

After checking in, they headed straight back to the large, high-ceilinged space that was the M.E.'s domain. The place was like a modern-day Dr. Frankenstein's lab, full of gleaming stainless steel, hoses, and drains.

He spotted the forty-something medical examiner dictating notes into a voice recorder, standing next to a body on one of several metal gurneys. A Caucasian female. Far too intact to be their Jane Doe.

The door swishing shut alerted Soames to their presence, and he clicked off the device to greet them. "Nice to see you both again, Charli, Church. Sorry, we never seem to meet under better circumstances, but that's the nature of the beast."

A genuine smile lit up Charli's face. "Good to see you too, Randal."

"Soames." Matthew greeted the medical examiner while wrinkling his nose. The lab didn't reek of dead bodies, but that was only because they were so loaded up with chemicals. A mishmash of gross crap that gave off a very specific pungent-sweet odor that stuck around long after he left.

Soames always reminded Matthew a little of a turkey in appearance, with his long, scrawny neck and a pair of thighs that were skinnier than one of Matthew's steak knives.

Matthew scowled. His *old* steak knives. Freaking Judy had taken those when she'd moved out.

"Let's start with the bad news." Soames always kicked off his report the same way, a habit that Charli seemed to appreciate but Matthew found a little corny. "As I'm guessing you inferred for yourselves, the body was pretty badly decomposed. Human remains and Georgia summers aren't a good mix. That means fingerprints might not be possible. Also, take a look at this."

The unusual grim note to the M.E.'s voice warned Matthew they weren't going to like whatever was inside the evidence bag Soames had just picked up.

"Lipstick?" Charli frowned at the small black cylinder visible within the clear plastic. "Was that found in the plastic container with the victim?"

"In a manner of speaking. I found the lipstick inserted into the victim's vagina. I'm guessing that's what the sutures were for, to hold the lipstick in."

Charli released a tiny gasp while Matthew's stomach heaved. He felt feverish.

Whoever had attacked their Jane Doe hadn't just murdered her but had also stuck a lipstick inside her and sewn her up like a damn pillow. He hated his next question. "Do you know if they did it after she was dead, or before?"

The grim expression on the M.E.'s usually jovial face answered before Soames ever opened his mouth. "Hard to know definitively based on the decomposition, but based on what I saw, I think it's reasonable to conclude before. I'll provide you with close-up photos so that you have the information on the brand and color for your investigation."

Seconds ticked away in silence as they all absorbed that horror. Matthew's mind kept shifting to his own daughter, and he wanted to break things.

"But there is good news?" Charli finally asked.

"Yes. Teeth are intact, so we can check dental records. I'll run them through NamUs, but do send me the names of the dentists who treated any missing persons you're looking at too, just in case she's not in the database, and I'll start working on getting medical releases."

Charli jotted the reminder in her notebook. "I'll send those along once I'm back at my desk. How long will matching dental records take, if it comes to that?"

"Depends. If the missing girl's family was proactive and had her information uploaded into the NamUs database, it should be quick. Maybe an hour or two. Less than a day for sure."

NamUs stood for the National Missing and Unidentified Persons System, a national clearinghouse and resource center for missing persons across the country. Funded by the National Institute of Justice, NamUs offered a variety of services, including the creation of a database for people who disappeared without a trace and free forensic services like odontology, which in layman's terms meant the study of teeth.

Concerned families could upload information about their missing loved one to assist with their identification. Distinguishing marks, significant medical history, x-rays, and the like.

"And if it's not in NamUs?"

"Then we're talking longer. Usually a couple of days, at least. It all comes down to how responsive the dentists who treated your list of missing girls are to our requests for records, so we can compare those dental records to our victim. And not to be the bearer of bad news, but in my experience, fewer people use NamUs than you'd think."

Charli met Matthew's eyes across the office and winced. None of this news pointed to them solving the case quickly, and her partner's frustration showed on his face. "Thanks for letting us know. Anything else?"

Soames nodded. "The other good news is that the larynx was also intact, and I was able to spot what I believe are two fractures in the greater horns of the thyroid cartilage."

Greater horns? Matthew was still puzzling that out when Charli replied. "You think she might have been strangled?"

Soames nodded. "I think it's a strong possibility."

Charli's brow wrinkled. "What else could cause that type of injury?"

"Suicide by hanging, although that seems unlikely unless she figured out a way to bury herself after death, blunt trauma to the neck. Maybe a bad fall if she landed just the wrong way, though not nearly as likely."

Matthew frowned. "Any way to tell for sure?"

The medical examiner sighed. "Not with the soft tissue as far gone as it is. Sorry. I was able to narrow the time of death down a little more for you, if that helps."

When Charli replied, her voice was so raspy that she had

to clear her throat and start over. "Every little bit helps, Randal. Thank you."

If Matthew didn't know better, he'd almost believe his calm, hyper-rational partner had gotten all choked up. But over what? A more accurate time of death? If so, that worried him almost more than the dead girl did. Charli was a little odd, but she was consistent in her oddness.

"Again, I can't give an answer with as much specificity as I like, due to the previously mentioned factors and also the body being sealed up tight, which eliminated analysis of insect activity or soil. The container and protection from insects and other predators would have decreased the rate of decomposition, but the heat and humidity crank the rate up. After taking all of those factors into account, the best TOD estimate I can give is the victim likely died sometime in May, probably early June at the latest."

"May." Charli exchanged a look with him that said they were on the same page.

Maddie Hanley had gone missing in mid-May, not long before school let out for the summer.

"Oh, and I saved the best for last."

Charli perked up, and Matthew's own hopes rose. That was Soames's jacked-up way of telling them he'd uncovered a useful bit of information. "You got something?"

"I do. X-rays showed an old fracture in the proximal phalange of the deceased's fifth metatarsal bone, left side."

Doctors were all the same. Using a whole lot of fancy words when all they really needed to say was "pinky toe."

"I'm still running a few final tests. I'll let you know if I find anything of interest."

After thanking Soames and reminding him to call when he got a hit on the dental records, Matthew and Charli left the lab.

Charli was quiet on their walk down the garish hall with

its loud patterns and colors, not even smiling when he cracked a joke about getting a suit made from the psychedelic chair material that reminded him of disco balls.

Matthew didn't like it. This was usually the time when his partner rehashed what they'd learned, repeating the new information aloud in the hopes that it would prompt one of them to have an epiphany.

Not today, though. Her posture was closed off, and her mind wasn't even in the same room. Distracted, which might mean nothing if he was paired with anyone else in the precinct, but for Charli? It was bizarre as hell. He liked to joke that this was her pit bull phase of the investigation, where she latched onto the case with a single-minded purpose, and nothing short of a crowbar could pry her off until they solved it.

Whatever was going on with her, he didn't like being on the outside. They were partners. She shouldn't bottle stuff up like this. "Charli, come on. Talk to me. You sure you're doin' okay?"

Charli stiffened like he'd jabbed her with a cattle prod. Her chest rose, and her shoulders went back. "I told you already, I'm fine. Although, I'm starting to get irked that you keep asking. I'm a big girl, Matthew. I don't need you to handle me like a fragile porcelain doll."

That was his Charli. Prickly as a porcupine at times and blunt as a brick wall.

He flashed her his palms. "Trust me, I know you're not a porcelain doll. Although, with that cute little haircut and big blue eyes, you can see where the confusion comes in." When she whirled, those eyes were anything but doll-like as they narrowed and flashed with temper. He shook his head. "Nope, you aren't allowed to be mad. Notice I didn't call you Smalls or mention you're about the same size as a porcelain do...oops, my bad."

His teasing had the desired effect. After a second, she relaxed, and her lip began to twitch. "You think you're so funny, don't you?"

"Maybe not *so* funny, but a little bit, like yea much." He held his pointer fingers about an inch apart and pursed his lips before stretching his arms wide. "Yeah, no, you're right. This looks way more like it."

Charli did that eye-rolly thing of hers but was full-on smiling when she turned away. He'd consider that a success. If she wouldn't talk to him, the least he could do was cheer her up a little. She'd been walking around lately like she'd seen a ghost.

A ghost Matthew was sure looked exactly like the childhood friend she'd lost when she was only a teen herself. Another young life cut short by some demented sicko.

He'd never admit it in a million years—mostly because if he did, Charli would kick his ass up and down the street—but fine, so what if he was a little overprotective? That had nothing to do with her competency. Mentally, Charli was tough as hell, and she practiced her MMA stuff regularly, so she could defend herself against most of the bozos out there who might want to harm her. None of that changed her petite size and build, though. If something happened to her on his watch...

His entire body clenched at the idea, like he'd just been hit in the gut with an intense stomach cramp after eating some bad shrimp. Nope, nuh-uh, never gonna happen. He'd take a spitting-mad Charli over an injured Charli any day of the week.

After the climate-controlled chill of Soames's office, stepping outside was like barging fully clothed into a steam room. His underarms started to drip immediately, and his button-down clung to his stomach like plastic wrap.

He grimaced and tugged the shirt loose from his waistband, hoping to hide his growing gut. Freaking Judy. He'd sported a six-pack and been fit as a fiddle up until she put him through the wringer. Cheating on him, dragging him through that nasty divorce with her awful, money-grubbing lawyer. Packing up and whisking his only daughter off to California.

Now Chelsea couldn't see him, even if she wanted to. Though, Judy had messed that up too, turning their four-teen-year-old into some kind of wind-up doll who spewed all the same crap as her mom.

He clicked the remote on his truck, resisting the urge to scoot past Charli to open the passenger door. His dad had impressed upon him from an early age to mind his manners around women, and that lifelong habit was a hard one to break. When they were first partnered up, it had taken Charli pinning him with her frosty stare almost every day for a month before he'd finally remembered to stop opening the door.

"You're my partner, not my Bumble date, Matthew. How do you expect the community we serve to believe I'm competent enough to be a detective if I can't even open my own car door?"

At the time, he'd been amused. He'd barely even heard of Bumble and was still married. Definitely not interested in his new, pint-sized partner romantically. He thought of her more as a daughter than anything.

He swallowed hard and tugged at his collar before turning over the ignition. As he reversed the truck out of the parking spot, his mind drifted back to Judy.

Yeah, maybe he had worked too much, but wasn't that better than the alternative? At least he wasn't some deadbeat husband who'd lounged around the house all day eating chips and drinking beer while his wife busted her ass at work and then came home too exhausted to cook dinner and look after the kids.

Besides, he wasn't the one who'd cheated. Shouldn't that count for something?

He didn't realize how long he'd gone silent until Charli's voice penetrated his reminiscing. "Who's quiet now? Anything I can help with?"

For a second, he tried to imagine how Charli would react if he fessed up.

Funny you should ask. I was just thinking about my ex and how maybe the reason I feel so overprotective lately is because I know my only possible value to someone as young and pretty as you is as the hulking, aging sidekick.

Matthew recoiled from the cringey version of himself and curled his free hand into a fist. He'd rather punch himself in the face every hour on the hour than dump that pathetic bunch of crap in his partner's lap.

"Nah, I'm good. Just thinking about Chelsea and how far away she is now."

He knew Charli wasn't big on physical displays of affection, so he was startled when she reached across the center console and gave his arm a quick squeeze.

Coming from her, that meant more than ten hugs from one of those bubbly, touchy-feely type women.

"I'm sorry, Matthew. You must miss her a lot."

Matthew nodded while guilt sat in his stomach like a rotting apple. Thing was, Judy had a point. He really had worked long hours and spent a lot of nights in his office, hunkered down over files. So much that Chelsea being gone didn't seem like all that drastic of a change.

His shoulders sagged as he waited on a light to turn green. Accepting that he'd been a shitty husband was one thing. The idea that maybe he'd also sucked as a dad cut a lot deeper, with a much sharper blade.

"Wait, pull over. Let's play a hand of blackjack first to see who's breaking the news. You in?" Charli raised her eyebrows as she waved the deck of cards at him.

It was one of the special little partner habits they'd picked up sometime during their first year together. Whenever an event came up that either they both wanted to claim dibs on or they both were desperate to avoid, they used a single round of blackjack as their decision-maker.

Matthew pulled into the closest parking lot and put the truck in park before settling back in the seat. "When am I not in?"

In this instance, they were playing to decide who was burdened with the crappy task of notifying Maddie's next of kin since they were almost certain of the victim's identity. Charli dealt the cards with a steady flick of her wrist.

In front of Charli was a six of hearts, while he showed a seven of clubs.

Charli stuck the tip of her tongue between her teeth, a cute-as-hell action he caught her doing every now and then when she was debating something.

Based on that alone, he decided she must have a high card in the hole. An eight, maybe a nine. Otherwise, she wouldn't be torn. They'd played enough that he could read her tells and knew she was conservative with her bets. She didn't like going over.

She stared at her card with a little crease between her brows before nodding. "I'm taking a hit."

She flipped a new card over onto her pile. A three of spades.

Her neutral expression probably would have fooled literally anyone else, but not him. That quick press of her lips together and glance down meant she was happy with her hand.

"Hit me."

The new card slapped down, revealing a nine of hearts.

"Dammit!" He flicked his bottom card over to reveal the seven of diamonds. Busted.

The smile Charli had been hiding broke free as she turned over her hole card.

"Oh, come on! An ace?" He smacked his forehead. That was why she'd been indecisive. Not because she'd worried about busting, but because she'd been debating whether or not to play the ace high or low.

As she collected the cards, Matthew sighed and pulled out of the parking lot with the upcoming task already weighing on his heart.

He really wasn't feeling up to breaking the news to this poor kid's family today, but just like with the rest of his life, he knew there was no sense arguing over the cards he'd been dealt.

10

As Matthew navigated his truck through the southwestern part of the Historic District, Charli almost regretted winning the blackjack hand. The previous times he'd lost, he griped in a teasing way right up until they knocked on the family's door, but today he'd acted deflated, like a vampire had stuck its fangs in him and siphoned out all the fun.

Guilt pricked her stomach. She hoped her recent moodiness hadn't contributed to her partner's current glum demeanor. She made a mental note to broach the topic in a day or two, once they'd both had a chance to catch up on sleep.

This area was a little more run-down than the northern and eastern sides of town, and the houses were interspersed in spots with apartment buildings. The Hanleys' street was modest but neat, and the house Matthew parked in front of was blue, with a balcony on the second floor that extended across the entire width of the home.

Neither of them spoke as they climbed the three steps that led to the porch. Charli smoothed her hair while

Matthew knocked, glad that her short, pixie style tended to stay put in the humidity.

A woman in her forties cracked open the door. Her dark blonde hair was pulled back into a messy ponytail, and the round glasses perched on her nose made her big brown eyes resemble an owl's.

Matthew took the lead. "Mrs. Hanley?"

"Yes?"

Matthew pulled his jacket back to show his badge. "We're with the Savannah Police Department. Mind if we come in for a few minutes?"

The woman's gaze flickered between Matthew and Charli before her eyes widened and enhanced the owl comparison even more. "Yes, of course. Is this about Maddie?"

"Let's get inside, and then we can talk." Matthew waited for Mrs. Hanley to step back far enough for his big frame to enter. Charli trailed in his wake, steeling herself for what was to come.

She hated this part with the entirety of her one-hundred-pound being. Very soon, the hope propping Maddie's mom up would be extinguished, and Charli remembered how awful that felt all too well. Like spending months teetering on a narrow shelf stuck near the top of a tall cliff, clinging to both a flimsy rope and the belief that a rescue mission was on the way...until a few words yanked the rope away and sent you plummeting over the edge.

Mrs. Hanley showed them to a floral couch with sun-faded blue petals and squat, sturdy feet that Charli checked before sitting down. As Matthew took a seat, Mrs. Hanley scurried off and returned with her husband, and the couple settled into a pair of blue upholstered chairs opposite them.

"They're from the Savannah police. I think they might have some news about Maddie." Mrs. Hanley updated the stocky, brown-haired man beside her before turning frightened but hopeful eyes at Charli and Matthew. "When Maddie first went missing months ago, I took a leave of absence from my job as an events coordinator. I just went back last week. Isn't it funny how things work out sometimes?"

Charli threaded her fingers together in her lap and squeezed. The hope in Mrs. Hanley's voice was painful.

Mr. Hanley's expression didn't match his wife's. His brown eyes were wary as he studied Charli. "Let's wait and see what they have to say, Martha." His voice was deeper than Charli had expected and held a faint trace of a northeastern accent.

Matthew touched an old knife wound on his neck, but that was his only visible sign of discomfort before he started in. "First off, I know this must have been a challenging few months, and I'm sorry for that. No one should ever have to go through what you two have."

"Thank you." Mrs. Hanley squeezed her husband's hand, her hopeful smile never wavering.

"This might sound strange, but I need to ask…did your daughter ever break any bones?"

After a few seconds of shocked silence, Mr. Hanley shook his head. "No, I don't think—"

"Yes, she did." Mrs. Hanley shot her husband an exacerbated look. "You might not remember, honey, but she dropped a brick on her little toe when she was, oh, eleven or so, I think it was? The thing swelled up like a dang tick, so I rushed her to the doctor. He said she'd broken it, but there was nothing much to do. They just heal on their own."

"Do you happen to remember which foot that was on?" Matthew said.

"Oh, wow, I'm not sure…" Mrs. Hanley pursed her lips. "If I recall, I think it was the left one?"

Charli stared at her hands while Matthew cleared his throat. "We came straight here from the medical examiner's office. A body was found yesterday. We can't be one-hundred percent sure until all the test results are in, but the preliminary findings suggest the body they found belongs to your daughter. We're very sorry to bring you this news."

Mr. Hanley squeezed his eyes shut and bowed his head, but Mrs. Hanley's expression didn't change. Not unusual. In Charli's experience, loved ones often needed a little time before the news registered.

When Maddie's mother did process what Matthew had said, her chin reacted first, with a localized quiver that gradually spread to the rest of her body. Hope was tough to defeat, though. Even as her body reacted, Mrs. Hanley shook her head. "No. No, that can't be right. That can't be our Maddie."

She whirled toward her husband, who was sobbing quietly in the chair. "What are you...stop that! Stop that this instant! She's not dead. Did you even listen to them? They said the results *suggested*. That means they don't know! It could be someone else. Right? Right?"

When she turned to face them, her head was up, her posture defiant.

Matthew's soft voice was at odds with his size. "It could be, but..." he held up his hand to stop Mrs. Hanley from interrupting, "you need to prepare yourself. The odds aren't in your favor."

"Come here, honey." Mr. Hanley reached for his wife, but she lurched away from his embrace.

"The odds aren't in our favor, but that doesn't mean *no* odds. Right?"

The couch creaked as Matthew sagged, but he was upright again before anyone but Charli noticed. "True, but I don't think—"

"If it was Maddie, shouldn't you know right away? I read that fingerprints come back really quickly now, with that automated system. And Maddie was printed for that babysitting program she did. Remember that, Ken? So, if it was Maddie, you'd have matched her prints by now. But since you don't know for sure, I bet that means her prints weren't in the system, which means it's not our daughter."

The denial also wasn't unique, but the circumstances in which they'd discovered the body were. Matthew hunched over his lap, giving off such miserable vibes that Charli stepped in.

Sometimes, the nicest thing you could do for someone was amputate their limb in one fell swoop. Otherwise, the residual part continued to die and turn necrotic slowly over time. Left unaddressed, the infection could spread to other limbs and organs, putting the entire body at risk.

Charli prepared herself to be the blade. "There are no prints, Mrs. Hanley. The body was too decomposed in the heat. The medical examiner will need to compare dental records to confirm the match, but based on your daughter's height, hair and eye color, previously broken little toe, and length of time she was reported missing, the body discovered out in the marsh yesterday almost certainly belongs to Maddie."

She started to offer her condolences, but the wail Mrs. Hanley unleashed drowned out everything else.

Charli clenched her hands tighter while Maddie's mom jumped to her feet and stomped around, yanking on her hair and scream-sobbing until her husband pulled her to his chest, which she clung to like her life depended on it.

On the couch beside her, Matthew was also unhappy, squirming and probably thinking ahead, along the same lines as Charli.

This was all tragic, but they still needed to interview this poor couple.

One time last year, after breaking the news of a man's

death to his wife, Matthew had turned to Charli in the car and asked if she'd rather spend every day of her life informing families that their loved one had passed away or watch someone get physically tortured.

Without batting an eye, she'd answered, "Physical torture."

At least with that type of pain, there was still hope for the person's circumstances to improve.

Dead loved ones didn't return from the grave.

After five brutal minutes and a shot of whiskey that Mr. Hanley dug out of a cabinet somewhere, Mrs. Hanley finally quit bawling. The whites of her eyes and eyelids were pink, and she was still sniffling and hiccupping, but at least she no longer seemed on the verge of collapse.

Matthew cleared his throat. "I understand this is a very difficult time, and I'm sorry that I have to do this, but we need to ask you some questions. Whoever committed this terrible crime is still out there, and I know we'd all like nothing better than to stop this person from striking again."

Matthew's wince told Charli he caught his flub, but it was too late. Mrs. Hanley lifted her red-rimmed gaze and pinned him with a death stare. "No, Detective, the thing I want more than *anything* else is to have my daughter back, alive and well."

She began sobbing again, and Matthew shot Charli a helpless look, which wasn't like him at all. He was usually the better one with people, always coming up with the right thing to say.

Her heart twisted. Poor Matthew. Had to be tough, breaking news like this when you had a teen daughter of your own.

When the noise abated enough, Mr. Hanley spoke. "Go ahead, ask your questions. We definitely don't want this son of a bitch out there hurting anyone else's daughter."

"Thank you." Charli slipped the photos out of her jacket pocket. "Does this brand of lipstick mean anything to you?"

She handed the evidence picture over to Mr. Hanley. Both she and Matthew scrutinized his reaction as he studied it. Terrible as they were, statistics didn't lie. The vast majority of missing children were runaways. Of the ones who weren't, most were abducted by a family member, and more than half of the murders where the killer was identified were committed by someone the family knew. That meant the Hanleys had to be considered as potential suspects.

Especially when that number rose to more than sixty percent when considering female victims in particular.

If Mr. Hanley was familiar with the lipstick, his expression didn't show it. He studied the photo for a few moments before shaking his head. "No, but that doesn't mean anything. I don't really pay attention to stuff like that. Honey, you see this before?"

Mrs. Hanley pushed her glasses on top of her head and scrubbed her eyes with the back of her hands before peering at the photo. She took a slightly longer look, but in the end, shook her head as well. "No. I don't think I've seen it before. Why?"

"This lipstick was found…with the body." The Hanleys would find out what happened to their daughter soon enough.

Maddie's mom gasped before grabbing the picture and tugging it closer. "I don't know…she has a lot of makeup. She started begging me to take her to the makeup place in the department store to try on all the samples the second she turned thirteen." Fresh tears brimmed in the woman's brown eyes. "She'd ask me which color eye shadow or lipstick looked better until I was about to pass out on my feet. I can't believe I'll never take her there again…"

Before the woman could break into another round of

uncontrollable sobs, Charli pushed another question in her direction. "I hate to ask, but could we get one of Maddie's old hairbrushes or a toothbrush? Something that would have her DNA to help facilitate a positive ID."

Sniffling, Mrs. Hanley asked her husband if he could run upstairs and fetch Maddie's hairbrush. She waited until he disappeared and lowered her voice. "Ken doesn't like to talk about this, but I just wanted to make sure you knew Maddie had apparently been talking about sneaking off with her boyfriend."

Like she'd flipped a switch, Mrs. Hanley began weeping again. Matthew shifted in his spot and avoided eye contact. Charli's throat thickened, and she suddenly found it hard to swallow. "We, um..."

Yesterday, Peter and Shelly Briggs had practically fawned over her, suffusing Charli with their gratitude for tracking down their missing kid. In their book, she'd emerged as the hero.

One day later and another missing child, only this story couldn't have a more opposite ending. No matter what else happened, Mrs. Hanley would forever associate Charli with her daughter's death.

As Charli witnessed the woman's pain, she berated herself for her cavalier attitude toward yesterday's visit with the Briggs. She'd acted like a jerk. That sort of unbridled gratitude might make her squirm, but the bottom line was that if parents wanted to thank her, it meant their children were still alive.

She'd gladly sign on for a lifetime of awkward gratitude over another single day of this heartbreak.

Matthew slanted an alarmed glance at Charli, almost certainly wondering why she'd stopped mid-sentence. "As my partner was saying, we did know about the boyfriend, and an officer already questioned him. He checked out, but we can definitely take another pass at him."

Charli didn't have a way to mime *because I feel like a big phony*, though, so she sat quietly with her hands in her lap. Mr. Hanley tromped back down the stairs, brandishing a purple hairbrush.

Charli thanked him and accepted the brush, sliding it into one of the gallon-sized plastic bags tucked into her pocket. She spent more time on the task than necessary, sealing the bag with a methodical precision to avoid Matthew's eyes. When he realized she wasn't going to rejoin the interview, he plowed through the questions on his own.

Mr. and Mrs. Hanley took turns answering the usual staples, but none of their answers revealed anything Charli and Matthew hadn't already read in the missing persons report. They wrapped up the session, rising and thanking the Hanleys for their cooperation.

Mr. Hanley asked if they could show themselves to the door and lock it behind them so he could get his wife upstairs to bed. He helped her stand and then guided his wife up the stairs, one slow, defeated step at a time. The image burned into Charli's brain before she pulled the door shut with a soft click.

She held up her hand as she climbed into the passenger's seat of Matthew's truck. "I know, I wasn't at my best, either. Looks like we're both having an off day."

His raised eyebrows said *no shit*, but wisely, her partner kept that sentiment to himself. "So, guess it's back to the drawing board."

"Yu-up." She leaned her head back against the seat and sighed. She'd hoped to find a lead but had only ended up with more questions. What kind of depraved mind would sew a tube of lipstick into their victim before killing them, and why?

Charli pictured the photographs the forensics team had taken of Maddie's body, all crammed into that plastic container.

She paused, hit rewind on her thoughts. "We obviously need to do an internet search on the lipstick, but I don't see that taking us far. That brand is huge, and that Happy Harlot color seems to be incredibly popular. They even sell it in drug stores. But what about the plastic container she was buried in? I haven't seen those anywhere. Maybe that will lead us to the killer?"

Matthew shrugged. "Dunno, but let's see if we can find out."

11

Charli stripped off her blazer the second she shut the front door and had her blouse halfway unbuttoned before she reached her bedroom. The ancient hardwood floor groaned in all the usual spots, reminding her a restoration was long past due.

The floor would have to get in line. She would be forever grateful to her grandmother, who'd willed Charli this house when she'd died, but the inheritance came with some headaches too.

Located in the Historic District, the home was in one of the nicest parts of town, surrounded on all sides by antebellum architecture and covered in a canopy of live oaks.

The downside also happened to be related to the house's location in the Historic District, which was a fancy way of saying the place was old. *Really* old, which also meant the property required a lot of TLC, time, and money. Unfortunately for the house, Charli wasn't exactly flush in any of those areas.

And in the event that her circumstances changed and those factors all came together? Due to the home's historic designation, she'd first need to gain a permit from the local Planning Commission before undertaking any renovations.

The only thing that sounded worse than spending her free time on a structural overhaul was spending that time on bureaucratic red tape.

After hanging her blazer in the closet, Charli stripped down, tossed her sweaty clothes into the woven laundry basket, and climbed into the shower. One of the few updates she'd made was the giant rain showerhead, which she used now to blast cold water over her body and wash the grime away.

Once she felt clean again, Charli toweled off and pulled on a pair of loose shorts and a t-shirt and headed into the living room. The decor throughout the house was what one of those fancy designers on the home improvement channel might refer to as eclectic, if they were bending over backward to be kind.

That fit because Charli's grandmother had been more than a little eccentric. She'd lived to suit herself and couldn't have given a fig about anyone else's opinion of her or her tastes. Every decade, she'd purchased new pieces that caught her eye, with no apparent concern for how they might all blend together.

The sitting room remained the only space that stayed true to the house's classical design. Antique furniture graced the cozy room, from elegant Queen Anne chairs, a cherrywood coffee table, and a pretty cream and mauve loveseat that Charli avoided like the plague.

She gave it the evil eye as she turned toward the living room. "One of these days, I'm taking you to Goodwill. Just you wait."

The threat was empty, though, and if the loveseat were truly sentient, it would know that by now. Charli's grandmother had loved that stupid piece so much that she'd made

Charli promise to never get rid of it. *"It's not Priscilla's fault you bounced around on her too much as a child and broke her leg. If anything, Priscilla should be mad at you."*

That all made perfect sense, except for the part where Priscilla was a stuffed piece of furniture that didn't have feelings while seven-year-old Charli did. That sudden crash had freaked her out, producing a nasty knot on her forehead when it bounced off the floor.

She might have recovered and made her peace with Priscilla if that had turned out to be the sole incident, but no. Three years later, the loveseat had attempted to maim her again, mixing it up by collapsing on the opposite side.

Too bad that was where her ten-year-old self, still suspicious from the previous incident, had been perched. No forehead bonks that time, but the sudden lurch had caused her to drop a glass. The cut on her foot when she'd jumped off the loveseat had earned her three stitches on the ball of her left foot.

After that, her grandmother had clucked her tongue and claimed Charli and Priscilla were just a bad mix.

Charli had agreed. From that day on, she'd decided Priscilla was a death trap in disguise and refused to sit on her again. As crappy as her building skills were, even she knew better than to slap even her light weight on four skinny little legs. Maybe if the builder had paid more attention to physics rather than carving scores of useless curlicues and flower petals into the wood, Priscilla would be less prone to maiming the unsuspecting souls who rested their weary bottoms upon her cream-colored elegance.

One of those bottoms would not belong to Charli, though. Never, ever again.

She left the austere dignity of the sitting room for the color explosion of the living room. Decked out in blues, purples, and greens, the space represented her grandmother's retro seventies phase.

Charli could take or leave the color scheme. What she loved were the velvety-soft fabrics on the chairs and couch. Plus, the bookshelves.

She sighed with pleasure at the floor-to-ceiling bookshelves that spanned an entire wall. One of the first things Charli had done upon moving in was pull a ladder over and rearrange all her grandmother's old romances and westerns to the highest shelves. The lower shelves she filled with the books she'd brought along, organized by subject—serial killer nonfiction, psychology, mysteries, and graphic novels —and within each category by author's last name.

Charli gazed longingly at a new hardcover about Randy Steven Kraft, the so-called Scorecard Killer who'd preyed on young men he found along California freeways in the 1970s, but pulled out her phone instead. She chewed her lip as she scrolled through her music app. Her go-to selection after work tended to be rock, especially when she was knee-deep in a brand-new case. Tonight, though, screaming electric guitars and pounding drums might send her right over the edge.

She skipped the rock and chose a playlist titled "Serial Killer Prevention" instead, which she'd loaded with more relaxing indie artists and ambient beats. Once the first notes kicked off, she headed to the kitchen, which resembled a fifties diner with black-and-white decor accentuated by splashes of red.

The appliances were from the last decade, though, a fact Charli thanked her grandmother for as she yanked open the stainless steel refrigerator and cold air wafted out. At least she shouldn't have to worry about replacing them anytime soon. Neat stacks of plastic storage containers and fruit arranged in a bin met her at eye level. She bypassed those in search of a refreshing drink. Reaching for a pitcher of lemonade on the bottom shelf, she spied a half-empty bottle of wine wedged into the far corner.

She hesitated before wrestling the bottle out. Unlike the meals in the storage containers, which she rotated each week, Charli had no idea how long the wine had been in there. After unscrewing the cap and sniffing, she shrugged. Smelled fine to her.

Her grandma had a set of old crystal wine goblets in the sitting room hutch, but washing the dust away seemed like too much effort, so she grabbed a green plastic cup and poured a small amount inside.

She sipped as she carried the wine into the living room, grabbing a coaster before setting them both on an end table. Her next stop was the storage closet near the stairs. She pulled her dry-erase board out, along with a small, labeled bin of markers and erasers, carrying both back to the living room. As always, she considered the soft electric-blue couch before rejecting it in favor of plopping down on the large, blue-and-green shag rug that looked like it had come straight off the set of a seventies sitcom.

Crossing her legs beneath her like she used to do in school, Charli popped the cap off a pen and scrawled "Madeline Hanley" across the top of the whiteboard. She filled in the space below with quick, five words or fewer descriptions of the facts of the case.

When she finished, she chewed on the pen cap as she studied what she had so far. Her gaze crept to the name at the top, and her mind began to drift. Back to Bonaventure Cemetery. Back to the day her best friend Madeline's mom had called with the news.

With a savage jerk of her body, she ripped herself out of the past. "Stop! This isn't about my Madeline right now."

Stopping was hard, though. The parallels between this case and her Madeline kept popping up.

None of that mattered. While the reasons for her distractions were understandable, she couldn't allow them to continue. This new Madeline deserved one hundred percent of her focus.

Her Madeline would have to wait.

Picking up the eraser, she wiped away the first name and wrote "Maddie" instead.

Erasing her mind wasn't quite as simple. She reached for her phone, tempted to call Matthew and take him up on that offer to talk. She recoiled and snatched her hand back before touching the device.

Matthew was a great partner, caring and kind, but how could he possibly help? He hadn't experienced anything similar in his life. No one Charli knew had. Dumping all of this on him ran the risk of making things awkward between them.

Sure, on some level, Matthew could relate to loss. After his wife packed up their only daughter and left him, Charli was certain he at least partially understood the void in her own life. But the sheer finality and brutality of murder created a divide in their circumstances Charli doubted anyone could fully understand. No, she was alone in this.

Charli assessed the probability of feeling better after talking about Madeline as very low. On the other hand, there was a high chance she'd regret opening up about her old friend the moment the words left her mouth.

She wasn't sure how much time passed before she realized she was staring blankly at the whiteboard, but she pegged it as long enough. Rising, she packed up the markers and carried them and the whiteboard over to the couch, plopping both down on the middle cushion.

"The least you can do is be useful in some small way."

After carrying her mostly untouched wine into the kitchen and dumping it down the sink, she trudged upstairs to her bedroom.

The two Madelines weighed on her when she climbed into the antique four-poster bed and closed her eyes, and as she drifted off to sleep, she worried she was failing them both.

"I'M SORRY!" Charli shot up in her bed with her heart slamming against her ribs under her sweat-soaked t-shirt, her ears still ringing from the screams. Darkness greeted her.

Nightmare. Just a nightmare.

A shrill noise pierced the quiet room. Charli froze before realizing it was her phone, ringing from the bedside table. She fumbled for the device.

The soft green numbers on the clock read a little after three in the morning.

Definitely not good news.

Heart still thundering in her chest, she peered at the screen. Ruth's name flashed, which only reinforced Charli's certainty. There were very few reasons for her boss to call in the middle of the night, and almost all of them involved more dead people.

Charli answered the call while plucking her wet shirt away from her chest. "Cross."

"Sorry to wake you, but we've got another body."

Less than forty-five minutes after Ruth's wake-up call, Charli was in her car, waiting for Matthew outside his apartment. He hurried outside, yanking the door shut and locking it behind him. It was the same routine he'd followed on the handful of other occasions she'd arrived to pick him up. He'd never once invited her in, but it was more than that. Matthew seemed to be actively trying to prevent her from even peeking inside.

Charli's gaze lingered on the blue door for another moment before she shrugged and turned away. It was a little odd he wanted to shield her from seeing his place, but she wasn't one to judge. Based on the sloppy state of her partner's truck, she suspected his apartment wasn't the tidiest, and maybe he was embarrassed by the mess.

The bigger the space, the more room for trash. That had been one of her mom's mottos and why she'd always insisted on carrying a small purse, even though Charli could never remember a time when her mom's purse, car, or home was anything other than tidy.

Charli's heart clenched. The memories seemed to operate

on a switch. As long as she didn't think about her mom, she was fine, but the second she did, the floodgates opened, triggering intense, painful pressure in her chest.

People told her one day the pain would fade, but Charli didn't want that, either. The idea of not hurting over her mother's death felt disloyal somehow. She told herself that wasn't logical, but it didn't help. Apparently, grief didn't follow a rule book.

During the first part of the drive, Matthew kept yawning, and Charli's mind shifted from her mom to the horrible dream.

When she realized she was stuck on the hateful, accusatory expression on nightmare Madeline's face, she shook herself. *Dream Madeline is imaginary, but Maddie Hanley is real. You can still find her killer.*

"What are the chances this victim was killed by the same guy as Maddie?"

Matthew yawned once more before responding. "Excuse me. And, hard to say without seeing the body, but the fact that she's another young female found near the same location? My gut says pretty damn high that this is our perp's work."

Charli still didn't give much credence to Matthew's or anyone else's gut, but in this particular instance, she happened to agree. It was too soon to draw conclusions, but the facts so far, skimpy as they were, pointed in that direction.

They were likely dealing with a repeat killer, and if they'd found two bodies already, they might uncover more.

The realization hit them both at once, banishing the last of the dream from Charli's brain and making Matthew sit up straight in his seat and utter a soft curse. "Damn."

That was all he said, but the single word summed up the current state of events succinctly.

Damn, indeed.

Reading about past serial killers was entirely different from potentially tracking an active one. In the books on her shelves, the stories had ended long ago. No future lives were at stake.

In real life, people would keep dying until the killer was found and captured. Until *she* found and captured him.

A heavy weight pushed on Charli's shoulders and settled deep into her bones, but the pressure was offset by the electricity pulsing through her veins. That was how early morning calls played out. First came the intense grogginess that triggered an adrenaline rush to fend off the fog. Once the epinephrine kicked in, Charli was always wired and raring to go.

Her body hummed as she turned onto the road that led to the new site. The marsh spread along the side of the road, eerie, dark, and still in the starlit night. At least, until they reached the crime scene, which was lit up with enough wattage and human activity to power a sports arena. Charli estimated they were about half a mile away from where the previous body was discovered.

Matthew squinted out the windshield. "I hate those damn lights. Makes me think I should be eating hot dogs and cheering on my team, not digging up dead bodies."

He reached to unclip the seat belt, but Charli cleared her throat, making him sigh. "I swear, you're the only cop I know who enforces the seat belt law. We're going like ten miles an hour now. Even if we crashed, I'd barely scratch my damn nose."

His hand dropped to his lap, though, so Charli ignored the grumbling and parked on the side of the road. As they headed over to the sleepy-eyed, uniformed cop who stood as a sentry to the scene, she kept one eye on the ground, wanting to avoid another bout of muddy boots if at all possible.

He waved them under the yellow crime tape that was once again affixed to a set of orange pylons, and they picked their way over to two death scene investigators who worked under Soames in the GBI's Coastal Lab.

"What've you got for us?" Matthew rested his hands on his hips.

Mike Stone, the taller and lankier of the two GBI agents on the scene, replied first. "Another body, more decomposed than the last one, so she's probably been here longer. Young, blue-eyed brunette female found naked like the last one. Found in the exact same type of storage container. No M.E. confirmation yet, but it appears she's got sutures in the same spot as the previous victim."

A pit opened in the bottom of Charli's stomach as she and Matthew exchanged a glance. That removed all but the tiniest sliver of doubt.

Their unsub had committed both murders.

"Is it time to bring in the cadaver dogs so we can search the entire area?" Charli asked.

Stone nodded. "Already put out the call."

Matthew shifted his weight from foot to foot, an indication her partner was just as concerned over these new developments as she was. "Who found her?"

"A couple of teens making a TikTok video. Can you believe that shit?" Mike shook his head like he was still trying to make sense of it all.

"Wait, seriously? TikTok?"

Matthew sounded far more surprised than Charli. Pretty much every teen she ran into lately had their face all but attached to an electronic device of some kind. Even when sitting together in little huddles, they all played on their phones.

She'd downloaded the app a while ago to see what all the hype was about. As she'd scrolled through some of the videos, she'd experienced a sharp pang in her chest. All that dancing and lip-synching. Had Madeline been alive today, Charli had no doubt her friend would have been a star.

"Yeah, they saw all the police commotion and decided to mosey on over and see what was up. We told them to get lost. So, they started poking around in the mud more than half a mile away, pretending to be some teen *CSI* shit or gravediggers or what have you, and wouldn't you know it? Little punks found another container. That's when they hauled their bony butts back to us."

Matthew shook his head. "Stranger than fiction, man."

Charli's mouth tightened. "You have a cause of death yet?"

The taller tech shrugged. "Hard to say given the state of the body, but no obvious wounds, just like the last one."

Matthew shuffled his feet again. "ID?"

"Negative. And before you ask, we don't have time of death narrowed down yet, beyond months."

Charli grasped at straws. "Any chance that trace evidence will be helpful?"

"Probably not. We took samples of everything we could, though."

Charli bit back a sigh. It wasn't the GBI's fault this killer was proving to be cunning. "Thanks."

Matthew and Charli spent the next forty-five minutes inspecting the body and the area surrounding the recovery site but didn't linger longer. Their forensics team and the GBI crew would go over every inch of the scene and surrounding area and photograph, bag, and tag anything of interest. She would only get in the way of their organized chaos.

Once the crew scouring the site processed the evidence they'd collected back at their respective labs, they'd document their findings. From that point on, Charli and Matthew were in the hot seat.

Back in her car, Charli checked the time. "It's still early. How about we grab a coffee and something to eat and figure out what our next steps are?"

Matthew nodded. "Yeah…we need to see how many other girls are out there."

Charli's heart squeezed. "And we need to find this guy before he strikes again."

CHARLI'S CAR smelled like fried eggs and hash browns as Matthew devoured his second breakfast sandwich from the passenger's seat in the fast-food parking lot. Charli had already finished her one and only sandwich and was sipping coffee from a white takeout cup, her brow creased as they worked through the list of Maddie's potential contacts. "Out of everyone, I think we should try the boyfriend first. Girls always tell them stuff, right?"

"I think we should start with Abby Lawrence. They were best friends, so if Maddie was hiding anything or keeping secrets, Abby's the one who'd know."

Matthew was a little taken aback by the vehemence in Charli's voice. Her chin jutted out, giving off the impression she was prepared to fight him on this point. Since he didn't feel strongly one way or the other, he gave in. "Yeah, okay, fine. Let's go talk to Abby."

Her shoulders visibly lost some of their stiffness. "Okay. It's coming up on six-thirty now. By the time we get there, it'll be around a quarter 'til. We should be able to catch her while she's getting ready for school."

She started the car and headed out of the parking lot, leaving Matthew to clutch his coffee and wonder what was playing out behind those blue eyes. Something was definitely up with his partner, and it bugged him she was holding him at bay. They were supposed to work together, have each other's backs.

How could he have her back when she was locking him out?

A little before seven, they parked and walked up to the front door of a modest two-story brick home on the west side of town. A girl with a blonde bob partially shaved on one side opened the door. "Hello?"

Charli showed her badge. "Are you Abby Lawrence?"

The girl nodded and eyed them warily. "Yeah. Am I in trouble or something?"

Matthew flashed her an easy smile. "No. We're here to ask a few questions about Maddie Hanley. We hear she was a good friend of yours?"

The girl blinked several times, and her brown eyes welled with tears. "Best. Maddie was my best friend."

Charli edged a little closer. "I'm very sorry for your loss, Abby. I know how much this hurts and how surreal this must all feel to you right now." His partner's expression was unusually soft as she gazed at the teen.

Abby sniffled and nodded. "Surreal is right. Like, I woke up a billion times last night, and every single time, I forgot at first what had happened. Then it would all come crashing back, and I'd feel terrible all over again." Another tear slid down her cheek.

"I won't lie, it's most likely going to be like that for a while." Charli inhaled a deep breath. "Gradually, though, the memories will soften, and the pain won't come as often. I wish it weren't so hard, but when you love someone, losing them hurts. What we want to do is make sure we catch the person who did this before he hurts anyone else. Can you help us?"

Abby bit her lip, peered over her shoulder, and cocked her head for a second before slipping out onto the porch and shutting the door. "Yeah, but we need to do it out here and be quiet. My mom worked a late shift last night, and she can be a real witch if you wake her up early, and that's the last thing I can deal with right now."

Charli nodded. "Right here is fine, Abby, thank you. Can you tell us a little about Maddie?"

Abby tugged at a lock of hair and hunched her shoulders against the door. "What do you want to know?"

Charli and Matthew led her through the usual rundown. Nothing much stood out until Matthew asked, "Do you know anyone who'd want to hurt her?"

The girl shook her head. "No, but…" She stared at her feet like she was suddenly mesmerized by her neon green toenail polish.

For a moment, Matthew was distracted as well. Neon green, like a lime Skittle had puked all over her toes. Whatever happened to normal colors, like pink? Or red?

Last time he'd seen Chelsea, she'd had some weird navy blue color on her fingers. It was like teens went out of their way these days to look weird. He didn't get it.

Then he clued into what Abby had said, and that familiar sensation pinged in his gut. "I know this is hard, Abby, but even the tiniest bit of information or smallest detail can sometimes help us crack a case. Only problem is, we won't know what might help until we hear it."

Charli chimed in, her demeanor still uncommonly gentle. "He's right. If you think you know of someone who might have wanted to hurt her or was hurting her, please tell us. Even if you're not sure. We'll get to the bottom of it, I promise."

Abby lifted her head. "I don't know if he wanted to hurt her, but I'm pretty sure Maddie and her dad got into it more than once. Like, they didn't get along at all. Maddie was always complaining about him. Their arguments got pretty intense sometimes, real screaming matches. She FaceTimed me crying once because he smacked her, and I'm pretty sure it happened another time too. For the last month or so, Maddie was talking about skipping town with her boyfriend. I sort of thought she was just venting, but now I'm not so sure…"

Matthew's jaw tensed. Funny, Maddie's dad had never mentioned anything about aggressive fights with his daughter when they'd questioned him.

'Course, there was a good reason for that if Ken Hanley was the killer.

"Can you tell us more about Mr. Hanley? What was he like? Did he ever act in a way that you thought was weird or made you uncomfortable?"

Abby toyed with a silver ring on her thumb. "No, I mean, not that I can remember. I didn't like it when they got into it when I was over, but that usually ended the second he remembered I was there. I don't think he liked fighting in front of other people."

Which made perfect sense if he had something to hide.

"Honestly, Maddie avoided him as much as possible, though, and she came to my house a lot more than I went to hers."

Charli nodded. "And what about her boyfriend? Any bad vibes there?"

The teen shrugged. "No, not really. They seemed like kind of a weird couple, but Kevin is okay."

Matthew was still fuming, stuck on Mr. Hanley. What kind of miserable son of a bitch slapped his teen daughter around? If Matthew's gut was pinging before, now his entire GI tract was sending up flares. "You ever see any weird storage around the Hanleys' house? Maybe in the garage or out back somewhere?"

Charli sent him a sharp glance, which he pretended not to notice. His partner had informed him multiple times in the past she didn't believe in hunches, but Matthew knew better. Big, logical brains were good, but he was convinced logic alone couldn't solve cases. Not without a little more of the human touch.

Otherwise, why not assign cases to a computer and let an algorithm solve them?

Abby's smooth forehead creased. "Storage? You mean, like a shed or something?"

Charli jumped in like she was afraid Matthew would elaborate. "Don't worry about that now, Abby. If you could tell us about any regular places Maddie went after school or on the weekends, though, that would be a help." She glared daggers at him, though he wasn't sure why. He'd never intended to reveal any specific details about the plastic container, only give Abby a nudge in that direction.

"I mean, as far as I know, she walked straight home every day. She hung out with Kevin or came over to my house. We'd go to the movies or the mall but not, like, all the time."

Matthew considered nudging a little more. Charli's peeved expression made him think the better of it. Best not to ruffle her feathers anymore, or else he could expect drama. Not the emotional blowup kind, because Charli rarely if ever gave in to those types of displays. More like she'd subject him to a frosty lecture on the fallacy of using hunches versus facts while her blue eyes sliced and diced him like sub-zero laser beams.

Some women, like his ex, got emotional when they were mad. Judy would turn into a firecracker, sparking off in every direction, loud and attention-seeking.

Not Charli. The more upset she got, the more she

reminded him of one of those robotic text-to-voice features. Her speech grew more precise, clipped, and her default to analytical thinking more pronounced. Almost like she turned off her emotions entirely.

Of the two, Charli's version of mad was by far the more unsettling. His ex's theatrics used to piss him off, get his own blood pressure rising. Charli's? Scared the ever-loving crap out of him.

Today, though, Charli seemed all over the place. More emotional than usual one moment, icy the next. If it were anyone but Charli, he probably wouldn't think much of it. Maybe monthly hormone fluctuations or bad news on the personal front.

But it was Charli, so he was concerned. He studied her as she thanked Abby for her help and then surprised everyone on the porch by asking the teen if she needed a hug. The girl nodded, her face crumpling as Charli embraced her.

Meanwhile, Matthew was afraid his jaw was about to smack the concrete. If one of the guys back at the precinct told him Charli had volunteered to hug someone, he'd have blown it off as a joke.

Had an alien invaded her body, like in one of those old sci-fi flicks he'd watched from under a blanket as a kid?

Charli stepped back first, and Abby gave a teary wave before disappearing into the house. When the door shut, Charli stood on the porch and stared at the brown paint. Long enough that Matthew started to worry she'd gone catatonic. He was just about to wave his hand in front of her face when she turned on her heel and headed back toward the car.

He studied the back of her head as he trailed her down the steps to the sidewalk, uneasiness squirming in his stomach like a school of live fish.

Something was going on with his partner, and he needed to figure out what.

Sooner or later, Charli had to release whatever she was bottling up inside. Matthew wanted to make sure that happened...before an explosion occurred.

13

Charli was aware of Matthew's sideways glances during the drive over to the Hanleys' house, but she didn't venture any commentary, and he didn't press her. She was grateful for that latter fact because she wasn't sure where a discussion right now would lead. Her chest was tight, and she felt itchy, but on the inside where she couldn't scratch, and also a little unstable, like a sandcastle at high tide, surrounded by a crowd of stomping kids.

She forced her fingers to quit clenching the steering wheel like her life depended on it and tried to draw in long, deep breaths. A difficult task since her body had decided to manifest her tension by emulating a Victorian corset.

When she'd first learned of the case, she'd figured the similarities between Madeline and Maddie would carry an emotional toil and tried to prepare accordingly.

None of her preparations had braced her for the soul-stabbing moment when she'd stared into Abby's eyes and witnessed her own heartache reflected back.

She bit her cheek, frustrated with herself. One of the

unwritten rules of being a detective was not getting too emotionally attached to a case or the people involved.

Piece of cake, right? Charli had thought so in the past. That wasn't to say she didn't experience empathy for the people she encountered throughout the course of her investigations. She absolutely did. Empathy while maintaining her emotional reserve. Safeguarding a healthy psychic distance was a tactic she believed helped her better approach cases from a place of reason. Of logic.

That was how her partnership worked. With his hunches and emotional reactions, Matthew was the intuitive part of the team, while Charli was more levelheaded and methodical. He charged in while she held back for more details. Their polar-opposite approaches could have resulted in disaster, but against all odds, they worked. Their strengths and weaknesses balanced out, meshing together better than anyone dared dream.

Anyone except for Ruth Morris. Charli bowed to whatever analytic technique her boss had utilized to pair the two of them. Their first few months together, whispers had flooded the precinct, with cops snickering as they wondered aloud if Sergeant Morris had finally lost her touch. Bets had followed over how long before Charli or Matthew or both stormed into their boss's office and begged to be reassigned.

As Charli was learning was often the case, Sergeant Morris had the last laugh. Not only had her latest partner assignment hit the road running, but within a year, they were solving more cases than anyone else.

Messing with their dynamic could upset the balance. Plus, bouncing around like an emotional ping-pong ball was a disconcerting experience Charli would rather not prolong.

The problem was, she had no idea how to get herself back on track.

She shook her head as she turned onto the Hanleys'

street. No, that wasn't true. She was confident she knew one way…solve the case.

Cars still lined the curb in front of Maddie Hanley's house, forcing Charli to parallel park in a tight spot a couple of houses down. Matthew rolled his eyes at her law-abiding antics. If her partner were driving, he'd have blocked the Hanleys in their driveway without a second thought.

They were climbing up to the porch when the front door swung open.

Mr. Hanley took one step out before rearing back, clearly startled. "Did we have an appointment today?" He looked at his watch. "If so, I must have forgotten. I'm just on my way out the door to work."

His button-down, collared shirt and gray slacks backed up his statement. Kenneth Hanley owned and helped manage a successful local restaurant. Charli wondered if all owners dressed like they were headed off to an office job or if Maddie's dad simply enjoyed business attire.

Matthew cast a subtle glance at Charli, and she gave him an equally subtle nod in reply, letting him know she was okay with him starting off the questioning. He turned back to Mr. Hanley, with a casual, hands-in-pockets posture that was belied by the animosity Charli read in his tight-lipped, no teeth smile. "No appointment, but we had a few follow-up questions that we need to have answered sooner versus later. Okay if we come in?"

Her partner used his size like a battering ram, crowding Maddie's dad into backing up and opening the door wider before the man even comprehended what was happening.

One of many instances where Charli regretted the genetic code that had programmed her to top out at a measly five feet. No matter how tough or pushy she was, she'd never come close to achieving the intimidation factor naturally gifted to a six-foot-two frame.

She followed the path Matthew blazed for them, trailing both men into the house.

Kenneth Hanley stopped a few paces short of crossing into the living room. "What do you need to ask?"

"We just had a few more questions about your daughter. Can we sit down?" Again, the question was only a formality. Matthew brushed past Hanley like he lived there.

Hanley glared at Matthew's back before remembering Charli. Standing there. Taking everything in.

When she fluttered her fingers at him and smiled, his nostrils flared.

Goodness, someone was testy this morning.

The return smile he eventually managed was pained, really more of a grimace. He pulled back his sleeve and directed a pointed look at his watch. "Like I said, I was just on my way out the door, but sure. I guess I can spare a few minutes."

"Thanks, we appreciate that." Matthew chose the same spot on the couch as before. Charli pulled out her notebook and squeezed past Hanley, who still hadn't moved. He also hadn't invited either of them to sit, but that was okay. She'd found most people were followers, or at least, prone to suggestion. If you wanted someone to perform a certain action, your best bet was to do it yourself first.

Social decorum helped too. Especially in a traditional place like Savannah.

She settled beside Matthew, pen in hand and ready to go. Now all they needed was Maddie's dad.

Mr. Hanley stared at the two of them. His jaw worked. He opened his mouth like he might protest, but at the last second, pivoted to perch on the edge of the chair.

Charli allowed herself another tiny smile before schooling her features into a more appropriate expression.

Hanley crossed his arms. "Now, what do you need to know?"

"To start with, can you tell us a little about your daughter? Was she easygoing, did she get good grades, was she polite or a mouthy teen? Give us a little snapshot of her personality."

Matthew started off with softball questions. The goal was to ease the subject into a false sense of security in hopes of catching him off guard with tougher questions later.

While Matthew talked, she assessed and took notes. Her partner sometimes poked fun at her for the notebook she carried everywhere. She didn't care. Memory was unreliable and transient. Subject to a variety of environmental influences, including time. Whereas, unless she dropped them in a lake or set them on fire, her notes held up.

She also paid attention to Hanley's intonation. His vocal fluctuations. Emotional triggers. Contrary to the teachings of pop culture, there was no hard science to back the usefulness of nonverbal cues. Nothing to support that rapid blinking or nose scratching meant a witness was lying, so Charli didn't spend much time on those.

"Maddie's personality? I'm guessing she was like most girls her age. Upbeat and sweet one moment, irritable as a wet cat the next. Not super shy, but not one of those social butterflies, either. She pulled mostly B's and a few C's." He paused and shrugged. "Sort of like your typical teenager."

Hanley scooted back in the chair. His shoulders relaxed. Good. After the initial shake-up, they wanted Hanley to lower his guard. The real test would come when Matthew veered into less comfortable territory.

"Ever get into any trouble at school? With other students or teachers?"

Mr. Hanley shook his head. "Not that I can remember."

"How about at home?"

Maddie's dad hesitated, scratched his chin. "Not really.

She got in trouble from time to time. Usual stuff, like not doing her chores, getting a bad grade on a test, sassing her mom. Grounded every once in a while. Like I said, she was a pretty typical teenager."

Still nothing to indicate Hanley was telling anything but the truth.

The couch moved when Matthew shifted his weight, draping an arm along the back cushion in a deceptively casual gesture. "How would you describe your relationship with Maddie overall?"

Another glance at his watch. "I don't know, strained? Teen girls can be a real pain sometimes. Maddie was no exception. Lots of screaming, crying, or that god-awful shrieking and giggling when her friends would come over. Someone should come up with a service that offers teen parents a way to soundproof their rooms. I swear they'd make a killing."

Beside her, Matthew emitted a soft noise that reminded her an awful lot of a growl. She was right there with him. How could this man act so callous?

She took three deep breaths and made herself let the judgment go. They were here to determine if Kenneth Hanley was a killer, not an asshole.

"Tell me, Mr. Hanley...do you really think *strained* is the right word for a relationship where the father hits his daughter?"

Matthew's softly worded question took a second for Hanley to register. Charli was ready when he did. First came the shocked intake of breath, followed by the brief rounding of his eyes. Next, his face and neck turned a blotchy red. His nostrils flared, and she braced for a defensive outburst.

Before that happened, his eyes closed, and he exhaled. He repeated that several times until his color returned to normal. "I don't know who've you've been talking to, but yeah, okay. I admit that Maddie and I got into it once or twice, and I lost my cool and hit her. I'm not proud of myself, but Maddie, she could really get mouthy sometimes, try a saint's patience."

Kenneth Hanley lifted his hands like he expected Matthew to commiserate with him, dropping them again over whatever he read on her partner's face.

"Which was it, Mr. Hanley? Once or twice? Or did it happen more than that?"

"Twice. Only happened two times. That's the god's honest truth." This time, Mr. Hanley shifted his attention to Charli, probably in hopes of gaining a more sympathetic audience. "Why is he asking me all this? Last I checked, it's not against the law to discipline your own daughter."

Actually, it was, but Charli needed to keep him talking so she let it slide...for now.

"I realize these questions might be uncomfortable, but it's our job to ask them anyway." Charli's tone was reassuring, though she was close to grinding her teeth. "The quicker you answer my partner's questions, the sooner we can be out of your hair."

"Yeah, all right." Her answer appeared to mollify him, but only a little. He remained on the edge of his chair when he fixated back on Matthew. "Can we keep this moving along? I really do need to get to work. We're having some problems with our seafood distributor."

"Sure thing, Mr. Hanley." Matthew was the picture of calm. Beneath that mellow exterior, though, Charli sensed a storm brewing. "If you don't mind, I'd like for you to tell us how those two incidents happened."

From the way Maddie's dad's eyebrows lowered, he very much minded, but after another glance at his watch, he started talking. "She was yelling at me, using foul language, and then, she stared right at me and dumped her soda out on the floor. I'd had a crap day at work, had to let go of an employee, and I just lost it, reacted when I should have walked away. I regretted my actions instantly, but of course, it was too late."

Matthew's jaw flexed. "Usually, those aren't isolated incidents. If you lost control once or twice, that means it's probably happened a dozen other times before or since. You can tell us now, or we can do this the hard way and haul you down to the station for questioning, your choice."

A lie. They couldn't haul Kenneth Hanley down to the station against his will without arresting him, and they didn't have enough to warrant that action. Charli kept her expression neutral, though, and didn't interject. Lying while questioning potential subjects wasn't illegal. An ethically gray area, maybe, but a tactic police used to their advantage all the time.

"I only slapped her across the face the one time. The other time, I only hit her arm. That's it."

Heat rose in Charli's chest, but she kept her composure. *Only.* The word was doing a lot of heavy lifting there.

With a deliberateness that seethed with restrained violence, Matthew straightened on the couch and braced his hands on his thighs. "Is it just me, Mr. Hanley, or are you not sounding particularly remorseful for a man who just discovered his only daughter was killed?"

The breath caught in Charli's lungs as she waited on Kenneth Hanley's response to her partner's provocation.

The man just stared at Matthew first before shaking his head and jumping to his feet. "This is bullshit. I'm done talking to you. I've gotta get to work. You need more, you'll need to speak to my lawyer."

Just to mess with him, Matthew took his time standing up, stretching, and patting his pockets as if checking for his keys and phone. Mr. Hanley grew more agitated by the second, but he was smart enough to hold his tongue.

When Matthew finally made it to the door, he turned back. "Thank you for your time, Mr. Hanley. You have a nice day now, you hear?"

The front door slammed before they stepped off the porch, rattling the walls and echoing in the humid morning air.

Once in the car, Charli turned over the ignition. She kept the gear in park and the engine idling until the front door flew open.

Mr. Hanley stalked to the black Honda Accord in the driveway. He wrenched open the driver's side door, flung a brown leather briefcase into the passenger's seat, and climbed in. The Accord's tires screeched as he reversed.

"I wonder if he forgot to eat breakfast this morning?" Charli waited until the Accord's taillights disappeared from her rearview mirror before shifting into drive.

"Why, you think he's got low blood sugar? You can go now."

She gave Matthew's chest a pointed stare.

"Yeah, yeah, I know. I swear, you're more of an old lady than my old Boy Scout troop leader." Despite his grumbling, Matthew pulled the seat belt across his body. "Well? What did you think?"

Charli waited for the telltale click before easing the car onto the road. "I think he owned up to hitting his daughter pretty quickly. He didn't seem especially upset by his behavior, but that's likely the case for lots of parents who live in this part of the country."

"Yeah, but he lawyered up."

She braked at a stop sign, signaling and checking the through street for cars before turning right. "Which is exactly what people are told to do in this situation."

"He didn't exactly come across as a guy who was grief-stricken by his daughter being killed, did he?"

Charli shrugged. "Hard to say. People process grief in lots of different ways. Plus, even if he isn't as remorseful as some parents, that doesn't make him a killer."

Matthew grunted and folded his arms. "Maybe not...but it makes him suspicious as hell."

14

" ... A breaking news report that two bodies have been discovered over the past two days in a section of the marshes by the Vernon River. The first body was discovered on Tuesday and has been identified as belonging to sixteen-year-old Madeline Hanley of Savannah. Madeline was reported missing back in May after she went to school one day and never came home. The second body was found early this morning in a location less than a mile from the first body. This victim has yet to be identified, but our sources tell us it's another young female."

I cranked up the volume with the remote.

"The Savannah Police Department is working in conjunction with the Georgia Bureau of Investigation to find the person or persons responsible for these crimes. No news yet on whether or not these two deaths might be the work of the same killer. We're told that Madeline, or Maddie as she was known by family, was found by birdwatchers, who were hoping to sight a rare bird but uncovered something far grislier. The second body was found by two local teenagers trying to make a TikTok video..."

I couldn't even feign surprise at the TikTok revelation. Teens these days were ruled by social media. They thought if they didn't post an event or experience on the internet, it didn't happen.

"We'll keep you up-to-date with any breaking news, so stay tuned…."

Once the special news bulletin ended, I clicked the TV off and sat in silence on the couch, waiting for the fear I'd always assumed would accompany this moment to grip me. My pulse did quicken, and a sudden restlessness invaded my legs, but that was from anticipation.

Seeing my accomplishments on the news had proven far more exciting than I'd ever expected. They'd found two of my buried treasures, which I knew would lead them to hunt for even more. Everyone was greedy that way. In that sense, the cops were lucky because I'd hidden extra Easter eggs for their hunt. They were digging up my hiding spots, each one hand-picked by me.

Energy surged through every cell, filling me like gas in an overflowing tank. If I'd realized how powerful this experience would make me feel, I might have sent the cops clues weeks ago.

I shot to my feet and headed down the hallway to my bedroom, pausing to straighten a small wrinkle in the blue comforter and check that nothing was out of place on the bookshelves before heading to the closet. I walked inside, squatted down, and removed the white boot box from the low shelf where I stored my shoes.

After carrying the box to the bed, I sat and opened the lid, peeling away the top layer of tissue paper. A gunmetal lockbox awaited.

My heart sped up as I opened the combination lock. Nestled inside were my official passport, ten one-hundred-dollar bills, my mother's wedding ring, and an old pocket watch that had once belonged to my father. All were strategically placed to prevent any curious eyes from digging further. I removed each item, one at a time, before pushing the concealed lever inside.

With a soft snap, the false bottom released. After removing it, I gazed at the remaining contents.

Five black cylinders of red lipstick. Three spools of my favorite fishing line. A packet of suture needles. An old cell phone.

I pulled the device out and scrolled through the pictures. Ah, there they were. My beautiful girls. Captured for all eternity by the wonders of modern technology. A good reminder that scientific advancement was neither inherently good nor evil. The outcome depended on how it was used.

I swiped the screen, reminiscing each time a new face popped up. Their pink-and-red painted lips, fitted tank tops and t-shirts, tight jeans, and leggings made me think of my daughter. Given the chance, would they all have been friends?

After running my finger down one rounded cheek, I smiled. Yes. I believed so. Though not exactly the same, they had a lot in common.

Same brown hair. Same full lips with a tendency toward pouting when events didn't go their way.

Angels in appearance with the hearts of devils. Down to every last one. Even my Tanya.

Especially my Tanya.

I reclined back on my bed and scrolled to the last photo. The last one I'd ever taken of her. Before that fateful day...

"This is all your fault, you know. You and that wicked friend of yours. Why couldn't you just follow directions?"

I was reading the paper when Tanya paraded into the living room. Her skintight black tank top was bad enough, but my gaze was locked on her lips. "Go to the bathroom and wipe your mouth off right now. I thought we agreed you'd never wear that ungodly color again."

Tanya tossed back her long brown hair. "I never agreed to anything. You just ordered me around like you always do."

My blood started to boil. Carefully, I folded the paper and set it aside on the coffee table. "Well, then, I'm ordering you again now. Go wipe it off. You look like a whore in that red color. Oh, and change your shirt while you're at it. That one's too small."

To my surprise, Tanya didn't make a move to do as I'd asked. Instead, she laughed. Laughed.

I rose to my feet and stalked closer. "You think this is funny?"

She shook her head. "No, I think you're funny. And also sad. Ashley told me the reason you're so worried about what I'm wearing is because you're a giant perv. She said you're always sneaking looks at her boobs when she comes over."

That manipulative little bitch. "Ashley is a slut and a liar. She's the one who gave you that damn lipstick to begin with."

"I know, and I think it looks great."

Rage flooded me like lava. I'd always known Ashley was toxic. I should have banned her from my house months ago. She wore those low-cut tank tops on purpose, to make me look. To tempt me. And then to call me a filthy name when I did, trying to corrupt my Tanya...

"I don't give a damn what you think. I said take it off, and give me the lipstick while you're at it, so I can throw it away." My voice continued to rise until I was shouting. "You will not leave this house looking and acting like a harlot!"

Her laugh was mocking. An ugly sound like a witch's cackle that echoed in my ears. "Too late for that. I already had sex with a boy. More than once."

Shock held me still. "You did not."

Her blue eyes blazed with defiance. "I did, and guess what? I was wearing this lipstick when I did! So, you're too late."

Her mouth kept moving, but whatever she was saying turned into an unintelligible warble. My rage boiled over, and I lunged.

"Shut your mouth, do you understand? Never. Say. Those.

Things. To. Me. Again." My fingers dug into her soft flesh more forcefully with each word I uttered. How dare she call me those names? Speak to me like that? Hang out with that awful girl who was no better than a bitch in season? "You need to learn some respect, do you understand?"

"Ah..." She made a little noise but didn't reply, so I squeezed harder.

"I said, do you understand?"

Her eyes bulged, but still, not a single word. She scratched at me, struggled, kicked. I didn't care. Within my fury, there was a heady rush as I exerted my power over her. Finally. No holding back. No lecturing or listening to annoying whines.

I was in charge here. It was past time Tanya remembered that.

Triumph tasted sweet on my tongue as I squeezed and squeezed. By the time I was finished, Tanya would never talk back to me again.

When I finally released her, Tanya collapsed to the floor and didn't move. After spending minutes trying to revive her, I finally gave up.

I'd been right, though. Tanya never did talk back to me again.

My real cell phone rang, yanking me out of the past. With a last reluctant glance, I powered off the old phone and tucked it back into the box.

"I'll visit again soon and tell you about the exciting new developments."

Once the hiding place clicked shut, I reached for my working phone. The prefix was familiar. Someone from the office.

"Hello?" My voice was pleasant, clear. There was little worse than shoddy phone manners.

"Hey, did I catch you at home?"

"As a matter of fact, you did."

"Oh, good. Can you bring that book in today that you brought up at the last meeting? I'd love to check it out."

"Of course, no problem. I'll pop it in my work bag before I head over."

After another brief exchange, I hung up and checked the time. Better get a move on. I'd never been late to work before, and I didn't want to start now.

Tardiness was another pet peeve of mine. So incredibly rude of people not to show consideration for others.

After grabbing the book and carefully tucking it into my leather satchel, I carried my loafers to the front door and sat in the beige easy chair to slip them on.

In light of the exciting news, today would prove challenging to my focus, but focus I would.

My job was important. Giving anything less than my full effort at work was rude.

Besides, the girls in my hidden phone could wait. They weren't going anywhere. Were no longer a threat to others or themselves. I'd made sure of that, by releasing them from their sinful temptations. My girls were safe.

Unfortunately, the world was full of girls just like them. Every day, it seemed like more popped up to take their place. Wild, and so very misguided.

They desperately needed my help, and I'd devote my life to saving as many as possible.

Those girls couldn't wait.

I cast a longing glance at the door of my bedroom. "Soon. I'll be bringing a new girl home to repurify soon."

15

"Maddie's dad seems like a person of interest."

Charli signaled before changing lanes to pass a delivery truck blocking part of the road. In her opinion, it was much too early in the investigation for anyone to be labeled a "person of interest." They'd barely had a chance to get started and were still waiting on forensics to analyze trace evidence, along with an autopsy and hopeful identification on the second body. They didn't have circumstantial evidence pointing to Kenneth Hanley yet, much less anything more concrete.

She shared as much with Matthew. "I think it's too soon to jump to any conclusions." She checked the time. It was a little after eight in the morning. "Let's head over to the school and talk to Maddie's boyfriend."

"Fine, but I'm just saying, I think Kenneth Hanley is a real—"

Charli's phone shrilled before Matthew could tell her what he thought of Kenneth Hanley, but that was okay. She was confident she could surmise the gist from his disgusted tone.

Bluetooth picked up: *Incoming call from Sergeant Ruth Morris, Savannah Police Department.*

On cue, Matthew chuckled. "I still can't believe you added Savannah Police Department. Were you afraid you'd forget where your boss worked otherwise?"

No. She hated leaving any blanks when completing her contacts. Matthew knew that, though. He just liked to razz her.

She ignored him and accepted the call. "Hello, Sergeant Morris, what's up?"

"Cross. Where are you?"

She slid an uneasy glance at Matthew, who clenched his teeth and pretended to cringe. Their boss never bothered to waste time with small talk, but there was an extra bite to her words that portended trouble. "Just leaving the Hanley's house, on our way to interview Maddie's boyfriend."

"I need you to put that on hold and return to the office ASAP. We've got a situation."

The line went dead before Charli or Matthew could ask for more details.

"Whatever it is, sure doesn't sound like good news." Matthew's voice was glum as Charli made a legal U-turn at the next light. "I wonder what's wrong now?"

Instead of wasting time playing guessing games that would lead nowhere, she redirected their focus to facts. "What do we know so far?"

Her partner adjusted his position in the seat, settling into the familiar routine. "We know we have two dead bodies. Both young women with long brown hair. Both buried in large plastic containers that very few suppliers sell in that size within our search radius. Both had their genitals sewn shut, and we're still waiting to see if our second victim also had a tube of lipstick placed inside her."

Charli sucked her tongue between her teeth as she

performed a mental review before adding to her partner's facts. "Both found buried in the marsh to the south of the Vernon River, a little less than a mile apart. Both dead likely for four or more months. One girl identified as Maddie Hanley from Midtown High School with injuries consistent with strangulation. Still waiting on details from the second victim. Anything else?"

Matthew grunted. "Yeah. The first victim's dad is a dick who admits to hitting his daughter twice and doesn't seem all that torn up about her death. He needs to be high on the suspect list."

She ignored the last comment. "We know Maddie had a boyfriend who, according to her best friend, she was thinking of running off with." After racking her brain for any other pertinent details and coming up short, she moved on. "What don't we know?"

"We don't know if her dad's alibi holds up, or if any neighbors heard them fighting."

Charli nodded. "Right. We also don't know if there's anything important in Maddie's cell phone records from before her disappearance. We'll need to get a warrant for those. We don't know much about her boyfriend, Kevin. Or how the two victims are tied together."

"Right. We need to find out how these two victims overlapped. Same school, same sports teams, friend group, same church, whatever."

Charli nodded as she turned into the precinct parking lot. "Let's hope Soames can get back to us quickly with an ID on that second victim." An ID would hopefully help them answer some of those burning questions and lead to creating a suspect pool. From there, they'd whittle away at the names until they found their killer. "There's a possibility we'll be investigating a third victim before long."

"Let's hope not. Maybe we scared Hanley before he had a chance to strike again."

And maybe your dad guilt over Chelsea moving away is pickling your brain.

"We have no way of knowing if Hanley is responsible yet." She parked the car in her usual spot and shut off the engine. "Besides, those girls have been dead for months, which means even if you're correct about Hanley, he had plenty of time to kill others before we visited him this morning."

That shut him up as they climbed out of the car, allowing some of the tension clamping down on Charli's chest to ease.

Matthew could very well turn out to be right. Kenneth Hanley might have killed his daughter, and even the other girl. At this precise moment, they simply didn't have enough evidence one way or another to draw conclusions.

And if they did go with that theory, what would Kenneth Hanley's motive be? Charli could buy the possibility that in a fit of temper, he lost control and strangled his daughter, but what about the second girl? Where was the motive there?

The fact was, they had no idea yet, and until they identified the second victim, it would be challenging to come up with one. Matthew was a skilled detective in so many ways, but his tendency to jump the gun and fixate on a particular suspect early on in the investigation was frustrating.

She climbed out of the car into a blanket of heat. The temperature must have risen again over the last twenty minutes. Charli's blouse stuck to her back by the time they escaped into the air-conditioned building. Matthew's skin glistened like he'd just stepped out of the shower.

Not even nine o'clock in the morning. Today was going to be another September scorcher. Statistically speaking, people were more irritable during the hot months than colder ones. Study after study across a range of disciplines all reached the same conclusion, making summer in the South an especially wild time to be a cop.

She sometimes wondered if that was the real reason people up in Canada had a reputation for being more polite. Maybe all that snow and cold kept their cortisol levels in check.

They headed straight up the stairs to Ruth's office, to find her glowering in their direction out the glass window.

Charli suppressed a groan as she and Matthew approached.

Just like she'd said. People tended to be crabbier when it was hot outside, and Sergeant Morris was no exception.

SERGEANT RUTH MORRIS straightened the files sprawled across her desk into a haphazard pile while she waited for her detectives to get their butts into her office. Going off their pinched expressions as they appeared at the top of the stairs, she gathered they were none too thrilled about being called in, but that was too damn bad.

Wasn't like she was all that keen on seeing their annoying mugs, either.

She steepled her fingers in front of her, scrutinizing Detective Cross for obvious signs of wear and tear as the pair headed toward her office. This case held a lot of similarities to Cross's friend's murder back in high school. Enough that she'd been wrestling over whether or not to yank Cross off and assign someone else with less baggage.

If Cross was buckling under the pressure, though, her blue eyes and bearing didn't reveal a thing. Ruth grunted. Not that she'd expected any different. Charli Cross was a hard nut to crack. So tough and expressionless at times that a couple of the patrol cops had taken to calling her Slate behind her back.

Ruth didn't put any stock in their bullshit. She was a Black woman in a job traditionally held by white men. In Georgia. Over the years, she'd been saddled with similar insults and much worse. And those were only the ones she'd heard.

Women in this line of work had to be tough, otherwise they wouldn't make it for very long after training. Cross was more than that, though. She was shrewd, and capable, and exceedingly trustworthy. Did she annoy the hell out of Ruth at times with those blue eyes of hers that seemed to constantly assess a person's every breath and movement? Sure. But so did every other cop in this place at one time or another.

Ruth would never admit as much, but Cross had a special quality that could go the distance. She didn't want to see her burned out over an old high school trauma.

With Matthew by her side, that was a distinct possibility. Ruth frowned as her gaze shifted to the tall detective shadowing Cross. That man was a workhorse, through and through. Old-school. Married to the job. Even back when he'd had an actual wife.

Ruth had paired them together in part to offset Charli's size deficit. Cross could hold her own, but the reality was, a lot of folks out in their neck of the woods were still a little backward. They didn't cotton to obeying a woman but tended to snap right to attention when confronted by a cop with a height advantage and a set of testicles.

Her eyes narrowed as Matthew sidestepped Cross to reach the door first. When he pulled it open, an expression of pure exasperation flickered across Cross's pixie-like features, reminding Ruth of a dark-haired, pissed-off Tinkerbell.

Another step and Cross's face smoothed, revealing

nothing as she headed for one of the two chairs opposite Ruth's desk.

Doubts needled Ruth's gut. Lately, she'd been plagued by concerns over whether or not the pairing had been a mistake. Matthew seemed a little too protective at times. A little too interested.

Ruth didn't know whether to laugh or curse. A damn schoolboy crush? No, she didn't think so. At Church's age, he probably thought of the petite detective more like the daughter he'd recently lost to the West Coast.

At least Cross seemed to have her head screwed on straight. And she was smart enough to hand Church his ass on a platter if he overstepped.

Ruth tabled the concern for now. They had more pressing matters to worry about.

"Sit."

As they settled into the chairs opposite her desk, she focused on Cross. Matthew was a good detective, but she'd bet her favorite purse this was the end of the road for him. She didn't see him rising any higher in the department, in big part because he didn't have the ambition. He liked being a detective and had no desire to change that status.

Cross, though…she was smart and driven to succeed. Both traits proven out by her meteoric rise within the department.

A sharp claw scraped beneath Ruth's ribs and vanished just as quickly. So what if she'd been twenty-seven when she'd achieved the rank of detective, while Cross had only been twenty-three? Maybe if Cross and Ruth had been climbing the ladder at the same time, she'd have reason to worry. At her age, though, the only things she needed to focus on were her pension and finding a suitable candidate to take her place.

Was Cross even interested in Ruth's job, though? The

woman was so private. Ruth doubted even Church knew. If anyone did, he'd be the one she'd tell.

If Charli wasn't interested, then Ruth had a challenge on her hands. She'd need to devote some time to figuring out exactly what might motivate an enigma like Cross to throw her hat into the ring.

Not yet, though. Ruth had a few more good years left in her.

She straightened in her seat and glared at the two detectives. Time to get down to business.

16

C harli faced Sergeant Morris with her hands folded in her lap. Was she imagining things, or was there really a calculating gleam in her boss's dark eyes as she surveyed Charli over the top of the metal desk?

Before she'd reached a conclusion, Sergeant Morris jumped to the reason for her summons. "The local media knows about the two murders. The story broke this morning." Matthew started to groan but cut the noise short when Ruth glared at him. "That was not an invitation for your theatrics, Detective. What it does mean is we can expect the news to spread quickly."

Charli kept her lips buttoned to trap in her own dismay. No wonder the sergeant was so upset. The media had a knack for making even the most even-keeled cops irritable, especially when it came to high-profile cases. Now, in addition to worrying about solving the murders, the police department would need to front calls from concerned locals and soothe their mounting fears. Once the public got wind of murders, everyone's blood pressure started to rise, and being the sergeant, Ruth was in one of the hot seats. The higher-ups would increase the pressure on her to solve this quickly, and she'd turn around and transfer that pressure to Matthew and Charli.

If the media stuck to the cold, hard facts, that'd be one thing. They didn't, though. Straightforward news reports often went out the window in favor of clickbait and speculation. Drumming up fear meant drumming up sales, and even in journalism, profit was king.

"Because of the media scrutiny that is sure to come, the chief went ahead and requested additional resources from the GBI, to help expand the search area down at the marsh." Sergeant Morris scowled her annoyance over this detail. Since she'd already asked the GBI to assist with forensics, Charli guessed that meant regular GBI agents had been called in. Her boss tended to get a little testy when the chief acted unilaterally, particularly when that matter involved calling for outside assistance.

Not that Sergeant Morris was alone in her dislike of such actions. Far from it. In Charli's experience, nothing brought a precinct together quicker than the threat of outsiders barging in.

Even she had to fight off a stab of annoyance. While she typically had no issue bringing in additional help when needed, she and Matthew had barely had a chance to dive into this case. Coordinating with the GBI could be tricky, depending on who they sent over. The more egos in the mix, the bigger the headache.

Matthew groaned. This time, Ruth didn't bother to reprimand him. "Are you kidding me? We just got started, and those snot nozzles are coming in to try to boss us around?"

He echoed Charli's thoughts, albeit a little more colorfully. She frowned. Although... "Wouldn't a snot nozzle be essentially the same thing as a nostril?"

Matthew rubbed his chin as a sheepish grin crept across

his face. "You know, you might be right. I never really thought much abou—"

A loud bang cut him off. Both of them jumped and directed their attention to Ruth, whose clenched fist was hovering over the desk for a second round, if necessary. "Sometimes, when I remind myself you two have the highest success rate of everyone in the department, I don't know whether to laugh or cry."

Charli cocked her head, bursting with curiosity over which one of the two her boss usually ended up doing. Matthew caught her just in time, jabbing her heel with his toe until she clamped her mouth shut.

Right. That was one of those questions she'd be better off keeping to herself.

"Is it too late to call the Geebs off?" Matthew used a hard G, riffing off the slang term for FBI agents. Charli returned his kick, only harder. Numbskull. How was his question any more tactful than hers?

"Pray tell, why would I want to go and do a knuckle-headed thing like that?" Sergeant Morris carefully folded her hands on the desk and stared him down until the silence grew uncomfortable enough for Matthew to shift his weight in the chair. "I'm already exhausted and we've only had this first case a couple days. Everything will be amplified now that we have a second body and media involvement."

"I get that, but—"

Ruth held up her hand. "Uh-uh. No buts. This is the way it's going to be. The pressure is being applied from the top of the food chain. In case you need reminding, you are not at the top. Not a whale, not a shark. More like one of those tiny fish, what are they called?" She snapped her fingers. "Minnows! As a minnow, you do as you're told, or else expect to get chewed up and swallowed by the bigger fish."

When Matthew opened his mouth to argue, Sergeant

Morris cut him off. "Let me stop you right there, Detective. If either one of you doesn't feel capable of playing nice with the GBI on this, then you can and will be pulled off the case. Do I make myself clear?"

The threat hit Charli with unexpected force. Her lungs seized up. Her heart pounded.

No! She had to stay on this case. For Maddie.

And Madeline.

She swallowed the burst of illogical panic and nodded. "Yes, Boss."

Matthew took a few beats longer to respond. "Got it."

His tone was so surly that Charli was tempted to kick him again. If his moodiness cost them this case…

She breathed easier when Sergeant Morris moved on. "Good. Then get out of here and back to work. I'd like a report by the end of the day on where we're at."

Charli sprang to her feet and hurried for the door, eager to get back to work. Matthew trailed behind, muttering as he went. "Minnow, my ass. At the very least, I'm a barracuda."

She bit back a moan at her partner's ill-timed humor. Her ankle flexed. That was it. He obviously needed another kick to get his attitude back on track. No, multiple kicks. From steel-toed boots.

"I heard that, Detective Church," Sergeant Morris called from behind them. "Now quit your fussing and get out, before I downgrade you from minnow to plankton."

It wasn't until Matthew continued mumbling under his breath as he stomped across the floor to their office that she realized he was actually peeved by that stupid minnow analogy. He confirmed her assessment by rattling the wall when he shoved the door shut behind him and throwing himself into his chair.

"I can't believe she called them in. It hasn't even been

forty-eight hours yet. How about giving us at least a few days before losing faith in our capabilities?"

Charli's forehead wrinkled. Why was Matthew taking this so personally? It wasn't like him to be so touchy.

She took that back. Six months ago, that would have been true. Lately was another story. "I don't think she did it because of a lack of faith. This case is going to blow up, especially if the second victim is also a local teen. I think she's just trying to manage perceptions."

His stormy expression didn't abate. "By bringing in more GBI agents? Watch out, next thing you know she'll be calling up the Feebs, bring in one of those profilers." His sneer made it clear what he thought of that idea.

Funny, because Charli actually perked up when he uttered the word. Her fascination with serial killers had led to a corresponding interest in profilers. "Would that be such a terrible idea?"

Matthew pretended to gag. "Hell, yes. Those ass ponies are nothing more than professional guessers. Every damn profile is almost exactly the same...organized white male who was abused by his parents as a child. I'd be happy to do that job for half their salary."

Charli didn't necessarily agree with that summation, but now wasn't the time to argue. Not when her partner was so agitated. "Instead of worrying about that now, I say we try to get as much legwork done as possible before we have to coordinate with them."

Matthew let the chair legs crash back to the floor and nodded. "Good idea. Maybe if we put our heads together and really crack down, we can solve this thing before we ever need to talk to them."

She didn't have high hopes of that happening, but she kept that to herself. "Since we're here, let's see what we can find out about Maddie's boyfriend before we go talk to him."

17

Charli kept her clenched hands out of sight in her lap as Janice Piper leaned against the doorjamb leading into her and Matthew's office. The older detective held a sheet of paper in her hands, presumably the facts she'd collected on Kevin Harding. Instead of just handing her research over, though, she insisted on reading it to them aloud, like they were five and she was the kindergarten teacher.

If the woman was so desperate for Matthew's attention, why couldn't she just tell him already? Preferably outside of work hours?

Charli filled her lungs with air and pictured her frustration dissipating like raindrops on a lake as she breathed out.

"Kevin Harding, age nineteen, lives at 1219 West Parker with his mom, Louisa Harding. Has an older brother named Scott, who lives in an apartment near downtown. Kevin's a senior at Midtown High. Played soccer his freshman and sophomore years. No records of any interactions with the police beyond a parking ticket in January. No school suspensions. He doesn't have classes on Tuesdays or Thursdays, so goes to work at Custom Craft Garage just off the I-95 outside of town."

Charli plugged the information into her map app. "Any other problems you could find?"

Janice glanced up from the page. "Nothing really jumped out at me to mark him as a troubled kid, but who knows? People are crap at that stuff. How many interviews have you seen of neighbors wringing their hands and saying how so-and-so always seemed so quiet and nice...right up until they ax murdered their entire family?"

Charli frowned. Janice had a point. She just wished they had more to go on. "Any idea why he quit soccer?"

The other detective shrugged. "No. Maybe he just got bored. What, you want me to ask around? Didn't think it was important."

"That'd be great, Janice, thanks." Matthew smiled at Janice, and the woman's cheeks flushed with pleasure.

Charli sank low in her chair. Wonderful, now she felt like a third wheel in her own office. If only telepathy existed. She'd blast the heck out of Matthew's head right now. Something along the lines of, *quit encouraging her or she'll start moving her desk in.*

Luckily, it didn't take long for Janice to slip back into her tough persona. "What the hell are you thanking me for? I'm just doing my job." She tossed the paper onto Charli's desk. "Later."

She left, but her perfume lingered. Some kind of heavy, musky scent that reminded Charli of her grandmother and made her long for a fan.

Matthew's chair creaked as he leaned back, resting his hands on his stomach. "So, what are you thinking? Do we interview this bonehead at school or wait and hit him up at work?"

Before Charli could decide, her phone rang and vibrated

across her desk. She checked the name flashing across the screen. "It's Soames."

Matthew sat up straight as she answered the call. "Hey, Randal. Matthew's with me, so I've got you on speakerphone."

"Hello again, Charli, Detective Church. I'm calling with some preliminary information on the latest victim. This a good time?"

She grabbed a pen and a legal pad. "Go ahead."

"My initial examination puts the victim between sixteen and eighteen years of age. We were able to gather some hair samples to compare with the database, but I'm not optimistic about that turning up a match."

Neither was Charli. The DNA database tended to be more useful for eliminating suspects from a pool than anything else. Most of the samples in the database came from crime scenes. The average law-abiding citizen would have no reason to be included.

"X-rays showed no previous fractures or otherwise notable deviations. Most likely, we'll have to rely on dental records to make a match."

Not ideal, but she'd been expecting as much. "Anything else?"

"I hesitate to say because it's near impossible to tell for sure, given the state of decomposition, but I'd be remiss if I didn't mention that I have my suspicions that both victims were sexually assaulted first. The x-rays indicated the victim recently suffered a fracture to the pubic bone. This appears to have happened antemortem and never had a chance to heal before her death. While the first victim did not have a fractured pubic bone, the other similarities with the sutures and lipstick would seem to indicate both victims were sexually assaulted while they were alive. Nothing I could ever prove in court, but…"

He trailed off, but his statement lit a fire in Charli all the same. Soames was very skilled at his job. If he suspected sexual abuse, then the girls had probably been abused.

Not only did their unsub kill his victims, he likely terrorized them before ending their lives.

A loud snap echoed in the small space. Matthew sat behind his desk with one half of a broken pen in each hand. She had little doubt if their killer walked in right now, her partner would stab him with the pieces.

"I understand. Thanks, Randal. Call me as soon as you learn anything else, no matter what time it is."

"Will do. I'll talk to you two later."

Charli ended the call. While grim, the M.E.'s observations energized her, stoking the flames in her belly until her entire body burned with determination.

Two girls were dead for sure already. By later that afternoon, the body count might be higher. As awful as that was, the worry that propelled Charli now was a more pressing one.

The killer had gotten away with murder and possibly sexual assault. At least twice. Maybe more. From her years of serial killer research, Charli ascertained their murderer was someone who most likely killed for pleasure or was driven by a deep-seated, maladaptive psychological need. From the accounts she'd read, those types were the least likely to stop on their own. Often, success would embolden them. Cause their behaviors to escalate.

If that were the case, then their killer would strike again.

A band wrapped around Charli's chest as she surged to her feet. That absolutely could not happen. Not on her watch.

She hadn't been able to save Madeline or Maddie or their current Jane Doe, but she could save the next girl.

She had to.

Her stomach growled, reminding her that their hasty breakfast had happened hours ago. Charli found that she burned off more energy when working stressful cases than usual, and as a result, needed to refuel her brain more frequently.

Matthew's forehead creased. "We going somewhere?"

"I need food. Let's head out now and grab something before we visit Kevin at the garage."

18

"That was a waste of time."

Not only had Charli and Matthew spent the past hour speaking to a surly teenager who didn't appear to have the ability to look a person in the eye, she now smelled like she'd been dipped in an oil pan. Felt like it too.

Matthew nodded. "Interesting what Kevin said about Maddie's dad, though."

It sure was.

Charli flipped open her notepad. "Called the man a dick. Said Hanley was 'always up in her business, and they fought all the time.'"

Matthew growled low in his throat. "Kid confirmed that Hanley knocked his daughter around a couple of times too. So much so, that she thought of running away."

They'd barely sat down at their desks in their office when Janice popped her head around the door. "We got the results back on those storage containers from that online distributer. No records of any being shipped to the greater Savannah area over the past nine months."

"Damn." Matthew cursed while Charli's stomach sank. This wasn't the news they'd needed.

"Yeah. Sucks. They were able to send us a list of all the orders for two or more containers made in the last nine months, and it's a beast. We're gonna be drowning in orders for the next week."

Janice had barely been gone a minute when a man appeared at their door.

"Detective Cross?"

She looked up from the spreadsheet she'd just started. "That's me."

He greeted her with an outstretched hand and a polished smile. "I'm Special Agent Preston Powell with the GBI. Nice to meet you."

At his desk, Matthew grumbled something under his breath she was glad she couldn't hear.

She forced a pleasant smile. "You too. Please have a seat. This is my partner, Detective Matthew Church."

The expression beneath Powell's sun-streaked brown hair remained pleasant as he dipped his head. "Nice to meet you, Detective Church." His expression didn't falter when Matthew only grunted in return.

Once the agent was settled in a seat, she swiveled her chair to face him. "So, what would you like to know?"

Despite the animosity rolling off her partner, Powell seemed at ease sitting in the chair he'd dragged between their desks. All his exposed skin was brown. Tanned from sun exposure. Coupled with the bleached hair, he could have easily passed for a surfer or beach bum.

The GBI agent was several inches shorter and likely a few years younger than Matthew. Beneath his jacket, his physique was compact and well-muscled. "How about you fill me in on the highlights so far, and we can go from there."

To Charli's surprise, Matthew volunteered. "Sure thing.

Just don't be too disappointed when you find out we don't have much yet. We just started on this case yesterday. We're still getting our bearings."

Her partner's tone was amiable as he launched into a monologue. Too amiable.

Charli narrowed her eyes. Did she even want to know what he was up to now?

Matthew droned on, glazing over the important points of their investigation, like Kenneth and Maddie's tumultuous relationship and their progress on the plastic containers, while gushing over the fast-food breakfast they'd stopped for that morning.

"You wouldn't believe how much of a difference real jack cheese makes on a breakfast sandwich until you've tried it yourself. And good quality bacon, cooked to perfection. Not too crispy, not too soggy. Otherwise, it can ruin the whole thing."

Charli's mouth fell open. Had the case pushed her partner over the edge? There was no chance the mush on their sandwiches that morning had been jack cheese. She hesitated to call it cheese at all. More like a cheese-like product. Dairy adjacent. And as orange as a crayon.

As for the bacon, she'd eaten higher quality at a bargain motel's free breakfast buffet.

Whatever drama was playing out in their office right now had nothing to do with breakfast.

She settled back in her chair, absorbing the rest of the show with morbid fascination.

"...and real potato hash browns instead of that fried cardboard crap you get at those big chains. Night and day, I'm telling you." Matthew rubbed his stomach for emphasis before switching gears and launching into a detailed description of the traffic they'd encountered on their way to and from the crime scene.

If Powell found Matthew's sandwich soliloquy or traffic updates frustrating, he didn't let on. His attractive features remained schooled in a friendly arrangement. The agent reclined in the chair like he'd never heard a more interesting lecture in his entire life.

Charli conceded a flicker of reluctant admiration for his congeniality. As Matthew prattled on and on without Powell's smile faltering, though, her patience began to wear thin. Why were they holding eye contact like that? Like a pair of dogs meeting for the first time? "Let me guess. This a new spin on a male pissing match except, instead of urine, you're trying to out-alpha each other through fictitious accounts of breakfast foods and obnoxiously good manners?"

After a brief delay, both men turned to stare at her with similar expressions of disbelief.

She crossed her arms. "What? Do you really expect me to waste my time pretending anyone in this room cares what kind of cheese Matthew ate at six o'clock this morning?" She directed that comment at Powell. "Which, for the record, was definitely *not* jack cheese."

Powell made a choking noise. She ignored him in favor of glaring at Matthew, who was doing his best to act confused. "You sure, Charli?"

She narrowed her eyes. Drummed her fingers on her bicep. Used silence to wait him out while he squirmed.

He broke first. "Fine! I admit it, that wasn't jack cheese. Just stop looking at me like you want to pull a Dahmer and eat my brain or something, okay?"

"Is this better?" Charli's smile was all teeth. "By the way, Dahmer ate thighs, organ meat, and hearts, but not brains. Those he used for drilling holes and performing makeshift lobotomies."

"Great," Matthew muttered. "I feel much better now."

Powell's throaty chuckle interrupted them. "I never

expected this assignment to be quite so entertaining." He turned to toss a question at Matthew. "Is your partner always so...forthright when dealing with colleagues?"

To her surprise, Matthew actually answered. "If by forthright you mean blunt as an unsharpened pencil, then yeah. That's Charli."

Two pairs of male eyes focused on her.

Well, wasn't this fun? In calling out their juvenile behavior, Charli must have inadvertently activated some male-bonding ritual. That was the only explanation that made sense.

She ran a hand over her hair. Granted herself a moment to breathe through the annoyance. Curved her mouth into a smile. "Did you know that Dahmer also soaked the genitals of one of his male victims in acetone and kept them in his work locker? Sometimes, I think about that when I'm having a rough day."

The way both men flinched in unison was deeply satisfying on a primal level. See? She could be a team player. Look at how she was helping them deepen their newfound bond.

Matthew recovered first. "That was a visual I could have lived without."

Powell nodded. "Same."

They traded a fleeting smile before Matthew remembered he'd decided to be pissy. "By the way, don't call her Charli. That's only for her close friends."

And just like that, the bonding ended.

Charli pinched the bridge of her nose and wished that, for once, the men in her immediate vicinity could be just a little less dramatic.

Her phone rang, creating a welcome distraction.

Thank you, Randal. She hit the speaker and swiveled back around. "Hey, Randal. You find out more for us?"

"I did indeed." All three of them stared at the phone in

Charli's hand, waiting for what the M.E. shared next. "After examination, I've concluded the second victim was also strangled."

Charli's pulse quickened. "Another thyroid cartilage fracture?"

"No, but there was a tiny fracture in the hyoid bone. In addition, the infrahyoid muscles were intact enough for me to note extensive hemorrhaging, which is common in strangulation cases, particularly manual. Combined with the evidence of trauma to the strap muscles, I feel reasonably confident saying she was strangled." He cleared his throat. "Also, as we'd expected, I recovered another tube of Happy Harlot red lipstick from where it was inserted into her vagina. Like the other victim, she was sewn up using sutures of a thick material consistent with fishing line."

Even though she'd been expecting as much, her stomach churned. "Thanks, Randal."

"Yup. I'll be in touch."

When the call ended, Charli's mind was racing. "So, in addition to the same plastic containers, vaginal suturing, and lipstick, we now believe both victims were killed in a similar manner." She churned the information around in her head, trying to tease out a connection she'd yet to uncover. "Our unsub likes to kill with his hands. That's personal, implies he knows his victims. He has some fixation on lipstick and sewing the girls up. If we could figure out why he follows this pattern, or why he's burying them in those specific containers, that could really help."

Frustration welled in her chest. They needed more.

Powell cleared his throat. "One thing I noticed when I read the report and looked at the pictures was that those containers sealed up pretty tight. Restricting airflow like that helps preserve bodies longer than leaving them out in the elements. No blow flies to lay eggs, or beetles, or other insect activity to eat at the soft tissue."

Charli dipped her chin in agreement. "Right, and no predators, either. The decomposition in that situation would be spurred on by heat and the body's own bacteria alone."

"Exactly. I think it's reasonable to consider that our killer buried those victims in those containers specifically because he was trying to preserve them longer, only he didn't realize how much humidity and heat would speed the process along by themselves."

She blinked. "That's an interesting idea, one I confess we hadn't evaluated yet." Of course, the question that followed was obvious.

If the killer was trying to preserve the bodies, why?

Matthew muttered out of the side of his mouth. "Thought you didn't like guesses."

At least, that was what Charli thought she heard.

She faced him, preparing to educate her partner on the substantive difference between educated guesses and gut instincts when her phone rang again.

"Hey, Randal."

"The dental records were in the system, so we got a match. The body belongs to Shana Feist."

"Thank you." Charli was already jumping to her feet as she hung up. "The last victim is Shana Feist. Do you have her file?"

Matthew sifted through the files on his desk before plucking one from the middle. "Got it."

"Let's go." She squeezed by the older detective, forgetting about Powell until she was halfway down the stairs. She hesitated for one beat before shrugging and descending the remainder of the steps at a brisk pace.

If Special Agent Powell was half the professional he tried

to portray, then he'd understand why they'd run out without saying goodbye. And if not? Well, that was his problem.

Their getaway plan hit an abrupt wall at the bottom of the stairs in the form of their boss.

Sergeant Morris stood beside a tall, lean woman who was a good decade younger. "Perfect timing. Cross, Church, this is Special Agent Evelyn Fields. She's here from the FBI."

"Detective Cross. Detective Church. I'm from D.C., but I'm here to act as a liaison for this case." The woman's dark hair was slicked back into a tight ponytail. Her severe style matched the precise, almost formal manner in which she spoke. Her navy pantsuit appeared fresh from the dry cleaner, and her black shoes gleamed. "As such, I'll be immediately convening a task force, consisting of the three of us and Special Agent Powell to start."

As Agent Fields's shrewd brown eyes landed on her, Charli kept her gaze trained straight ahead and her expression neutral. She didn't dare peek at Matthew. Her partner's most loathed FBI feature might be "profiler," but "task force" was a close second.

Once, he'd bitched for an hour straight about how he was sure the entire FBI would fold if it weren't for "picking locals' brains by creating a task force and then taking all the credit for themselves."

"Now that that's settled, I think it's a good time to fill me in on where you were headed in such a hurry. It might be best if we all go together. I find that spending time as a unit while out in the field is the quickest way to get to know each other."

Matthew sucked down a noisy breath. "You've got to be kidding, right?"

Evelyn Fields's attention shifted to him. "Excuse me, Detective Church? Were you asking me a question?"

Under that withering brown stare, even Matthew hesitated. "Uh..."

"What I'm sure my partner was trying to express was his surprise. We've never sent four people to break the news of a family member's death before. We always figured that would run the risk of overwhelming the parents by creating too big of a crowd, but if that's the way the FBI does it, then of course, we're happy to follow your lead."

The FBI agent's head swiveled back to Charli, who met her eyes without blinking while everyone nearby seemed to hold their breath. She counted down ten seconds in her head before Fields broke the tense silence. "No, I think two officers is plenty for that assignment. You and Detective Church can continue on with your plan while Special Agent Powell and I head out to the burial sites and see if we can assist on that front."

Charli nodded. "Perfect, we'll do that." She pivoted as soon as she uttered the words. It wouldn't do to let Agent Fields see her smile.

"Oh, and Detective Cross? Please report back as soon as you leave that household so I can tell you where to meet us. Then we can rendezvous and share our first findings as a team."

Charli cringed inwardly, but on the outside, her posture never changed. "Will do." She quickened her pace, desperate to reach the door and disappear out of range before Agent Fields made another awful suggestion.

As she reached for the door, Charli was grinding her teeth. Sharing information was fine, but working as a team? No, thanks.

Even back as early as grade school, she'd hated the group assignments. Too many cooks in the kitchen equaled a bunch of wasted time arguing over who did which task and when and how they did it.

One partner was already a stretch, but she knew Matthew. The two of them trusted each other and balanced each other out.

Adding Fields and Powell to the scale would throw their dynamic out of alignment.

In turn, throwing their dynamic out of alignment would likely lead to a delay in solving the case.

Charli waited until they were almost to her car to comment. "You were right."

"I often am, but what in particular are we talking about this time?"

She paused with one hand on the door handle to peer at her partner over the top. "I'm talking about 'task force.' That really is one of the stupidest concepts I've ever heard."

Her partner started guffawing as she climbed behind the driver's seat. He didn't stop until they were two blocks away.

19

Charli stood on the porch and stared at the bright blue door while Matthew rang the doorbell.

As they waited, she clasped her hands in front of her, trying without success not to speculate on the kind of family who'd use such a joyful color on their tidy, two-story home.

A happy one. A loving one.

An image of Shana Feist's decomposing body rotting away inside the plastic container popped into her head. Matthew had won the blackjack round this time. She'd held on sixteen, and he'd taken a third hit on fifteen and landed a five. Her turn to break the news.

"Coming!"

Footsteps accompanied the call on the other side of the door. Charli pushed aside the awful visual of their dead daughter. She couldn't let any of that show on her face.

Calm. Controlled. Professional. Shana's parents deserved nothing less and so, so much more. More than Charli could give them.

They deserved a daughter who was still alive, and she

couldn't help but believe she'd failed them in that regard. Just like she'd failed Madeline.

The door swung open. A woman with freckled skin and short, reddish-brown hair stood in the opening, a slight furrow between her brows as she took in their attire. "I'm sorry, but we already have a church and aren't interested in changing."

She started to push the door closed.

"Wait. We're with the Savannah Police Department."

Charli's command made the woman pause. She hurried to pull her jacket aside, and the woman's gaze locked on her badge. "Are you the parent or legal guardian of Shana Feist?"

The woman's entire body stiffened. "Yes, I'm Sarah Feist, her mother."

"I'm Detective Cross, here with Detective Church. Is your husband home?"

The furrow between Shana's mother's brows deepened. "Yes, he's working from home today. Why? What is this about? Is it Shana?"

Charli flexed her fingers. Released them. "Do you mind if we come in and wait while you get your husband?"

Mrs. Feist nodded but didn't move from the spot. "Did you find her? Is she okay?" Her blue eyes searched Charli's face. For a sign, any sign, that the news was hopeful. That her daughter was alive.

Charli squeezed her hands so tightly, her bones ground together. False hope was a terrible thing. More painful by far than ripping the bandage off in one quick motion. She gave the tiniest shake of her head.

The woman's lip started to tremble.

Charli gentled her voice. "I think it would be a really good idea if you got your husband so we can talk to you both at the same time."

Mrs. Feist nodded again and opened the door to let them

in. "Wait here, please."

Charli and Matthew hovered in the entryway while she disappeared down a hallway to the right.

"This sucks." Matthew's muttered comment didn't make her feel any better. It wasn't like she needed the verbal reminder about how bad this situation was. Dread had turned her stomach into a block of cement.

Breaking the news to loved ones was never fun, but when the murder victim was a kid...

Charli drew in a deep breath and prepared herself for what was to come. No matter the age, no loving parent wanted to outlive their child, but murder went beyond illness or a car accident. Finding out your son or daughter was intentionally brutalized and killed by another human being? That level of pain could never be matched.

Mrs. Feist reappeared with a sandy-haired man wearing wire-rimmed glasses and a short-sleeved Wildcats t-shirt behind her. They stopped more than ten feet away, as if coming any closer might make the news hit harder. After an awkward silence, Mr. Feist cleared his throat. "My wife says you have news for us?"

"This might be easier if we all sat down."

Lip still quivering, Mrs. Feist pointed wordlessly to a pair of beige chairs on the left. Not out of rudeness. At least, Charli didn't think so. She guessed Shana's mother didn't trust herself to speak without breaking down.

Charli and Matthew took the chairs and waited for the Feists to sit on the matching couch.

Once everyone was settled, Charli wasted no time. "As I think you've gathered, Detective Church and I are here to deliver some painful news about your daughter, Shana Feist."

"No!" Mrs. Feist started sobbing before Charli could even finish. Her husband grabbed his wife's hand and made soothing noises.

"Shh, sweetheart, let's hear them out." He nodded at Charli to continue.

"A body was found buried in the marsh by the Vernon River at around three o'clock this morning. We've since received confirmation via dental records that it belongs to your daughter, Shana."

"Oh, god." Mr. Feist's whispered reaction was soon over-powered by his wife's wails. He murmured to her until she quieted before turning back to them. "Do you know who did it?"

"Not yet, but we promise that finding the person responsible is our top priority." Even to her own ears, the promise wasn't enough.

"How..." Mr. Feist paused, his Adam's apple bobbing as he swallowed. "How was she killed?"

Charli forced her gaze to remain steady. "Based on injuries to her neck, we suspect she was strangled."

Mrs. Feist whimpered while her husband stared at the floor. His shoulders hitched back as he sucked down a deep breath. Like he was preparing himself for something terrible.

Please, please don't ask. You'll never be able to un-hear the answer.

But when he lifted his head, Charli read determination in the set of his jaw. She braced herself for the question she knew was coming.

"Do you think it was a man who killed her?"

"Yes. As of now, we have good reason to believe a man is responsible."

Mr. Feist's hands started to shake. "Did...was she...did he hurt her before he...killed her? You know...*touch* her?"

Sitting there, gazing into those eyes that pleaded with her to say no, Charli's heart splintered into pieces. Beside her husband, Mrs. Feist was cringing, as if waiting for a blow.

The truth stuck in Charli's throat. How did you tell

someone that their daughter had almost certainly suffered a violent, sadistic sexual assault, possibly multiple times before she was murdered?

She selected her words with care. "The decomposed state of your daughter's body has made the exact nature of her injuries very difficult to ascertain with any degree of certainty, but there are some findings that do make sexual assault a possibility."

Shana's mom wailed. After a dazed few seconds, Mr. Feist sprang out of his chair to kneel at his wife's feet, wrapping his arms around her waist. She bowed her head over him while they cried. They stayed locked like that for several minutes, filling the living room with their pain.

Charli clenched her hands together even tighter, digging her fingernails into the opposite knuckles to fight the burning behind her eyes. Crying would be self-serving. A way to release her own pain. The Feists didn't need that, not from her.

What they needed was a calm, levelheaded detective. One who would find and stop the person who'd snatched their daughter from them.

Cold comfort in the face of their loss, but that was the most she or anyone else could offer now. After Madeline's murder, Charli was convinced cold comfort was better than none at all.

She waited until they'd regained some semblance of composure. She didn't need Matthew to tell her this part sucked too.

After providing them with a list of bereavement resources and information on who to contact to help them transfer their daughter's body, Charli pressed on. "I hate to intrude on you during such a difficult time, but we really need to ask you some questions. Whoever did this is still out there, and we need to stop him before he hurts anyone else."

Mrs. Feist held up a finger, rose on unsteady feet, and vanished back down the hallway. She returned with two wadded-up balls of toilet paper. One she shoved into her husband's hand, the other she clutched in her own. After a loud sniffle and a swipe at her nose, she nodded. "Okay. We'll try."

They'd been at the Feist's house, what, five minutes now? And Charli already felt drained.

In retrospect, she almost wished they'd let Fields and Powell make this visit.

Almost.

"To start, can you tell us a little about your daughter? What was she like?"

Mrs. Feist's lip shook again. She gave a helpless shrug as tears flooded her eyes.

Mr. Feist cleared his throat. His gray eyes also glistened. "Shana is…was, a good girl. Laughed a lot, got good grades. Never got into trouble at school, did her homework and chores on time without us nagging. She's so thoughtful and sweet. *Was*. God. I can't believe…I don't…" He choked up, pausing to clear his throat again. "I don't understand why anyone would want to hurt our little girl."

The words stabbed Charli like a knife to the throat. Long ago, Mrs. Ferguson had uttered close to the same exact thing to her. Also in a clogged, broken voice.

Why would anyone want to hurt my sweet little Madeline?

Charli's years on the police force had yet to provide her with an answer. Not one that helped ease the pain.

She averted her gaze and said nothing. What was the point? None of the platitudes that good-intentioned family friends and teachers had shared after Madeline died had worked for her. Sometimes, they'd even made her feel worse.

Had filling the silence with absurdities like, *"Sometimes bad things happen to good people"* ever helped anyone ever, in the history of these types of visits? If so, Charli would like to meet those people, if only to ask them how.

"We read in her file that she went to the park one afternoon and never came home. Can you tell us anything else about that day? Was she meeting someone?"

Mr. Feist shuddered. "No, not that we're aware of."

In fact, Shana's missing persons file that Charli had remembered to grab right before heading out of the precinct covered most of these questions. The Feists had remained adamant that Shana would never run away. A Levi's Call had been triggered at the time.

Weeks had stretched on with nothing to show for the statewide alarm that accompanied a child abduction.

Charli didn't know the detective who'd conducted the missing persons report, though, and reports were only as thorough as the detective who filed them.

"Did she act out of the ordinary at all, like get dressed up or fix her hair or makeup more than usual before leaving?"

Mrs. Feist shook her head. "No, she just headed out with her phone and earbuds and said she was going for a walk over to the park. Dressed in her exercise shorts and a t-shirt, like usual."

Charli's internal radar pinged. "Like usual? She went on this same walk often?"

"Yes. Usually both weekend days, and a couple of times during the week, but those moved around based on how much homework she had."

Charli finished jotting down her note before continuing. "She disappeared on March twentieth, correct?"

"That's right. Before dinnertime."

"You mentioned she frequently took walks on most Saturdays and Sundays. Do you know if the timing of those walks tended to stay consistent, or did that vary?"

"Shana liked to stick to a routine." Mrs. Feist paused to

blow her nose. "She'd leave around four o'clock, give or take a little, so she could be home by dinner, which we ate around six. She was only ever late one time that I can remember, and she called to let us know first. Like my husband said, she was a good girl. Kind, considerate."

Mrs. Feist's face crumpled again. Charli took that opportunity to share a glance with Matthew. His grim expression reflected back her own worries.

Their killer had already shown he was organized and smart. From what her mother said, Shana Feist had a routine. There was every chance their killer had scouted out his prey ahead of time. Tracked her movements, recorded her schedule.

Chosen just the right moment to pounce.

Charli took careful notes as the Feists responded to her follow-up questions. Shana wasn't involved in organized sports. She took intermittent piano lessons, but in her own home. Charli took down the instructor's name and number but didn't hold out much hope when she found out the teacher was a seventy-year-old woman who'd taught Mrs. Feist when she was younger too.

Unlike Maddie, Shana didn't attend Midtown High but a nearby charter school called Innovation Arts and Tech High. The names of Maddie's friends and boyfriend didn't ring a bell. None of the photos of those same people sparked any recognition with the Feists, either.

According to her parents, Shana didn't have any enemies or even get into arguments with anyone. Matthew showed them a photo they'd printed off the internet of the exact brand and color of lipstick the killer had sewn inside their daughter. Charli heaved a relieved sigh when Matthew told them only that the lipstick had been buried with Shana.

Eventually, they'd learn the truth. That was a horror that could wait for another day.

Both Shana's mom and dad shook their heads in bafflement at the image. They claimed their daughter barely ever wore makeup. The only time Sarah Feist remembered Shana putting on lipstick was over spring break when she was trying to catch the eye of a cute guy, but she'd given it up after a few days as "too much work."

Once she'd exhausted every avenue she could think of at the moment, Charli asked if she and Matthew could look through Shana's room.

Sarah Feist raised a hand to her throat and glanced at her husband for support.

His chest heaved, but in the end, he nodded. "I don't see why not...as long as you ask before taking anything."

"I promise we would never take anything without your permission."

"Okay, then." Reed Feist pushed up from the chair with effort, like he'd aged fifty years within the last half hour. "Follow me."

Charli and Matthew trailed him single file as he led them down a narrow hallway. His footsteps thudded on the hardwood floors, slow and heavy. She wondered if he'd ever move any other way again.

What about Madeline's mom? Does she walk that way now? All slumped and broken? Oh, that's right, you wouldn't know, since you were too much of a coward to keep in touch.

Reed Feist opened the last door on the right but didn't go inside. "This is it. I don't...I'll be in the living room if you need me."

Shana's dad turned sideways to squeeze past Matthew, scrubbing his eyes with his palms as he went.

Charli's heart wrenched. She wished there was something she could say to ease his pain, but there wasn't, so she cleared her mind and slipped into analytic mode.

Her emotions wouldn't help them find clues in Shana's

room. A calm, level head might. She dug a pair of latex gloves from her pocket and pulled them over her fingers. A white-framed, full-sized bed with a purple comforter set split the room in half. "You take the right side. I'll take the left."

Matthew grunted his agreement as he pulled on his own gloves.

Before getting started, Charli surveyed the interior. Besides the bed, the other furniture included two matching white nightstands, a six-drawer dresser, and a blond desk near a closed door that likely led to a closet. The walls were painted a soft lilac color, and white shelves were layered above the desk.

A soft robe covered with pink flamingoes hung from the back of the door. A pair of white flip-flops with a daisy design sat beneath the desk. An empty coffee cup rested beside a Chromebook, along with a half-empty pack of gum, scattered papers, a hairbrush, a couple of cotton balls and a bottle of nail polish remover, and a few other odds and ends.

A book bag leaned against the dresser. On the nightstand, a copy of *The Handmaid's Tale* waited to be finished, with a bookmark dangling out at the midway point. A retainer case sat next to that.

The entire room gave the impression Shana had only stepped away for an afternoon or a night or possibly left on a short trip but was expected back any day.

Fresh sorrow plucked at Charli's ribs, but she shoved the feeling away. She could unpack it again later. Once she was home.

For now, she needed to devote all her energy on focusing. On what was in the room. On what wasn't.

"You good?"

"Yup." Charli had to be good. Another girl was counting on her.

They split off to opposite sides of the room. Charli

started with the desk while Matthew took the dresser. She began on the left side, picking through every piece of paper. A few were blank, a few more were half-finished drawings of anime-style girls with big eyes and funky hair. A couple of old math assignments. No notes.

She found a green spiral notebook beneath the loose papers. The first ten pages were full of doodles and song lyrics. The next few held more drawings. Beyond that, the pages were blank. Charli flipped through them all just to make sure. She turned the notebook upside down and shook. Nothing fell out, so she moved on.

A unicorn statue. A box of fancy colored pencils. An assortment of colored permanent markers in a small rainbow bucket. As far as Charli could tell, nothing that pointed to Shana's killer.

Charli moved on to the drawers. The top one squeaked as she pulled it open. Inside was a pile of thin, paperback how-to-draw manuals. Everything from anime figures to portraits to horses. She flipped through each one to check for papers or notes. All were empty.

A metal box labeled "Artist's Pastels" held true to the claim. In the back corner was another pack of gum and scattered throughout were more colored pencils. No diary or notebooks. No photos.

She squatted down to reach the bottom drawer. A blue paper folder was on top. Charli opened the pages to find honor roll certificates and a few graded papers tucked inside.

Excitement zinged through her veins when she spotted a small purple book with gilded pages. *Diary.*

As she thumbed through the pages, her initial rush faded. The lined pages were untouched.

She replaced the diary and picked through the remaining items. A paint set. A box of hair bands. A nail polish kit, still new in the box. Nothing that immediately jumped out at Charli as relevant to their investigation.

After checking beneath the desk and drawers for anything hidden away, Charli rose with a loud sigh.

Matthew glanced up from the book bag he was rifling through. "Nothing yet?"

"No. You?"

He shook his head.

Charli turned back to the desk. A bulletin board was situated just above the writing surface and right below the shelves. Shana had pinned photos to the board, along with a few memes she'd printed off the internet.

She studied each photo with care. Shana and the same three girlfriends appeared in several of them. Another couple were of Shana and just one of the other girls. Shana and a black-and-white cat. A landscape photo of the ocean. Another of downtown Savannah. None of Shana and any boys, blond or otherwise.

The last photo Charli inspected stole her breath away. She stared at the image, her pulse throbbing in her throat.

The image showed Shana and a short, dark-haired girlfriend posing in front of a statue of a large angel, one that Charli recognized.

That picture had been taken inside the Bonaventure Cemetery.

Charli wasn't sure how long she stood there before Matthew nudged her shoulder.

"Everything okay? You look like you saw a ghost. Whatcha looking at?" He turned his head to follow her line of sight. "Ah, shit. That's where your friend was abducted, right?"

Her mouth was so dry that swallowing was hard. "Yes." Her voice came out like a squeak. She cleared her throat, irritated by her show of weakness. "You don't think it's relevant, do you? Related?"

Matthew's eyebrows shot up toward his hairline. They both knew it wasn't like her to be so hesitant. "To your friend's old case? Probably not. You know kids, they love that cemetery. But I can ask the Feists if we can make a copy of that picture if you like."

His voice was gentle, like he was speaking to an injured animal. She hated when people talked to her like that. Like she was delicate and might break at any second.

"If you're finished with your side of the room, go through the bookshelf while I check out the closet." She scooted past him to open the closet door. Mostly to hide her flaming face. "And I'm sure you're right. I doubt the cemetery is relevant. We should get the names of the other three girls in those photos, though."

Shana's closet was a small walk-in. Charli flipped the light switch to illuminate the contents. For a teen, the space seemed reasonably tidy. Clothes hung along the far and right sides. All but a couple of pairs of shoes sat on a double rack along the bottom of the left side. Sweatshirts and t-shirts were on the built-in shelves above the shoes. Most folded, with a few balled up and shoved on top.

Another shelf ran along the top on all three sides. Instead of clothing, Charli spotted a few baseball caps in one corner and an army of stuffed animals. All lined up in a neat row, staring back at her. Almost like Shana had decided she was too old to keep them on display in her room anymore but too attached to stuff them in a box.

Starting on the left side, Charli worked her way through the shoes. Converse, flip-flops, Ugg-style boots, athletic shoes. Nothing too wild. None hiding any clues or anything at all.

She was pulling sweatshirts off the shelf and digging through pockets when Matthew entered.

"Want me to start on the right si…Jesus, that's creepy!" He froze in the open doorway, his mouth fixed in a horrified circle as his head swiveled to take in all the stuffed animals. "Don't you think that's creepy? All those beady little eyes watching us. Just waiting for us to turn our backs so they can attack."

Just like that, Charli's previous embarrassment faded. She might have ghosts yet to wrestle, but at least she wasn't freaked out by a bunch of cotton stuffing and buttons. "Don't worry, I'll keep you safe."

"I'm going to hold you to that." After a long, exaggerated shudder, Matthew began searching through the clothes.

She finished the lower shelves and joined him. Hangers squealed every so often as they pushed them along the bar, checking pockets on jackets and pants. Making sure nothing was hidden behind the clothing.

When the last garment was checked, Charli battled the disappointment sucking at her like a vacuum by backing away until she blocked the closet entrance. Using her arm, she pushed her blazer back and rested her hand on her hip. Just above her gun.

Matthew frowned. "What's going on?"

She kept her expression neutral. "I'm watching your back like you asked." When he continued to look perplexed, she elaborated. "One of us has to check out those higher shelves, and since I don't see a step stool handy, it's not going to be me."

A beat passed before Matthew groaned. "You've got to be kidding me."

"Nope. But I promise I'll be right here. Ready to shoot the stuffing out of one of those little Gremlins if they even think about trying to steal your soul or dive-bomb you from behind the moment you turn your back."

Matthew narrowed his eyes at her. She flashed an innocent smile in return.

"Great, thanks. I didn't want to sleep tonight anyway." He was shaking his head as he picked up the first animal—a purple-and-blue hippo with improbably long eyelashes—and began checking it for hiding spots. After deeming the hippo clear, he replaced it on the shelf and moved on. "Catch."

Charli caught the blue, floppy-eared dog an inch away from her face.

Together, they worked through all the animals. Two had holes, but their initial excitement disappeared when they found nothing inside beyond cotton stuffing.

Matthew replaced the last one on the shelf and followed Charli out of the closet. "I guess that's it. Either Shana wasn't the type of girl to keep secrets, or else she was a pro at hiding them."

Hands on her hips, Charli made one last, slow circle in the middle of Shana's room. "Nothing in the backpack, under her bed...in her bed?"

"Nope. Already checked. There, and between the mattresses."

She nodded. "Let's go over the floor for any loose boards and check the vent, then I guess we're done here."

Neither of them was surprised when nothing turned up.

If her room and parents were anything to go by, Shana Feist had lived something of a charmed life up until the day she'd disappeared. If there was a clue or hint as to a darker, more sinister presence in Shana's life hidden within her room, Charli didn't see it. The bright colors, art, and sketchbooks. Lived in but neat. Photos with friends. Certificates. All of it pointed to a well-adjusted, lucky girl.

Then again, people would have said Madeline was lucky

too. Right until the day a killer abducted her in broad daylight, then murdered her.

A shiver tracked down her spine. Charli turned back to Shana's desk. Pushing onto her toes, she leaned over and snagged a photo of Shana and her three friends at school, and another of Shana and a freckle-faced girl holding up paintings and grinning inside a gymnasium of some kind.

As she was replacing the pin, her gaze drifted to the photo from Bonaventure Cemetery. Her stomach cramped.

Not from a gut instinct or a hunch. More of a reminder.

Don't fail another girl.

She grabbed Shana's laptop and a couple of the photos and headed for the door. "Let's ask the Feists about the other kids in these photos and get going. Before the stuffed animals have time to plot revenge."

But as she walked down the hall, even Matthew's muffled curses behind her weren't enough to banish the guilt circling her like vultures.

There was only one way to do that.

Find the killer.

BACK AT THE PRECINCT, Matthew and Charli bypassed the stairs and headed straight for the office in the left corner of the building that housed the tech guys. They still needed to contact Powell and Fields, but they needed a few minutes to process everything away from the agents first.

Matthew popped his head into the open doorway. "Knock knock."

A young guy with brown hair that always flopped into his eyes greeted him. "What's up?" The tech didn't bother lifting his head from one of five computer monitors arranged like a spaceship console in front of him.

"Hey, Artie, we come bearing gifts."

Magic words. Artie's head popped up, and as predicted, his hair flopped into his face. He used both hands to shove the strands behind his ears which, going from experience, Matthew guessed would stay put for all of twenty seconds. Thirty, tops. "Detective Church! Detective Cross! Oh, look, another laptop."

Matthew handed him the computer, along with the chain of custody card, watching to make sure Artie filled it out. "Did you manage to get anything off of Maddie Hanley's laptop yet?"

Artie tossed his pen to the side. "Yes, give me just a sec." He swiveled his chair and rifled through about ten piles of papers arranged along the far side of his desk before grabbing one. "Here you go."

Matthew accepted the papers and watched as the tech fired up a silver laptop with a Lenovo logo. "If you want to sit, I can walk you through what I found."

Charli dragged a chair over to the side of the desk so she could view the screen without Artie pivoting it back and forth. Matthew followed her lead and scooted in.

The tech clicked through and showed them Maddie's various accounts. Email, both personal and student. Rarely used for anything other than Amazon purchases or assignments. Some photos, most of them from when she was younger.

"Any more recent photos?"

Artie shot Charli a *sorry* expression. "No, that's all. Recent ones are probably on her phone. Since there aren't any stored in Google Drive, I'm guessing she had an iPhone."

Matthew grimaced. "According to her parents, she did."

"No password for the iCloud?"

"No."

There was a moment of silence during which all three of

their expressions were equally grim. Unless they figured out Maddie's password, breaking into the iCloud was nearly impossible. "So, no texts, either."

Artie brightened. "No, but most kids don't use traditional texting much these days. Maddie did a lot of messaging through Instagram. I consolidated all the messages and printed them out, along with the messages in her video game chat. Glancing through them super quickly, I didn't notice anything out of the ordinary. Some cursing, lots of innuendo. Some complaining about her parents. No threats or ganging up on other players to try to get them banned or anything that made me think *hmm*, though. Seemed like your typical high school girl."

Typical high school girl...except for the part where she got murdered.

"Any messages to her friends or boyfriend about running away?"

"Some, but I got the sense that it was mostly her blowing off steam." Artie lifted a shoulder. "I've seen teens say a lot more dramatic things on their public social media accounts than Maddie did in private."

"So, nothing that raised any red flags for you?"

"Sorry, not really. But maybe you'll find something."

Artie's doubtful tone suggested otherwise. Matthew rubbed his neck. Was a smoking gun too much to ask for?

Charli's calm expression showed no signs she was similarly frustrated.

Then again, Charli was a pro at keeping her feelings in check. A little too much of a pro at times, if you asked him.

"Did Maddie have any Discord accounts where she messaged or chatted with friends that you noticed or other accounts like that? I'm sure you know so many more than we do."

Under Charli's compliment, Artie visibly preened. "Oh

yeah, I know about loads of those. *Loads.* Based on her history, though, Maddie stuck mostly to the 'gram. Here, let me show you."

Matthew exerted a lot of effort to refrain from rolling his eyes. Not that Artie would have noticed if he had. At the moment, the tech was far too interested in showing off for Charli to bother with Matthew.

The tech brushed his bangs back behind his ears as he prattled on. Next time Matthew showed up in this office, he was bringing a bag of hair clips. Maybe some of those thick, elastic things that Chelsea used to leave all over the house. What were they called? Bunchies? No, scrunchies, that was it.

Matthew watched Artie's display with growing amusement. He'd witnessed Charli shut down unwanted male attention from much more impressive catches than the young computer whiz over the past three years. Often with an icy finality that made him wince in sympathy even as he laughed.

The puppy-eyed tech had gone off on a tangent, rattling off the names of all the new, "cutting edge" texting apps out there that kids used these days. Eyes shining like he'd written the code himself.

Matthew shifted impatiently in the chair. Enough already. As entertaining as Artie's peacocking was, they didn't have time for this.

He opened his mouth to interrupt, but Charli beat him to the punch.

"Okay, well, thanks for the info. We've got to get back to our office and go through these pages." She grabbed the papers Artie had printed for them off the desk. Her pivot was so swift Matthew doubted she'd had time to catch the man's crestfallen expression.

Even if she had, it wouldn't have made a difference. Whether on purpose or not, his partner had a tendency to ignore any expressions of emotions that didn't fit into her schedule.

Matthew flashed the dejected tech a sympathetic smile. "Thanks, Artie. Later."

"Yeah."

He had to hurry to catch up to Charli. For someone with legs so much shorter than his, she could really cover ground when she wanted.

She paused in front of the door to the stairs, her shoe tapping an impatient beat on the concrete floor. When he was close enough, she shoved a stack of papers at him. "Here, you take half, and I'll take half. We need to get through these ASAP and see if anything stands out."

He grabbed the pages reflexively. "You get bossy when you're stressed."

Charli snorted. "Please. I'm always bossy."

"Hold up!"

Fields's hollered command set Matthew's teeth grinding together. Ahead of him, Charli's shoulders went rigid, and the slender hand curled around the doorknob tensed. Matthew half-expected his partner to ignore Fields altogether and head up the stairs, but at the last moment, she released the door and turned to where the FBI agent rushed over. Powell hurried behind her like a dog on a leash.

Matthew's stomach soured. The two of them had materialized out of thin air. Like they'd been on the lookout for them. Nothing good could come of that.

Not that he expected anything good to come from the bristly agent.

"I'm glad I found you." Evelyn Fields's mouth shifted into what Matthew figured was her approximation of a smile.

He offered her the same in return. "Funny, I wasn't aware we were lost."

Charli didn't bother pretending. "We just returned from

Cyber and were headed to our office. Did you need something?"

"In order to increase our efficiency with this investigation, I've decided we should consider reorganizing. Why don't you and Matthew pitch in and assist with research? Janice Piper could use all the help she can get digging through those lists of container purchases. Plus, we have the lipstick to research and the fishing line."

Her flinty gaze dropped to the papers in Matthew's hand. "Are those the printouts from what Cyber found on Maddie Hanley's laptop?"

Matthew fought the urge to lie. "Yeah."

"Excellent. If you both want to hand them over to Preston and me, we'll get started on that right away."

She extended her hand toward Matthew, palm outstretched and waiting.

Matthew eyed the pale skin like it belonged to a cobra. His jaw set. "No."

"I beg your pardon? Is there a problem, Detective?"

Fields's feigned innocence was like gasoline on a fire. Matthew glared at the agent while digging a finger under his collar. "I don't know, why don't you put those Feeb investigative skills to work and you tell me?"

Charli shifted her weight beside him, her gaze darting between him and Fields like she was witnessing a tennis match. He sensed her unhappiness with the current friction in the room but noted with triumph that she made no move to hand over Maddie's records, either.

"What my *Feeb* skills tell me is that we all want to catch the asshole who's apparently been running around Savannah for the past year murdering teen girls, and in order to do that, we need a plan. Like it or not, I was the one called in to assist and head up this task force."

Heat blazed up Matthew's neck. He was so mad, he could

feel his pulse pounding beneath his belly button like some alien baby trying to escape. Who the hell did this lady think she was?

This. This was exactly why he hated the freaking Feds. Always barging in, acting like they knew everything. Treating the locals like they didn't have two brain cells to rub together.

"If you think we're going to just sit back and let—"

"Whoa, let's hold up here a second, give everyone a chance to calm down." Powell sidled between Matthew and his would-be dictator, holding his hands up like he was refereeing a football game.

If that FBI wannabe thought he could force Matthew to toe the line, he was in for a rude awakening.

His partner had also shifted her attention to the GBI agent. "I wasn't aware everyone was in need of that opportunity."

Powell's forehead creased as he stared at Charli. He scratched his neck. The GBI agent was clearly taken aback by Charli's blunt retort. Trying to decide whether or not she was mocking him.

Good luck with that. When Charli retreated behind that inscrutable expression, there was no telling what was going on inside that calculating mind of hers. Over three years together and Matthew was in the dark as often as not.

Powell chose the wise course of action. He skirted Charli's comment and moved on. "Look, this is a tough situation. We're all a little on edge. I know we all feel the heat, but Agent Fields is the one whose feet will be held to the fire as the head of the task force."

Fields stood up just a little straighter, appearing pleased with Powell's narrative so far.

Meanwhile, Matthew braced himself for the stream of bullshit that was sure to follow. *Blah, blah, Fields is the leader, blah, blah, she gets to call the shots, blah blah, that's why I'm shoving my head so far up her ass I can see her tonsils.*

"But with all due respect, Agent Fields, Detectives Cross and Church have a significant head start on this case. They know the area, and they've interviewed several of the families. Wouldn't it make more sense to grab a few extra hands on deck from records, maybe even Cyber or unis, to dig through those transactions, and let them stick to what they're doing?"

Matthew's jaw almost came unhinged. Was the Geeb actually defending them? And if so, why?

Even Charli's lips parted in surprise.

All eyes shifted to Fields. Three against one now. She shot Powell a quick glare before throwing her hands in the air. "Fine. But only if you," she pointed at Powell, "round up those extra hands on deck to search transactions."

Without another word, Fields sped away. Probably returning to whatever little web she'd woven in some dark corner of the precinct to prepare to devour her next victim.

Powell stayed put, like he was waiting for a damn medal or something.

"Appreciate it." The tight-lipped reply was the best Matthew could muster. He trusted the agent's sudden alliance about as much as he did those contestants on *Survivor*. Even if Powell was acting to their benefit now, that didn't mean he wouldn't stab them in the back as soon as circumstances shifted.

Maybe the GBI agent had a beef with Fields. Maybe he wanted to get in good with the chief. He likely had motives that Matthew couldn't begin to decipher. Whatever. Matthew and Charli were good for the interim. That was all that mattered now.

That, and the fact that he was still pissed as hell at Fields's power play. "I'll see you back in the office in a few, Charli."

He left his partner studying Powell like he was one of those fetal pigs from biology class and stomped up the stairs. Fields's obnoxious voice echoed in his head, egging him on.

"Like it or not, I was the one called in to head up this task force."

Yeah, well, guess what? He didn't like it. Not even close. And he wasn't about to drop the whole thing, just because Powell intervened for who knew what reasons and talked some sense into the Fed.

He burst through the exit onto the second floor and stormed straight into Ruth Morris's office.

Ruth lifted her eyebrows at the way he barged inside without knocking but spared him a lecture. The sergeant rested her hands on her metal desk. "Yes?"

"That...*agent* you summoned from the FBI just tried to turn Charli and me into paper pushers. On our own damn case! That woman's a freaking menace. If it weren't for Powell, we'd be stuck in our office for eight-hour shifts, reading through a buttload of online orders." Just talking about Fields's bullshit out loud had Matthew seeing red again. "You've got to do something about her. She's a dictator in the making."

"I understand your frustration, Detective, but what would you have me do?"

"I don't know. How about ship her back to where she came from with a return to sender label taped on her a...mouth."

Matthew's split-second amendment from ass to mouth appeared to do little to soothe his boss's ire.

Sergeant Morris slapped her hands on the desk. "In case you hadn't noticed, there's a serial killer using our city as his hunting grounds. He's snatching up our children. We're facing down a full-fledged shit storm when the news hits all channels. A massive panic throughout the streets of Savannah. I want this guy found yesterday, and I don't care who the hell brings him in, be it you or Fields or the man on the moon."

"And Charli and I can bring him in, but not if our investigation is being hobbled by the Feebs." Matthew paced the length of the sergeant's desk. "You know how good Charli and I work together. We don't need the FBI and GBI trying to reorganize us. All they'll do is slow us down."

"And I'm not saying you and Detective Cross don't have the freedom to investigate. By all means, do what you need to do. Work your magic."

Some of Matthew's agitation drained away. He stopped pacing and faced Sergeant Morris. Her hands were still resting on the desk, her dark eyes unfazed.

He read between the lines and sighed. "But the agents aren't going anywhere, right?"

"You're smarter than you look, Detective Church. That's right. No one is going anywhere until this murder is solved."

Her phone rang. She made a shooing motion with her hands before picking up the call.

Matthew crossed the brown carpet for the door.

"Hold up, Detective."

The sudden sharpness of her voice made his gut clench. He turned back as she switched the call over to speaker. "Okay, go ahead, John."

"Like I was saying, we just dug up another body. This one is only a quarter mile or so from the second one. Same type of container. We're going to—"

Matthew didn't stick around to hear what John was going to do. He raced over to Charli, who was standing behind her desk with a fresh cup of coffee.

"Let's go. They just found another body in the marsh."

20

———

The truck careened around a corner as Matthew accelerated into a right turn at breakneck speed. Charli had to grab the overhead hand grip to avoid a collision between her skull and the passenger window.

"Is there an emergency you didn't tell me about? Or were you just thinking my pulse was a little low and needed a late afternoon pick-me-up?"

Matthew changed lanes. "Yes. The emergency is that we can't let Fields and her Geeb sidekick beat us to the scene."

Questions popped into Charli's head, the main one being: *Why? Why couldn't they let Fields and Powell beat them to the scene? Why did it matter who got there first? Why hadn't they coordinated with the two agents to begin with before leaving the precinct?*

The query she settled on was none of the above. "Why are you acting so weird?"

After a few seconds, Matthew barked a laugh as though she'd shared a hilarious joke. "Hey now, are you allowed to ask that anymore? What if I'm just differently brained?"

She wasn't joking, but that was okay. His failure to meet

her eyes was telling.

If her partner didn't want to talk about why Fields's presence bothered him so much, that was his call.

As long as his hang-ups didn't end up biting her in the ass too.

The marshland stretched along the road, green grasses ruffling in the summer breeze. The odor of sulfur and mud seeped into the truck's interior, courtesy of all the activity and digging. When the crime scene appeared up ahead, Charli's stomach dropped.

Media vans. Everywhere.

"I guess now it's a real party." Matthew shook his head as he turned left across the street and pulled up along the side of the road.

She wanted to comment that, next time, she'd prefer a better party venue. Preferably one with fewer dead people... and reporters. The camera crews spread out on the civilian side of the yellow police tape like a pack of hyenas.

One of the hyenas noticed them walking up and broke off from the pack. A man with carefully styled brown hair and a hungry expression.

Charli used the yellow police tape like a beacon, keeping her eyes glued straight ahead.

"Detectives, can you tell us if they've found any more bodies?"

Other reporters caught on and swarmed around her and Matthew, checking for the weakest point of entry.

A microphone appeared in front of Charli's face. She swerved to avoid colliding with it and continued on her path. The reporters shouted over each other and kept pressing in, tight enough that Charli felt claustrophobic.

"No comment." Matthew repeated the words several times.

Charli's own throat was too dry to make a sound.

As a detective, she'd dealt with reporters before. Never her favorite experience, but she appreciated the service they provided. Usually.

Not this time, though. The swarm hit too close to home, dragging her back to those awful weeks after Madeline died.

How many times had she opened the front door of her house, only to find another journalist camped out on the sidewalk? Always with a cameraperson waiting to start recording the second she appeared and a journalist ready to charge her, microphone wielded in their eager hand like a sword.

The questions were what haunted her, though. Even ten years later.

"Hey, Charli. Can you tell us about the day you saw Madeline Ferguson abducted?"

"Did you see the guy who grabbed your friend?"

"How does it make you feel, knowing that your best friend was kidnapped right in front of you by the same person who likely killed her?"

So many times she'd wanted to turn on them and yell, "How do you think it feels?" Instead, she'd clamped her lips together as instructed by her parents and ignored the reporters while she trembled from the force of her silent screams.

Her entire body tightened like the jaws of a steel trap. She tuned out their questions, the press of their bodies, and focused on that yellow ribbon.

Fifteen feet to safety. Ten feet.

"Come on, get back now! I don't want to have to tell you again." A uniformed cop had stepped toward them with his hand out, reminding the reporters to stay on their side.

Five feet.

Matthew lifted the tape up, chuckling. "Media's a cluster as usual, but at least we beat Fields and Powell to the scene."

As she ducked beneath the barrier, Charli snapped. The journalists, Madeline, the three dead girls were all bad enough, but her partner's misplaced chuckle was the thing that really triggered her.

She walked far enough until she was sure they were out of earshot of the reporters before stopping and pointing. "Look."

Beside her, she sensed Matthew's puzzlement, but he played along. "Okay, I'm looking. What's going on?"

She ignored his question. "What do you see?"

"What do you mean? I see the marsh. The river in the background. A bunch of people from forensics gathered around a pile of mud and a plastic bin that I'm guessing contains a dead body."

Her nod was curt. "Exactly. A dead body. The third one, to be precise. Likely belonging to another teenage girl."

"Yeah, I know all that already. What's this all about?"

Finally, Charli turned to face him. Her voice remained level and at a conversational volume, two facts that were completely at odds with the anger scalding her chest right now. "I don't know what your issue is with Agent Fields or Agent Powell, and at this precise moment, I don't care. What I do care about is solving this case. Can you hang up your grudge until after we've done that? Three dead girls, Matthew. Maybe more."

Matthew stared at her, then averted his gaze and shook his head before facing her again. When he opened his mouth, she hoped he would tell her what the hell was going on with him lately. Instead, he grunted. "Yes, I'm aware."

Charli's eyes narrowed. She almost never argued with her partner, but right now, she was having a hard time believing that. The constriction in her chest reminded her to take deeper breaths and rein in her wild emotions.

After several exhalations, she tried again. More calmly

this time. "Whatever you think of Fields, remember she'll have access to resources we won't. The very least we should be doing is playing nice so that she'll share."

If anything, this attempt to logic Matthew out of his grudge backfired. His mouth thinned, and he didn't say a word.

Charli latched onto the one subject that might help her partner see reason. "If this were Chelsea, wouldn't you want all law enforcement officials working together to help solve the case?"

Matthew jerked back as if she'd struck him. "Jesus, Charli. Did you really just ask me to picture my own daughter as one of these rotting corpses shoved into plastic bins by some sick fuck with a lipstick fetish?"

She shook her head, frustrated. That wasn't what she'd meant to imply at all. If she had, she would have used those words specifically. "No, I—"

But Matthew was already stomping off.

After an epic eye roll that was wasted on her partner's back, Charli trudged after him. If he wanted to pout, fine by her. As long as he quit his stupid game of one-upmanship with Fields and company.

Another twenty yards away, the forensic photographer was still snapping photos of the body inside the container, so Matthew veered over to Soames. The GBI medical examiner stood farther from the crime scene than usual. The reason slapped Charli in the face after another couple of steps. Or more like, attacked her mucous membranes with the noxious reek of decay.

She blinked rapidly to keep her eyes from watering and focused on breathing through her mouth. Without knowing any details, she could already guess this victim had been dead for a lot longer than the last two. Not a great indicator of what they might hope to recover in terms of evidence.

Ahead of her, Matthew stopped, and his shoulders spasmed. His arm flew up to cover his nose. When he started walking again, his pace was slower, and every so often, his shoulders flinched again.

Charli guessed her partner was gagging. He almost certainly wasn't the first one at this scene to react that way, and she doubted he would be the last.

"We've got to stop running into each other like this." Even the M.E.'s attempt at humor fell a little flat.

Charli's smile was just as obligatory. "Let's hope this is the last time for a while."

When Soames didn't make his usual "you wound me" response, she knew things were bad.

"Anything yet?" Matthew's voice was muffled from speaking into his arm.

Soames shook his head. "Not really. I can perform a quick examination of the body once the photographer finishes up, but I can tell you right now, I won't see much here. Based on the liquid I noticed, this victim is well into the active stage of decomposition. I'll need to get that container back to the lab so I don't risk losing evidence."

That gelled with the stench. The liquefaction stage was a late stage of decomposition, when the internal organs autolyzed and turned from a solid state into mush. "So, probably dead longer than the others?"

"That's a safe bet."

Matthew didn't spare her a glance or acknowledge her comments in any way. Charli wasn't sure if he was still upset or worried that too much motion might make him hurl. "I'm going to take a quick look around. I'll be back when you start your exam."

She started out across the grass, skirting the crime scene and pulling out her notebook to scribble off a quick illustration of the burial site in relation to the river. She pivoted, studying the spill of green swamp grass that lined the river until she located Maddie's burial site, which she added to her drawing.

The site where they'd discovered Shana's body was located around a bend in the opposite direction. Giving the forensics team a wide berth, she picked her way closer, until she got a better idea of the orientation in relation to the road and river.

She smoothed her hand over her hair and sucked her tongue between her teeth, studying the stretch of land. Wondering what, if anything, she was missing.

Did the area hold a special meaning or significance to the killer? Or had he chosen the location because the water-moistened soil was easy to dig up, and there were rarely many people around?

The hairs on the back of her neck began standing on end. Her head whipped up as she reached back to rub the spot.

Before she could question the impulse, she whirled, scouring the surrounding area.

Nothing there. Of course there wasn't.

She shook her head at her own jumpiness. "Better watch out, or you'll be parroting Matthew's hunches in no time."

After another slow circle, she headed back. The photographer had finished documenting the body and surrounding area, and Soames was walking toward the burial site. Matthew lagged behind, stopping every few steps to turn his face away and shudder.

As she crossed the swampy grass to meet them, she spotted two figures beelining toward them from the direction of the street. They arrived at the same time.

Fields's flushed cheeks and rigid spine radiated indignation. Behind her, Powell appeared cool by comparison, the usual unassuming smile on his handsome face.

Charli suspected he used his bland, congenial expression

as a tool to lure people into revealing too much. He might play the part of an easygoing, relaxed agent, but she'd be surprised if a razor-sharp mind wasn't lurking beneath that bland mask. You didn't become a GBI investigative agent without also possessing some hard edges.

If he was irritated, he hid the emotion well. Unlike Fields.

The FBI agent's glare found a target on Matthew's face. "I hunted all over the precinct for you two when I got the notification about this body, but you were nowhere to be found. I should have known better. I don't appreciate my time being wasted, especially not when lives are on the line."

"Yeah? Well, I don't—"

Charli cleared her throat. Matthew stopped talking and turned his head. She widened her eyes, gave a single jerk of her head. Her partner shoved his hands into his pockets and muttered under his breath.

Fields cupped a hand to her ear. "Was that a response, Detective? If so, you'll need to speak up."

Matthew's shoulders heaved with the force of his sigh. "I said, sorry. We should have informed you."

The FBI agent's stunned silence only lasted a few seconds before she leapt back in. "You're right, you should ha—"

"My partner and I aren't used to checking in with anyone besides Sergeant Morris, but we'll try to do better from here on out."

Charli's interjection had the desired effect of interrupting Fields's griping. She'd made her point. Matthew had apologized. Beating him over the head with the same point he'd just acknowledged wouldn't bring any of them closer to finding the killer...although it might make Matthew dig in his heels and switch back into his odd belligerence.

No one needed that. Least of all the dead girls.

For a second, she feared Fields was going to argue further, but before she could start, Powell slipped in.

"Since it sounds like we're all on the same page now, why don't we give Dr. Soames our undivided attention?" He put his words into action by moving closer to where the M.E. was squatting by the open container, presenting Charli and her two feuding companions with his back.

Although her hope was that, after this, they'd manage to downgrade their status from feud to détente.

Fields's narrowed gaze swept Matthew's face once more before nodding. "As long as 'trying to do better' means doing better, then sure. Let's move on."

Her stiff-legged gait showed that Agent Fields wasn't ready to completely let it go yet, but that was her problem, not theirs.

As long as Matthew kept up his end of the bargain—and Charli would make sure of that—then Fields would have to get over herself. All their personal squabbles or vendettas or whatever the case of the animosity between them was, it was all meaningless compared to finding and stopping a serial killer.

When they joined Powell, Soames was in the process of positioning his associate. "Can you hold the flashlight right there...yes, thank you, that works."

The photographer stood on the other side, waiting to hit record. Not that there was much to see with the body still tucked inside the storage bin. The video was mostly to provide a detailed record of when the body had been touched, by who, and how, to ensure if the case ever went to trial, the suspect's defense attorney couldn't cry foul.

Soames crouched in front of the circular opening. "Okay, go ahead and start recording."

Charli and the others quieted as Soames began to speak for the recording, providing his name, date, and time, along with the names of everyone present.

The medical examiner went through and named

everyone in attendance before moving on. "I'm about to perform a preliminary inspection of a body that was recovered from a shallow burial site east of Rose Dhu Road and just south of Schley Avenue, approximately fifty yards off the road in the marsh adjacent to the Vernon River. I will be conducting this inspection without removing the body from the plastic container it was sealed in due to the advanced degree of decomposition making removal in the field without losing portions of the corpse doubtful."

Even Powell grimaced at that visual. Matthew scooted a few steps back, as if ducking behind her might help save him from the stench. Not likely, when he towered over her by at least a full foot. Unless he'd decided to risk public humiliation by crouching behind her like a small child playing a game of hide-and-seek.

This close-up, the sweet, foul odor of rotting flesh was so strong, Charli could almost believe she was taking a steam bath in a spa for cannibals. As soon as she got back home, she'd be stripping off these clothes, tossing them in the washer with extra bleach, and scrubbing off in a hot shower until her skin turned bright pink.

Even Soames paused to turn his head and take a breath before continuing. "Initial impression of this body is that it belongs to a young female in the active stage of decay." He leaned in closer. "Liquefaction of tissue and internal organs is noted throughout the body but especially in the abdominal region and is consistent with the brown fluid puddling beneath the back and pelvis."

A muffled groan came from behind Charli, and Fields blanched. Charli bit her cheek to keep from shuddering. The dead bodies they usually encountered had stopped fazing her a while ago. None of them had ever been described as swimming in a lake of melted flesh goo, though.

"Minimal insect activity noted..."

Still paler than usual, Fields glanced at her watch before huffing an impatient sigh. Matthew jingled the change in his pocket.

Besides Charli, Powell was the only other non-M.E. office observer who remained quiet and still.

"Hey, Drake, would you mind getting an evidence bag ready?"

Charli tensed, her fingertips tingling. Fields and Matthew stopped fidgeting. Powell's eyes might even have narrowed a fraction of an inch.

After once again instructing his associate where to hold the flashlight, Soames leaned back into the opening. His arms moved as he fussed with something inside. "I'm now observing what I suspect is foreign material within the body...a type of sturdy thread or line. I'm removing a foreign object from the mass of tissue inferior to the pubic arch that likely once formed the vaginal canal..."

Soames emerged from the bin, rocking back on his heels. Held between the fingers of a latex glove covered in viscous brown goo was a small black cylinder.

Lipstick.

"For the record, I've extracted what appears to be a tube of lipstick." The M.E. checked the bottom and read. "Made by BeautyDay, number fifty-five in the shade Happy Harlot."

Soames dropped the lipstick into the evidence bag his associate held open before catching Charli's eye. His usual jovial face was grim.

She gave him a curt nod, dread stretching all her muscles to the breaking point.

The third victim lined up with the two others. Same container, stitching, same exact shade of lipstick.

Looked like their murderer had officially leveled up.

21

The chaos on the marsh in the distance filled me with an excited buzz. All those police officers out there, digging and running around like chickens with their heads cut off. All because of me.

My vantage point at the edge of the construction site provided me with the perfect view. A little higher than the marsh and too far away for them to notice me without a pair of binoculars like the ones I pressed to my own eyes.

Same as every other weekday, the banging and electric grind of power tools had cut out promptly at five o'clock. The workers filed out shortly after, leaving the dirt lot deserted by five-fifteen. The owner was probably adamant about avoiding overtime, which coalesced perfectly with my needs.

I leaned against the Explorer's hood, power rushing through my veins. All the previous times I'd come here to oversee the unveiling of my girls, I'd played it safe and watched from inside the SUV. No one else had ever driven up here, and I preferred this unencumbered view. With the way their little police bodies scattered this way and that along the swamp grass and mounds of muck, I almost felt like I was directing a play.

A half-smile tugged at my lips as I sketched out a quick plot.

Act one: the painstaking selection of my girls and my capturing process.

Act two: their repurification before I set them free.

Act three…well, that would cover the scene before me now. A bunch of hapless officers digging up my girls and running themselves ragged in their vain attempts to discover who'd placed them in the earth.

Of course, law enforcement would be hoping for a fourth act. A clincher where they could don their capes and play the hero by capturing the person responsible.

My smile dimmed. What they lacked was the imagination and conviction to comprehend that I was a hero too. Only my methods for addressing the moral decay eroding the very fabric of our society were far more radical than running around with a badge playing cops and robbers.

One day, I hoped more like-minded citizens rose up and tackled the rot invading our children like a historical plague. For now, though, I acted alone. Repurifying one girl at a time.

I watched those little bodies move around the grass. "You can look, but you won't find."

I'd been very careful. I'd cleaned their bodies with a bleach mixture before interning them into the bins, which I'd brought with me from the old farm back in Virginia. No easy way to trace those containers back to me. I'd burned all their clothing. Offloaded all their busted phones and SIM cards in different dumpsters across Savannah.

The media vans were new today. I gave a rueful sigh. "I bet you love all that attention, don't you, my pretties?"

I refocused on the figures clustered around the latest

container the police had uncovered, frowning when I only counted four. The medical examiner and his lackey, a photographer, and the tall detective. All men.

"Now, where did you wander off to, I wonder?" After shifting my field of vision to the right, I spotted the short-haired, female detective. "Ah, there you are."

There was something about her. So restrained, yet I sensed a rebellious nature lurking beneath her masculine suit and sharp gaze. Unlike most of the other imbeciles there, she never made a repulsed face when greeting my girls or acted like she was close to vomiting. She clearly took the matter seriously and handled the situation with the respect it deserved.

For some reason, she'd wandered away from the others, surveying the marsh from multiple directions before bending her head over that little notebook she kept handy.

When I figured out what she was likely doing, a throaty chuckle rumbled from my lips. "Aren't you an industrious little bee, sketching out all the burial sites? I applaud your initiative, though you're wasting your time. I'm afraid there's nothing telling in the placement of my girls beyond my own convenience."

As I continued spying, the detective's head shot up from the notebook. One hand went to the back of her neck, rubbing the skin left bare by her childish haircut.

Almost like she'd sensed my presence.

As if to prove my point, she whirled, throwing up a hand to shield her eyes as she scoured the stretch of land between us. I held very still, my breaths turning shallow. At the same time, the crotch of my jeans grew restrictive as I hardened.

Could she see me?

A few moments later, she shook her head before heading back across the grass to rejoin the others.

I released a giddy laugh. "Aren't you a feisty one?"

The detective was far too old to be one of my girls. That didn't mean I couldn't appreciate her all the same.

She reminded me a little of one of my girls from back in Virginia. My first one after Tanya.

"Now, there was another one who was petite and spunky."

While keeping my binoculars focused on the activity, I allowed my mind to wander back to that first night with Ashley.

I waited in the corner of the parking lot across the street from the bowling alley, beneath an overgrown tree and well out of range of the streetlamps that spilled light along the sidewalk. The dashboard of my SUV informed me two hours had already passed. I stretched my arms and changed the channel until Frank Sinatra crooned from the speakers. A singer from better times, when every song wasn't about sex or dropping F-bombs. When girls and women were classier and didn't flaunt their bare midriffs and butt cheeks all over the internet.

I'd waited in this same spot on three previous occasions while doing reconnaissance. All three times, Ashley left the bowling alley no later than seven-fifteen. My guess was her parents told her to be home by eight. Her house was a little more than half a mile away. I'd clocked it myself. I guess they figured such a short walk was safe in our small town, even with the daylight so close to disappearing.

That probably explained why they didn't notice how, on at least two of the three occasions, Ashley had clearly been under the influence.

A figure emerged from the bowling alley's entrance. When she stepped into the light, my pulse quickened.

Long, dark hair. Tight white tank top. A skirt so short that she'd probably been giving everyone a show whenever she bent over to pick up a ball, which was undoubtedly her intention.

Ashley was starting her walk home.

Adrenaline flooded my veins and urged me to rush, but I knew better. Timing was key. I waited, watching her sway down the sidewalk, the little bit of weaving she did back and forth telling me she'd been successful in her attempts to manipulate older men into buying her beer.

Once she disappeared from sight, I set my phone timer for four minutes. I'd timed the drive before, as well as her walking pace. The ideal point of pickup was just after her next turn. That short segment took her by a large, undeveloped plot of land. No streetlights, no nosy neighbors. The perfect place to strike.

When the timer clanged, I turned over the engine and reversed out of the parking space. I took a left onto the main street and made a quick right, observing all the traffic laws and speed limits.

No other cars passed me as I cruised up to that first turn and made the left. I held my breath until I spotted her just a few yards ahead.

Exactly where I'd hoped she would be.

Not wanting to trigger any alarm bells in her head, I didn't ease off the gas behind her, instead driving past at the normal speed before glancing in my rearview mirror and feigning surprise. I hit the brake hard and pushed a button on the door until the driver's side window rolled down, poking my head outside. "Hey, is that you, Ashley?"

She stopped and blinked up at me.

I waved. "It's Tanya's dad, remember?"

That nudged her alcohol-soaked memory. "Oh, right! Hi. Whassup?"

"Nothing much, just heading over to a friend's house to play some poker. You need a lift? Your house is on the way."

Ashley hesitated, glancing down the street. My heart sank. This was the only part of the scenario I had no control over. My hands gripped the steering wheel hard. I didn't like this feeling of uncertainty in my stomach. If she said no, I'd have to make a quick decision. Either modify the plan at the last second and grab her or drive off empty handed.

The tension flowed from my muscles when she shrugged. "Sure, why not?"

Again, just as I'd hoped, she walked around the front of the SUV and climbed into the seat next to mine. That made me happy. If she'd chosen the seat behind me like I was the unofficial chauffeur, the way Tanya used to do, I wouldn't be able to strike like I needed to. I would have been forced to modify my plan or abandon it altogether.

Too many variables in play.

She settled in the seat and gazed up at me expectantly. "Ready?" Her skirt rode up her sleek thighs. Any higher and she'd show me exactly what color panties she was wearing.

Assuming she was wearing any at all.

Ashley reached up to tug at the fabric, but I saw right through her ruse. Drawing my attention there on purpose, like the little attention-seeking whore she was.

My smile widened. "I will be ready, just as soon as you put on your seat belt."

Her eye roll was such an exact replica of Tanya's that I might have believed my own daughter was sitting there...if I hadn't strangled the life from her blue eyes five weeks ago.

As Ashley turned her attention to the metal clasp, I reached into the pocket on the driver's door and grabbed the syringe, hiding it beneath my left thigh.

Once the metal clicked, I nodded. "Good girl." I eased the SUV into drive and crawled along the street.

My nerves fired off tiny explosions. My body's way of informing me I was venturing into uncharted territory. I'd meant to jab her as she was fussing with the seat belt, but in the moment, the notion was unsatisfying.

Too easy. I wanted more time to witness fear spark in those blue eyes. To lap up the emotion like a cat laps up a saucer of milk.

This was the girl who'd sent my Tanya down a path from sweet, wholesome girl who obeyed her dad to makeup-wearing floozy who flaunted her body to attract boys.

Ashley's terrible influence had led directly to Tanya's death. Her terror was only fair and would make her subsequent rehabilitation so much sweeter.

I hit the childproof lock and continued driving.

"How does Tanya like boarding school? Didn't she go to like Europe or something?"

I smiled. "Tanya is exactly where she needs to be."

Ashley was barely listening at this point. She was too busy watching a video on her social media feed. I had to repeat my comment before she replied. "She's so lucky. My parents would never let me go somewhere cool like that by myself."

I doubted that very much, unless it was about the money. From what I could tell, Ashley's parents couldn't be bothered to keep tabs on their daughter at all. Such a sad state of affairs.

While driving, I sneaked wary glances at her phone. Another miscalculation on my part. All it would have taken was a single text to a single friend or family member informing them I'd given her a ride home to ruin all my carefully laid plans.

Any girl with an ounce of self-preservation or common sense would have done as much.

Ashley clearly had neither.

I passed the turn-off for her house and continued down the road until we reached an undeveloped stretch of land. After tapping the brakes, I glided the SUV to a stop beside a giant tree.

Ashley was so intent on her phone that it took her a good ten seconds to glance up. She automatically reached for the door handle before she stopped, frowning out the windshield at the darkened street ahead. "This isn't my house."

Stupid girl. Even now, she sounded more annoyed than scared.
"No, it isn't."

She waited, like she expected me to give her more. When no reasonable explanation for the stop was forthcoming, her demeanor changed. I saw the exact moment when fear crawled into her pouty, beer-impaired head. Her movements turned jerky as she fumbled with the seat belt clasp.

"That's okay. I can just walk home from here." The seat belt whizzed free, and she grabbed the door handle. One yank. Two.

Of course, the door didn't budge.

Her dry swallow was audible. An elixir to my ears. "I...I think the child lock is on. Can you unlock my door for me, please? I can walk from here. It's fine."

Such nice manners...when she decided such things were worth her while.

When she peeked up at me, her usual sulky expression was absent. Her eyes were round.

My smile widened. I lifted the hypodermic needle filled with the horse tranquilizer I'd diluted based on my best guess at her body weight. "I'm afraid I can't do that, Ashley."

She stared at the needle, and those painted lips parted in preparation to scream. I lunged, jabbing the needle into her arm with one hand while clamping my hand over her mouth with the other.

Once I plunged the drug into her muscle, I tossed the needle into the back seat and used my other hand to subdue her. We grappled for control of her cell phone before I wrestled it from her hands and threw it on the floorboard.

She bucked beneath my hands, her nails clawing at my back over my shirt.

I pressed my mouth close to her ear and whispered. "Go ahead and fight. It'll push the drug into your system more quickly."

Like the follower she was, Ashley went still. I chuckled to myself. The girls these days. So mouthy and certain they knew everything worth knowing, yet none of them possessed the first idea how to think for themselves.

They all needed a crash course in the things in life that truly mattered. Real values. Not social media 101.

"I'm going to show you the error of your ways."

She flinched at that, jerking her arms in a renewed attempt to escape. Her motions were slower, though. Clumsy and weak. The powerful tranquilizer was powering her responses down, like a laptop slowly going to sleep.

"That's it. Rest for now."

Motion in the distance dragged my attention back to the marsh. While I'd been busy reminiscing, two new players had joined the others on the field. A woman and a man. Both dressed in suits.

They stood a little apart from the detectives I was familiar with. The body language between them and the feisty, short-haired detective and her much taller partner made me think they weren't part of the original investigation. More like outsiders.

I tapped a finger to my chin. "Is that you, FBI? Coming to rain on my parade?"

I wasn't sure what to think about that. Part of me was flattered. Part was annoyed by the inconvenience.

The medical examiner was stooped over by one of my burial tombs. A short time passed before he rocked back, clutching something in his hand.

I spun the binoculars until the focus sharpened on the plastic bag. A small, black cylinder was inside.

"A little rude to take a girl's lipstick from her, don't you think?"

A peek at the petite detective's face when she turned away made me smile. "Why the serious face? Are you not a fan of that shade of red?"

Red. That reminded me. My smile lingered as I returned to Ashley.

The air was musty and cool when I opened the door to the storage cellar and climbed down the stairs. At the bottom of the steps, I paused, inhaling through my nose. Beneath the odor of neglect, I detected the sharper, more pleasing perfume of Ashley's sweat mixed with one of those sweet body sprays that teen girls favored.

If only they understood they didn't need artificial products to enhance their natural beauty. So much money wasted on perfumes and deodorant when their own unique scent was so much more intoxicating. So pure.

Ashley was in the same position I'd left her in last time, pressed against the back of the chair I'd bound her to and watching me with wide eyes.

My first few attempts to educate her on her transgressions hadn't gone over very well. The first time, she'd still been too drugged to do much more than mumble, so I'd left so the poor girl could get some rest.

She'd spent the entirety of our second visit begging me to let her go, so frantic in her pleading that she hadn't taken in a word I'd said.

I stepped closer. "I have a good feeling that the third time is going to be the charm. Are you ready to let me instruct you on the mistakes you've made with your misguided, whorish ways?"

Those blue eyes stared up at me. So lovely. So sweet. "I..." She paused to clear her throat. "I'm sorry, could I have a drink of water? My mouth is so dry."

Her voice was softer than usual. Submissive.

Exactly the way girls should be.

"Of course, I'm not a barbarian. I'm sure it's from all that screaming you were doing earlier." I shook my head as I crossed over to the set of metal shelves where I kept a water bottle with a straw ready just for this purpose. "I told you that screaming was futile. You know there's no one within several miles of this farm, so I'm glad you finally decided to spare your poor throat."

I crouched down near the chair and held out the water bottle until she could reach the straw. She sucked down greedy gulps.

"Ah, ah, careful. You wouldn't want to choke."

She paused for a breath, and I pulled the bottle back, pleased.

Now we were getting somewhere. If only parents taught their daughters to listen and cooperate, the world would be a much better place.

"More?"

At her nod, I put the straw back within reach, pleased with our progress. Twenty-four hours in the cellar had done wonders for her disposition. Maybe parents should consider this before—

Water sprayed my face. I stumbled away, swiping furiously at my eyes.

The ungrateful little bitch had just spit on me.

When I opened them again, Ashley was sneering.

"I hope you choke to death, you fucking creep! You can take your instructions and shove them up your ass because I'm not going to listen. Do you hear me? I'm never going to listen, so fuck you! No wonder Tanya got the hell out of here. She probably wanted to get as far away from you as possible."

My body pounded with fury, but unlike Ashley, I had control of my emotions. I walked over to the shelves and ripped off a paper towel to wipe off my face. "You know, I tried to give you a chance. Tried to make you comprehend how your obsession with having people look at you was rotting your soul and ruining your life. I can leave our time together knowing I did my best, but growth requires active participation from both parties."

After tossing the paper towel into the trash can lined with a paper bag that was destined to eventually be burned to ashes, I opened an old box and pulled an object out before turning back to her. "Speaking of Tanya, do you remember this?"

She stared at the lipstick I held between my fingers. "No, why would I?"

I pulled off the lid and slid it into my pocket. A few turns of the bottom pushed the red lipstick up.

Bright red. Clown red.

Or, as the name on the bottom proudly proclaimed, Happy Harlot.

My thighs clenched with a mixture of anger and excitement. "Funny you should ask. This is the lipstick you convinced my daughter to buy against my explicit wishes. Does that ring a bell?"

She swallowed hard, but stubborn to the core, refused to answer.

My heartbeat quickened. That was okay. After all, there was no joy in breaking a mare that was already saddle trained.

I strolled closer, enjoying the way her eyes grew wider with each of my steps. I stopped a few feet away. After regarding me warily for a good twenty seconds, her shoulders began drooping with relief.

The next moment was when I pounced.

I lunged forward, straddling her thighs and curling my free hand around her throat. Squeezing until my fingers sank deep into that warm, fragrant skin. I squeezed tighter and tighter, choking her until the whites showed around her irises. Her mouth gaped open in a desperate bid to suck down more air.

Perfect.

As she gasped, I painted her open lips with methodical strokes. "Tanya did get out of here, but not the way you think."

Stroke.

"If only you hadn't given her this lipstick."

Stroke.

"If only she'd listened to me when she'd had the chance and wiped that horrible color off."

Stroke.

"You had your chance, but you insisted on choosing the path of disrespect and self-loathing."

Stroke.

"Now you'll end up in the same place as her...buried at the far edge of our land, where no one but me will ever see you."

Ashley's pretty blue eyes were all but bugging out of her head when I released her neck, studying my handiwork while her harsh gasps for air rent the serenity of the cellar.

The bright red color emphasized the soft, wanton curve of her lips. Desire shot into my groin, exactly as she'd always intended.

My hands shook with regret. "Just look what you made me do. All I ever wanted was to teach you girls the virtuous path, but you refused to learn."

The longer I stared at that lush, scarlet mouth, the quicker my regret disappeared.

I'd done my best. She'd made her decision. "If you insist on acting the whore with that filthy mouth, then who am I to treat you otherwise?"

Ashley's wheezing subsided. She started to whimper. "You killed her. You killed Tanya."

Tears leaked from eyes that were defiant only seconds ago. When I leaned forward, she squeezed them shut. I wrenched her jaw until they jerked back open.

"Oh no. This is what you wanted all this time, wasn't it? Male attention, to tell you how pretty you are? To pant after you like a dog after a bitch in heat?"

Ashley tried to protest. I put a finger to her lips. "Shh, don't bother lying. We both know the truth."

Still holding her jaw, I pushed my nose to her neck and inhaled. Her sweat overpowered the perfume now. So beautiful and fresh.

I dug my fingers into her soft hair and wrenched her head back, smiling into her beautiful face.

"Guess what? Looks like today is your lucky day because you have my undivided attention now."

When I blinked out of the memory, my palms were sweating, and the crotch of my jeans had grown uncomfortably tight. I readjusted myself. The hunger throbbing inside me wasn't so easily satisfied, though. A quick scan of the marsh revealed that while the uniformed officers and a few of the forensics crew lingered, the others were gone.

That was my cue to vanish too. This would be my last time to the construction site. Too many reporters sniffing around now. Plus, that little detective had stared over this way. As thrilling as our interaction had been, I didn't want to take any chances. No doubt such a busy little bee would discover my little viewing spot sooner than later.

As I climbed into my SUV and the engine rumbled to life, I bid a fond farewell to my secret viewing spot. I'd hoped that moving to a city almost ten times the size of my last town would enable me to fly under the radar for at least another year. With the way events were transpiring, I'd be lucky to last out the year.

The FBI snooping around the last town to investigate my missing girls had been enough to convince me to acquire papers and an ID under a new name. They were tucked into a locked case back at home, which was hidden behind a loaf of bread in my pantry. Ready to go whenever I was.

Hopefully, none of those items would be necessary. Any departure that required their use all but guaranteed my need for a career change. The fine state of Georgia required all employees in my field to be fingerprinted as a condition of employment.

I cruised onto the main street and sighed. As upsetting as it was, I was inclined to believe I was close to overstaying my welcome in Savannah.

At the next light, I turned left. Fifteen minutes and several more turns later, and I was cruising toward Peach State Pizzeria.

The sight of the cute little brick business sent anticipation flowing up my legs and pooling with delicious warmth beneath my belly button. That giddy sensation from earlier returned full force.

I spared the structure a quick glance as I cruised on by. No slowing or stopping.

Not quite yet.

I didn't need to peek inside to picture the dark-haired girl who scurried around carrying pizzas to diners. Bending low over tables when delivering plates and shaking her ripe, firm ass while she sashayed away.

Yes, the time to flee Savannah was quickly approaching.

First, though, I could make the time to repurify one more wayward girl.

22

"Wanna talk about it?"

Charli didn't take in much of the scenery on the drive back to the precinct. Much of Matthew's anger seemed to have eased, but the residual tension between them lingered enough that he'd cranked up the volume on his country station in lieu of talking.

She glanced at Matthew. The thing was, she did want to talk about it. And also didn't.

She blew out a long breath. "I was just thinking about the similarities between these victims and Madeline's case."

Matthew latched onto her train of thought. "You're back to wondering if it could be the same guy?"

"Yes."

He nodded. "All right. Lay it on me. What are the similarities?"

Charli repeated the ones she'd come up with. Matthew appeared to mull those over for half a block. "What about the differences?"

She extended a finger with each response. "No lipstick. No stitches. Madeline was abducted in plain sight in front of witnesses. As far as we know, no witnesses have come forth in any of the other cases. Madeline's body wasn't buried in that same kind of plastic bin."

A van swerved toward their lane. Matthew swore and laid on the horn before replying. "My take is that the differences in these cases are a lot more significant than what they've got in common. The lipstick, stitches...that's the killer's signature. Seems to me like the only big factor in common apart from their age is the burial site, which is easy enough to explain. Two different killers both decided the marsh would be a great place to hide a body."

She hesitated, but only for a moment. "Agreed."

Charli turned her head to stare out the passenger window, her neck still as stiff as a board. She hadn't lied. She'd just neglected to share the remaining worry that gnawed at her brain like a termite in a fence post.

What if the killer hadn't yet formed a signature when he'd kidnapped Madeline? Murderers evolved just like everyone else. If the guy they were hunting had just started out on his murder spree ten years ago, he'd had plenty of time to finesse his skills and rituals since then.

Like someone hit a play button in her head, the image reel started up. The man tossing Madeline into the back of the gray creeper van. The squeal of tires as he accelerated away while Charli raced hopelessly after them.

Her fruitless attempts to nag the detective in charge to find her friend.

Weeks spent hoping and praying and avoiding the press.

That awful day when hope died. When Marcia Ferguson's devastated, choked-up voice wailed down the phone line that the police had found Madeline's body.

Why would anyone want to hurt my sweet little Madeline?

Charli relived the guilt that had crashed over her like a building crumbling in a massive earthquake, stealing her appetite and motivation to get out of bed in the mornings. Burying her for weeks in the rubble of depression and shame.

She was still reliving the past when Matthew parked the truck outside the precinct. She climbed out of the vehicle, shaking her head. Poor Mrs. Ferguson. Not only had her only daughter been stolen from her, but her daughter's best friend had been too guilt-stricken post-tragedy to check in. She'd exchanged a few words and a hug at Madeline's funeral, but after that, she hadn't followed up with Mrs. Ferguson even once. No visits. No phone calls. Not even an email or a letter.

The familiar weight of guilt attached to her spine on their walk to the precinct entrance, pressing on her until each step was harder than the last. Teenage Charli at least had the excuse of youth and immaturity. What was her excuse now?

In the past two days, Charli had spoken with two sets of grieving parents about their dead daughters. Complete strangers. Sure, that was part of the job, but the fact remained she was a grown woman now. One who was perfectly capable of setting aside her own emotions in order to do the right thing.

If Charli pooled all the time together into a single lump, she'd spent weeks, maybe even months, at Marcia Ferguson's house growing up. The woman deserved more. From the universe, and definitely from Charli.

She hadn't realized she'd stopped walking until Matthew opened the front door and waited.

When she still didn't move, his eyebrows joined above his nose. "You coming?"

The sun had almost disappeared, indicating sunset was just around the corner. Definitely well past the end of her shift. A fact that was typically meaningless during the thick of a meaty case when both Charli and Matthew were known to camp out in the office and run on a couple hours of sleep.

Charli tried to picture herself stepping inside and jumping back into the case. Her mind rebelled, refusing to focus on the other victims for longer than a heartbeat before shifting back to Marcia Ferguson. Now that the notion of calling Madeline's mom was in her brain, it refused to leave.

Still, she wasn't sure which one of them was the most surprised when she shook her head. "No, I need to go home."

The handle slipped free from Matthew's grasp. "You're going home?" He gaped at her like she'd just informed him she was ditching work to go on a last-minute vacation to Fiji.

"Yes, home. You know, that place in the Historic District where I live when I'm not at work?"

"Haha, very funny." He scratched his ear and frowned. "You sure you're okay?"

Define okay.

"I will be once I take care of this one thing." She hoped she'd be okay after that. Or at least, okayer. Not that okayer was a word, but Charli blamed the inexplicable idiosyncrasies of the English language for that over her own linguistic failings.

"Right." Matthew's face still held the dazed expression of someone who'd just regained consciousness after a bonk on the skull. "Well, good luck."

"Thanks. Text or call if you get any breaks."

"Yeah." Shaking his head, Matthew turned and reached for the door before jerking to an abrupt stop. "Hold up...are you seriously stranding me with Fields and Powell tonight? You always stay late to work cases. What happened to all that rah-rah-rah, go team, Kum-ba-freaking-yah crap from earlier?"

He scowled at her over his shoulder. Charli studied his

stormy countenance, baffled yet again by his over-the-top knee-jerk reaction to working with the FBI and GBI agents.

Perplexed and growing more annoyed by the second, Charli took a deep breath. Instead of snapping back that only one of them needed to work on their Kum-ba-freaking-yah crap—and it definitely wasn't her—Charli held her tongue. Matthew's ex had moved his only child all the way across the country. The age of the girls in their current case had to be eating at him. Just like the case hit a little too close to home for her due to her past.

They were both on edge. Understandably so.

"Yes, I'm seriously going home because I need to take care of something I've been putting off for a long time before I'll be able to focus again. By your own admission, you know I wouldn't be leaving if it wasn't important."

Their stare-off lasted only a couple of seconds before Matthew relented. "I know." He directed his scowl at the concrete near his feet. "Doesn't mean I have to like it."

Charli snorted. Some days, Matthew's decade on her seemed to grant him more than ten extra years of wisdom and maturity.

This was not one of those days.

"Remember to text with any updates."

She turned and started walking for her car before Matthew mumbled a sulky, "Fine" at her back.

And her dad thought she should date more. Please. As much as Charli loved Matthew in a platonic sense, she was more than happy to leave his messy butt at the office when she came home. And that was when her work spouse was acting like his usual, good-natured self.

The idea of dealing with an actual spouse's mood swings at home after completing a hard day's work? Charli shuddered as she shifted her car into gear. Thanks, but no thanks.

Her life was fine just the way it was. High drama at work, low drama at home.

Well, except for Priscilla. The good news was that the ornery old loveseat couldn't talk back.

Once Charli returned home, she threw her clothes in the washer with extra detergent and headed straight to the shower. It took twenty minutes of scrubbing and three hair washes until she deemed her pores and hair follicles free of rotting body stench.

After drying off, she changed into her pajamas and headed back to the kitchen, where she drank a glass of lemonade and fixed a turkey sandwich. She wiped off the countertop, sorted the mail, and put the clean dishes away. As she straightened the already tidy bookshelves and was halfway through a grocery list, she gritted her teeth and shoved the paper to the side.

Procrastinating would only increase the number of knots twisting in her stomach.

"You came home to make a call, so make the damn call already."

She poured a half glass of wine, took a sip, and headed into the living room. After settling on the couch—the good one, not the death trap just waiting for another opportunity to drop her on her ass—she pulled her phone from her pocket.

The number came to her in a heartbeat. Faster than her own. A remnant from thousands of childhood calls.

One more gulp of wine for courage later, and her fingers tapped in the numbers.

Even though it would only be delaying the inevitable, a big part of her hoped no one would answer. Like over half the American population, Mrs. Ferguson could have finally ditched the landline. Or maybe she was out to dinner or already asleep. In that case, voice mail still counted as trying, right?

Marcia Ferguson answered on the third ring. "Hello?"

The familiar soft-spoken voice hit Charli like a shock-wave, transporting her to the past like a time machine.

Mrs. Ferguson, smiling as she asked what trouble Charli and Madeline had gotten into that day.

Mrs. Ferguson, reminding them to turn the lights off at midnight if they wanted pancakes the next morning.

Mrs. Ferguson, recounting a story from her school days while Charli and Madeline giggled and tried to picture her ever being that young.

"Hello? Is someone there?"

Charli unstuck her tongue from the roof of her mouth and cleared her throat. "Um, yes, sorry. Hi, Mrs. Ferguson, it's Charli." She glanced down at her hand to find herself clutching her BFF pendant and released the gold heart. When several seconds passed with no response, Charli hurried to fill in the gap. "Charli Cross. Madeline's old friend from high school?"

"Yes, dear. I know who you are. You were at my house every other day, once upon a time. I know I must seem old to you, but I promise I haven't lost my memory yet."

Charli squeezed the phone tightly. *Off to a perfect start. Well done.* "No, it's just…been a while since I talked to you last."

She cringed. A *while*? Exactly who did she think she was fooling?

Another brief pause. "Yes, it has been. Ten years to be precise."

An awkward silence followed. Longer this time. Long enough that Charli started questioning whether or not she'd made the right choice in calling at all.

Too late now. Unless you want to add "hanging up on your

dead friend's mom" to your other transgressions, you're stuck. Deal with it.

Charli swigged another sip of wine. "Right. Well, I've been thinking about Madeline a lot lately, and you, and wanted to reach out and check in."

She braced herself. Madeline's mom had every reason to mock her feeble attempt or ask why Charli thought she needed her now after a decade had passed before hanging up.

Any of those options or worse were no more than she deserved.

"I'm glad you did. I think about you a lot too."

Tension Charli didn't even realize she was carrying in her neck and back melted away. She sagged into the couch as ten years' worth of guilt poured from her mouth. "Mrs. Ferguson, I'm so sorry that I didn't call sooner. I wanted to, so many times, but I just couldn't. I was afraid I'd only make things worse by reminding you I was still alive while Madeline wasn't and how I wasn't able to save her. I was scared you blamed me as much as I blamed myself, and I didn't want that to be my last memory of you. Not with Madeline gone." She sniffled and rubbed the tears off her cheeks. "I'm sorry, you must think I'm an awful person."

This time, the pause was mercifully short. "Oh, Charli, of course I don't think that. No one in the family blames you. How could we? You and Madeline were both only girls. The only person I blame is that monster who stole my baby away from me. If anything, I was worried that you were upset I didn't check in on you. I was the adult, after all."

Charli blinked. Never once in the past ten years had that notion ever popped into her head. That, more than anything else, helped her cling to the possibility Mrs. Ferguson was telling the truth about not being upset.

"So, we both spent the last decade thinking the other one was mad that we didn't call?"

Mrs. Ferguson sighed. "It definitely sounds that way. I think I saw this plotline once on an old episode of *Seinfeld*."

Charli giggled. She'd forgotten all about that. Mrs. Ferguson used to joke that every mishap came straight from a *Seinfeld* episode. And every single time, Madeline would roll her eyes and smile.

Madeline.

Charli's laugh turned back into a sniffle. Madeline's mom joined in. Soon, they were both crying, then laughing, then laugh-crying while they exchanged memories of Madeline.

Before long, Charli was yawning. "Excuse me."

"No need to apologize. We've been on the phone for almost an hour, and I bet you've been busy at work lately."

Charli gaped at the time on her screen. They really had been on the phone for just shy of an hour. "We have had a lot on our plate this past week."

"I'm sure. I saw on the news how they discovered those bodies in the marsh. I can only imagine how that brings up old memories for you as a detective."

Charli flinched. "You too, I'm guessing."

"Oh, yes, of course. As long as I live, I will never understand how people can do such horrific things."

Charli's impulse was to answer, "Same." Only, in order to do her job, she often had to put herself into the mind of the people performing those horrific acts.

Luckily, Mrs. Ferguson spoke again without Charli needing to drum up a socially acceptable reply. "I hope you find the person responsible soon."

"Me too." That much she could say with a clear conscience.

"Well, I'm so glad you called. Maybe we should make it a habit to check in on each other a little more often from here on out. What do you think?"

Charli smiled. "I think Madeline would like that." A

static-filled, scratchy noise filled her ears, followed by a clatter. "Mrs. Ferguson, are you still there?"

Madeline's mom was breathless when she answered. "Yes. Sorry about that, I dropped the phone. I might not think I'm old yet, but my fingers don't seem to agree. Too many years of knitting catching up on me, I guess."

Charli's heart twinged. Back in her high school days, Mrs. Ferguson had a basket of knitting with her pretty much everywhere she went. Charli had always been drawn to the vibrant colors and soft creations. "I'm sorry to hear that."

"Oh, I'm doing fine. Don't you worry about me."

After another brief exchange and promises to not let another ten years go by before speaking again, Charli hung up. As she washed out her wine glass in the kitchen sink, she hummed an old song under her breath. All that angst she'd wasted over calling. Now, she felt so much freer. Like speaking to Mrs. Ferguson had unlocked the door to Charli's invisible prison cell.

The conversation had also cleared the fog from her mind. Plus, that screaming sense of dread? Gone. Or at least, quiet for now.

Charli climbed into bed feeling more relaxed and at peace than she had since before the case had started.

Tonight, she'd get a good night's sleep. Wake up refreshed and ready to track down a predator.

23

The precinct was buzzing the next morning when Charli bounded up the stairs to the second floor. As predicted, she'd slept well. Her clear head and lighter conscience infused her body with energy.

She hurried toward their office, eager to jump in. Today was off to a good start. If she kept the momentum going—

Matthew stuck a pin in her excitement as soon as she crossed the threshold. "You see this?"

Charli clocked his glum expression and sighed. "This" clearly wasn't a new puppy photo or a funny meme. "Give me a second."

Once she put her bag in the proper place, she turned back to inspect the unhappy thing on his phone screen that he was so desperate to share. She scanned the headline of *The New York Times*.

Two Teen Girls Discovered Buried in Savannah Swamp; Third Body Yet to Be Identified.

She blew out a breath. "Okay, the national media has picked up the story. It was only a matter of time. That headline could be a lot worse."

"Oh, just wait." Matthew pulled his phone back and hit a few buttons before turning it back toward Charli's face.

Three Dead Bodies and Counting...Does Savannah Have a Serial Killer on the Loose?

Her gut clenched. "Okay, that's definitely worse." Once a journalist or reporter put the "s" word out into the universe, there was no sticking that genie back in the bottle.

"Things are going to get ugly, and fast."

Charli had no arguments for that. She clutched at the dregs of her waning optimism. "Well, I guess that means we need to get our butts in gear."

Ruth popped into their doorway. "I couldn't agree more about upshifting your asses. That means you should both be pleased to hear we'll be starting morning briefings with Agents Fields and Powell in the conference room."

Matthew cringed. "Define *pleased*."

Ruth pinned him with the full force of her murder face. Matthew held up his hands. "Just a little joke."

Charli doubted that but didn't volunteer her opinion. This reaction represented a huge improvement over yesterday's meltdown. She'd take whatever small win she could get. "When is the meeting?"

Ruth jerked her thumb over her shoulder. "Now."

Charli grabbed her pen and her case file and sprang to her feet. At this point, she didn't care if Matthew took offense to her eagerness because the truth was, this briefing was a relief.

Sure, the team approach might not always be her favorite, but she *was* a fan of the organized approach. Especially now. Fields and Powell's arrival had wrought enough chaos to last Charli the rest of the year. Next year too.

Finally, maybe they could all pull together to solve this case. Catching this killer required a coordinated effort. Each agent and detective pooling their respective strengths.

That couldn't happen when everyone was running off on their own, keeping secrets, and competing like they each represented a different country in an Olympic event.

More cooperation. Less infighting.

She hurried after Ruth for the conference room, hoping Matthew was on the same page.

When they entered the room at the back of the second floor, Fields and Powell were already seated on the far side of the scarred wooden table that had squatted in that same spot since at least the nineteen fifties.

Charli greeted them both before slipping into an empty chair near the rolling whiteboards at the front of the room. Matthew plopped into the chair behind her.

Ruth took her place standing at the head of the table, shuffling through a couple open files and withdrawing a photo. They'd already created a murder board, with Maddie's picture and information on the first whiteboard. Shana's picture smiled at them from the second.

On the third whiteboard, she picked up a black dry erase marker and printed "Jane Doe" in block letters. Ruth clipped the new photo beneath the name. It was a gory picture of the insides of the barrel.

Everyone in the room tensed as the urgency of catching their killer slapped them in the face again. How could anyone do this to teenage girls?

"Let's get right to business. As I'm sure you're all aware by now, the national press has picked up this story and run with it. That means we can expect to be under a microscope from here on out until we catch this rat bastard. We no longer have time for infighting," her sharp gaze bit into Matthew before swerving to Fields, "and can't afford to make any mistakes. The longer this drags on, the bigger the negative public perception for all of us...and since none of our organizations can afford another hit to our image when almost half the population is screaming to 'defund the police,' that means not allowing this to drag on. I'm assuming we can all agree on that point?"

Once Charli and the others all nodded or voiced their concurrence, Sergeant Morris continued. "Excellent, then let's get started." Using the marker as a pointer, she jabbed the whiteboard under Maddie's photo. "Tell me what we know about Maddie."

They went around the room, filling in the data while the sergeant wrote. Once everyone agreed they'd created an exhaustive list of the details they'd collected, they moved on to Shana and completed the exact same exercise.

By contrast, the space they filled on the Jane Doe board was only a couple of lines.

Charli took careful notes in her notebook. Even though she'd started her own lists, she wanted to make sure she hadn't missed anything. Besides, research showed writing utilized a different part of the brain than speaking or reading. Rewriting the information could potentially shake an idea loose...or better yet, trigger a new connection.

There was a reason some of the other kids at her high school had poked fun at her meticulously kept notebooks back in the day. Funny how some of those same kids had come crawling to her to copy her notes before the final exams.

Sergeant Morris studied her handiwork before pulling another blank whiteboard out from behind the others. "That's a good start. Now let's talk about what we don't know. What do we need to find out?"

Matthew's chair creaked as he leaned over to whisper in Charli's ear. "Did you know we had rolling whiteboards in this precinct?"

All too conscious of the sergeant's sharp eyes, Charli opted to respond by shaking her head.

She did jot herself a note.

Find out where Sergeant Morris hides the fancy whiteboards.

"Detective Church. Did you have something you wanted to share?"

That right there was exactly why Charli hadn't answered Matthew verbally. Ruth Morris was like that one teacher who'd always been able to bust the kids who were goofing off, even with her back turned.

"Yes." Matthew lied with admirable aplomb. "We need to figure out how the killer is picking his victims."

The sergeant jotted a quick shorthand note on the empty board.

Finding victims, how?

The marker screeched when she underlined the line twice, making Charli flinch.

"And how do we do that?" Sergeant Morris asked the question with her back to them, pen poised an inch above the board.

Charli leaned forward. "Find out where there's overlap between the victims, if any. Sports, jobs, clubs, friend circles, family, church. Anywhere they might have come into contact with each other."

"Good." Her boss scrawled another shorthand note, thankfully skipping the underlining. "Where do we start?"

Matthew chimed in first. "Missing persons reports, although I went back over those last night, and nothing stood out. No friends in common or anything like that."

"Then get a new pair of eyes. What else?"

"Read back through the parent interviews to check for any crossover."

Sergeant Morris nodded at Powell. "Right, and if you aren't sure, then schedule a follow-up interview. Next?"

"Schools." Charli spoke at the same time as Fields. She dipped her chin at the agent, indicating she had the floor.

Fields continued. "Interview their teachers from last year at both schools, talk to counselors. Any staff who might have insight. Some teachers can be pretty astute, so maybe someone will have noticed something weird, or one of the girls confided in them about something that will make a connection."

"Good."

As Morris made another notation, Charli volunteered again. "We need to map all the known locations for each victim so far and cross-reference them, plus keep plotting them as we learn more details. Could be the killer is picking the victims based on geographic location."

The sergeant straightened from the whiteboard to shuffle through the files scattered near her end of the table. She extracted a paper and unfolded it to reveal an enlarged map of Savannah. "Here you go, Detective Cross. Why don't you use the map I suspect you've already started and transfer your data points onto this one? That way, we can all benefit from your attention to detail."

Based on her boss's bland tone, Charli couldn't tell if the statement was a compliment, a gentle ribbing about not sharing, neither, or both, all rolled into one. What she did know was that everyone's eyes were on her as she withdrew said map from the folder in front of her and walked up to take the map and the container of colored pushpins that Morris offered her.

The rest continued to discuss the most urgent investigative angles while she shoved the pins into the correct spots on the map. Blue for Maddie. Red for Shana.

Midtown High, Maddie's home address, best friend's address, Kevin's home address, and his brother's apartment, all blue.

Innovation Arts and Tech High, Shana's home address, the address of the family she occasionally babysat for, the park where she'd been headed the day she'd disappeared, and the locations of where her three best friends lived, all red.

The last points she marked were the approximate locations of where their bodies were found in the marsh. To that area, she added a third green pin to mark the spot where their Jane Doe was found.

She was just stepping back to get a better perspective when her phone shrilled from her pocket.

Grimacing, she scooted to the side so the others could have an unobstructed view as she checked to see who was calling.

Her pulse picked up. "Hang on, everyone. It's Randal."

The others quieted as she answered the call. "Hey, Randal. I'm in the room with the others. Is it okay to put you on speaker?"

"Yes, but no need to bother, I'll be brief. We got an ID back on the body, confirmed by dental records. Her name is Regina Pugh."

"Regina Pugh." Every room occupant sat up straighter when Charli repeated the name.

"That's it. That's all I have for now."

"Thank you. The ID should help us out."

"I hope so. Good luck."

Charli hung up and turned to face the rest of the room. "At least we've got a name."

Morris clapped her hands together. "All right. What do we know or what can we find out about Regina Pugh, anyone?"

Matthew answered as Charli rushed back over to her chair. "That's one of the misper cases we read. Another local girl. I think Detective Piper caught the case."

"Anything else?"

Charli flipped her folder back open and pulled out the missing persons file for Regina that she'd printed out. "I have her information right here." She scanned the page. "She was fifteen when she disappeared. The mom reported her as missing," she performed a quick mental calculation, "around seven months ago now. None of the names listed on this page look familiar, but she did attend Midtown High."

Sergeant Morris used her palm to erase "Jane Doe" and wrote Regina instead. After jotting down their new victim's age and name of her school, she popped the cap back on the pen. "Is that everything for now?"

Charli didn't respond. She was too busy gaping at the picture in the file before dragging her gaze up to the photos of Maddie and Shana on the boards. Her hands flexed.

"They could all pass for sisters." Charli's revelation was barely a whisper.

Morris nodded. "That they could."

Three girls. All with long brown hair, blue eyes, skin on the pale side. Pretty.

Without exchanging a word, everyone in the room recognized the truth.

If the killer was selecting his victims from all around the area based on appearance alone, their attempts to track him would be near impossible...until he slipped up and made a mistake.

Charli curled her fingers around the table edge. They had no idea if that was the case or not. More likely, he was using multiple criteria to pick victims. Appearance, and another factor.

If that was true, then they needed to find that additional factor.

Fields and Powell stuck their heads together and whispered. Matthew shot sideways glances at Charli like he wanted to whisper too but was afraid she'd bite his head off. Sergeant Morris glared at the murder boards as if that might force them to provide answers.

Meanwhile, Charli was anxious to get to work. She slapped the file shut and stood. "Given this new information, I think our priorities for now are clear. We need to interview Regina Pugh's parents and conduct interviews at the victims' schools, giving priority to Midtown High since two of the three girls went there."

Matthew wasted no time pushing his chair back and standing. "I'm with Charli."

Across the table, Agent Fields rolled her eyes as if to say, "no shit." Powell's handsome face wasn't quite as relaxed as usual.

Sergeant Morris nodded. "Good plan. Agents Fields and Powell, any objections to tackling the parent interviews this time?"

When both of them shook their heads, she turned to Charli and Matthew. "That leaves you two heading to Midtown High. I'll call ahead and let the principal know you're on your way and that we'd appreciate their full cooperation."

"Would you mind calling over to Innovation High too? Agent Powell and I can head there once we finish talking to Regina's parents."

Charli left the room as Sergeant Morris was still agreeing with Fields. Matthew followed close on her heels.

Three girls were dead. If they hurried, maybe they could solve this case before they dug up more bodies. Or the killer struck again.

24

Matthew trailed Charli up to the sprawling, two-story brick building that fronted the entrance to Midtown High. A six-foot-tall metal fence blocked off the school from the front parking area and funneled visitors to the main entrance through the office.

An intercom to alert someone inside was affixed on the wall below a video camera, but Charli bypassed that and pulled the handle on one of the electronic double doors. The door squeaked open, making Matthew frown. All the safety features in the world wouldn't do a lick of good if they weren't utilized properly. Right now, anyone could wander into the building off the street.

Cool air enveloped Matthew when he entered the school's lobby area, helping to dry the sweat droplets that had already started forming on his forehead. Today was set to be another scorcher.

A middle-aged brunette with round glasses in blue frames and pink cheeks sat behind the long wooden counter, engrossed in whatever was on her computer monitor. She didn't even glance up when they were only a couple feet away.

He shook his head again, irritation rising in his chest. Where was the school resource officer? The Savannah-Chatham County Public School System had its own campus police department, which meant every high school usually had an off-duty or retired cop working as a security guard. Whoever was assigned to this school was slacking on the job. Probably too busy harassing some poor kid for bringing a vape to school. He made a mental note to call into their headquarters later.

The receptionist still hadn't noticed them, and part of him wanted to reach over and yank the monitor out of reach while he made her answer a series of questions. The first one was, *why go to the trouble of installing security features if you don't monitor the front door?*

With the follow-up being, *haven't you seen the news?*

Of course, those actions would likely result in the school filing a complaint and refusing to talk to them, so instead, Matthew leaned his elbows on top of the counter. "Hello."

The woman's focus didn't budge from the screen. "For early pickups, sign in on the monitor, please." Without sparing them a glance, she pointed to the right, where a tablet was propped up on a stand and attached to an external keyboard.

Charli spoke up first. "We're not here for an early pickup. We need to speak with Principal Moen."

The mention of the principal's name pulled her away from the screen. "Do you have an appointment?"

"Our boss called ahead." Matthew flashed his gold shield. Charli did the same.

"Oh, you're the two detectives from Savannah PD?" The woman made a clicking noise with her tongue. "Why didn't you say so? Hang on, let me see where he wants you to go."

Her cross voice took the cake. He turned to Charli with an incredulous expression, only to find his usually unflappable partner glaring at the woman like she wanted to jab her with a number two pencil.

Guess this case was pushing both of them close to their breaking points.

When the receptionist finished speaking into the phone, she pointed. "Principal Moen says to head straight to the conference room. Down that hallway, take a right, first doorway on your left."

"Thanks."

Matthew followed Charli through a narrow hallway with a low ceiling to a room with an open door. A thirtyish woman with bleached blonde hair wearing a fitted coral dress was already seated behind a long wooden table that took up almost the entire room. She popped to her feet when they entered.

"Hi, you must be the detectives. I'm Lainey Ashe, one of the guidance counselors. Please, come sit wherever you like."

Charli and Matthew selected chairs opposite the counselor. A closer inspection of the woman's face revealed that her eyes were pink rimmed.

He hazarded a guess. "Were you Maddie Hanley's counselor?"

"I was." She sniffled. "It's so awful what they've been reporting all over the news. Those poor girls. Do you have any leads?"

The question ended on a hopeful note. Matthew offered her a regretful smile. "I'm sorry, we aren't at liberty to discuss those kinds of details in an ongoing investigation, but I can say we're doing everything in our power to find the person responsible for these deaths and bring them to justice."

"Of course. I was just hoping for a bit of good news."

Charli's chair squeaked as she fidgeted uneasily beside

him. He didn't blame her. Every word he'd just recited made him sound like a total bureaucratic ass. Worse still, they made him feel like one. Those were the rules, though, and hey, he could take comfort in the fact that, in this particular case, the legalese mumbo jumbo was probably a lot more comforting than the truth. The last thing the concerned public wanted to hear right now was that, so far, the Savannah PD had no idea who was running around Savannah, savaging the community's teenage daughters.

Or if another girl would soon go missing.

Beneath the table, he clenched his hands into fists. "I hear you. Hopefully, we can share some good news soon."

He hadn't meant to imply that good news was imminent, but Ashe's wobbly smile told him that was exactly how she'd interpreted it.

"Sorry I'm late." A short man with a mustache and wire-rimmed glasses hurried into the room and grabbed an empty seat on the far side of Lainey. "Vincent Olsen, guidance counselor."

After Matthew and Charli introduced themselves, Lainey apologized. "I'm sorry, the others should be on their wa...oh, here they are now."

Matthew swiveled his head toward the door.

A bald man with wide shoulders paused just across the threshold while he surveyed the room's occupants. His gray button-down looked fresh from the dry cleaners, his black slacks still creased. Compared to his pristine appearance, Matthew's suit probably appeared as if he'd slept in it.

He glanced at his rumpled charcoal trousers and frowned. Come to think of it, he did seem to remember dozing off on the couch in front of the TV a few times over the past few weeks without bothering to change his clothes first. When was the last time he'd dry-cleaned this thing?

Judy used to handle all this stuff. He needed to come up with a better routine.

When the man locked eyes with Matthew, his mouth tipped up into a politician's smile. "You must be Detective Church and Detective Cross. Welcome to Midtown High. I'm Gary Moen, the principal, and skulking behind me is Vice Principal Rosa Blankenship. Ms. Blankenship, scoot on out to greet our guests."

His stop was so abrupt that the shorter woman trailing him almost ran into his back.

With effort, the vice principal squeezed herself between the wall and Principal Moen's body without managing to brush up against him. She was a short woman dressed in a no-nonsense navy blue pantsuit, with dark hair pulled back into a severe bun. Her attire matched the serious expression drawn across her face. "Nice to meet you both. Thank you for coming. Please, feel free to call me Rosa."

After introducing herself, the woman rounded the far side of the table to settle in an open spot close to the window. Even though there were several other open chairs, Principal Moen took the empty seat at the head of the table. Along with his obnoxious entrance, that told Matthew a lot about the man's views on his own importance.

The first thing Moen did after sitting down was make a big show of pulling back his sleeve to consult a silver watch. Matthew almost snorted out loud. People like that slayed him.

Yeah, we get it, buddy. Your time is very valuable.

Of course, that wasn't what he said. "Thank you all for arranging to meet us on such short notice. We appreciate your cooperation."

The principal folded his hands on the table and heaved a sigh. "Yes, well, your sergeant was rather…persuasive about the urgency of this matter." His mouth turned down at the corners, letting them know he wasn't especially happy about their boss's phone call.

Cry me a river.

"As I'm sure you know by now, three bodies belonging to teen girls have been discovered in the marshes. One of those girls was Maddie Hanley, who was a student here last year. In light of her murder, we're reopening the missing persons investigation into another one of your students, Regina Pugh."

Until Fields and Powell confirmed that they'd notified the parents, Charli and Matthew would keep Regina's identity as the third victim under wraps. No mother or father should ever have to find out their child was brutally murdered by way of a phone call from another parent or worse, from a journalist thrusting a microphone in front of their face and launching a million rapid-fire questions.

In Matthew's experience, bad news always spread faster than good.

The principal's nod was impatient. He checked his watch again. "Your sergeant told us that too."

Matthew's jaw clenched. He'd officially run out of patience. "I'm sorry, is there something more important you need to be doing right now? A student from your school was abducted and murdered. Two others were murdered in the same way. Savannah is dealing with a serial murderer who targets teen girls. Forgive me, but I'm hard-pressed to think what you have on your schedule that could be more important than that."

The other man reared back in his chair as if shocked. He quickly glanced around the table and glowered at the other staff members, none of whom would meet his eyes.

Matthew figured Moen was the kind of guy who wasn't used to having his authority challenged, and if so? Too damn bad.

When the principal turned back to Matthew, the politician's smile was paired with narrowed eyes. "I am aware of the tragic deaths, Detective. Just as I'm sure you're aware that I have more than fifteen hundred other students here to monitor and try to keep safe. We are taking this situation very seriously. In fact, I have a video meeting with the district board in a bit to hash out ways to be proactive about safety."

Charli leaned forward. "You could start by making sure your office workers keep the front door locked and check all IDs before allowing adults on campus. We had to all but bang on the counter when we arrived for your receptionist to acknowledge our existence."

A tiny snort came from Rosa Blankenship. "Sounds about right."

Moen sent her a sharp glance before straightening his perfect collar. "I'll take that under advisement. Now, what do you need from us?"

"For starters, we'll need copies of both Regina's and Maddie's schedules from last year. Also, any information on clubs or sports they were active in, names of students they hung out with, that sort of thing."

"Rosa, did you print up their schedules?" Moen barked the question at the vice principal without bothering to turn his head.

"Yes, I have them right here." Rosa opened a manila folder and plucked two papers out. She slid them across the table.

"Thank you. That's very helpful." Charli directed her gratitude toward the vice principal while Matthew grabbed the schedules. When his partner resumed her inspection of Moen, all traces of warmth fled her expression. "What about the rest?"

"Lainey and Vincent should be able to tell you about any extracurriculars. As for friends, well…" Gary Moen shook his head. "Like I mentioned before, this is a big school. I don't have time to pay attention to which students are buddying up."

Somehow, Matthew didn't find the fact that Moen was clueless regarding the social dynamics on his campus shocking at all. The man probably believed such matters were beneath him. He turned to Blankenship. "What about you?"

The vice principal gave a regretful shake of her head. "Sorry, I tend to know more about the students with disciplinary issues and maybe a few of the high achievers. The kids in the middle of the spectrum often slip under my radar."

Charli glanced up from her notepad. "Neither Maddie nor Regina had disciplinary issues?"

"Not that I can recall, no."

"What about excessive absences or tardies?"

Rosa retrieved two more pages from the manila folder and slid them over. "I checked after Principal Moen informed me of your visit. If you look, you'll see both girls had a few absences and tardies but nothing flagrant enough to raise any red flags or trigger a letter from the school district."

Lainey Ashe typed on her keyboard. "Just double-checking my records on Maddie...sorry, no clubs or school sports are showing up for her."

Matthew's attention shifted to Vincent. The man stroked his mustache before shaking his head. "I'll have to double-check back in my office, but to the best of my memory, Regina wasn't involved in anything apart from the Gay-Straight Alliance, but that's more of a social club than anything else, where students get together and chat."

Beside him, Charli's pen scratched across the paper as she took dutiful notes.

"What kinds of kids were they overall? You mentioned

they didn't have any disciplinary issues, but what about personalities? Popularity? I understand you might not know the names of their friends, but surely someone noticed whether or not they had friends at all or if they might have been bullied."

Lainey glanced around the table first before answering. "I can only speak for Maddie, but she was always respectful whenever I interacted with her. Outgoing, giggled a lot. I definitely saw her around campus with a few other girls, sometimes a boy, so I don't think she was a loner or one of the super popular ones."

"Was the boy she was with Kevin Harding?"

The counselor's eyebrows scrunched together. "Tall kid, pretty face, looks like he woke up on the wrong side of the bed? If so, then yes."

Matthew traded a glance with Charli. That definitely sounded like Kevin. "Ever get a weird vibe from the two of them?"

"Honestly? No, not at all. Not like some of the couples I've seen around."

Matthew nodded before addressing Vincent. "What about Regina?"

Vincent adjusted his glasses. "She never triggered any alarms for me. Seemed like a nice girl. Wasn't super bubbly but also wasn't one of those kids who couldn't carry on a conversation without looking like they want to curl into a ball and disappear."

Matthew frowned. The counselor made it sound like there were a lot of high school students who fell into the latter group. He took a mental note to check in with his ex and make sure Chelsea didn't end up like that. "Friends?"

"Any time I saw her, she was usually with Lauryn Hall." His shoulders drooped. "She told me she wanted to go out of state for college. Said she'd lived in Georgia her entire life so far, and she wanted to see what else there was."

Silence stretched across the room following his words. Matthew's chest ached, and he guessed they were all experiencing variations of the same depressing thought.

Regina Pugh might never have the chance to make her dream come true.

Only Matthew and Charli knew with one-hundred-percent certainty that Regina's dreams were dead.

Charli's stiff shoulders reminded him of how difficult this case must be for her. Were all her own friend's unrealized dreams spinning through her head right now?

Across the table, Lainey Ashe dabbed at her eyes with a tissue. Everyone acted like the wind had been knocked from their sails, with the exception of the principal, who merely appeared impatient.

After a few more questions, Matthew thanked them for their time. "Next, we'd like to interview their former teachers."

Gary Moen consulted his watch. "Can't this wait until after school? I'd prefer not to disrupt any classes. Gossip spreads like wildfire on high school campuses, and that's the last thing we need right now. We already have the press calling for comments on Maddie."

Matthew forced himself to take a calming breath. Not easy given what a tool this guy was. "I hear you, but I suspect the last thing you really need is another dead student. If you think the gossip will kick up from us talking to teachers…"

The other man flinched. "Right. Of course, we want you to do whatever you think you need to do, Detectives. I simply request you go about your business with the least disruption possible." Gary Moen pushed his chair back and rose. His politician's smile was back, a little worse for wear.

"Now, if you'll excuse me, I have a meeting. I'll leave you in Rosa's capable hands."

Everyone was silent as he swept from the room. Once the door snicked shut behind him, Rosa Blankenship spoke up. "Lainey, can you print up the current schedules for Maddie and Regina's teachers from the previous year? Specifically when they have open periods and lunch."

"On it." Clicking followed as the counselor tapped at the keyboard.

"Thank you." The vice principal faced Matthew. "I know Gary can come across as a little...callous sometimes, but he's not wrong about the gossip, or press. I've been fielding calls since Maddie Hanley's body was identified, including from concerned parents. The students have definitely been whispering about her death in the halls. I hope we or any other school don't end up with any more dead students."

"We're all on the same page there, and we'll do our best to avoid pulling teachers out of class. None of us are helped by creating a mass panic situation."

Vincent nodded. "Amen to that." Several seconds passed. "Do you need us for anything else?"

Matthew waved him off. "No, we should be good for now, thanks."

Chairs creaked while all three of them climbed to their feet.

"Good luck. I hope you catch him."

Vincent made the comment on his way out. Lainey murmured a similar one before leaving.

Blankenship was the last to go. "I'll be in my office if you need anything else. Don't hesitate to ask. And please, feel free to use this room as long as you need."

"Thank you."

Once the door closed behind her, Matthew blew air from his cheeks. "Well? Sense any weirdness?"

Charli scowled. "You mean, other than the fact Principal Moen seemed more worried about public relations than dead girls?"

"He was a piece of work, wasn't he?"

"That's one way of putting it. Apart from that, then no, not really."

Matthew grunted. Unfortunately, that was the same conclusion he'd drawn. "Let's take a look at these schedules and see what we find."

He put the papers side by side between them, so they could both view the details. Charli caught the overlap first. "There," she pointed at a name on Maddie's schedule before dragging her finger over to Regina's, "Blake Baldwin. They both had him for P.E."

"Blake could also be a female. We'll need to check that." As she circled the names, Matthew found another overlap. "Looks like they both had Mariela Lynch for Spanish too. Though with the lipstick and stitching, I doubt we're looking for a woman."

Charli underlined the Spanish teacher's name. "Agreed, but we should still interview everyone if possible. Not like we're swimming in leads."

She slapped the pen against her notepad, frustration that was echoed in the tension radiating down his neck. Ever since they'd landed this case, he'd been experiencing a tight pressure between his shoulder blades, one that was steadily growing with each passing hour.

He kneaded the knot in the back of his neck and sighed. When Matthew had delivered his warning to Gary Moen, he hadn't embellished the truth. Either they found this monster soon, or another girl would likely die.

Sadistic freaks like this rarely stopped killing. Not once they developed a real taste for it. This guy would keep murdering teen girls until he was caught or dead himself.

Charli checked the time on her phone. "Doesn't look like anyone has a free period right now, but this shows Baldwin's class meets on the field. That's less disruptive than popping unannounced into a classroom. We could tackle him together since he had both girls in class, then divide the list up from there?"

"Works for me."

They stood and wound their way from the building, passing outdoor basketball courts and tennis courts enclosed by chain-link fencing. The baseball fields were empty, but on the soccer field, a group of students was racing up and down the grass, dribbling soccer balls around orange pylons before turning around and heading back to pass the ball to the next person in line.

"That must be him." Charli motioned to a man close to Matthew's height who stood about ten feet back from the running students. "He looks a little older than the rest of them, and he's the only one wearing a baseball hat."

As they drew closer, Matthew's gut clenched. Not due to the man's attire—although the gray t-shirt and navy athletic shorts were a little on the tight side—but because of the group of five girls who flocked around him, giggling and nudging each other. "Appears Mr. Baldwin is pretty popular with a specific demographic."

"I noticed that."

The sun blazed down on them as they trudged across the grass. Matthew swiped the back of his hand across his forehead, wondering if maybe he'd chosen the wrong profession. Here he was, stuck outside in the heat in a suit, while the gym teacher over there got to trot around all day in his workout clothes.

He pictured spending eight hours a day trying to teach kids a little older than his daughter how to play various sports and shuddered. On second thought, he'd stick with his long sleeves. At least half of the dozen times he'd spent instructing Chelsea on how to properly throw and catch a baseball had ended in tears or screaming.

When they were within earshot, Matthew called out. "Blake Baldwin?"

The man turned, flashing them a dimpled smile. "That I am." When he removed his sunglasses to hook them on his collar, the girl closest to Matthew released a noise somewhere between a giggle and a sigh.

Not that Matthew made a habit of checking out other men, but Blake Baldwin had a pair of the clearest blue eyes he'd ever seen. Combined with the defined cheekbones and square jaw of a male model and a fit, muscular build to match, Matthew could see how some of the students gravitated toward him.

He was young too. Probably no more than five years older than most of the seniors. "We need to talk to you in private. Can you step away for a minute?"

"Sure thing." Baldwin blew his whistle in two short bursts. The students performing drills stopped in the middle of the field. "Take a water break, then line up in two rows opposite each other and start on those passing drills we did last time."

His little horde of fangirls lingered. "Go on, ladies, you too. I expect to see some hustle out there during this next exercise, okay?" He shooed them away with his hands.

The tallest blonde girl flashed him a cheeky salute. "Whatever you say, Mr. Baldwin." They all took off after that, giggling and chattering, several of them glancing over their shoulders at Baldwin as they sashayed across the field.

Baldwin turned back to Matthew with a wink. "Teen girls, what a trip. Gotta love 'em."

Charli tensed beside him. Probably thinking the exact

same thing that was blazing through Matthew's head right now.

As long as you don't love them too much.

Matthew led them a good twenty feet away from where the students milled around, distrusting Baldwin's fan club not to eavesdrop.

"So, what's up?" Baldwin's posture remained at ease as he regarded the two of them.

Charli introduced them both as detectives. Was it Matthew's imagination, or did the man tense? "We need to ask you a few questions about Maddie Hanley and Regina Pugh. Both girls took your P.E. class last year."

The smile slipped from Baldwin's face. "Oof, yeah. Maddie Hanley. I saw the news about her. Horrible thing." He braced his hands on his hips and shook his head.

"What can you tell us about Maddie? And Regina?"

A furrow formed between Baldwin's eyebrows. "Not much. Neither of them really stood out in my class, you know? They weren't especially motivated. Hang on a sec."

He cupped his hands to his mouth. "Hey, Ashley, Jayden, come on now! You can both pass better than that in your sleep. Let's see some hustle out there, people!" He clapped his hands twice before giving his focus back to Matthew. "Sorry about that. Those two are on the soccer team I coach. Some days they put in a hundred and ten percent, but others, it's like pushing two teen-sized boulders uphill."

Baldwin gave a good-natured chuckle at his own joke. Neither Matthew nor Charli cracked a smile.

Matthew jingled the change in his pockets. He didn't like the idea of this guy touching teen girls, whether it was to push them up a hill or otherwise.

"What about their friends? You ever see them hanging out with any of your other students around campus, or each other?" Charli held her pen at the ready.

Baldwin shrugged. "Not really. I don't really pay much attention to who's hanging out with who, know what I mean?" He cupped his hands again and yelled. "Hey, Brooke, what was that? Come on, now! Pay attention to where your teammate is!"

Was this man delaying their questions on purpose?

Matthew took a deep breath, reminding himself that getting in this guy's face wouldn't promote cooperation. "Ever hear them or any other girls in your classes talk about feeling like they were being watched or say anything that in retrospect might have been a red flag?"

The P.E. teacher pulled the hat off his head and ran his fingers through his thick, wavy hair, reminding Matthew of the spot on the back of his own head that was steadily growing thinner with every passing year.

After appearing to consider the question for several seconds, the teacher finally shook his head. "No, man, can't say that I did. I make it a point to not overhear what my students are saying, though. Enough to make your ears burn."

Baldwin accompanied that statement with another wink, making Matthew's hackles rise. The longer he was around this guy, the less he liked him. He kept picturing Chelsea as one of the girls who'd flocked to Baldwin like sheep to a shepherd. The image soured his stomach.

Charli handed the teacher a business card. "Thanks for your time. If you think of anything else, call us immediately."

He glanced at the card before tucking it into his pocket. "Will do. See ya 'round." After giving them a salute very similar to the one from his student earlier, Baldwin jogged back over to the field.

Matthew tracked the teacher's retreat before pulling out his cell phone and dialing Janice. "Hey, do me a favor and get someone to get me a background check on Blake Baldwin, a P.E. teacher and soccer coach at Midtown High."

"You think he's a suspect?"

When Baldwin reached his class, he was immediately swarmed by several students. All girls.

"Not yet, but there's something off about him. Worth looking into."

Charli poked his arm. "Ask her to do a background check on the other male teachers while she's at it."

Matthew gave her a thumbs-up. "You hear that?"

"I heard." Janice sounded put out. "I love it when your partner acts like I'm her personal assistant."

Matthew knew better than to comment on that. "Thanks, see you back at the precinct."

When he hung up, Charli was waiting. "What do you think is off about Baldwin? Apart from all the female attention?"

Matthew didn't have a straightforward answer. The one he did have was guaranteed to make his partner roll her eyes, but he went ahead and said it anyway. "Nothing concrete, but I've got a gut feeling about him. Come on, let's talk to the rest of the teachers."

He turned toward the campus in time to miss any eye rolls aimed at his back, but she managed to convey her skepticism with a loud snort anyway.

25

Charli parted ways with Matthew in the corridor, with her taking on Maddie's teachers and her partner taking Regina's. She was pretty sure his boxers were still in a wad over Baldwin, but she trusted him to tackle the rest of the teachers on the list with an open mind.

The P.E. teacher had come off as just this side of sleazy, but no more than many of the uber attractive men Charli had run-ins with over the years. When you had an ego the size of a small planet, you tended to believe any person was available to you with a snap of your fingers.

Could she see Baldwin having consent issues? Absolutely. Serial killer tendencies with a side of sexual sadism? She wasn't nearly so sure.

When she reached a beige door with the number twenty-nine, she stopped and gave three sharp raps. She pulled it open without waiting for a response. "Dwayne Potter?"

The brown-haired man sitting behind the desk held up a finger. "One second." He finished scribbling something across the top of a paper before setting the pen down. "Sorry, I'm in the middle of grading tests. What can I do for you?"

"Charli Cross, detective with Savannah PD. My partner and I are on campus today interviewing teachers in a murder and missing persons investigation. Do you have a few minutes to talk to me about Maddie Hanley?"

"Of course, of course. Here, let me get you a chair." He leapt to his feet and grabbed an empty chair from a student desk.

"Thanks." Charli performed a quick scan of the classroom on her way to the seat. Dwayne Potter appeared to favor sharing quotes from famous authors and historical figures. Just like when Charli was back in high school, most of them were from men.

Gandhi. Churchill. Calvin. Mandela.

"What can you tell me about Maddie?"

Potter's shoulders lifted and lowered as he heaved a heavy sigh. "Not much, I'm afraid. Maddie was an average student, mostly B's and C's that ended in C's on her report card because of missing assignments here and there. She didn't participate much in class discussions."

"Did she ever get into trouble in your class?"

Potter shook his head. "Not really."

"Does 'not really' mean that she sometimes did get into trouble, but nothing major?"

"Nice catch." Potter's patronizing smile raised her hackles. If he patted her on the head and said "good girl," this interview might head south, quick. "I occasionally had to reprimand her and a couple of the boys in class for whispering during lecture. These kids somehow believe sitting in the back row renders them both invisible and inaudible to human ears. You know how it is."

Potter smiled, and Charli smiled back even though, on a personal level, she had no idea. She'd always done her best to pay attention in class and chose the front row whenever possible like the total nerd she was. "So, Maddie was a little bit of a flirt?"

The history teacher dropped his gaze to the desk, as if hesitant to share.

Charli was pretty sure she knew why. This type of reaction wasn't uncommon when conducting interviews about murder victims. "I know it can be difficult to feel like you're criticizing the dead, but I promise you aren't betraying Maddie by telling me these types of details. If anything, you're helping us get one step closer to finding the person who killed her."

Dwayne Potter nodded. "Sorry, of course you're right. It just feels wrong somehow." He cleared his throat. "Anyway, yes, 'flirt' would be a good way to describe her. Then again, you could use that word to describe several girls in my classes."

"What about the boys you mentioned? Did you ever get a sense they got tired or upset by her flirting, maybe wanted something more?"

The history teacher lifted his eyebrows. "We are talking high school boys here, right? Their hormones are running so wild at this age, they want more just by looking at a stick figure drawing of a girl. That's why I've always been a fan of school uniforms, if only to help prevent students from being distracted."

The argument was common enough in Georgia that Charli could perform a loose translation: girls should cover up at school so as not to tempt and distract poor, innocent boys with sinful horrors like bare shoulders or too much thigh.

She bit her tongue. *Let it go, so what if he's a little sexist? You have more important items on your agenda.* "Let me rephrase. Did anything about these boys' interactions strike you as particularly odd or charged in some way?"

He scratched his chin. "Not really, no. But now that I'm thinking about it, I did notice them lag behind a few times after the bell rang. Almost like they were waiting so they could follow her out." He lifted his palms. "Then again, maybe they were good friends outside the classroom."

Not much meat to that story. Still, Charli liked to check every possibility off her list. "Do you happen to remember their names?"

"I do, but only because those two did manage to get into a fair amount of trouble. I probably had to yell their names at least once or twice a week."

Charli wrote down the names, making a note to review their social media accounts to check for red flags.

None of her remaining questions revealed anything new or noteworthy, so she thanked Potter for his time, handed him a card, and headed for the door.

"I hope you get some answers soon."

"Thanks, me too."

Once the door shut behind her, Charli checked the next name on her list. Willa Mayfield, Maddie's geometry teacher.

"Let's hope you or one of her other teachers has something more useful to share than Potter did."

As she neared the end of her final interview, Charli realized her earlier hope wouldn't come to fruition.

"Is there anything else you can tell me about Maddie?" She faced Mike Drummond across a utilitarian metal desk that was a dead ringer for the ones used by teachers back when she attended high school.

While the English teacher stroked his neatly trimmed beard and pondered her question, Charli's gaze wandered one last time over the boxy classroom. His desk was that kind of haphazard tidy people often associated with teachers: papers and books everywhere but stacked into piles. A silver picture frame faced away from her, so she could only see the little black kickstand rather than the photo inside. A computer and a mug with the school logo were the other two items on top.

Like Potter, Drummond's walls were crammed with quotes. Unlike Potter, witticisms from Shakespeare and Mark Twain competed for space with words by Toni Morrison and Maya Angelou, and the black bookshelves at the back of the room held a huge variety of titles. Everything from the quoted authors to Gillian Flynn to a whole row of books Charli recognized as young adult.

"I let my students pick the books they want to read. That's why there's such a variety. Studies have shown teens are more likely to do the reading instead of looking up a summary in SparkNotes if they get to pick books they're actually interested in."

"Schools needed a study to tell them that?"

Drummond's lips twitched. "Apparently so."

"Huh." That probably explained why she'd ended up reading nothing from the current century during her high school years. So many stories written by middle-aged men, most of which had put Charli to sleep. "Did you remember anything else?"

"Not off the top of my head, sorry."

Charli held back a sigh as she stared at the mostly blank notebook page. So far, none of the teachers or staff had given her much. Their stories about Maddie fit in with what Blake Baldwin had shared. Maddie didn't stand out. She wasn't a star student or a failing one but didn't seem especially motivated to be in class.

The words teachers had used to describe Maddie ranged from "funny" and "sweet" to "nice girl, but more interested in boys than homework," and Charli's personal favorite, "just biding her time until she graduated and went to work at a fast-food chain."

With teachers like that last one, it was no wonder Maddie hadn't put in more effort.

She smoothed her jacket. "That's okay. I appreciate your time."

Mike Drummond rose and offered his hand to shake, but Charli scooted the chair away. "Sorry, fighting off a cold."

She waited until she rounded the desk to hand him her card. "Call me if you think of anything else." Her eyes found the framed photo near his monitor that she'd been eying from the rear throughout their interview, and her pulse gave a little leap.

The picture showed Drummond and a second man grinning side-by-side on a boat.

The boat wasn't what piqued Charli's interest, though. It was the pair of large, gaping-mouthed silverfish they both held. Or, more specifically, the thin, white line the fish dangled from. "You get a chance to do much fishing during the school year?"

Drummond followed her line of sight. "Not as much as I'd like, but I try. One of the things that keeps me sane enough to work. Do you fish?"

"No, but my brother, Sebastian, is visiting for a while and was talking about trying to sneak some fishing in." Charli didn't have a brother, but if she did, Sebastian seemed like a nice name. Law enforcement were allowed to lie, and Charli usually only did so in order to relate to the person she was talking to. "Where do you go? Do you have your own boat or rent?"

He named a nearby lake. "My friend and I own a boat, but they rent them at the marina too."

Charli jotted the information down. "Thank you, I'll pass that on."

When she left, her head was pounding while her shirt was plastered to her back. The air-conditioning hadn't been performing optimally, turning the low-ceilinged room into an oven.

She'd held onto the weak hope that one of the female teachers might have caught something her male peers missed, but she was disappointed. The only new detail had come from Willa Mayfield, who had wrinkled her nose and claimed both Maddie and Regina liked to push the dress code boundaries and dress a little provocatively upon occasion.

Given the geometry teacher's modest attire—a loose floral-print dress with a high neckline and calf-length hem, paired with old-school, low-heeled pumps—Charli didn't put much stock in the comment. Her last interview subject, Mariela Lynch, confirmed as much when she repeated the remark without naming names.

The pretty Spanish teacher had snorted. "If by provocative they meant that Maddie dressed like eighty percent of the teen girls in the country, then sure." She'd tucked a strand of light brown hair behind her ear before shaking her head. "I swear, every time I think we're finally emerging into modern times, I hear something like this and weep."

All in all, none of the interviews turned up much. None of the teachers had been able to recall any overlap between Maddie and Regina or remember anything troubling.

The only details of interest remained the fishing photo on Drummond's desk and the boys from Potter's classroom, but all of that was flimsier than a straw house in a tornado. Matthew was right. Baldwin was the most interesting find by far. That still didn't make him a suspect.

She followed the corridor back to the main office, texting

Matthew along the way to see if he'd finished yet. Hopefully, her partner's interviews had yielded better results.

Her phone pinged.

Done. Meet me at the truck.

When she passed by the front desk to reach the parking lot, the receptionist made a point of glancing up this time.

Good. If nothing else, maybe at least the staff would be more vigilant going forward.

Country music blasted from Matthew's pickup truck when she opened the passenger door. He dialed back the volume as she climbed in. "Well?"

"Not much." She quickly filled him in on Drummond, the boys in Potter's class, and the geometry teacher's comment about the way the girls dressed. "You?"

"Maybe. I decided to do a little poking around about Baldwin, and two of Regina's teachers definitely had a reaction when his name came up. One of them clammed up, but Regina's English teacher said there'd been some talk when he first arrived a year ago. I couldn't get any more out of her, though, so I hit up the guidance counselor again afterward."

"And?"

"After a little prodding, she lowered her voice and admitted she'd heard when he'd applied for the job there might have been some weirdness with his old school, some kind of baggage, but the principal was tight-lipped, and they'd been desperate at the time because the last P.E. teacher left without giving notice."

Charli drew her eyebrows together. "Surely if the baggage was anything that bad, the school wouldn't have given him a good reference?"

"You know how it is. No one wants a scandal or the responsibility...they just want to make the trouble someone else's problem." When her expression remained skeptical, Matthew sighed. "Think about how often police departments let bad cops resign instead of forcing them out and reporting them?"

Much as it pained her to admit it, Matthew had a point. She could name two cops off the top of her head who'd left under those exact circumstances. The practice was a frustrating holdover from the old boys' network of the past. One Charli personally hated, since the practice often ended up biting the new precinct—and the public—in the ass. Bad cops didn't magically change their stripes just because they moved to a new town. They took their crappy tactics with them.

If that happened with police, it probably happened in other professions. "Did she say anything else?"

"No, the principal walked by then, and she changed the subject. She wouldn't say anything else after that."

Charli considered that information while Matthew drove them back to the precinct. There could be something to his line of thought. Principal Moen definitely came across as the type of administrator who'd go to great lengths to avoid a scandal...but still. Even if Baldwin had committed some disciplinary violation, that didn't make him a killer.

The secrecy around his hiring did make him worthy of follow-up, though.

Once inside the precinct, she and Matthew split up. He headed straight to Janice to see if there was any progress on the background checks while Charli retreated to their office to do a little digging on the two boys Potter had mentioned.

She found one of them on Instagram. His photos and captions didn't sound any alarm bells. None featured any of the dead girls. The other boy didn't appear to have a social media presence. She copied their names to a blank page, adding the names of the other students mentioned by teachers as being friendly with the victims. Jayden, Ashley, and Brooke from Baldwin's P.E. class went on the list too. Tomorrow, they could start interviewing them.

Next, she hunted down the phone number for the marina Drummond mentioned. Half an hour later, she'd learned Mike Drummond owned a small speedboat with no below-deck storage. The manager she spoke with said the teacher was there a lot over the summer and more sporadically during the spring, but he'd never seen him with any girls, only another man.

Frustrated, she headed back to the conference room where they'd all met that morning.

She wondered if Fields and Powell had made more progress. "Not like they could have done much worse," she muttered.

The rolling whiteboards were still spread out in front of the table. Charli reviewed the information on each victim again before turning to study the map.

A few fruitless minutes later, she pulled out her phone and typed in the information she knew about Blake Baldwin. She found the right one in under a minute. His home address was a little trickier.

After coming up empty-handed, she shot off a text to Matthew: *Shoot me Baldwin's address when you get it.*

Another two minutes passed before he sent her a reply with the information.

She added the pin to the map before stepping back and folding her arms. Baldwin lived less than half a mile from the Hanleys, but that put him on the opposite side of town from the Feists.

When nothing else popped out at her, she scooted farther away, closed her eyes, and opened them again.

Nope. Still nothing. No overlap, no obvious patterns. Unless the fact that the three pins representing the victims' addresses covered the west, north, and east sides of Savannah counted as a pattern. Could that be some kind of code, suggesting the killer's next victim would come from the south? Or was she so desperate to find a clue that she was making things up? Because she was definitely desperate.

Groaning, Charli clasped her hands together behind her neck. "And you give Matthew a hard time for his hunches. Next thing you know, you'll be reading tea leaves to find the murderer, or better yet, calling in a psychic."

Her gaze was drawn back to the tight cluster of three pins near the Vernon River.

The marsh. He'd buried all three victims within three-quarters of a mile of each other in the same stretch of wetlands. Could there be something about the crime scene they'd all missed?

If she stood here twiddling her thumbs while staring at the map any longer, she might be driven to do something drastic. Like, say, google crystal balls.

She turned her back on the whiteboards and headed for the door. Hopefully, Artie down in Cyber was having better luck than her.

A SHORT TIME LATER, Charli trudged back up the stairs. She'd sat in Artie's little command station for the better part of the past hour, scouring Shana's photos and in-app messages. The most exciting thing she'd found was a picture of a cat wearing a pair of hot pink sunglasses. Nothing had appeared off. Although, she wasn't confident she'd even recognize "off" if she stumbled across it, short of a man holding up a tube of lipstick with a big arrow pointing to his face. There just wasn't enough to go on.

Her mind wandered back to the marsh, and from there, the construction site. If their killer wanted a viewing point for all the hoopla he'd instigated, the dirt lot was perfect.

On her way up the stairs, she checked her phone. No

voice mails yet from the foreman. She typed up a quick reminder to call back tomorrow for that list of employee names and background checks. Although, their killer was smart. Too smart, maybe, to attach himself to the site by name.

That didn't mean he couldn't be sneaking in after hours.

She dialed down to the front desk. "Hey, it's Cross. I need someone to push through the paperwork to get security cameras installed at a construction site ASAP. It's for the Marsh Killer case." Matthew jogged up as she was rattling off the address, his cheeks flushed. Charli wasn't sure if it was from exhaustion or because he hated when the press gave serial killers such cringy names. "Notify me as soon as you get the approval. Oh, and can we send a patrol car by after hours? Tell them to take down the license and vehicle information of anyone they find and call me immediately."

Charli hung up and gave him her full attention. "What's up? Background checks show something?" She motioned to the files in his hand.

He lifted his other hand, showing her his phone. "I've got Lainey Ashe on the line." He closed the door. "She wants to talk to us in private about Baldwin."

26

I slouched behind the wheel in the dark, keeping my eyes trained on the stretch of sidewalk ahead while Nat King Cole crooned from the speakers. A streetlight provided soft illumination of the area beyond where I'd parked by the curb, in front of a house with a "For Rent" sign poking out from a weedy patch of dirt in the front yard.

The dashboard clock showed the time as a little after eight o'clock. I'd been sitting here waiting since before the sun had started to set a good fifteen minutes ago. What little light lingered in the sky was rapidly fading. Within the next ten minutes, this little neighborhood would be in full twilight, something I'd noted during my previous visits over the last few weeks, just like I'd charted all the other pertinent details. If I'd learned one thing from teaching, it was the importance of planning ahead.

I knew her route home from the pizza parlor to her house well enough to walk it blindfolded in my sleep, along with the time I could expect her to appear within each particular segment.

Without fail, she left work promptly after her shift finished at seven forty-five, always setting foot out the door no later than eight. Her walking speed varied depending on whether or not she was reading something on her phone, chatting with a friend, or listening to music, but not by much. On each occasion I'd timed her, she'd arrived home within sixteen to twenty-one minutes. The only outlier was the time she'd jogged part of the way, when she'd completed the route in fewer than fourteen minutes.

I'd planned for this occasion with meticulous care. I was confident I had all the details down. The biggest lingering uncertainty in my head was one I couldn't control...what if she got a ride home tonight?

The concern didn't come from left field. My girls were still the leading news story across all the stations. Good thing I was packing up and leaving soon. Even if I'd been able to stay in Savannah, hunting would have become so much more difficult. Too many frightened parents concerned about their darling daughters' safety after a lifetime of neglect.

"And where were you when they needed you most, to teach them about moral safety, hmm?"

I checked the clock again. Ten after eight. Five more minutes before I could expect her to strut down the sidewalk like a little tart in those skintight black pants she wore to work with her fitted red uniform tee.

I shifted my body in the seat as excitement drummed through my veins. She would show up. I had faith. After all, if the trained peace officer who'd come out to the school today couldn't figure out who I was or stop me, that had to be a sign that my cause was just.

I'd faced the officer as politely as could be, answering all those questions while concentrating on not getting a hard-on that would be difficult to explain away. Certain doom had been only a few feet away from me and had been none the wiser. The thrill of deceiving them was intoxicating, like guzzling a glass of champagne on a hot day.

The only experience that surpassed that one in terms of dizzying, walking-near-the-edge-of-a-cliff delight was when I captured and repurified one of my girls.

My pulse ratcheted up in anticipation. This would be my last girl in Savannah, so I needed to make it special. Back at my old house on the farm, I'd stashed all of them in the cellar. Sadly, my house here didn't have a cellar to speak of... but it did have an attic. At first, I was hesitant to use it for those purposes because of the heat, but the high temperatures had turned into one of my favorite parts.

So much sweet, delicious sweat. I shivered, remembering how damp and perfect Maddie's skin had been. Glistening and pure, like her body was cleansing itself under my watch.

"But I messed up a little with you, didn't I? Too much tranquilizer." I sighed. Tragic, really. Poor Maddie had never fully recovered from her dose, so she'd never had a true opportunity to repent. I checked the syringe in the center console for the tenth time.

For my last girl in Savannah, I was going out on a limb. I'd halved the tranquilizer dosage from what I'd used before. That way, she'd still have some fight left in her. Hopefully, a lot of fight. I'd even decided to go a step beyond and zip tie her hands in front of her when I locked her in the attic rather than behind her like the others. That ought to make her extra feisty.

Even the mere thought of the fear that would etch itself across her face while she attempted to shove me away sent blood surging between my legs.

Up ahead, movement grabbed my attention, but it was only an older woman heading out from her house and onto the sidewalk. I ducked low in the seat when she started in my direction, heartbeat accelerating. The tinted windows should do their job, unless she was one of those busybodies who took it upon themselves to snoop through every unknown vehicle in the neighborhood.

Peeking through the openings in the steering wheel, I waited as she crossed the street and cut through the alley on the opposite side. The stranglehold on my lungs released when she disappeared from sight.

Eight-sixteen gleamed from my dashboard. Two minutes behind her usual schedule. Disappointment tunneled through my heart.

Maybe my luck had run out, and she really had gotten a ride tonight.

"I'll give you five more minutes." Any more than that and I'd be forced to abandon ship. Straying too far from the plan was too dangerous at this juncture.

At eight-seventeen, she appeared beneath the streetlight. My pulse gave a little jump for joy.

Even in the dim light, the way she carried herself and her lithe, freshly bloomed body reminded me of my daughter. Just like she had that very first day I'd laid eyes on her back in May.

Only selecting girls from my school would have been too obvious, so I'd had to branch out. Luckily, my side gig also put me into contact with plenty of other girls who were ripe for the picking.

A car cruised down the street, headlights forming an eerie glow on the dark road. The girl's eyes tracked the car until it disappeared before continuing toward me.

My breathing quickened. My fingertips tingled. Her vigilance as she drew closer only made her more enticing.

"You'll be my last hoorah in this town...we'll have to make sure it's a memorable one."

JENNY WITHERS WAITED until the car disappeared down the street behind her before walking down the sidewalk again. She was probably being silly, letting her mom's warnings get to her. Yeah, they'd found three dead girls in the marsh, but that was, what? Three girls out of however many tens of thousands who lived in this city?

The reassurance allowed her to relax a little. In less than ten minutes, she'd be home. Her mom worked until eight forty-five at the grocery store, or else she would have picked her up. She'd tried to get Jenny to wait at the pizza place once her shift ended, but no, thank you.

By the end of her workday, she smelled like a salami stick. She couldn't wait to get home and shower.

In the past, she'd rarely worried about anyone bothering her on the walk home. Tonight, though, the street appeared darker somehow. More foreboding.

Or maybe she was just a big wimp, like her friends said. She was the only one in their group who refused to watch horror movies.

In the distance, a car alarm pierced the night. She jumped, her head whipping in that direction. The shrill ringing stopped a few seconds later, making her laugh at her nerves.

See? Not a boogeyman. Just some idiot accidentally setting off their own alarm.

Officially spooked, she picked up her pace. For the next few weeks, she'd take her mom up on that offer of a ride. No big deal. She could sit in the back and do her homework while she waited. She'd survive an extra hour of smelling like spicy pork.

Homework, ugh. After her shower, she had a buttload left to do. That's what she got for signing up for honors and AP classes this year. Getting out of work on time tonight had been tougher than usual. Her boss had pulled her aside and made her go over the weekend's schedule for the third time and all but sign her name in blood that she'd show up for the Saturday afternoon-evening shift.

Once she promised—also for the third time—that she definitely wouldn't flake at the last second to attend the first high school football game, he'd finally let her leave.

Football was fine and all, but she much preferred the tips she'd earn from the packed restaurant before and after the game. She already had a little more than a thousand dollars saved. Pretty soon, she'd be able to afford a cheap car. Besides, the after parties were much more fun than sitting in the bleachers sweating her butt off. She'd leave work in plenty of time to hit one of those.

She hurried on, jumping again when the driver's side door of the SUV she was passing creaked open. She veered over to avoid being hit, shaking her head.

Idiot. It's just someone coming home from work and taking their time getting out.

It wasn't until a man climbed out that she could pinpoint the reason for the hairs on her arms lifting.

The SUV was parked the wrong way along the curb.

She registered the dark bandana covering the lower half of the man's face an instant before he lunged. The next events occurred so fast she could barely distinguish them from each other. Strong fingers clenching around her upper arm. A sharp pinch in her shoulder. A gloved hand clamping over her mouth as he wrestled her forward.

On the few occasions Jenny had ever pictured this moment in her head, she'd always reacted instantly, her reflexes as quick as a cat's so she could catch the assailant off guard and escape.

In reality, the man was the one with lightning-quick reflexes. Jenny was only just comprehending what was happening when he yanked open the door behind the driver's seat and shoved her inside.

Her adrenaline was kicking in when he slammed the door shut and hopped into the driver's seat. She lunged for the door, reaching the handle an instant after the click.

It took her several fruitless pulls to understand what the click represented.

The child locks had engaged.

Her heart beat like a sledgehammer, hard and furious beneath her ribs. Giving up on the door, she punched the button for the window.

Also locked.

Panic crawled inside her. She started to scream, and a man screamed into the SUV at the same time, accompanied by the high-pitched wail of an electric guitar. The music was so loud that her first reaction was to throw her hands over her ears and cringe.

You don't have time for this. Get out of here, now!

Terror needled her skin and drove her forward. She beat her fist into the back of the man's skull, pulling his hair. A black object appeared in the driver's right hand, stopping her short.

A gun.

She froze, her eyes glued to the weapon. A metallic flavor filled her mouth. Her first wild thought was she could somehow taste the gun until the pain registered.

Not metal, blood. She'd bitten her tongue.

The man turned down the volume enough so she could hear him over the music. "Settle down, please, or I'll have no choice but to put this to use...and we both know you'd be horrified if I ruined your pretty skin by putting a bullet in it, wouldn't you? Now, get back in your seat, and put your seat belt on. You can never be too safe."

Goose bumps exploded across her skin at his soft laugh,

but she did as she was told, her eyes glued to the gun. Her body felt funny, like the time she'd had two beers on an empty stomach over the summer. Almost like she was floating.

It took her clumsy fingers five tries before the buckle latched. Her head swung toward the window, and with a start, she realized the car was moving. When had that happened? Where were they? "What did you give me?"

She wasn't really expecting an answer, so she was surprised when he replied. "Don't worry, just a little something to take the edge off and keep you calm. I decided we'd be more productive if I gave you less than poor Maddie. You can thank me later."

Maddie. Why did that name sound so familiar?

The reporter's voice from that news channel her mom was glued to last night echoed through her head.

...the body has been identified as belonging to Madeline Hanley, known as Maddie to her friends and family...

Terror threatened to choke her. She had to concentrate on breathing to suck down enough air.

Gun or no gun, she couldn't just sit here and await her fate. She'd end up in a hole in the marsh.

She kept her eyes locked on the driver, waiting for an opening while digging her nails into her palms. Harder and harder, gritting her teeth against the pain.

When she couldn't take any more without crying out, she opened her hands and rubbed her right thumb against her left palm. It came away wet.

Quietly, she wiped the blood on the car seat, pushing hard to smear it in good.

Her mom liked to watch *CSI* to relax when she wasn't at the restaurant. One of the few times Jenny had joined her, a girl had used this trick to help the cops find the killer.

She wished she could remember if they'd found her alive or dead.

Her mind drifted. When her floating head cleared again, the car was still going. Had they been on the road for seconds? Minutes? Hours?

The gun. She should try to wrestle the gun away. If she could just jump out, she could run for help...

A glance out the darkened window showed her a street she didn't recognize. Still. She could knock on someone's door. Surely they'd let her in. Help her call nine-one-one.

Her boneless fingers were grappling with the buckle when the SUV turned off the street. She got a quick impression of a long, deserted driveway and a two-story house with a triangular roof like a gingerbread house.

Am I Hansel or Gretel?

She jerked her head to keep herself alert and clawed at the metal.

Faster. Hurry, or it will be too late.

The engine shut off. The window showed they were inside a building. A garage. When had that happened?

She tensed her legs the best she could as the world careened before her eyes. When the lock clicked open, she wrestled with the handle and lurched outside. Her feet hit the ground hard and wobbled, but she managed not to fall. She staggered two steps away before his hand tangled in her hair, and her scalp screamed in pain.

Fight. Run. Do something.

Jenny struggled against the man's grip, but he yanked her hair until tears sprang to her eyes.

"That's it, fight. It makes the repurification process so much more delicious."

His hot breath filled her ear, making her shudder. She started to scream, but he slapped something sticky over her mouth.

Next, he bound her wrists together as easily as if she were a plastic doll.

As he dragged her into the house, she began to pray.

Please, someone, help me. Give me the strength to stay alive.

27

Sergeant Morris ambushed Charli and Matthew in their office just as they were finishing their call with Lainey Ashe.

"Good, you're both here. Fields and Powell just got back twenty minutes ago. They're waiting in the conference room."

The groan slipped out before Matthew could prevent it, earning him a sharp look. "Sorry, but isn't one task force meeting a day enough?"

Morris crossed her arms. "I don't know, Detective. Are you minutes away from making an arrest?"

"Well, I have a potential lead I'm going to check out..." At her arched eyebrow, he gave up, shoving his hands into his pockets. "Fine. Can we make it quick, though? I really do need to get on the road."

"And who's the one holding us up at the moment?"

With that quip, Morris executed a neat about-face and headed for the stairs. When they reached the conference room, Fields and Powell were waiting. Matthew slumped into an open seat. He could already tell by the FBI and GBI agents' subdued energy and tight-lipped faces they hadn't experienced any more success with their investigation than he and Charli. This whole exercise was a waste of time.

Charli brought the others up to speed on their day, finishing with what they'd just learned from the guidance counselor. "Lainey Ashe said that Blake Baldwin left his old school abruptly because of a scandal involving one of the students there. Specifically, that he was having sex with a student."

Matthew growled under his breath. "And apparently, the principal knew about this rumor and hired the bastard anyway."

Sergeant Morris moved over to the murder board and wrote "Blake Baldwin" in block letters. "What's the principal's name?"

Charli answered first. "Gary Moen."

Morris wrote that name down next. When Matthew frowned, Morris tapped the words with her marker. "If the principal was aware that he was hiring a predator, he could be one too."

Made sense.

Evelyn Fields picked up the conversation, sharing the results of her and Powell's day. Her lips were pursed as she consulted her notebook. "Regina Pugh's mom was a bust. She works long hours at the pancake house and didn't seem to know much about who her daughter hung out with or where she was at any given time. The dad lives out in California, divorced. We contacted the local PD, and they're going to send someone out to interview him, but I think that's a dead end."

Matthew checked the time. Almost fifteen minutes gone. He wished he had a fast-forward button to speed Fields up. She appeared to enjoy hearing herself talk.

She blathered on about searching Pugh's room next. No

laptop, but they'd taken a cheap tablet and left it with tech. They hadn't found anything else of interest.

"One of the male teachers at Shana's charter school was arrested for domestic assault six years ago, but the charges were dropped. We plan to dig deeper into that. No flags on the rest, but we'll keep looking." Fields stopped and closed the notebook. "That's about it for now."

Finally. Matthew grabbed the table, preparing to vault out of his chair the second Morris dismissed them. "Can I head out now, Boss? I want to drive up to Statesboro, see if I can't find someone from Baldwin's old school willing to talk."

"Hold up a second." Morris tapped a single finger on the table as she studied him. His hair rose. He didn't like that thoughtful expression on her face, like the gears in her devious mind were whirling. "Agent Fields? Do you have plans this evening?"

Fields picked up her notebook and waved it in the air. "If by plans you mean...am I going to hunker down here and pore over my notes and the boards, then yes, definitely. As for normal people plans? No."

Ruth Morris's lips curved into a tight smile, and Matthew braced himself. *Here we go.* "Instead of doing that, I think you should partner up with Detective Church while he pays his house visits in Statesboro. I'm not inclined for one of my detectives to head that far out of our jurisdiction on this case solo, and it might be good for the two of you to work together."

Morris ended with the satisfied smirk of a woman who understood she'd backed the people around her into an inescapable corner. Matthew's throat worked, but nothing came out. What was there to say?

He shot his boss a sour glance, wondering how much she knew about his and Fields's history. Was this her misguided attempt at therapy-by-fire? Or was she pissed at him for some reason and getting her revenge by pairing him up with an FBI agent?

His only consolation prize was that Fields was in the same boat. If she refused, she'd come across as petulant and self-absorbed. A red flush crawled up her throat, and her hands gripped the notebook like she wanted to chuck it at someone.

"Well?" Morris prodded. "Will that work?"

Go on, do it, his mind urged. *Tell her no.*

Almost like she could read his mind, Fields locked eyes with him. Her nostrils flared. "Yes, that works."

Matthew issued a silent groan while Sergeant Morris clapped her hands together twice. "Excellent. I'll leave you all to it."

THE FIRST PART of the car ride passed without Matthew uttering more than a few monosyllabic words in response to Fields's queries. After five minutes of that treatment, she'd huffed an exasperated sigh and switched on the radio.

A country station. The last forty minutes had passed in comparative bliss, with Fields focusing on the road and Matthew focusing on Tim McGraw and Willie Nelson.

When the GPS instructed them to exit the interstate in two miles, the FBI agent finally turned the radio off. "Are you really going to pout for this entire trip?"

Matthew settled back into the seat and closed his eyes.

"Nice. Very mature." The *click-click-click* of the turn signal filled the car. She changed lanes before trying again. "I don't see how you completely ignoring me is going to help us solve this case, though."

Her long-suffering sigh was what prompted Matthew to open his mouth. "Oh, I'm sorry, are you saying you need my help this time? If I recall correctly from the previous time we worked together, Savannah detectives were, and I quote, 'so backward it's a wonder they ever see their own feet.'"

Fields's jaw fell open. "What in the world...?"

She started laughing, making him clench his teeth. "I'm glad you think your shitty joke is still so funny."

"Sorry, I'm not laughing at that. Just...is that why you've been acting so pissy this entire time?"

"That, and the fact that you got the powers that be to remove me from the case just when I was making headway." Matthew glowered at her profile, so he caught the surprise that flitted across her face.

"Okay, now I have no idea what you're talking about."

He wanted to call her a liar, but her expression was making him reassess. "So, you're saying you had nothing to do with me being taken off that murder case five years ago?"

She pulled her right hand off the wheel and lifted it in the air. "None. Scout's honor."

He narrowed his eyes. Debating. "But you aren't denying the shitty joke?"

Fields hesitated a second before sighing. "No. But I said *detective*, singular. Not *detectives*."

A muscle twitched near his jaw. "Is that supposed to make me feel better? That you singled me out?"

"I wasn't talking about you. I was talking about Jimmy Reynolds. That little asshat made the case a living hell for me with all his sexual innuendos and other assorted bullshit. I couldn't get away from him quick enough." She tapped her fingers on the wheel. "Though, to be honest, part of me did assume you were tainted with the same brush since you two seemed pretty chummy and all."

Matthew digested her words in silence, unease growing in his stomach. He'd never witnessed Jimmy say anything like that to women himself, but ever since the other detective had retired, there'd been rumors flying. Matthew hadn't paid much attention to them. Until now.

Fields slid a sideways glance his way. "Who told you I got you removed from the case, anyway?"

Matthew leaned back in the seat. "Jimmy." He'd been played. He felt like a tool.

"Hmm." Thankfully, that seemed to be all she was going to say about that. "Now, can we focus on this case and Baldwin?"

"Sure."

It was late before they headed back to Savannah, the sun having set hours ago. He was tired and hungry and also exceedingly glad that Fields was typing away on her tablet instead of finding the need to talk about how pointless their day had been.

His phone rang, and Matthew tapped the button to put it on speaker. "Yeah?"

It was Charli, and her voice was grim. "Another girl has gone missing."

28

When Charli pulled up in front of the squat, one-story house where Jenny Withers lived, every window blazed with light. The curtains twitched as she climbed out of the car, and the front door flew open after only a few steps up the crumbling brick walkway.

"Are you with the police?" A woman half a foot taller than Charli with a frizzy ponytail and frantic eyes appeared in the doorway. She peered over Charli's shoulder, as if hoping her daughter might pop up behind her. Her face fell when she realized Charli was alone.

Charli pulled her badge out as she approached. "Detective Charli Cross. Are you Angela Withers?"

The woman nodded. "Yes."

When Charli reached the porch, the shell-shocked mom didn't move. "Can we go inside?" she prodded gently.

Angela Withers blinked and gave her head a little nod before scrambling backward, clearing a path. "Sorry, my head is all over the place right now. I have a really bad feeling about this. My Jenny would never worry me on purpose. Something has to be wrong."

The fear thickening the other woman's voice was so tangible, it was almost like a separate entity.

Charli's gut twisted. She remembered the panic all too well. How overwhelming the emotion could be, making it impossible to think straight.

Days passing by with no news. Hope steadily dripping away like a slow leak until only numb resignation was left.

Charli smoothed her jacket, rubbing her fingertips over the soft material to banish the memory's emotional residue. Madeline was long gone, but Jenny Withers wasn't. If Charli did her job right, Jenny's mom would never experience that same soul-crushing void.

Angela Withers hovered on the threshold of a small, boxy room that opened into an equally boxy kitchen, with drab, worn furniture that was brightened by a handful of colorful throw pillows and framed posters on the walls. Large, half-burned candles flickered from plastic holders, giving off a citrusy aroma. The overall effect was a little messy but in a warm, lived-in way.

Somewhere outside, a car door slammed shut. Mrs. Withers jumped like a scalded cat before racing to the window.

Her shoulders slumped as she turned away. "Just the neighbor."

Jenny's mother was still wearing her light blue work shirt and khaki work pants with a name tag pinned to her chest. She twitched and trembled to the point Charli worried she might collapse. "Why don't we sit down? You look like you've been on your feet all day."

"I have, but I don't know if I can sit still right now."

"Would you mind if I sat down? It's been a long day for me too."

To Charli's relief, her ploy worked. Mrs. Withers led her to one of two padded barstools tucked behind a narrow kitchen counter. She waited until Charli settled into one before plopping down in the other one.

"Can you tell me what happened?"

Mrs. Withers shook her head. "I came home from work, and Jenny wasn't home. She's always home before me. Always."

"What time did you get home?"

"Same as usual, nine o'clock. I knew I should have picked her up from work. I told her to wait there for me after her shift ended, but she didn't want to. She didn't want to wait that long to shower, plus she said the walk was good for her." The other woman chewed the skin next to her thumbnail. "We only have one car, and my shift doesn't get off until eight forty-five on Tuesdays and Thursdays. She's always walked home before now, and everything was always fine."

Charli softened her voice. "We aren't sure everything isn't fine now, Mrs. Withers. Is it possible Jenny went to a friend's house after work and forgot to call? Or maybe a boyfriend's?"

Angela Withers's ponytail swished from the force of her head shake. "No. Not Jenny. It's been just the two of us for a while. We look out for each other. She'd never not come home without texting or calling me first. Plus, look at this." She tapped on her phone before shoving it under Charli's nose. "Her Find my iPhone app stopped between here and work. She's never turned her location services off in the whole time she's had that phone. There's no way she'd start tonight, knowing so many girls have...are..."

She trailed off with a shudder, unwilling or unable to put her worst fears into words.

Determination poured through Charli, hardening her resolve. "I promise, we're taking this very seriously and dedicating all our resources to finding your daughter. You did the right thing by calling. We have patrol officers out now, canvassing Jenny's route home. They'll be checking any surveillance footage from home security systems and video doorbells. We're optimistic that given the narrow window, we'll be able to find Jenny and bring her home."

If Jenny truly had been snatched by the Marsh Killer, they needed to capitalize on this opportunity. All the other girls were long dead by the time they'd discovered their bodies, whereas Jenny had only been missing for two hours.

That gave them a real chance. Both to save Jenny and prevent the loss of other innocent lives.

"Did Jenny ever mention anyone bothering her at work? Fellow employees, customers?"

Angela Withers gave a helpless shrug. "Every once in a while, she complained about a customer making a mess or not leaving a tip, but other than that, no. She liked working there. She was saving up to buy a car."

Her chin sagged to her chest, but not before Charli caught the gleam of tears. "What about Jenny's dad? Any chance he picked her up?"

The woman's mouth twisted. "And risk paying the child support he's back-owed for the past ten years? No. Gus split when Jenny was six and never looked back. Last I heard, he was living down in Florida with some stripper."

Charli jotted a note, even though she expected that avenue to be a dead end. "Did she mention being scared of anyone at all lately? At school, during extracurriculars, anywhere?"

Mrs. Withers shook her head. "No. Nothing. We talked about safety a little because of what's been going on, but that's it." She rubbed her palms down her face and moaned. "I can't believe this is happening."

Sensing the other woman was close to a breakdown, Charli cycled through the remaining questions as quickly as possible. At the end, she tore a blank page from her notebook and pushed it in front of Jenny's mom, along with a pen. "Here, why don't you make a list for me, with the names of all of Jenny's good friends, teachers, anyone she interacts with on a regular basis or has mentioned by name. Then, write down her activities over the past six months. Sports, club meetings, anything you can think of, along with the location and dates if you have them. While you're doing that, I'd like to do a quick search through Jenny's room, if that's okay."

"Y-yes, I can do that." Angela Withers clutched the pen like it was the one thing tethering her to safety. "Jenny's room is down the hall on the left."

Charli exhaled a relieved breath. When people started to panic, the thing she often found the most helpful was assigning them a task. Hopefully, Jenny's mom would be too busy coming up with a list to succumb to a full-blown panic attack. "Got it."

As she headed for the hall, someone knocked on the front door. Angela Withers leapt to her feet, one hand pressed to her chest. "Jenny?"

The woman's desperate hope fractured a tiny piece of Charli's heart. "I'll get it. That's probably my colleague with the GBI." Sure enough, when she opened the door, Preston Powell stood on the porch.

He followed her inside, where Charli made quick introductions while studiously avoiding eye contact with Angela Withers. She didn't want to witness the bone-crushing disappointment she guessed was etched all over the frightened mother's face.

"You're just in time to help me search Jenny's room. Mrs. Withers is going to work on a list for us." Charli all but dragged the agent down the short, narrow hallway. Instead of the usual school portraits, the walls were lined with candid photos of Jenny and her mom over the years, most filled with laughing, smiling, hugging, or some combination of all of the above.

When Charli stopped outside Jenny's room, there was a hard lump beneath her sternum.

"What was that all about?" Powell's sandy eyebrows rose as he stared at where Charli's fingers were still curled around his forearm.

Charli let go, her cheeks burning. Apparently, she'd been in such a big hurry to escape Angela Withers's pain that she'd basically accosted the GBI agent. "I'm sorry. I shouldn't have done that."

Powell leaned against the doorjamb. His lips quirked into a bemused smile. "I appreciate the apology, but it's unnecessary. I'm mainly curious about what prompted it. Is something wrong with Mrs. Withers?"

She brushed by him to enter the small room. "No." *But something is clearly wrong with me.* "She's understandably distressed, though, so I'm trying to keep her busy while we get this done."

"Smart." He straightened. "Let's get to work."

Compared to Shana's room, Jenny's was much simpler and less expensively furnished. No two pieces matched, making Charli guess they'd been hand-me-downs or acquired as the funds became available to buy one piece at a time. The bed consisted of a mattress and box spring on a metal frame, with no headboard or footboard. A rumpled black comforter with an abstract design in white covered the top. A blond dresser listed to one side, and the drawers inside were all crooked. The desk was constructed of white particle board resting atop spindly, metal legs.

Their search of Jenny's room progressed more quickly than Shana's because Jenny had fewer than half the possessions. The only laptop was a Chromebook with a Chatham Public

School sticker affixed to the outside. School issued, so Charli doubted they'd find anything of value on it. Districts usually restricted the websites that students were allowed to access.

A fist clenched around Charli's stomach, harder and harder with each passing minute. No drawers in the desk, so no place to hide journals or notes. The closet was another dead end. They found no secret hiding spots, no drugs, no condoms, or unusual photos. As with the other girls, there was nothing they could ID as a smoking gun. Nothing that even elicited mild alarm. When they finished searching, the only items they walked out with were the Chromebook and a few photos.

She paused at the end of the hall and turned to Powell. "Can you ask Mrs. Withers if we can borrow these and start filling out the paperwork to activate a Levi's Call? I need to call Sergeant Morris."

"Will do."

Charli watched Powell focus his easy smile on Jenny's mom before pulling out her phone and stepping out onto the front porch.

Sergeant Morris skipped the niceties when she answered. "Any luck with Mrs. Withers?"

The fist in Charli's stomach squeezed tighter. "Not yet. Nothing in Jenny's room, either. Where are we on the canvassing?"

A disgruntled sigh. "Same. We've got ten patrol officers out there now going door-to-door."

The grimness coming over the line matched Charli's own mood. This was their big shot. If they failed to find the killer now...

She stamped down the thought. "While Agent Powell's working on the Levi's Call, I'm going to grab a list of names I had Mrs. Withers provide. I'll shoot you a photo of it. Maybe someone will have a lead by the time I get back to the precinct."

"Wouldn't that be nice?"

Her boss's tone didn't hold much optimism, though. So far, digging into the other girls' known acquaintances had resulted in diddly squat. There was no reason to believe Jenny would be any different.

Charli hung up and sagged against the front door. No leads yet. Here, or out on the street. Where the hell had Jenny disappeared to? She'd been walking home through a residential neighborhood. Surely someone had seen or heard something, or a video camera doorbell would have caught a glimpse of what happened to the girl. Unless their killer was a ghost, and Charli didn't believe in those.

Not the literal kind, anyway.

After straightening her shoulders and injecting a confidence into her bearing she no longer felt, Charli headed back inside to check on the list.

29

J enny huddled in a ball in the corner, eyes squeezed shut while she rocked back and forth and waited for the man's footsteps to retreat.

This isn't happening this isn't happening this isn't happening.

When she peeled open her eyes, she hadn't magically transported back to her nice, safe room. Instead of reading fanfic in her bed or playing cards with her mom on their lumpy old couch in front of an episode of *Schitt's Creek*, she was sitting in a cramped attic room with a weird triangular ceiling that was low on the sides and higher in the middle. Plastic zip ties dug into her wrists, binding them tightly together in front of her.

She swallowed hard and winced. Her throat was raw from all the screaming. The man had laughed when he'd visited her, telling her she could scream her head off all she wanted because the first thing he'd done when moving in was insulate the room to make it soundproof. Jenny wasn't sure if he was lying or not, but she'd spent hours pounding on the walls and yelling for help, and no one had come.

Sweat dripped from her forehead. Lifting both hands as a

single unit due to the zip ties, she wiped her skin with her forearm. Not that she should have bothered. It was so damn hot in here. All she was accomplishing was smearing the sweat around.

The room was stark and creepy. Apart from her, the only items were an uncovered mattress, a plastic cup and water pitcher, and a single light bulb that dangled from a fixture at the peak of the ceiling. She would have broken the glass and used one of the shards as a weapon, but there was nothing to use as a ladder. The mattress was no help, even if Jenny could have forced herself to touch it, with all those yellow mystery stains dotting its surface.

Her stomach heaved. No way in hell was she sleeping on that. She'd take her chances on the wooden floor.

You really think that mattress is there for sleeping?

Jenny's gaze fell on the remains of her red work t-shirt, and a tremor wracked her body.

"Now, now, don't pretend this isn't exactly what you wanted all those times you paraded around in your tight shirts and short shorts, smiling at men with that pouty little mouth. You wanted people to look, so here I am. Looking.*"*

That was what the man had said when he'd visited her with a long, jagged knife gleaming in his hand. At first, she'd been terrified he was going to slit her throat open.

What he'd done instead was almost worse.

After backing her into a corner and pinning her arms to her stomach with his thigh, he'd grabbed a handful of her shirt.

"Don't move or I might slip and slice your pretty skin."

Jenny had gone still as a statue. Too afraid to breathe as, with a faraway smile, he'd sliced the material from sleeve to collar. First one side, followed by the other. By the time he'd backed up far enough to cut the front of the shirt in half, she'd been too shocked to move.

Hot shame poured over her. Like an idiot, she hadn't tried to fight. Done nothing as the pieces of her shirt fell away, and she sat shivering and sweating in her pink bra.

With one finger, he'd traced the skin beside her bra strap. She'd frozen even more. Felt herself detached from her own body.

Instead of attacking her, he'd collected a sweat droplet on his fingertip and brought it to his nose. Sniffed.

"Almost time, but not quite yet. A little longer and then you'll be ready."

The man didn't specify what she'd be ready for, but Jenny wasn't stupid. The way his eyes crawled over her bare skin left little doubt as to what he had in store. It wasn't a matter of if he'd return and finish what he'd started, but when.

Get up. Get up now.

Clumsily, she climbed to her feet, her bound hands all but useless as she stumbled across the floor to the tiny attached bathroom. Her brain was still a little fuzzy from the drugs he'd injected into her, and the sweltering heat of the room didn't help.

The mirror over the ancient sink was one of those weird, metal kinds that distorted your face like a creepy Snapchat filter.

Ugh. Snapchat. If only she had her phone. As if through a hazy fog, Jenny had flickering memories of the man taking her phone from her when he threw her into his car. He'd shattered the device under his heel, and if she didn't act, she'd be as dead as her phone.

Between the funhouse mirror effect and the single light bulb casting weird shadows, her reflection could have doubled for the poster from a horror movie. Her face was out of proportion. All wavy. Too long and thin. Her eyes were weird too, and her mouth was stretched impossibly wide and appeared disturbingly red.

She shivered. The lipstick. After cutting off her shirt, the man had pulled a black tube from his pocket. She'd regained control of her muscles by then, enough to try to yank her head away, but he'd grabbed her hair and pulled until tears sprang to her eyes.

"Don't play games. You want the attention. Just like the others."

He'd pressed the lipstick hard against her lips. When he was satisfied with his work, he'd kissed her with his gross, wet mouth. Stuck his tongue between her lips. She'd almost gagged, but he'd been excited. She could feel him pressing up against her, and part of her had wanted to die.

Awkward with her bound hands, she tore off a piece of toilet paper and rubbed her mouth until her skin burned. When she still felt dirty, she turned on the faucet and stuck her entire face under the running water, filling and spitting the lukewarm liquid from her mouth until it felt like her own again.

She hated the red lipstick. She hated this place. She hated that disgusting, perverted man.

"I need to leave for now, but don't worry. I'll be back soon," he'd licked his lips, making her stomach heave, *"and we'll finish up. You're filthy now, but that's okay. They all were until I repurified them."*

Jenny switched off the faucet, shuddering while panic raked her with sharp claws. Repurified? She didn't know what that meant.

What she did know was that those other girls had ended up dead.

Stark certainty crept along Jenny's spine. If she didn't escape, the man would kill her. After he forced her to do other things first.

A scream barreled up her throat. Jenny wanted to pound the walls again but knew that screaming and banging were pointless.

They won't help. Do something useful. Anything.

There was no point in checking the door again. She'd heard all three locks click as he'd engaged them. She'd spent minutes earlier kicking the door with her feet, slamming the wood with her arm. All she had to show for it was a bruised, throbbing shoulder.

Jenny dropped her forehead against the makeshift mirror and gathered her racing thoughts.

She might not be able to escape, but if she could free her hands, she had a chance. Especially if she found a weapon of some kind.

Lifting her head, her gaze swept the bathroom. She'd watched a YouTube video on how to escape zip ties once with her friends but hadn't paid that much attention. Something about putting pressure on the middle point, between her wrists.

The stupid yellow counter was rounded, so that was out. She'd already tried the edge of the metal mirror. Bolted down.

That left one last option.

With her hands zip-tied, even pulling the toilet paper off the bar was awkward. She ended up dropping the roll on the floor.

Her fingers curled around the metal hanger, and she yanked up and down, using momentum to help pry it off.

Sweat dripped down her back, her neck, into her eyes. Her wrists ached over the unnatural angle. She wanted to stop and take a break but was afraid if she did, she might give up completely.

The squeaking was rhythmic. She found herself singing the lyrics to that old kiddie song her mom used to sing to her in time to the beat. Over and over again.

Twinkle, twinkle, little star...

Her vision blurred. A knot clogged her throat. What if she

never saw her mom again? Would she even know what had happened to Jenny? What if they never found her body?

"No no no, stop it." Tears streamed down her face as she whispered the words. "Don't give up."

She pushed harder. The bar squeaked louder. Finally, when her wrists felt like they were close to snapping, the bar broke free. Jenny stumbled forward, laughing and sobbing at the same time.

The metal rod wasn't very sharp, but she tucked it into her pocket anyway. If she got the chance, she'd shove one end into his eyeball…or his nuts.

She turned her attention to the base plate, and hope bubbled in her chest. That edge looked a little sharper. Or at least, not as dull.

Jenny positioned her wrists on either side of the plate, inhaled, and slammed down.

Pain rattled her joints and seared her skin where the plastic dug in, making her whimper. The zip ties held.

Jenny drew in another breath. Tried again. Same result.

After too many tries to count, her wrists were on fire. Tears streamed down her cheeks. Now what?

She studied the metal plate. If pounding didn't work, maybe she could use the point as a saw.

Minutes later, her arms ached when she held her hands up to her face to check her progress. The plastic was scratched, but barely. She was no closer to freeing herself than when she'd started.

Jenny collapsed onto the toilet and buried her face in her bound hands. This time, she didn't try to hold back the angry, terrified sobs.

There was no way out. No weapons, no escape, no help on the way.

She was almost certainly going to die in this attic.

It was just a matter of when.

30

Charli rushed back to find the precinct in utter chaos. Several uniformed officers raced through the building while others shouted to be heard on the phones. By the front desk, she passed a small group of agitated civilians, two of the women red-faced and throwing their hands in the air as they yelled at the officer who'd been unlucky enough to draw the current shift.

After dropping off Jenny's Chromebook with Cyber, Charli bounded up the stairs. She ran into Sergeant Morris at the top.

"This all because of Jenny Withers?" Charli gestured to the commotion below.

"Yes. We have all hands on deck, got OT approved to call in some off-duty patrol officers to help man the phones. We're getting swamped with calls from the Levi's Call, even though the number in the announcement goes straight to the GBI." Sergeant Morris's lips puckered like she'd sucked on a raw lemon. "People can't follow the simplest directions anymore."

Charli frowned. In all the excitement, she hadn't stopped

to think about who'd do intake on the calls. "Did we assign someone to coordinate with the GBI so they call us with any legit-sounding leads?"

The sergeant's eyebrows shot up. "As a matter of fact, *we* did. Believe it or not, Cross, this isn't my first rodeo."

Her boss's tone was sharp enough to cut glass, and Charli flinched. She wasn't sure where the "we" business had come from. That was one of her own personal pet peeves, dating all the way back to kindergarten when Mrs. Martin had squatted down and told her, *"Now, Charli, don't you think it's time we shared that book? You've had it all day."*

In those situations, "we" almost always meant "you," and for the record, no, Charli hadn't agreed that it was time to share.

"Sorry, Boss, I'm a little more wound up than usual." With everything else going on, she didn't need to step on Morris's toes. The sergeant could get extra prickly if she believed an underling was questioning her judgment. "I wasn't trying to be obnoxious. I was asking because I honestly didn't know the answer."

Her response seemed to soften her boss's posture a little. "We have someone here serving as a liaison to the hotline. We should be informed of any tips immediately."

"That's good." Charli glanced around the second floor. "Speaking of the GBI, is Agent Powell back yet?"

"No, he's talking to a potential witness from Jenny's route home."

Charli's back stiffened. "Why didn't you tell me? I could have gone over and met h—"

This time, Morris only lifted a single dark eyebrow, but that was more than enough to shut Charli up.

"Not that I need to explain myself, but you'd just walked in when I got the call saying they might have a witness to the kidnapping. Powell was just leaving Jenny's house, so it made sense to have him detour over there."

Charli deflated. "Oh. That does make sense."

"You think?"

Her boss's clipped tone informed Charli she was skating on thin ice, but she was past caring. Finding Jenny was a frantic need inside her. One that superseded everything else. "What about Matthew? Have you heard from him yet?"

Her boss's nostrils flared. "Detective Cross, this may come as a surprise to you, but I am not your personal assistant or messenger. If you want to know where Detective Church is, I suggest you call him yourself."

"Right. I'll do that." Charli's cheeks warmed. There went that tendency of hers to bulldoze right by social cues when she was stressed. Still, her embarrassment wasn't strong enough to banish the impatience shooting through her limbs.

Powell was in the field. Fields and Matthew were who knew where. Meanwhile, minutes kept ticking by, each one reducing the chances they'd recover Jenny Withers before something terrible happened. Before Angela's daughter suffered the same fate as the other missing girls.

"Now, can I go back about my business, or are we going to stand here all night while you grill me over how I do my job? Remember, I haven't retired yet."

Charli did a double take. Retired? Where did that come from? That idea hadn't even been a blip in Charli's head. She couldn't picture anyone else filling Sergeant Morris's desk, now or at some nebulous time in the future. "No, go ahead, sorry. I'll be in the conference room if Powell calls with an update."

Her boss was shaking her head and muttering under her breath as she strode back to her office, but Charli had already moved on. Maybe studying the map one more time would lead her brain to finally click the missing pieces together.

Barring that, she'd help contact the names on the list Jenny's mom had provided and hope one of them could offer a bread crumb.

She added Jenny's pins to the map. Her home, the pizza place. Her school.

Charli stood back. Stared. Searched for some type of pattern. Shook her head while an invisible wrench tightened her muscles like they were screws.

"Nothing." She let out a frustrated slow sigh. "There's nothing there."

Even her fleeting idea about a directional component to how the killer chose his victims was a bust. Plotting Jenny's house didn't fill in the pattern. Neither did pinning the pizza place where she worked.

They were missing something. *She* was missing something. A piece that linked the others together. And she needed to find the missing link, quick. Before Jenny ended up like Maddie, Shana, and Regina.

Before she ended up like Madeline.

Apprehension shivered across Charli's flesh, an instant before her phone pinged. A text from Matthew: *We visited Baldwin. He's on a date right now. Alibi for tonight is solid.*

Her stomach dropped. There went her hope that Baldwin might be the culprit, small as it was.

After stepping back and staring at the map again for several minutes, her head began to pound. She rubbed her temples.

Come on, Charli. Think. Connect the dots.

Only, the longer she stared at the map, the more hopeless she felt. She couldn't make sense of any of it. Meanwhile, each heartbeat that pounded in her ears served as a visceral reminder that Jenny only had so many heartbeats left. Unless they found her. Quickly.

On the board, Jenny's photo morphed into Madeline's face, her friend's mouth opened in an eternal scream.

The colored pins blurred while all of Charli's doubts and fears descended, buzzing around her like a swarm of wasps. They formed an angry tornado as they swallowed her, blotting out the light and stinging her with a litany of failures.

See, you're doing it again. You failed Madeline. You failed her mother. You failed the three dead girls. Now you're going to fail Jenny and Angela Withers too. You should have listened to your dad, picked another career. At least that way, he'd be happier, and the person standing in this room would be a real detective, like Matthew or even Powell. Maybe then Jenny would already be back home safe and sound.

Charli squeezed her eyes shut and slapped her hands over her ears. Like that would somehow save her from an attack originating inside her own damn brain. Other voices from her past chimed in, echoing through her skull like a pessimistic chorus. Friends, students, coworkers, even her own family.

"You, a detective? Please. Bad guys will gobble you up and spit you out."

"I don't know, Charli, are you sure about this? It just doesn't seem like the right job for someone like you."

"Get a load of Officer Slate over there. Who the hell does she think she is, trying out for a detective shield already? If she wasn't such a cold bitch, I'd bet she was banging her way up the ladder, but who'd wanna tap that? She'd probably freeze your pecker right off."

Charli wasn't sure how long she stood there as the memories swarmed, buzzing and stinging away. What she did know was that at a certain point, the doubting voices stopped chipping away at her confidence and began having the opposite effect.

If she'd listened to the doubters, she never would have joined Savannah PD in the first place. Never would have become a detective. So many people along the way hadn't believed she could—or should—follow her dreams. Yet here she was. She'd already exceeded all their expectations. Succeeded when they'd believed she'd crash and burn.

Those voices didn't matter. They never had.

With her senses hindered, Charli's thundering heartbeat commanded her focus. Still too loud. Too fast. That was okay, though. A problem she knew how to handle.

She slowed her breathing. Pictured the oxygen flowing through her body, traveling down her arms and legs, coursing into her fingers and toes. Noticed how her muscles loosened with every single breath.

When her pulse returned to normal, she straightened. Some of the loudest negative thoughts lingered, but they were manageable now. More offstage whispers than center stage heckling into a microphone.

She recited facts. Logically, she knew she was a good detective because her percentage of solved cases was higher than anyone else in the city. She cared about Savannah and its residents. She did her absolute best not to bend the law to serve her own purposes and dedicated hours of her free time to the job.

Was she perfect? No, but no one expected her to be. Standing here incapacitated by guilt and self-doubt would only help the murderer and hurt Jenny.

There was no time for breakdowns. Not when Jenny Withers's life was at stake.

When Charli opened her eyes, her mind was clear. Her body calm. Her logic in place. Yes, time was a factor, but she wasted more time panicking than she did allowing herself space to consider all the information. Step-by-step. Piece by piece.

Charli sifted through the serial killers she'd researched in the past. There were all types, from impulsive to organized, mentally ill to cold and calculated.

The burial site and method proved the Marsh Killer had a dark purpose and was very organized. Almost certainly acted and lived alone, to have the freedom to assault the girls and perform his macabre stitching and burial rituals.

The killer might work alone, but she didn't.

Madeline's face materialized behind Charli's eyes, causing the old doubts to resurface. She raised her chin. She'd been a teenager herself when Madeline was snatched. No training. Taken completely by surprise.

This was different. *She* was different.

Her phone rang. It was Matthew. She didn't even say hello but jumped straight to the point. "I'm standing in front of the murder boards right now. Hang on, let me put you on speaker."

"I'm going to do the same so Fields can listen while she drives."

"Okay." Charli hit the button and set the phone on the table. "I'm looking at a couple of the photos we got from the medical examiner. Maybe we need to go back to the beginning, to the killer's motivations. The lipstick, the stitching. What do those signify?"

"That he's a sick fuck?"

Matthew's comment was followed by a snort from Fields. For a brief moment, Charli wondered how their road trip together was working out. Neither of them was dead, which she took as a good sign.

"At the very least, I think it means we're dealing with someone with a chip on his shoulder when it comes to women...or girls, as the case may be."

Charli nodded her agreement to Fields's contribution. "Agreed. The lipstick seems a little harder to assess. Is it symbolic in a literal sense, as in he has a hatred of makeup or was abused by someone who wore a lot of lipstick, or is it figurative? The stitching feels more blatant to me, like he's making some kind of statement about virginity...or railing against sexual promiscuity."

A few seconds of silence followed before Matthew spoke. "Maybe he was raised super religious and either got a girl pregnant or has a teenage daughter who got pregnant, and that set him off?"

"Maybe." Her partner's theory was as viable as any. That was the problem. Too many ideas, with no quick way to narrow them down. "What can we say with confidence about the killer so far?"

"He's organized." Fields cleared her throat. "And almost certainly has a well-above-average IQ since he's yet to be caught. Probably lives alone."

"He selects his victims based on a specific look. Teenage girl, long brown hair. Blue eyes."

Matthew's voice grew thick, and Charli wondered if he was thinking of his daughter.

"Right." Charli studied the map and chewed her cheek. The two pins at Midtown High kept jumping out at her. "Since he's intelligent, he's almost certainly trying to throw us off the trail...but his victims have to fit certain criteria. That's not easy to do unless you're somewhere where you come into contact with a constant supply of potential victims. Either where you live or work."

A pause before Matthew replied. "Like at a high school?"

Something clicked in Charli's head. "Not just a high school...Midtown High. That might explain why two victims came from there. Because that's his easiest way to locate girls who fit his criteria."

"But since picking only girls from the place he worked

would be too obvious, he might have made a point to outsource two of his victims, which explains Shana and Jenny." Fields's voice was thoughtful. "That makes sense, especially in the absence of finding any outside links between all of the victims."

"Okay, but even if we're running with this, we still need to figure out the link to Shana and Jenny."

Charli didn't let her partner's pessimism smother the excitement igniting in her chest. Instead, she dug through the file and pulled out the teacher interview notes she'd compiled from their visit to Midtown High.

"I'm going back over the list of male teachers now. You said Baldwin has an alibi...Drummond had that fishing photo, but nothing else about him seemed off..." Her finger moved as she skimmed down the page. "Michaels is happily married with three kids under the age of six so that seems unlikely...Potter."

She stopped.

Looking back, he'd made a few comments that could fit the profile. The thing about girls wearing uniforms to keep from distracting the boys. Implying that Maddie had flirted with the boys in the back row.

When she shared that with the others, Matthew made a dubious noise. "Okay, but I bet I could find you five other teachers with those same beliefs without exerting too much effort."

Fields's voice came over the line. "I have to agree. I'm not sure those types of attitudes are anything out of the ordinary."

Charli braced her hands in the small of her back and arched her spine before pacing a circle around the room. "I know. That was my initial reaction too. I think there's something else about Potter that's bugging me, but I'm not quite there yet."

"Whoa, hold up. Is it possible that my partner is finally admitting to experiencing a, wait for it, *hunch?*"

Charli turned away from the phone. "Shh, you're interrupting my train of thought."

Matthew snorted but remained quiet while the gears in her head whirred.

The vice principal had mentioned Potter was old-fashioned, but again, not unusual in this part of the country.

So what, then?

Using her finger as a marker, Charli read through the notes she'd typed up under Potter's name. She stopped midway through when two words jumped out at her.

Volleyball coach.

"Charli, you still there?"

"Hang on a sec."

She stared at the page, a glimmer of an idea forming in her head. Still clutching the paper, she walked back to Shana's board. In the photo from the art class at the community college, Shana and another girl were holding up their paintings and smiling into the camera, but Charli was more interested in the background.

In the frame behind them, they'd captured a girl dressed in a tank top and shorts leaping by a net, reaching for a ball over her head and out of view.

When Shana's mom had mentioned that the community college had hosted a range of classes for high schoolers that weekend, Charli hadn't thought much about it.

Staring at the photo now, though...

"I might have found something. It's a long shot but worth following up."

After giving them a quick rundown, Charli ended the call and punched in a new number.

One ring. Two.

"Hello?" The voice was sharp with worry.

"I'm sorry to call so late, Mrs. Withers, but it's important. This is Detective Cross."

"Detective? What's wrong? Do you have news about Jenny?"

"Not yet, but we're working hard to find her. I'm calling because I wanted to ask you a question. Did Jenny ever attend any classes off campus, specifically at Savannah Mesa Community College earlier this year?"

"No, I don't think so." Charli was already deflating when Mrs. Withers continued. "She did attend a clinic at the community college over the summer, though."

Charli tightened her grip on the phone. "Do you happen to know if volleyball was one of the course options?"

"Why, yes, it was." Surprise raised the pitch of Mrs. Withers's voice. "That's the one Jenny took. Jenny's best friend wanted to go and dragged her along. Why do you ask?"

Charli ignored the question. *Too soon,* she told herself. *It's too soon to get excited yet.* Her ricocheting pulse didn't listen. "Do you happen to know who taught the class?"

"No, but I'm pretty sure she mentioned it was a coach from one of the local high schools. Please, tell me what this is about."

Still not a smoking gun, but at least Charli's hand was starting to heat up. Her call waiting beeped. "Thanks for the information, Mrs. Withers. I'll be in touch." She clicked over to the other line. "Detective Cross."

"Yeah, this is Officer O'Brian. I was told to cruise by that new construction site off White Bluff Road, near the old Baptist church?"

Her heart beat faster. "That's right. Did you see something?"

"Big blue van, turned out to be press. I checked their credentials. They're legit. Local station."

Disappointment pinged inside her. "Thanks for checking.

If you want to give me their name and contact info—"

"Wait, there's more."

He paused, as if enjoying the drama of the situation. Charli wasn't nearly as thrilled. "And?"

"And I asked if they'd parked there more than one night, and they said yeah. Said the night before, they saw someone else. They saw a guy in a baseball cap drive off in an SUV as soon as he spotted them."

"Did they get a good look at his face?"

"Nah, said the windows were tinted, and they weren't really paying that much attention."

Charli issued a silent prayer. "What about the make and model of the SUV?"

"Black or maybe dark blue. Full-sized. Possibly a Ford, but they won't swear to that."

"Got it, thanks for calling." Charli hung up before he could respond and made a call downstairs. "Hey, I need someone to pull up DMV records for me. It involves the Marsh Killer case."

She rattled off Potter's name and current address as she headed to the stairs, hanging up after telling the officer to text her once the info was collected.

The information shouldn't take too long to acquire. In the meantime, Charli figured she could get a head start by driving over to Potter's place now and take a peek. She'd text Morris once she was already on the way. Just in case her boss was inclined to tell her no.

As Charli hurried out the door, a hint of a smile plucked at her lips.

Maybe Matthew was right. Maybe there was something to this hunch business.

Not that she'd ever admit as much. She'd rather lick a stranger's hand every day for a month than put up with her partner's insufferable "told-you-so" attitude.

31

T*hump. Thump.*

I lounged on the bed with my arms folded beneath my head, staring up at the ceiling and waiting.

"That a girl, keep up that fighting spirit."

Giving Jenny a reduced dose had been a genius move on my part. Just enough to keep her subdued on the ride here, but not enough to prevent her from whipping herself into a frenzy once she was safely tucked away in my holding area.

Ten seconds stretched into twenty. Twenty into thirty. Disappointment was just starting to curl in my stomach when the noise came again. More of a rapid banging this time.

Absorbing the sound, I smiled. "That's the way. Get yourself nice and worked up. All the better to sweat."

I reached for the cup on the nightstand and took a long sip of lemonade. Forget TV. Who needed that kind of artificial stimulation when I had my own built-in entertainment right here?

Thump.

I shook my head at the ceiling. Did she really think I

couldn't hear her up there, performing her silly antic acrobatics in what was surely some misguided attempt to escape? A tap-dancing elephant would have been quieter. Jenny was lucky I wasn't the vindictive sort of man who'd want to punish this type of behavior.

I didn't begrudge her the attempts. Especially since there was virtually no way she could free herself from the attic without a key.

Thump. Thump.

"What are you doing, you little slut?"

An image popped into my head of her sitting in that bright pink whore's bra with sweat dripping from her chin, down her back, her thighs as she rolled around and struggled to free herself from the zip ties. A wave of heat washed over me. I pictured lapping the sweat from her skin, tasting all that delicious purity as her body cleansed itself of sin, and shuddered.

Soon, Jenny. I'll visit you again very soon. But first, I'll give you time to work yourself into a lather, like a wild-eyed, untamed filly who's lashing out at the touch of a saddle.

There was nothing more satisfying than bringing such a spirited creature to heel.

I felt a pang of remorse when I dwelled on how limited our time together would be. Without the police and FBI hot on my trail, I'd draw the taming experience out. Give Jenny a chance to accept the halter and truly embrace the repurification process. Mind, body, and soul.

I could already tell this time would be special. My stomach tightened in anticipation. Ever since my experience with Tanya's friend in the farmhouse cellar, I'd kept my girls subdued with the tranquilizers. At the time, the spitting incident had bothered me more than I'd let on. I'd matured since then, though, coming to realize the fight would make the submission so much more rewarding.

Bang. Thump.

I licked my lips, smiling. Jenny was definitely a fighter, and despite our diminished window of opportunity, optimism sang in my veins.

What an accomplishment it would be, to tame that misguided spirit into something befitting a proper young lady, especially under the gun like we were.

Instead of turning a sow's ear into a purse, I'd be attempting to mold a low-class, attention-seeking whore into a respectable young lady. Like my own personal Eliza Doolittle.

"If we had more time, I bet I could teach you to fetch my slippers too."

I stretched and checked the clock. It was getting late. As much as I'd like to enjoy more of Jenny's struggles, I had work in the morning. I didn't dare skip for fear of drawing further law-enforcement scrutiny, but tomorrow would definitely be my last day at work. After that, I'd have the weekend to finish up with Jenny and make my escape.

The idea of what was in store for me sent a shiver of excitement racing across my skin. I sat up and clicked on the TV to enjoy one last bit of the hoopla I'd caused before turning in for the night.

"Police presence is heavy in this neighborhood, as officers go door to door in search of information on the disappearance of local teenager Jenny Withers, who never came home after her shift at a local pizza parlor ended tonight..."

As the reporter babbled away, I adjusted my alarm, moving my wake-up call an hour earlier than usual. Five a.m. That would give me a little time to visit Jenny before work. Give her a little taste of what was in store and motivate her to sweat and struggle while I was on campus.

With that in mind, I rose and padded over to the closet, where the white cardboard boot box awaited my upcoming festivities. I opened the lid and removed the gunmetal lockbox I kept stored inside. A few spins of the combination lock, and it clicked open.

Inside rested my subterfuge. To the unknowing, the contents of my locked box held value and were deserving of a secret and secure home. But their value to me rested in how successfully they fooled others and kept prying eyes from investigating further. Under the false bottom of the box was the real treasure.

Red lipsticks. Fishing line. Suture needles.

My fingers trembled with excitement as I stroked my index finger down the taut wire. Yearning stretched and tugged at my chest.

"You won't have to suffer much longer in that filthy, unclean shell, I promise. I'll make sure you're pure again before sending you on your way."

I was just getting ready to lock the box back up when the reporter jerked my attention to the TV screen.

"...may have found a lead, according to one resident."

The female reporter shoved a microphone into the face of an elderly woman. "I was walking back from a friend's house when I could've sworn I heard a girl scream. Some awful angry music came on right after that, so I figured my mind was playing tricks on me until the police came knocking on my door asking if I'd seen a teenage girl or noticed anything weird."

The reporter gave a somber nod. "And what did you tell them?"

"Same thing I just told you. That I heard a scream coming out of one of them big SUVs. Black, or maybe dark blue. Wish I'd gotten the license plate."

The reporter reclaimed the microphone, but there were no more details to share.

My blood ran cold.

Yes, there were sure to be a lot of dark SUVs in Savannah

and many more in the state of Georgia. The net was narrowing, though. Much more swiftly than I'd anticipated.

I cast a disappointed glance at my bed. No sleep for me tonight. To be extra safe, I needed to move up my timeline. Clear out of Savannah by tomorrow morning at the latest.

I pulled a pair of latex gloves out from beneath my sink before returning to the lockbox, selecting one of the spools, a suture needle, and the opened lipstick I'd used on Jenny earlier.

"Looks like tonight is your night, Jenny. I won't be going to work tomorrow after all, so we can stay up late and get started on your transformation right away."

32

A t the GPS's bidding, Charli turned off the two-lane highway and bumped down a back road that probably hadn't seen a construction crew in several decades. Her headlights cast an eerie glow over large, drooping trees that swallowed up the yards on either side, blocking her view of the scattered houses set back on rambling dirt driveways and making the street appear deserted.

Potter's house was the last one on the left. Charli eased off the gas about twenty yards back, catching a flash of what appeared to be a vacant lot filled with waist-high overgrowth next to it before shutting the headlights off. She pulled to the curb on the opposite side of the street.

After sliding her Glock into her shoulder holster and double-checking her jacket pockets for the taser, she eased open the door and climbed out, using equal care when closing the door before creeping down the street.

The DMV information had come back as a match on the drive over. Dwayne Potter drove a five-year-old black Ford Explorer. Sergeant Morris had told her in no uncertain terms she wasn't to knock on Potter's door or attempt to enter until backup arrived.

She hadn't said anything about checking the place out.

Morris was working on obtaining a search warrant, but the speed was dependent on how quickly they could wake a judge and get them to sign off. Jenny Withers was running out of time. If Charli could find something before the cavalry arrived that gave her probable cause to enter the premises, she could potentially save a life.

Potter's driveway was a long, dark tongue bisecting the trees before disappearing beyond their leafy blanket. Charli debated switching on the mini flashlight in her pocket before deciding against it. If Potter was awake inside the house and on the lookout, the beam of light would be a dead giveaway.

Yeah, and so will screaming out in pain over a twisted ankle, Charli thought after she tripped over an uneven spot.

Double-checking the terrain before every step made the fifty-or-so-yard approach feel like forever, but caution was key. Charli's eyes gradually adjusted to the darkness. Beneath the soft, moonlit glow, Potter's house was dark, neat, and unassuming. A tidy little three-story with a gambrel-style roof.

She checked the time on her phone, guessing it would take Matthew and/or Powell another fifteen minutes to arrive. Just enough time to do a little reconnaissance. That way, when the others arrived, she'd have prescreened the perimeter for any booby traps. Hopefully find something that solidified their case.

Gun in hand, Charli crept first to the window set into the garage door. She flicked on her flashlight.

Potter's black Explorer took up half the space. The other side was mostly empty, save for hooks in the wall holding gardening tools and a single camping chair and a row of shelves holding a few cardboard boxes. Compared to most garages, the space was oddly barren.

Next, she skirted the front of the house to the side yard, picking her steps along a bumpy stone path to the wooden gate that protected the backyard. No lock, but closed. Without a warrant, venturing beyond this point could be hairy.

There was no law preventing her from peeking over the top, though. Just her short legs.

Taking a chance, she climbed up on the rotting wooden planter that ran alongside the path before ending at the fence. Her boot wobbled on the soft, uneven surface, and she pitched forward, grabbing the gate to keep her balance.

Once her pulse quieted, she secured her footing and switched on the flashlight. The beam fanned out across a grassy, tree-laden yard.

At the end of a sweep, the light bounced off something solid. Maybe fifteen, twenty yards back. Not a tree, but shiny.

A shed.

She traced the beam along the side, exposing tidy rows of metal sheeting. The door was around the corner to the right. The flashlight showed it was ajar, a padlock dangling from the latch.

She squinted when the light fell on a white object just inside. Hard to know from here, but if she had to guess, she'd say it was a plastic barrel of some kind, or a container. A large one.

Maybe even the same size as the containers they'd dug up in the marsh.

Charli's breathing quickened as she hopped down from the wall. She squeezed the metal handle, bracing herself for the squeak. The gate swung open with barely a peep as if recently WD-40'd.

Taking slow, cautious steps, Charli followed a series of

crude, square stepping-stones embedded in the dirt along the side of the house to a large, open backyard. To her left, three steps led to a wooden deck, which in turn led to a set of French doors inlaid with glass.

Cheap plastic blinds formed stripes across the glass until their stopping point, halfway down. Charli crept up the steps and crouched so she could peer inside.

The interior was completely dark. Using her penlight, she spotted a kitchen counter off to the right and a couch to the left. No signs of life.

She eased back down the stairs and performed a quick visual sweep of the yard. Beside the fence that backed up to the vacant lot squatted the large, metal shed. After one last look over her shoulder into the darkened house, she headed to the enclosure. A dog barked in the distance, but other than that and the chirping of crickets as they scraped their wings together, the night was quiet.

Charli began circling the enclosure until she reached the door. The flashlight illuminated the object that originally caught her eye, and she held back a triumphant gasp.

Two plastic containers sat side by side. Up close, she could see the oversized round lids on the front in the flickering light.

Exactly like the makeshift coffins they'd found Maddie, Shana, and Regina buried in.

It's him.

Sweat trickled down the back of her neck while Charli ran the beam along the rest of the shed, starting up high. A metal toolbox on a shelf. A rake. A long-handled shovel… possibly used to dig in the swamp? There was something dark caked on the bottom, but dirt wasn't an unexpected finding on a garden tool.

Relief swelled like a symphony. She'd snap a few photos first, then call into the station for more backup.

Finally. They were going to catch this asshole.

As she fumbled for her phone, a crunch came from behind her.

"Put your hands in the air where I can see them. If I so much as think you're reaching for a weapon, I'll shoot."

33

"Come on, dammit! Pick up!" Matthew cursed when Charli's phone went to voice mail again and ended the call with a jab of his finger. "Can't you drive any faster?"

"Not safely, unless we want to risk the siren."

Fields's reply was far too calm for Matthew's liking. That didn't mean the agent wasn't right. They had no idea what was happening with Charli right now at Potter's house. If she was doing reconnaissance, there was a chance bursting onto the scene with sirens blaring could put her in danger. A small risk, probably, but not one he was willing to take.

Or she could be in danger already.

"Hang tight. We're almost there." Fields shot him a quick smile. "Your partner strikes me as very capable and cautious. I'm sure she's fine."

Matthew grunted by means of reply. He was too stressed to argue. Yeah, Charli was usually cautious and rule-abiding up to a point...beyond which she sometimes defaulted to "Charli logic."

If it came down to following procedure versus potentially

saving a life, though, all bets were off. Especially if the life in question was a kid's.

His knuckles were white as he curled his fingers around the door handle, preparing to jump out the second they pulled up.

He wouldn't be nearly so worried if Fields hadn't received a call from another FBI agent right after Morris alerted them that the DMV confirmed Potter drove a black Ford Explorer.

The agent had shared some disturbing news. In the twelve months before Potter moved to Savannah from a smaller, more rural town in Virginia, three teenage girls had gone missing.

One of the three was Potter's own daughter, Tanya. Apparently, the teacher had told the locals she'd gone away to live with relatives in Norway and finish high school there, but records didn't show that Potter had any family there.

What records did reveal was that his old residence was located on a small horse farm. The type of place where animal tranquilizers and oversized food bins wouldn't be out of place.

He glanced over his shoulder. Once he was sure Powell was still right behind them, he turned back around and punched redial.

Come on, Charli. Answer the damn phone and tell me you're waiting for us out front in your car.

Two rings, followed by a beep.

"You've reached Detective Charli Cross. I've stepped away from my phone..."

Matthew stabbed the end button and gritted his teeth. "Faster."

❄

POTTER's casual tone made sweat bead across Charli's neck. Her fingers twitched. Did she dare risk going for her Glock anyway?

A click followed. The sound of a bullet loading into the chamber.

Pulse throbbing in her throat, Charli lifted her hands in the air and began to execute a slow turn to face Dwayne Potter.

As promised, he was pointing a handgun at her heart from about six feet away. No one needed to be a good marksman to make a shot from that short of a distance. Her gaze dipped to the barrel before rising to his face. The expression there sent a chill skating over her flesh.

Maybe it was the darkness distorting his shadowy features, but Charli didn't think so. Instead of anger or worry or any number of understandable reactions, the history teacher appeared pleased.

The chill threatened to ice over into full-blown panic, so Charli recounted all the reasons she had to remain calm.

Powell and Matthew both knew where she was and were on their way. And even if they weren't, panic would only put her life—and Jenny's—at greater risk.

"Snooping around in my backyard? I expect that from some of my students, but from you? I find myself very disappointed."

Charli's eyes remained glued to the gun. Potter could choke to death on his disappointment for all she cared, but she didn't want to agitate him, so she remained silent.

"Now, slowly, remove your gun and put it on the ground."

Again, Charli assessed the risks as she reached for her weapon. Again, she decided the chance of Potter shooting her before she even disengaged the safety was too high. She squatted down and set the gun at her feet.

"Kick it away."

She complied.

"Good, now turn your pockets inside out and do the same with whatever's in there."

There went her taser and phone.

The gun barrel tracked her every move as she did what Potter asked.

"I've been watching you dig up my girls, you know." His tone was conversational, at complete odds with the situation. "Did you feel me watching that one time? You turned around, almost like you could sense my presence."

Charli flashed to that last visit to the marsh.

Why had she spun around? Not because she sensed his presence. She didn't believe in that kind of thing. "The construction site. You've been watching us from there."

"Probably not the most prudent decision, but I couldn't resist. I didn't want to disrespect my girls by not being there when they finally gained all the attention they'd been seeking."

Keep him talking. Someone will be here soon.

"Your girls? Is that what you call them?"

His soft chuckle snaked around her. "As much as I'd love to stand here chatting all night, I'm aware that I have limited time." As he was talking, he pulled something from his front pocket. "Now, stand very still. I'd hate to put a hole in that pretty head."

Syringe. He had a syringe.

Charli's heartbeat galloped. What the hell was that? GHB? A tranquilizer? Potassium chloride? Fentanyl? Too many possibilities. All of them ending with her either incapacitated or dead.

Basically, if he injected her with whatever was inside that needle, she was screwed. If he shot her with the gun in his other hand? Also screwed. Potter was a sociopath who murdered teen girls.

"That's it, don't move. I promise you'll only feel a little sting."

She filled her lungs with air. She had one chance to get this right. One.

To avoid the needle and bullets, her timing would have to be perfect.

Her muscles coiled as she kept her gaze glued to the syringe until he was within striking distance. Distraction. Let him believe her only focus was on the needle.

She held still. Waited for the needle to plunge through her jacket.

The instant the material pulled on her shoulder, Charli attacked.

She spun right and grabbed for his gun hand, bending his wrist back hard. He grunted, and his grip loosened just as a sharp pain pricked her upper arm.

Crap.

Too late, she jerked away from the syringe. At least some of the drug entered her body, burning as it spread.

Her fingers were wrapping around the gun when pain exploded in her left cheek. She stumbled and the gun went flying.

Potter turned and lunged for the weapon. Charli grabbed a handful of his shirt and yanked him back before whipping her left leg out and sweeping his knees out from under him. Potter toppled forward, managing to catch hold of her jacket on his way down. Together, they crashed to the ground, the impact rattling Charli's teeth and kneecaps.

The gun was less than ten feet away. Potter began crawling, and Charli launched herself onto his back, wrapping her legs around his waist and her arms around his neck. She tightened the chokehold, squeezing with all her strength.

He tried to buck her off, but she held on...even when he

flung himself to one side and she hit the ground hard, causing her ribs to shriek.

Her breathing was ragged, and her arms and legs trembled as she counted down in her head. She refused to let go, holding tight while he clawed at her skin and writhed.

A wave of dizziness hit her, and her hands slipped.

Hold on. You need to choke him out and get him into restraints...before whatever he dosed you with kicks in.

Almost impossible with the adrenaline surging through her body. If she didn't want to risk Potter getting free, she had to slow her galloping heart.

A soft, floating sensation was already tugging at the edges of her consciousness. Urging her to just let go and drift.

Charli tightened her grip, forcing herself to take long, even breaths. She refused to allow her fuzzy mind to dwell on what might happen if she passed out first.

34

Fields sped down a darkened, bumpy road. Trees whizzed by the windows. Up ahead, their headlights bounced off a lone car's bumper and license plate.

Matthew stiffened. "There's her car."

Fields tapped the brakes but continued past. "His house is up on the left." She steered them in that direction, pulling across the driveway entrance before coming to a complete stop.

Seconds later, Powell appeared next to the driver's window. "What's the plan?"

The lot was completely dark. Matthew's hair rose. He didn't like this. Not one bit. "Let's fan out. I'll take the front. You two go right and left. If we don't find her in a quick perimeter sweep first, we'll meet near the garage and go to plan B."

He didn't tell them that his plan B was busting into the house, warrant or no warrant. They'd probably try to talk him out of it, and he'd just as soon not waste their breath. If it came down to preserving the case or Charli's life, he would pick Charli. Every damn time.

Luckily, neither of them asked. They were too busy double-checking their weapons. "Ready?"

Matthew met Fields's gaze and nodded. "Let's do it."

As silently as possible, they all jumped out of the car and hurried forward. Matthew took the middle, scanning the tree-covered yard, whispering as he went. "Charli? You here?"

Crickets chirped in their high-pitched chorus, but his partner didn't respond.

He continued across the grass, his gut slowly filling with lead despite his best pep talks.

Charli is fine. She's a pro. She'll probably call or text any second now.

His phone showed no new messages. And yeah, his partner was damn good at her job, but Potter was an anomaly. Not the kind of criminal they were experienced with. Most of the killers they apprehended were motivated by passion, or survival, sometimes greed. In many of those cases, alcohol played a role.

Cold-blooded serial murderers were a completely different breed.

"Dammit, why couldn't you wait?" Matthew already knew the answer to his muttered question, though. Jenny Withers. Charli's number one priority would have been saving the teen before Potter could abuse her and strangle her to death.

Matthew couldn't even get mad. In Charli's place, he would have done the same damn thing.

That realization didn't ease his worry.

Matthew reached the house and crept to the garage to peer inside. The sight of Potter's black Ford Explorer loosened the strap around his lungs. Charli's car and Potter's car were here. That was a good sign.

Unless Potter had a second car not registered in his name.

Matthew slipped over to the front porch. The door was

locked. Windows flanked either side, but curtains blocked any view into the interior.

"Charli?"

No answer.

The strap binding his lungs cinched tighter again as his mind took him to a dark place.

What if Potter already had Charli inside? Overpowered her, knocked her out, taken one of those lipsticks—

Matthew jogged back to the front door and pulled out his gun.

Screw waiting. If there was any chance his partner was in there, he was going to act now.

He clicked off the safety and was aiming at the doorknob when Powell shouted, "She's back here!"

The alarmed note in the usually mild GBI agent's voice shot ice straight into Matthew's heart. Taking the three porch steps in a single stride, he raced to the side of the house. The gate was wide open, leading into a large, tree-filled backyard. He swept the flashlight back and forth until the beam landed on Powell. The GBI agent knelt next to two slumped bodies, one on top of the other.

No. Please, God, no.

The agent's hand was on the petite figure's neck who appeared to be astride the man on the ground. The agent was feeling for a pulse.

Panic crystalized in Matthew's veins, his arteries solidifying his blood into a million sharp, static edges that tore at his insides with every breath.

Powell's shoulders slumped, and Matthew released a strangled cry. "Charli?"

The GBI agent's head popped up. "She's okay. Just out of it. At first, I couldn't tell…"

He didn't need to explain further.

Matthew sank to his knees, his body weak with relief. As

he swept the flashlight to her face, the beam of light landed on a cylindrical object. "Looks like he injected her with something." He pulled out his phone and called nine-one-one, barking out an order for an ambulance for an injured officer.

Fields jogged up. "Everything okay?"

"Think so. Looks like Detective Cross was drugged. She managed to cuff him first, though." Admiration colored Matthew's voice.

After a beat, Fields replied. "See, Church? I told you she had it under control." The FBI agent was smart enough to turn away before he could glare her down. "Stay with your partner. Agent Powell and I can go inside and look for Withers."

Powell shot him a questioning look. Matthew waved him on. "Go, see if the girl's in there. Charli would be pissed if you didn't."

The GBI agent rose to his feet, taking one step to follow Fields when a slurred voice made him stop. "Charli would beee piiished. Why?"

All three of them turned to stare at Charli, who was slowly rolling off Potter and onto her back, rubbing the back of her skull and moaning.

CHARLI'S HEAD pounded like someone was setting off explosives inside her brain. Her mouth was cotton dry. She cracked open her eyes, cringing and jerking away from the bright light that stabbed her retinas. "Stop!"

"Sorry, Charli." Mercifully, the light lowered. She blinked until the residual flashing spots faded. "You okay? You feel hot or anything?"

A large hand pressed to her forehead. She lifted her arm

and swatted the offensive appendage away, annoyed when she missed by a mile and ended up slapping her own arm. "The hell's wrong with you! I'm not sick."

The hand left Charli's head. "Well, excuse me for being worried. Christ, Charli. You scared the shit out of me."

Matthew's words swam through her head, her brain throbbing as she tried to decipher the meaning. "Where am I?"

"You're in Potter's backyard, don't you remember? You drove out here before everyone else like a knucklehead and started poking around."

Potter? Why did that name sound familiar?

"Do you remember anything about the case? Teenage girls turning up dead. Dwayne Potter's Ford Explorer matching witness reports. Jenny Withers going missing."

Charli gasped and shot up into a sitting position. "Jenny! I need to go—"

Matthew's hand landed on her shoulder. "Hey, stay still! I don't think you should be—"

Charli clapped her hands to her ears, only her aim was too far forward and she ended up slapping her cheeks instead. "Shh! Your big man voice hurts my ears."

"My big…you mind if I record this for posterity's sake?"

She frowned up at him. Or rather, she frowned at all three of him. "You can't laugh just because you're big and tall, s'not fair. S'not fair anyway. If I was as tall as you, I could vomit at crime scenes and nobody would care."

Matthew turned his face away. His shoulders shook.

Charli's heart twisted, and she patted him on the head. "I'm sorry, don' cry."

His shoulders only shook harder.

She opened her mouth to try again when a siren blared in the distance. She tried to concentrate. Something important was happening.

Teenage girl. *Jenny.*

Head swimming, Charli staggered to her feet. She managed one step before the world tilted, and her arms windmilled in an effort to keep from losing her balance. Matthew grabbed her waist from behind. "Easy does it."

Irritation bubbled up her throat, and she smacked at his hands. "Lemme go. Gotta go find Jenny."

"I don't think—"

"Lemme go!"

A second of hesitation. "Okay. Don't say I didn't warn you."

He released her, and she lunged forward. Wobbly, but on her feet. "See?"

"Charli—"

"Shh! You can't stop me!"

Triumph propelled her through another few bobbling steps...until her forehead slammed into something solid. "Ouch!" Pain lanced her head. Ringing filled her ears. She jerked back and tripped over her own foot. Once again, she would have hit the ground if Matthew hadn't prevented the fall.

"Maybe I can't stop you, but that tree trunk certainly can." He lowered her to the ground as flashing blue-and-red lights flickered into the yard. Voices followed. "Hey, we're back here!"

Charli was still sitting on her ass when paramedics and uniformed officers came rushing through the gate.

While the paramedics asked her a billion questions, Matthew directed the uniforms over to escort Potter back to the car. "Send more officers into the house. We have a potential victim and two agents inside."

One of the paramedics shined a flashlight into her eyes. She flinched and batted at the instrument. "No!"

"Yeah, sorry, I think whatever Potter injected her with made her a little crabby and light-sensitive."

She stuck out her tongue in the direction of Matthew's voice before reaching up to touch the end with her fingertip. "Tongues are weird."

Matthew's voice lowered. "Is she going to be okay?"

Charli scowled. "I can hear you." She directed her attention at the paramedic, who immediately wiped the smile off his face.

"You should be fine, Detective Cross. I'm guessing he tried to dose you with some kind of tranquilizer but looks like some of it spilled on your jacket. You'll probably be loopy for a little bit, but it'll wear off."

More shouting came from the front of the house. Charli tried to lurch to her feet.

"Will you please sit down for now? Can you tell her to quit acting like an Olympic sprinter?" Matthew lowered his voice again. "Better yet, maybe we could give her the rest of that tranquilizer."

"Heard that too."

Before she could argue more, Powell jogged up. A big smile split his face. "We found her, and she's okay. Extremely freaked out and with a few scrapes and bruises, but otherwise in one piece. They're taking her to the hospital now."

Relief pulsed through Charli. No one would have to show up to Angela Withers's house and shatter her heart. Her daughter was going to be okay.

"Thank Christ. There, you see that? They got Jenny out without you breaking a leg...hey!" This time, she managed to stand up before Matthew could stop her. "Did you hear what I said? Jenny's okay. There's no rush."

Charli took one careful step, followed by another. "We need to help them search and gather evidence before we interrogate Potter. Make sure this never happens again."

Matthew darted in front of her, lifting his palms. "Whoa, hold up. Fields and Powell are here, plus the GBI mobile crime lab and forensics team are on the way."

Charli moved to the left. Her partner moved with her. "Stop. I can still help."

"Maybe. Or seeing as how you're still a little altered, you could make a mistake and contaminate the crime scene. Is that a chance you're willing to take?"

She raised her chin and scowled up into his big, only slightly blurry face.

"Or," he continued, "we could leave the crime scene in those very capable hands and take you to get some food and caffeine. That way, you might be ready to question Potter in an hour or two."

Charli considered her options. In the end, there was no contest. After casting a regretful glance at the house, she nodded. "Fine, let's go eat. You're buying."

35

Several hours and multiple cups of coffee later, Charli faced Dwayne Potter across a utilitarian table in one of the precinct's interrogation rooms. Potter sat erect in the plastic chair with his hands folded in front of him, acting every bit the prim and proper high school history teacher.

If not for the handcuffs attaching him to the cuff bar and the bolts attaching his chair to the floor, Charli could almost believe they were sitting across from each other in a coffee shop. One with an appalling interpretation of minimalist decor and really crappy fluorescent lighting.

Despite the bleach used to clean the space, the room always reeked of body odor, urine, and stale coffee. Charli sipped from her fresh cup while flipping through the file in front of her.

Inside the interrogation room, every minute felt more like twenty. By the time five had passed, most detainees were fidgeting like a three-year-old during circle time, their anxiety rising as the silence lengthened. Charli, Matthew, and Potter had been in there for ten minutes already without anyone uttering a single word.

The chair beside her creaked as Matthew shifted his weight. She'd wanted to interrogate Potter solo to start. Matthew had argued, probably worried she still needed a babysitter after the tranquilizer. No amount of persuasion on her part could convince him otherwise, so they'd struck a deal.

He'd accompany her in the interrogation room but follow her lead.

Potter had noticed Charli out in the field. Had planned to tranquilize *her* instead of shooting. That gave her an opportunity to capitalize on whatever freaky interest the killer had in her.

Metal rattled across the table. Next came a deep sigh. "As exciting as this all is, it's quite early in the morning, and I'm tired. If you're not going to ask me any questions, I'd like to be returned to my cell."

Matthew snorted. "And I'd like a Ferrari and an all-expenses-paid trip to Tahiti with a supermodel, but that's not happening anytime soon, either."

Charli flinched, casting her partner a reproachful look. "Sorry. It's late, and we're clearly all getting a little crabby." When she turned to Potter, she nibbled on her lower lip. "I was just catching up on your file. Would you like to start by telling me about how you picked th…your girls?"

"I'm afraid I don't know what you're talking about, Detective. How I picked who, now?"

His smarmy smile raised her hackles. She did her best to ignore the sensation, wrinkling her brow to feign confusion. "'My girls.' Isn't that what you called them earlier, in your backyard?"

The smile didn't change. "I'm afraid you must be confused. Do you think it's possible you're suffering from a TIA, or perhaps you're still groggy from the sedative I administered?"

Matthew leaned forward. "You admit to injecting Detective Cross with a substance of some kind?"

"Of course." Potter's quick agreement made Charli's eyebrows shoot up. "In self-defense. I woke up to an intruder in my yard...how was I to know you were a police officer? It was dark out there."

Charli's fingers twitched. Potter was toying with them. With Jenny's statement, they had him dead to rights on kidnapping and sexual assault of a minor. Unfortunately, everything else so far was circumstantial. The plastic containers, the mysterious disappearance of his own daughter, the lipstick and fishing line Fields and Powell found inside the house...it *should* be more than enough for a jury to put him away for life and then some.

"Should" being the operative word. Every cop had a story about a slam-dunk case that ended up dead in the water once it went to trial.

One person could be unpredictable. Twelve people? That was more like utter chaos.

Without Potter confessing to killing those other girls, there was no guarantee he'd spend the rest of his days behind bars.

The one good thing they had going for them at the moment was Potter's ego and enjoyment of pushing their buttons. Even so, he'd eventually grow bored with their dance and lawyer up.

They were on a clock.

Charli nudged Matthew's foot with her shoe, prompting her partner to chuckle. "Must suck, knowing you got bested by Tiny Tot over here."

He jerked his thumb at Charli, who gasped before lowering her voice to a stage whisper. "Would you mind not saying stuff like that in here, Matthew? It's really unprofessional. If I wanted you to treat me like an idiot, I'd dress like one of those hooker-wannabes you date." She made a big show of squaring her shoulders and exhaling before pasting a smile on her face. "Sorry about that, Mr. Potter. Partner stuff. Let's get back to—"

Matthew swore under his breath. The words were soft but clear within the quiet of the room.

"Prissy bitch."

Charli closed her eyes. When she reopened them, Potter was studying her with heightened interest. She pressed her lips together. "Matthew, please step out of the room and go find yourself something to eat. I've got this for now."

Her partner's glare was full of loathing. After a quick peek, Charli busied herself with straightening the file.

A few seconds passed before he snarled. "Fine." The chair squealed as he jumped to his feet. The room echoed with the slam of the door when he stormed out.

Charli smoothed her collar. Patted down her hair. Filled her lungs with air and released it. Once she finished, she folded her hands together and gave Potter a tremulous smile. "Sorry, my partner gets a little hangry sometimes."

"Why'd he call you that?"

She frowned. "Call me what?"

"You know." Potter leaned closer, dropping his voice to a whisper. "Prissy bitch."

"Oh, that." Charli ducked her head. "It's nothing. Just…"

"Just…?"

Charli nibbled her lower lip again, craning her head like she was checking the two-way mirror behind her. "I guess you could say Detective Church has a type when it comes to women. He says I dress like a nun, like the fact that I don't choose to show a lot of skin is a character flaw or something." She grimaced and muttered to herself. "Why am I talking about this?" Forcing a bright smile to her lips, Charli smacked a palm on the table. "Anyway. Let's get back to what we were talking about—"

"He's wrong."

She blinked. "I beg your pardon?"

Potter dipped his chin toward the door. "Your partner. Modesty isn't a character flaw in women…far from it, in fact."

"Thank you. That's what my mom always taught me, but these days not many people seem to agree. Especially women my age or younger." Charli bit her lip again before lowering her voice to a conspiratorial whisper. "I understand, you know. Or at least, I think I do. Why you did what you did."

"Go on." Potter went unnaturally still, his expression sharp and predatory as he assessed her.

Charli's pulse pounded, and her fingers twitched toward her holster. She double-checked his wrists. Still safely cuffed. "So many girls these days don't act the way they should. The short shorts, belly-button rings. Doing that awful, twerking dance." Ringing filled her ears. "You were trying to teach them a lesson, weren't you?"

At least fifteen seconds passed without Potter replying. Charli bit her cheek and picked up the pen. Her strategy had failed. Not that she was surprised. The tactic had been a long shot from the start.

"Teach them a lesson…and help them."

The soft statement renewed her hope. She widened her eyes. "Help them, of course! I should have guessed, given that you're a teacher. That's a helping profession."

Potter's face lit up. "Exactly," he breathed. "So many of these girls today, they have no adults to guide them. To help them differentiate right from wrong and instruct them on the importance of preserving their virtue, for themselves, and so they don't lead others into temptation."

Charli bobbed her head. "It's so frustrating, watching

them debase themselves the way they do. I have to tell you, Mr. Potter, I was shocked when we visited the high schools. I'd realized things were going downhill, but some of those outfits..." She gave a delicate shudder. "Plus, the vulgar way they talked. My daddy would've beat me with the belt if I said a tenth of what I heard on campus that day."

"Yes, yes." Potter nodded, eyes gleaming over having found a kindred spirit. "This is what happens when we spare the rod for too long. The children spoil."

Charli flipped to a photo in the file. "Is that what happened with your daughter, Tanya? Did her mother spoil her beyond redemption?"

Potter sucked in an audible breath as she slid the picture across the table. He stared at the pretty, dark-haired girl's image. A tremor wracked his shoulders.

"I was a teenage girl not that long ago." Charli tried to inject sympathy into her words. Not an easy task, given the disgust flooding her system right now. "I remember how awful we all could be. Mouthy, ungrateful, self-absorbed. Strutting around like we were God's gift to the planet. Was Tanya like that? I'm betting she must have been very difficult to provoke someone as helpful as you. I get it, though. It's always easier to lose our temper with our loved ones when we see them doing wrong."

"That's so true." Potter's gaze remained on the photo. "And my Tanya was definitely a handful."

Charli noted his use of past tense referring to his daughter. She was close. So close. "You told a bunch of people she was off at boarding school in Norway. But she couldn't have been since the FBI found her body in Virginia. They think she's been dead quite some time. Since before you moved to Savannah, in fact."

His chin whipped up at that. "They found my Tanya?"

"Yes," Charli lied. "And I'd like to understand what

happened. Like I said, I bet she was acting up. Not behaving like a proper young lady at all." With effort, she softened her voice. "Please, tell me what happened, Dwayne. Help me understand. Otherwise, they're going to use that nasty word when they talk about you in the news, one we know isn't true. Not when you were only trying to help."

Potter stiffened. His cheeks flushed. "Those girls, they're all Jezebels. They needed me to show them the right path. To help them repurify themselves."

Satisfaction curled Charli's fingers. Almost there. "Can you tell me how that worked, so I can explain it to the judge and the reporters when they question us?"

His gaze drifted back to his daughter's photo. "Attention. They were all starved for attention. I helped show them the perils of that path, how their outfits and lipstick and flirty little looks can strip men of their self-control, lead them to sin."

Charli would give anything not to have to ask the next question. "And how did you do that, Dwayne?" When he didn't speak, she prodded. "Did you give them a firsthand demonstration? Otherwise, girls just don't listen, do they? The only way for them to learn is if they experience the consequences of their actions."

His chin jerked up and down. "I had to show them what they did to men, parading around like that. The lust they inspired."

"I know you did." She almost choked on the vile words, clenching her hands in her lap. Much as it pained her to admit, launching over the table and wrapping her hands around Potter's throat would be detrimental to their case. "So, you showed them by having sexual intercourse with them?"

Potter shrugged, but Charli didn't let that trip her up.

"What about the lipstick and fishing line? Was that part of the repurification process?"

His eyes lit up again. "I knew you were a special woman when I first saw you in the marsh, Detective Cross. You really do get me, don't you?"

That was probably the single most repulsive statement anyone had ever made to her. "I think I do. You used the fishing line to sew them back up as a symbolic means of returning them to a chaste state." She scrunched her brow into a frown. "Although, I'm not sure I quite understand the significance of the lipstick. Can you help me? Was it just that the color was so whorish?"

"That, and it's the shade Tanya's friend told her to wear against my wishes. Instead of listening to her father, my daughter slutted up her mouth in siren red."

Charli's spine stiffened. She chose her next words with care. "And you couldn't let that go, could you? Tanya had to be punished?"

"Yes." Potter's voice was hoarse. "I didn't mean to hurt her, but I was so angry that I saw red. I told her time and time again that only whores wore lipstick that color. The first time she borrowed her friend's in that garish color, I made her wipe it off. She wasn't happy, but she did. But she kept hanging out with that girl until, one day, she called me a pervert and insisted that's why I wouldn't let her wear makeup or dress like a floozy. Then…then she told me I was too late anyway. She'd already had sex with a boy, so she'd earned the red lipstick. I snapped. The next thing I knew, my hands were wrapped around her throat, and she'd stopped moving…" A sob wracked his body. "My poor Tanya. Why couldn't you listen to me? If only you'd obeyed, like a good girl…"

His tears inspired nothing but disgust in Charli's heart.

Dwayne Potter was the ultimate victim blamer. None of his actions were his fault. "So, you killed her and buried her…"

"Out on my property by the north fence, yes. Where the agents found her."

Charli didn't bother telling him that Tanya's body hadn't been recovered yet. Though she imagined that would change soon. Morris and Fields were likely already on their phones, calling for agents and officers to descend upon Potter's old property.

"You didn't bury her alone, though, did you?" Another educated guess, based on the number of girls who'd gone missing within a fifty-mile radius of Potter's old farm before he moved to Savannah. Charli rattled off a few of their names. "I bet it was tough on you, stumbling across all those girls who looked so much like Tanya. So tough that you sent some of them to join her."

The way Potter's hands flexed like he was remembering them wrapped around a girl's neck made bile fill Charli's throat. "Only the ones who needed repurifying. Starting with that bitch friend of Tanya's who gave her the lipstick. Ashley was always over at our house with her butt hanging halfway out of her shorts and her tank tops showing off her cleavage. An attention-seeking little whore, just like all the others." He laughed, low and deep. "I gave her the attention she wanted. By the end, she recanted her mistakes, but it was too late. She had to pay for what she did to my sweet, innocent Tanya. They all did."

Funny how quickly Potter had switched narratives, transitioning from helper to punisher in the blink of an eye. "How many, Dwayne? How many girls paid?"

"Jenny Withers was going to be number seven."

The pen shook in Charli's hand. Six girls. Dead…because of him.

Potter gave a woeful shake of his head. "Now, what will

become of poor Jenny? Who will repurify her, cleanse her of her sins?"

Charli pushed a yellow legal pad toward him, along with the pen. "I don't know, but if you write down the names of the girls you repurified, along with a brief statement telling us what you did, maybe I can figure out a way for Jenny to visit you."

There was no way in hell Jenny Withers would come anywhere near this foul man unless it was to face him down in a courtroom, but Potter appeared too excited by the prospect to sniff out the lie. "That would be wonderful. I didn't get to finish, but maybe she could still be redeemed..."

Potter's smile made Charli want to break things. Starting with his teeth.

She curled her fingernails into her palm, waiting for the violent impulse to subside. For one of the first times, she understood how a law enforcement agent could, in a moment of weakness, lose control over their emotions and attack a suspect or detainee who wasn't an imminent threat.

All those young lives, ruined. All because this asshole subscribed to some archaic beliefs about sexual purity equating to moral virtue.

All because his fragile little male ego couldn't handle it when his daughter had failed to obey.

And because the only way he knew how to stop his sexual attraction to girls who resembled his late daughter was by strangling them to death.

When Potter hesitated, pen in hand, Charli gave him one last push. "If you don't write your version, everyone's going to believe the same thing as Tanya's friend. You don't want them to say you're one of *those* men, do you? You know," she lowered her voice again, "a pervert? Or worse..."

When his jaw set, Charli worried she'd gone too far.

Then his pen hit the paper, and he began to write.

TWO HOURS LATER, Charli walked out of the interrogation room, weary to the bone. Her butt hurt from sitting on the uncomfortable chair, and her brain hurt even more from dealing with the sick psychopath who liked hurting girls.

"Good job, Cross. Signed confession for six murders... couldn't ask for more."

Charli smiled at Matthew. In his incredibly wrinkled suit, he looked about as good as she felt. "Good job for all of us."

He blew out a weary sigh. "Yeah...we saved a girl tonight."

Charli clapped him on the shoulder. "We sure did." She examined Matthew's face, concern flooding her at how pale he looked. How sad. "Then why don't you look happier about it?"

Matthew was quiet for a few long minutes. "This case has made me think about Chelsea a great deal."

Charli's heart squeezed for her partner and friend. "You should go see her."

The corners of his mouth tipped up. "That's what I'm thinking too. In fact, I bought a ticket on the first flight out," he looked at his watch and frowned, "in only a couple hours. I'm going to take a few days off."

She just stared at him. In all the time that she'd known him, he'd never taken a day off. This case really had been harder on him than she'd thought.

"Do you need a ride to the airport?"

His pale face reddened a bit. "Janice is going to drop me off. Save me some long-term parking fees."

Janice, ugh. But Charli forced a pleased smile. "That makes good sense."

Matthew raised a fist, and Charli bumped it. "Safe travels, my friend. I'm not even pissed that you're leaving all the paperwork to me."

He laughed. "Are you kidding? You love paperwork."

Her partner wasn't wrong.

Matthew's face turned serious, and he stuck both hands in his pockets. "Charli…"

When he didn't go on, she raised an eyebrow. "What?"

He squeezed her shoulder. "Call your dad."

Charli's throat grew tight, and emotion scalded her eyes. She blinked to keep any sign of tears away. "I will. Now go." She fluttered her hand. "Scoot."

After Matthew had cleared out, Charli sighed deeply as she sank into her office chair, the door closed against the noise. As tired as she was, she knew she wouldn't be able to sleep until she'd at least gotten started on the piles and piles of paperwork that were in her immediate future.

Her stomach was growling when a knock sounded on her door. Hours had passed, and it was nearly lunchtime. No wonder she was starving.

Ruth came in before Charli could open her mouth. She looked grim.

Oh no.

"Sergeant Morris. Is there something wrong with the case?"

"No, that's all wrapping up smoothly. I'm here about another matter." Charli's heartbeat returned to normal as she waited for Ruth to elaborate. "We have another case. A young man was just found hanging from inside his own stable."

The End
To be continued…

Thank you for reading.
All of the *Charli Cross Series* books can be found on Amazon.

ACKNOWLEDGMENTS

How does one properly thank everyone involved in taking a dream and making it a reality? Here goes.

In addition to our families, whose unending support provided the foundation for us to find the time and energy to put these thoughts on paper, we want to thank the editors who polished our words and made them shine.

Many thanks to our publisher for risking taking on two newbies and giving us the confidence to become bona fide authors.

More than anyone, we want to thank you, our readers, for clicking on a couple of nobodies and sharing your most important asset, your time, with this book. We hope with all our hearts we made it worthwhile.

Much love,

Mary & Donna

ABOUT THE AUTHOR

Mary Stone

Mary Stone lives among the majestic Blue Ridge Mountains of East Tennessee with her two dogs, four cats, a couple of energetic boys, and a very patient husband.

As a young girl, she would go to bed every night, wondering what type of creature might be lurking underneath. It wasn't until she was older that she learned that the creatures she needed to most fear were human.

Today, she creates vivid stories with courageous, strong heroines and dastardly villains. She invites you to enter her world of serial killers, FBI agents but never damsels in distress. Her female characters can handle themselves, going toe-to-toe with any male character, protagonist or antagonist.

Discover more about Mary Stone on her website.
www.authormarystone.com

Donna Berdel

Raised as an Army brat, Donna has lived all over the world, but no place has given her as much peace as the home she lives in with her husband near Myrtle Beach. But while she now keeps her feet planted firmly in the sand, her mind goes back to those cities and the people she met and said goodbye to so many times.

With her two adopted cats fighting for lap space, she brings those she loved (and those she didn't) back as characters in her books. And yes, it's kind of fun to kill off anyone who was mean to her in the past. Mean clerk at the grocery store...beware!

Connect with Mary Online

facebook.com/authormarystone

goodreads.com/AuthorMaryStone

bookbub.com/profile/3378576590

pinterest.com/MaryStoneAuthor

Made in the USA
Coppell, TX
13 November 2022

86290450R00193